WANDERING
STARS

WANDERING STARS

SHOLEM ALEICHEM

Translated from the Yiddish by
ALIZA SHEVRIN

VIKING

VIKING

Published by the Penguin Group
Penguin Group (USA) Inc., 375 Hudson Street,
New York, New York 10014, U.S.A.
Penguin Group (Canada), 90 Eglinton Avenue East, Suite 700, Toronto,
Ontario, Canada M4P 2Y3 (a division of Pearson Penguin Canada Inc.)
Penguin Books Ltd, 80 Strand, London WC2R 0RL, England
Penguin Ireland, 25 St. Stephen's Green, Dublin 2, Ireland (a division of Penguin Books Ltd)
Penguin Books Australia Ltd, 250 Camberwell Road, Camberwell,
Victoria 3124, Australia (a division of Pearson Australia Group Pty Ltd)
Penguin Books India Pvt Ltd, 11 Community Centre,
Panchsheel Park, New Delhi–110 017, India
Penguin Group (NZ), 67 Apollo Drive, Rosedale, North Shore 0632,
New Zealand (a division of Pearson New Zealand Ltd)
Penguin Books (South Africa) (Pty) Ltd, 24 Sturdee Avenue,
Rosebank, Johannesburg 2196, South Africa

Penguin Books Ltd, Registered Offices: 80 Strand, London WC2R 0RL, England

First published in 2009 by Viking Penguin, a member of Penguin Group (USA) Inc.

1   3   5   7   9   10   8   6   4   2

Translation copyright © Aliza Shevrin, 2009
Foreword copyright © Tony Kushner, 2009
All rights reserved

LIBRARY OF CONGRESS CATALOGING-IN-PUBLICATION DATA
Sholem Aleichem, 1859–1916.
[Blonzende shteren. English]
Wandering stars / Sholem Aleichem ; translated from the Yiddish by Aliza Shevrin.
p. cm.
ISBN 978-0-670-02052-2
I. Shevrin, Aliza.   II. Title.
PJ5129.R2B4613 2008
839'.133—dc22   2008029028

Printed in the United States of America
Set in Adobe Sabon

For
my husband,
HOWIE,
loving companion
and
fellow wordsmith

Contents

PART II:
WANDERING STARS

Foreword*

I should have advised you not to write a novel. Your tastes, and your genre, lie elsewhere. And I doubt that there is anything as romantic in the lives of our people. They are so different from the rest of the world that one must understand them perfectly, before attempting to write about them!

Reb Mendalle Mocher Sephorim, in a letter to Sholem Aleichem, quoted in the dedication in Aleichem's novel *Stempenyu* (TRANS. HANNAH BERMAN)

Mastery of an aesthetic form is a form of possession—it's a manifestation and expression of power, confidence, security, authority. When we encounter a perfect poem, play, novel, or sonata, when we're audience for a masterpiece, a work of art that's as full a realization of the potential of its form as we imagine is humanly possible, we're very likely witnessing the triumphant culmination of a journey. Behind the creation of a masterpiece lies a history of aesthetic experimentation, innovation, and refinement built upon antecedence, tradition, and heritage, and this history and its apotheosis constitute a meaning apart from the work's expressive content. For instance, when a perfect novel irresistibly and entirely enfolds its audience within its stratagems and its artificial cosmos, it may describe fragmentation, devastation, entropy, and collapse (the perfect expression of the

---

In which, reader, plot will be discussed and meanings considered, so perhaps first you should read the novel—and you must read it! It's a blisteringly funny, extraordinarily moving, revelatory chronicle of the Yiddish theater of the early twentieth century!—and then if you feel inclined, come back to me.

imperfect being one of art's essential purposes); but in the mastery of form required to create it, the work also describes wholeness, completion, and community. We apprehend the deep social coherence whence that mastery of form most likely emerged.

People who, through accident or evil human action, stand outside social coherence and community, who are or feel themselves to have been dispossessed or disenfranchised, may, if they happen to be artists, find in a perfected aesthetic form what they've been searching for: wholeness, completion, home. But first-arriving immigrants in a new world will inhabit their homes differently from the native-born who built them. The strangers will inhabit their new homes with a dislocated angularity that betrays unfamiliarity, uneasiness, an uncertainty about tenancy rights and the terms of the lease. The bric-a-brac, or I should say *tchotchkes,* they've brought with them, redolent of other, alien histories, of the old, lost world, will soon be unpacked to inappropriately decorate the new occupants' digs. "Look at the mess they've made of that nice house," the native-born neighbors will say. "Those people, they don't take care of their things."

Ignoring the objections of the finical or the xenophobic, the unentitled refugee artists take shelter in alien forms and settle in, making the unfamiliar their own. They experiment, innovate. They carry the perfected form toward what lies beyond perfection, toward something new.

If you recall my last letter, I mentioned a writer who was staying with me in my boarding house. He writes for the papers and makes a living from it. The way it's done is, he sits and writes and sends it off and gets a kopeck a line when it's printed: the more lines, the more kopecks. Well, I thought it over and asked myself: Good Lord, what does he do that I can't? What's the big trick? After all, I went to school just like he did and have a better handwriting—why not give it a try and toss off a line or two for the Jewish papers? What can I lose? No one will chop off my head. The worse that can happen is, I'll get no for an answer . . . P.S. If with God's help I get ahead with my writing—that is, if I acquire the literary reputation I soon hope to—I'll ask the editors to advance you a few rubles. I wish

you, my dear wife, to benefit equally from my new
line of work. It's more honorable than business, which
is why it pays an honorarium and not a commission.
It's an easy way to make a decent living.

Sholem Aleichem, *The Letters of Menakhem-Mendl*
and Sheyne Sheyndl (TRANS. HILLEL HALKIN)

The reader of *Wandering Stars* can, if this is the kind of thing the reader likes to do, catalog its imperfections, of which there are enough to keep any literary scorekeeper busy and happy. Time lurches wildly in Aleichem's novel, and the narrative along with it. The opinionated, distractible narrator, when he's doing his job, rather than taking a rest while allowing letters written by the characters do the storytelling, seems less interested in his two protagonists than in the fantastical secondary cast that surrounds them. And who can blame him? The secondary characters are magnificent, men and women cooked up out of wit, terror, panic, hunger, chutzpah, pathos, and spleen (especially spleen), effortfully and arduously *cooked*—peeled, chopped, boiled, or fried—rather than dreamed up or imagined.

That this is a knotty, knobby, odd novel of fits and starts and sudden jolts is possibly due to its serialized newsprint origins and its lateness in Sholem Aleichem's writing life; or possibly conventional wisdom and Reb Mendalle Mocher Sephorim are right about him, and Aleichem is found at his best in his short stories and occasional pieces. We might thus consign his novel to culture's remainder table, unless we consider how appropriate its strangeness is to its subject. Though like many other, more perfect novels, *Wandering Stars* is about love, it's about love between Jews who work in the theater. So it should be strange and imperfect. Theater is almost never perfect; its imperfections, its incompleteness and its tawdriness, are among the principal sources of its power. And do I need to tell you that life for Jews isn't perfect? I don't.

But at Zolodievka the fun begins, because that's where
you have to change, to get onto the new train, which they
did us such a favor by running out to Kasrilevke. But
not so fast. First there's the little matter of several hours'
wait, exactly as announced in the schedule—provided,
of course, you don't pull in after the Kasrilevke train
has left. And at what time of night may you look for-
ward to this treat? The very middle, thank you, when

you're dead tired and disgusted, without a friend in the world except sleep—and there's not one single place in the whole station where you can lay your head, not one. When the wise men of Kasrilevke quote the passage from the Holy Book, "Tov shem meshemen tov," *they know what they're doing. I'll translate it for you: We were better off without the train.*

> Sholem Aleichem, "On Account of a Hat" (TRANS. ISAAC ROSENFELD)

Wandering Stars traverses the Jewish diaspora at the beginning of the twentieth century, its impoverished and imperiled shtetls and overcrowded urban ghettos, separated by vast, unwelcoming, perilous distances. At the heart of Aleichem's novel is the romantic tale of Leibel Rafalovitch, the rich man's son, and Reizel Spivak, the poor cantor's daughter. They're a pair of strange, imperfect, or rather incomplete creations, and they provide the book with a shadowy, indeterminate heart. Their early days are beautifully detailed, but the years of their maturing and their respective apprenticeships as artists are fitfully and asymmetrically glimpsed. As a consequence, their subsequent stellar achievements seem improbable, impalpable, and dreamlike—as do Leibel and Reizel, or as they are called by the end of the novel, Leo and Rosa, themselves. Unlike the other characters, they're disturbingly gossamer, dreamed up rather than cooked.

It would be easy to conclude that its vague, dreamy, partially visible, partially occluded protagonists are a serious flaw in *Wandering Stars*, a dreadful violation of the rules of the novel-writing rule book. But before reaching this conclusion, consider that Leo and Rosa are stage performers. Performers finesse the fleeting moment. Theirs is the art of the ineffable, and their accomplishments, likewise; hence the truism that the performer's offstage life is often as unstable, shadowy, improbable, and impalpable as anything she or he does onstage. Eric Bentley, in his *Pirandello Commentaries*, observes that "if a novelist's characters have something a playwright's do not, and the latter's need the actors to fill them out, the playwright's characters have something the novelist's do not: they are not only characters, but roles." Perhaps the two main characters of this novel about the theater are not properly considered characters at all but stage roles, waiting to be filled. Or, in writing roles instead of characters, perhaps Aleichem advances a corollary to Bentley's observation: that the living actors who fill playwrights' roles are to normal (non-stage-performing) people what playwrights' roles are to a novel's characters. Without insulting actors, whom I count among my best friends and on whose talents I depend for my livelihood, perhaps the actor shares to some extent the incompleteness of the stage roles he or she will, by acting, complete.

> *The house had an attic, and the groom, in high hat, frock coat, and white gloves, climbed up there and hid. She stood on the stair below and the balcony scene from* Romeo and Juliet *began—but a little the other way, Romeo above and Juliet below.*
>
> *"Adler, come down," she called.*
>
> *"I'm afraid," I answered.*
>
> *"What are you afraid of?"*
>
> *"You will do me some harm."*
>
> *"Come down, I will do you no harm."*
>
> *"Swear it."*
>
> *"I swear it by my dead father."*
>
> *I came down the stair. We looked at each other, fell into each other's arms, wept. In the rooms inside, musicians were playing, young people dancing. In the end, she went her way.*
>
> Jacob Adler, account of his wedding day, *A Life on the Stage* (TRANS. LULLA ROSENFELD)

Aleichem's novel, as is evident in the modern openness in its pages, is a product of the Haskalah, the Jewish Enlightenment that began in the eighteenth century and flourished in the nineteenth. But not for many years after our author's final works would casting off sexual reticence and delicacy become a literary (not to mention social) option in Jewish communities of the diaspora. Meanwhile, delicacy and reticence retained their authority, and so transgression remained a highly potent spice.

As I was reading *Wandering Stars,* its lovers reminded me of another pair from Haskalahic Yiddish literature. S. Y. Ansky's play *The Dybbuk,* virtually contemporary with *Wandering Stars,* is equally unshapely, strange, and remarkable. Khonen and Leah, *The Dybbuk*'s lovers, are introduced, driven worlds apart, and cross worlds to find each other again, just like Leibel and Reizel. Like *The Dybbuk,*

Wandering Stars derives its dramatic power from desire born of apostasy, and desire's postponement. Like *The Dybbuk, Wandering Stars* is a love story during the telling of which the lovers spend almost no time together. *The Dybbuk*'s moment of reconciliation and gratification is fiery, mystical, and tragical-ecstatic; the wandering stars of the novel finally meet in a touchingly, realistically anticlimactic scene at the Bronx Zoo. In both play and novel, the long-awaited reunion of lovers is, for the audience, for the reader, shockingly brief.

This unsettling brevity can be attributed to the plot mechanics of moralism, to sexual repression reasserting itself, drawing the curtain or slamming the door and putting an end to transgression. The transgressors are banished, and the audience's romantic or prurient expectations are disappointed, while other expectations, for tragedy in *The Dybbuk* and for an unsentimental realism in *Wandering Stars,* are satisfied.

I'd like to propose that the abrupt conclusions are meant to address another expectation, neither moral nor emotional but political and teleological. Since the days of the first singing of the Psalms, Jewish art about lovers, torn asunder, yearning for one another, sanctifying heart and memory as love's tabernacle, seeking and perhaps finding one another, contributes its share to the great Jewish historical narrative of exile and Zion, the protracted Jewish anticipation of Moshiach, the desire for and the continually, painfully deferred return to Jerusalem. And this seems to me especially the case for a Jewish novel about lovers with *wandering* in its title.

In Ansky's play and Aleichem's novel, the lovers reunite and immediately disappear; just as the desired one is finally obtained, the scene is rudely snatched away from us. After such a terribly long and bloody time, after so much waiting, the precise nature of Moshiach, Zion, Jerusalem has, for Jews in the modern world, become obscure, as will the precise nature of any object of endlessly deferred desire. If the heart of all diasporic tales of desire is desire for home, there's a special, specific poignancy in averting the eyes at journey's end, as both Ansky and Aleichem seem to do. It's as if, after such a terribly long and bloody wait, obtaining the object of our desires has become almost impossible to vividly imagine, as if reunion with the loved and lost one has become almost unrepresentable, recognizable only in its elusiveness, in its receding and vanishing.

Indeterminacy in art reminds us that the world is unpredictable, contingent, and malleable, which can be a blessing for people needing alternatives, change, and escape. But all blessings are mixed blessings, as every Jew knows. In catering to a then-new appetite for indeterminate endings, Aleichem showed himself to be a modernist. We moderns, Jewish and otherwise, know that for us to survive, the world must change, and to the extent that we can, we must change the world; indeterminacy means that there's a reason to try. In a Jewish novel, however, an inconclusive conclusion has for its readers an awful, heartrending familiarity: still we are not saved. Even those of the strongest faith must face an affliction of doubt and ask whether, for Leo and Rosa, for us, there will only ever be wandering.

> *Yesterday I read my new play* The Truth *to the actors. They want to present it this coming Friday, and I have only three acts. But I'm not worried—I'm doing my part and I think not badly, and they'll have to work it out, I can't add much to it.*
>
> *While I was reading the third act, a tragi-comic scene took place—they all cried. Feinman's head fell on the table and he started to scream, "I can't stand it! I can't stand it!" The actors predict that it will be successful.*
>
> *If it isn't, my boy, it's all over.*
>
> Yiddish dramatist Jacob Gordin to his son Alexander, quoted in Beth Kaplan, *Finding the Jewish Shakespeare*

Seedy and lowbrow, its company morally ambiguous if not downright appalling, the Shchupak-Murovchik Yiddish theater troupe in *Wandering Stars* blows into the little shtetl of Holeneshti like a calamitous storm, overturning everything it encounters; it too is a product of the Haskalah, a herald and an agent of progress, change, liberation. Like any revolutionary force, the Shchupak-Murovchik Yiddish theater troupe shatters structures both familial and communal, quotidian and sacrosanct; it devours and destroys lives, and sets people free.

All blessings are mixed blessings, as every Jew knows. The Enlightenment, modernism, and technology brought us liberation and fascism as well. The trains that transported us out of the shtetls later transported us into the camps, so though you might argue with the wise men of Kasrilevke, mentioned several paragraphs earlier, it's easy to understand why they concluded: we were better off without the train.

The refugees of Holeneshti who haven't perished in the storm, in pogroms and anti-Semitic purges, will wander forth, displaced, liberated by the catastrophe of change, shtetl dwellers becoming ghetto dwellers becoming artists, cosmopolitans, socialists, or Zionists, or frequently both. Once free, free to wander; once wandering, longing for home. The exilic dialectic spins on.

Theater works its rough, emancipatory magic on Leibel and Reizel, awakening appetites and dreams. It pitches them headlong into a clamorous and convulsive world, where their outsides grow fast and their insides seem hollow, puffed full of air like balloons. They will never be happy, but so what? Who is? Unhappiness they share with their extravagantly unhappy, breathtakingly kvetchy, gloriously cursing supporting cast.

The people who people *Wandering Stars* are for the most part verbally, emotionally, and sometimes physically violent. They've all been severely knocked about, and they give as good as they get. Nearly everyone's a hysteric, driven by financial desperation to obsessive, frenzied plotting, hondling, hyperbole, and fraudulence. They're engaged from birth in a ferocious, unceasing struggle, determined survivors of murderous oppression, crushing poverty, and ignorance. Their world is, unsurprisingly, blazing with rage.

Hysteric, and hence hysterically funny. Aleichem uses laughter to transform rage into an occasion for joy, and in the process laughter itself is transformed, it becomes destabilizing and dangerous. The laughter Aleichem provokes is exceedingly provocative: not complacent but startled, not reassured but astonished. Laughter such as this doesn't answer anything, it asks everything; it doesn't settle anything, it throws everything in the air. Within such laughter, rage is very much alive, and through such laughter, a raging cry for justice can be heard. Once heard, the cry becomes uncontainable. This, too, is an emancipatory magic.

Wandering Stars is a great novel about theater, an invaluable account of the Jewish theater of the diaspora, but it's equally a brilliant exploration of liberation's outrageous, tumultuous motion through human society and the human soul. Epic and intimate, wide open and claustrophobic, Aleichem's perfectly imperfect novel tears, mends, and re-tears its narrative voice along with its characters' lives, as it tumbles us all, characters and readers and narrative, toward the future, toward, should we be so lucky (we should be so lucky!), something we can call home.

TONY KUSHNER
September 2008
New York

A Note on the Translation

Wandering Stars was first translated into English by Frances Butwin in 1952 and has been out of print for many years. On the suggestion of the noted Yiddish scholar and Sholem Aleichem authority Dan Miron, I undertook a new translation. Professor Miron brought to my attention that the previous translation had significantly abridged the novel and even had, in addition to its serious omissions, a changed ending.

Upon reading the original in Yiddish, I fell in love with this little-known epic. Here Sholem Aleichem depicts an antic troupe of Yiddish actors as they travel from a small town in Bessarabia, across Europe to London, and finally to New York. Posing special challenges to the translator is the way their Yiddish takes on colorations of the languages of the places where they temporarily live. While in London, some characters incorporate British phrases into their Yiddish as a way to impress others with their "upper class" speech. The phrase "all right" peppers their conversations. How can the translator convey to the reader that this is, for them, a foreign phrase embedded in the characters' own language and a sign of their efforts at acculturation?

This problem is intensified once the troupe arrives in New York's Lower East Side. There the performers take over many Americanisms and Yiddishize them. How to convey this? To write English with a Yiddish accent mischaracterizes how it sounds to the Yiddish speaker, to whom it seems quite right. Simply writing the words in English fails to convey what the speaker is attempting, but that is sometimes the only solution. One pompous character, giving a speech in Yiddish, addresses his audience as "Ladies and gentlemen," which in the text is written in Yiddish letters but spoken in English, where it is lost in translation.

I thank my weekly Yiddish Lunch Group for their help and Rivka Rubinfeld, my daily walking companion of almost twenty-five years, for her help with Hebrew words.

Special appreciation goes to Steven Spielberg, whose generous funding of the digital library of the National Yiddish Book Center in Amherst, Massachusetts, made it possible to have a perfect Yiddish copy of this novel.

Thank you, as well, to Janet Biehl, the most awesome copyeditor ever.

I wish to thank the faculty and graduate students of the University of Michigan Judaic Studies Department, with whom I meet weekly to enjoy reading aloud from the wealth of Yiddish texts. These dedicated scholars are all multilingual and have been most generous in their help.

I would like to give special thanks to John Siciliano, my editor at Viking/Penguin, whose help and support have been invaluable.

I am grateful to Howie, my husband of nearly sixty years, who has always been my in-house editor and other set of ears. As a published poet, he enjoys contributing the translations of the poems and ditties that Sholem Aleichem loved to include in his work. I dedicate this book to him with deep gratitude, admiration, and devotion.

ALIZA SHEVRIN
May 2008
Ann Arbor

PART I

ACTORS

The Bird Has Flown

One bright Sunday morning toward the end of summer, Leah the cantor's wife awoke with a start. She suddenly remembered it was Sunday, market day. Glancing out the window, she saw broad daylight. "What's the matter with me! It's late!" she exclaimed. She dressed hurriedly, splashed water over her fingertips, ran through her morning prayers, grabbed her basket, and sped off to the market, afraid she would miss all the bargains.

It was a beautiful morning. A warm sun bathed Holeneshti in its golden rays. Once she reached the market, Leah was like a fish in water—she was in her element. The sheer size of the Holeneshti market was something to behold. The Moldavian peasants had brought in sheep's milk and cheese, and great quantities of vegetables from their gardens—corn, greens, and cucumbers, all selling for a song, as well as onions, garlic, and bitter herbs. With all these plentiful choices before her, Leah quickly negotiated a basketful. And the fish! A heaven-sent bargain! She had not planned to buy fish, but suddenly there they were. But please imagine what fish—tiny, skinny, scrawny little things, all bone, barely a mouthful, but so cheap it would be a shame to turn them down. No one would believe it! Yes, Leah was having a lucky day at the market. Of the one ruble she had brought, quite a bit was still left. With so much still unspent, she thought she would surprise the cantor with a gift—ten fresh eggs. *Yisroyeli will appreciate that*, she thought. It would be enough to make ten throat-soothing honey *gogl-mogls*. The High Holidays would be here soon—*He'll need them to keep his throat in good shape. And how about candies for my Reizel? She loves sweets, confections, snacks—bless her, what a delight that girl is. I only wish I could buy her new shoes. The old ones are worn through and through—useless.*

With these thoughts spurring her on, the cantor's wife hurried from booth to booth until the rest of the ruble had melted away like snow. Only then could she finally relax and go home.

As she neared her house, she could hear the cantor practicing singing his prayers: "*Mee-ee-ee ba-a-a-esh u'mee-ee-ee bamayim!*" That sweet familiar voice had given her pleasure for so long, but she never tired of it. Yisroyeli the cantor was practicing a brand-new *U'netaneh tokef* to chant for Rosh Hashanah. He was not one of your great cantors with a worldwide reputation, but in his own Holeneshti he was famous enough. You can be sure the town would never have exchanged him for the greatest cantor, not even one with his own choir, nor let him go for a million rubles! But that's neither here nor there. Yisroyeli the cantor also taught on the side—without it the family would never have been able to manage. Luckily he was a fine biblical scholar with a talent for teaching Hebrew. In addition, God had blessed him with a fine hand to pen letters for those who could not write. He had ten students, the richest children in town. One of his prize pupils was the son of Benny Rafalovitch, the richest man in town. Two incomes are nothing to sneeze at. Nonetheless, despite his chanting and his teaching, he and Leah often did not have enough to eat for *Shabbes*. Still, they would not die of hunger— somehow they would find a way.

Arriving home, carrying a full basket from the market, perspiring, Leah was surprised to find that her daughter did not show her face. Usually Reizel was already dressed and washed, her hair combed, running to greet her. She'd poke around in her basket: "Mama, what did you bring me?" "Wait a minute," Leah would say, "what's the hurry? First let me get your father his glass of chicory."

That was what the cantor's wife was expecting today. But the house was quiet, strangely quiet. Reizel was nowhere to be seen or heard although the door was open. Was it possible she was still asleep? The cantor continued to warble, reaching the highest notes with a sob, "Ach, *mee-ee-ee ba-eysh umee-ee-ee bamayim!*" And again, "*Mee-ee-ee ba-a-esh umee bamay-ay-ay-ayim.*"

Quietly, Leah tiptoed into the house and set the basket down in a corner. So as not to disturb her husband in his work, she busied herself at the stove, all the while muttering: "God in heaven! Is she still asleep? These young girls! The students are coming to class any minute now, and she'll be walking around half-naked right in front of them. She thinks she's still a child.

"Yisroyeli! Yisroyeli? No, he can't hear me. He's too wrapped up in his *ba-eyshes* and *bamayims* prayers this morning, God help us! Someone might think they're stuffing his pockets with gold for his chanting. And here Reizel walks around in worn-out shoes, may I suffer her pains. How long is she going to sleep! I have to wake the child up!"

With these words, Leah hurried to the curtain that divided the room and listened quietly for a moment. Then she slowly lifted the curtain with two fingers. She peered in the bed, looked toward the open window—and froze, unable to speak. Feeling as if someone had struck her heart with a stone, she turned to her husband:

"Yisroyeli!"

The intensity of her voice immediately stopped Yisroyeli's singing. "What is it, Leah?"

"Where is Reizel?"

"What do you mean, where is Reizel? Isn't she asleep?"

* * *

Within half an hour the news had spread through the town about the cantor's misfortune. People streamed into the house to find out what had happened. "Is she really gone? How is this possible? How could this have happened?"

For the rest of the morning the town seethed like a kettle: "Have you heard? The cantor's daughter is gone!" "What do you mean? Where has she gone?" "Gone—as if she had sunk into the earth."

And the cantor? How to describe him? He neither cried nor spoke. He stood in the middle of the room like a statue, staring at the empty bed mutely, as if words and even reason itself had failed him. His wife, however, was tearing around the town like a madwoman, wringing her hands, beating herself in the head, crying out to the heavens, "My daughter! My child! My precious!" Trooping after her, the townspeople helped her search. They hunted everywhere, in every corner—across the bridge, in the cemetery, in all the Wallachian gardens, and even in the lake. Gone!

Half dead, the cantor's wife was carried home to a house full of people, all talking about the tragedy that had befallen the cantor in his own home. Some pulled back the curtain to gaze at the empty bed and the open window. "So it was from here the bird flew away?" they wondered. Leave it to the people of Holeneshti to come up with a clever way of putting it.

CHAPTER 2
She Faints Away

Every Jewish town, no matter how poor, must have its own Roth-schild. The Rothschild of Holeneshti was Benny Rafalovitch. To tell you all about his wealth and position would be too much. It will suffice simply to describe how many sat at his table. Each and every day at Benny's table you would find no fewer than twenty people: sons, daughters, sons-in-law, daughters-in-law. All were handsome, healthy, well-fed souls with full round faces. Among them was also an old grandmother whose head shook from side to side, as if saying "No no!"; a nursemaid, pale as an underdone roll but with a flush high on her cheeks; and a young man, a distant relative, who over-saw the household accounts. This young man's name was Simcha but everyone called him Sison v'Simcha, which means "joy and glad-ness." Not that he was such a happy creature—on the contrary, he was by nature a cheerless, melancholy sort with a sleepy demeanor. He had black, shiny hair, puffy eyes, and a constantly stuffed nose that made it difficult for him to properly pronounce his *m*'s and *n*'s, and his full and thickly mustached upper lip didn't help.

We will have the opportunity to become acquainted with this family in due time, but in general we can say that theirs was a wealthy, happy, lively household that was most fond of eating. When it came time for them to eat, one could have gone deaf from the uproar, the din, the clatter of spoons and forks.

At the head of the table, like a king, sat the master of the house himself, Benny, a Bessarabian Jew with a substantial belly and a beard that grew horizontally. Yes, it parted to the left and to the right, not like an ordinary beard, and it refused to lie flat as it should. But he could do nothing about it, try as he might!

When Benny ate, he threw himself into it—nothing could distract him. He hated doing two things at once anyway, but when eating he refused to be bothered about anything else. He spoke very little but didn't mind when others spoke. When a clamor erupted at the table, he would shout, "Quiet down, you scamps! Better look into your prayer books and pay attention to what you are reciting!" By this he meant they should look into their plates and pay attention to what they were eating. It was his way to speak elliptically. For instance, he called a horse a "fellow," money was "shards," a wife was a "disaster," a son

was a "kaddish," a daughter a "blister," bread a "thread," a house
an "attic," an alcove a "hole"—and so on. One could have created a
whole new dictionary from Benny Rafalovitch's vocabulary.

At the opposite head of the table sat Benny's wife, Beylke, a, tiny,
frail, quiet woman, unheard and unseen. Looking at her, you would ask
yourself: *Was this the woman who brought into the world all these children?* But don't be fooled—this tiny woman bore on her shoulders the
weight of the entire household. Always busy, she took on everyone's pain
as her own. She asked nothing for herself but instead devoted her life
to her children. In this respect she was following in the footsteps of her
aged mother-in-law, whose head shook in a constant "no no." This old
mother had apparently been created to remind people of their death.

Having lost almost all her senses, the grandmother still had
one—a sharp eye. She saw everything before anyone else did. So
no one besides her had noticed that the youngest boy, Leibel, was
missing. Scanning the long table with her sharp eye, the old lady had
noticed it immediately. Her head shaking, she exclaimed, "Where in
the world is Leibel?"

They all looked around and saw that Leibel was missing. They
began searching for him everywhere. "Where is Leibel?" they all
wondered.

As long as Benny's household had existed, it had never happened
that a child was missing from the dinner table. The father became
angry and commanded: "Let them bring the young lamb from the
flock!" Benny meant that they were to bring the youngest one from
the *cheder.* They sent a messenger to Yisroyeli the cantor's *cheder* to
bring Leibel home for supper.

The Rafalovitches were already eating the last course, the fresh
corn, when the messenger returned with the news that Leibel had
not gone to the cantor's house that day and that a tragedy, may it not
happen here, had befallen the cantor and his wife: their daughter,
their only daughter, had vanished during the night without a trace.

This news hit the family like a bombshell. They sat staring at
one another. What each of them was thinking at that moment was
hard to know—they kept their thoughts to themselves. Only the old
lady, who was used to speaking her mind, said loudly and clearly, as
her head wobbled: "Have a look in the desk drawer. I could swear
that in the middle of the night I heard someone stirring in the dark
while the young man"—she indicated Sison v'Simcha—"was snoring so loudly he could have woken the dead."

Old people have such odd ideas! What did she mean, Sison v'Simcha was snoring? If a fly were to alight in the room, he would have heard it, so light was his sleep! Still and all, the sleepy bookkeeper stood up with effort, took his time wiping off his hairy upper lip with his greasy hand, and fished a ring of keys from his trouser pocket. Slowly, unhurriedly, he unlocked the middle drawer of the oaken desk, peered inside—and stood paralyzed. His sleepy, puffy eyes seemed to glaze over, and he could not speak so much as a word.

Benny came to his aid: "For God's sake, speak!" he thundered, so loudly that Sison v'Simcha began to shake.

Though tongue-tied and snuffling through his stuffed nose, the bookkeeper found words: "Believe me, these keys were with me all night, in my pants pocket. Believe me, I didn't sleep a wink, heard not the slightest noise. Come see for yourself—the drawer is now empty, not a trace!"

At these words someone at the table uttered a stifled scream, keeled over, and fell into a faint.

It was tiny, frail, quiet little Beylke.

CHAPTER 3

Holeneshti Goes Wild

Holeneshti was in turmoil. It seethed. It boiled. Holeneshti was going wild.

Imagine, in one day so much happening! Two scandals at once! And what scandals they were! And such an oddly matched pair: the poor cantor's daughter and the richest man's son. Was it just a coincidence?

Holeneshti set to work. Shopkeepers locked up their shops, teachers left their schoolrooms, workers laid aside their tools, and housewives abandoned their stoves. All went into the town center to gather in small circles, filling the streets. It looked just like a *Shabbes* after *shul*. Rumors flew, there were endless speculations, and story after story was told, impossible to put down on paper, because no sooner did one person tell a story than someone else told another, and then a third person with yet another story would butt in to clip their wings, saying they were both idiots. No one knew what had become of the young couple. But adding to the jumble was a fourth person who pronounced that the third barely knew more than a corpse. Leave it to him—he would give you the final word! A lengthy disquisition followed built on his own surmises, borrowing from both Rabbi Akiva's literal and Rabbi Hillel's commonsense rules. But the crowd was not convinced. According to commonsense rules, his explanation did make sense, but then what? It led nowhere.

Then yet another person was heard from, a blond man with dull eyes who elbowed his way in and posed a perplexing question: "Hear me out, Jews. I want to ask you something. Tell me, I beg you, how is it that our young couple decided to disappear on the very same Saturday night that the Yiddish acting company left town?"

"What does that have to do with it?"

"What does that have to do with it? Maybe the Jewish actors have something to do with it."

"Stop repeating everything. Say something sensible!" The crowd burst out laughing.

The blond fellow with the dull eyes felt insulted. "You can bray like donkeys for all I care. If you're all so smart, then tell me: What were the actors doing last week in Yisroyeli the cantor's house? If you can't figure it out, why don't you ask the cantor?"

"And pour more salt on his wounds?"

"Then stop talking nonsense, and follow what I'm saying. If you ask me, I'll tell you exactly what the actors were doing at Yisroyeli's. They had learned he has a daughter, and a beauty too, who can sing. Knowing the cantor is a poor man, they asked him to let her join the company and promised they would make something of her. Well now, does that make sense?"

"It does make sense. But what about the Rafalovitch boy?"

"This I cannot figure. My head is splitting just thinking about it. It's possible that Benny Rafalovitch's son, who studies at Yisroyeli's *cheder*, is in love with the cantor's daughter and went along with her. How else would a young scamp like that get involved in such things? Maybe the girl duped him, with the consent of her father and mother. But we all know the cantor, and he is not that kind of person. Could it be his wife? It's possible. Who knows what a woman can do?"

"Quiet down! The police chief is coming!" someone in the crowd exclaimed, pointing. The police chief sped by in a spanking-new, squeaky carriage that was decorated with many bells and was drawn by a pair of white horses that the crowd recognized as Rafalovitch's.

Sitting alongside the police chief in the carriage, huddled in terror, was Yechiel the *klezmer*, who had performed with the acting company during its stay.

The sight of the carriage with Benny Rafalovitch's horses and Yechiel the musician suddenly made the words spoken by the blond fellow with the dull eyes so believable that the crowd gravitated closer to him in order to hear his words, which soon made sense.

Now that the Holeneshti Jews are on the right track, having found in the Yiddish acting company the key to this strange mystery, we leave them to their stories. Let them sharpen their wits while we go back a few weeks, to the moment when a Yiddish acting company arrived in Holeneshti, for the first time ever since Holeneshti became a town and Bessarabia a province.

CHAPTER 4

A *"Real Character"*

Some three weeks earlier word had spread in Holeneshti that a Yiddish acting company was arriving. No one was particularly excited by the news. "What is this?" the Holeneshters said among themselves. "Actor types, comedians—who needs them?"

One might easily assume that the townspeople were spoiled, that they had known theater all their lives and had grown weary of it. But to be honest, they had never witnessed a single performance and could not have begun to tell you what theater really was. Then again, where is it written that you have to see everything with your own eyes in order to have an opinion? For what reason did God endow a person with intelligence? A Jew understands more important things, thank God. A Jew is not a peasant.

One fine morning a strange character arrived in Holeneshti. He was wearing an orange and dark blue-green cape with a threadbare, crushed cap on his head, and he was carrying a battered valise. When he let it be known that he was looking to rent a space for a theater, he was immediately surrounded by curiosity-seekers, not because the fellow himself was such a curiosity—that's beside the point—but simply because they were curious about what he was up to.

The man, short and clean-shaven, looked around with shrewd eyes at the town and its Jews. To those gathered around him he said in an odd hoarse voice, his threadbare crushed cap sliding up and down: "Obviously, as I look around, I see that our ancestor Adam never observed a *Shabbes* here."

Just a few ordinary Yiddish words, no? But you had to see for yourself the effect they had. Suddenly, helplessly, everyone was holding his sides with laughter. At first the fellow was startled by this reaction and watched them in silence, as if they were out of their minds. He waited till the laughter died down and then spoke to them more earnestly. On the road to the town he had begun to feel pangs of hunger. His stomach was empty, and he was beginning to feel faint.

"Tell me, my dear friends, do you know where I can find a little something to fill my belly?"

Again, the words were ordinary, but the way he spoke them had the townspeople rolling on the ground.

"I am not joking. I just need something to fill my face."

That was all they needed. Those last words resulted in nothing less than stomach cramps brought on by too much laughter.

Within half an hour all of Holeneshti had repeated those last words: "Something to fill my face"—ha ha ha!

"A real character!" they said, wiping away tears of laughter. "A strange character, and a strange cape, and a strange cap, and a strange way of speaking. You could die laughing!"

The fellow searched till he found what he was looking for—a good inn that served food. After polishing off a shmaltz herring and downing a glass of Bessarabian wine, he contentedly smoked a cigarette and chatted with the landlady, a pretty, dark-skinned woman named Necha. Did she have a husband, he wanted to know, or was she a widow or a divorcée, or was she simply unmarried? Necha giggled and turned away from the strange character. The man took his walking stick, pushed his crushed cap down on his forehead, stuck his hands in his pockets, and left the inn. Strolling toward the center of town, he kept an eye out for a likely place for a theater.

As he walked, a clutch of barefoot youngsters who had discovered that they loved the theater followed him step by step. Then he came to a courtyard, where he spotted a large, wide, empty stable with an iron roof.

This is the stable God created on the sixth day of Creation for a Yiddish theater! he said to himself, and entered the courtyard.

That was Benny Rafalovitch's courtyard and Benny Rafalovitch's stable.

CHAPTER 5
A Pair of Letters

Holeneshti did not have to wait much longer for a Yiddish theater. The "real" character came to an understanding with Benny Rafalovitch about renting his stable, and they agreed on a price. Then he sent off a letter to his people that we now reproduce exactly, word for word, in the same language in which it was written:

> *My dear friend Albert* in this letter I am letting you know that I am in Holeneshti a town in Bessarabia as big as a yawn full of people who wolf down cornmeal mush and guzzle wine as if it were water but Moishe will go to the theater if it's the last thing he does and I've rented a theater you could find it in London and a stage so big you can drive a sleigh and horses across and covered with an iron roof so not a drop of rain can leak through the landlord of the theater is called Benny stuffed with money like a sack of sawdust but all he wanted was a deposit so I told him he should cool his heels because in a day or two I am getting mail and I found pretty cheap lodgings and a landlady a little doll eat and drink as much as you like and everything on credit so don't be an idiot and don't let grass grow under your feet and right away send out the sets and playbills and stop whatever you are doing and come right out with the whole troupe and for God's sake don't depend on the pawnshops because it's already been three weeks and nine days since we worked and we'll all die of hunger you can get an engagement here as easily as Hotzmach eats a tasty pot roast on an empty stomach say hello to Hotzmach for me the devil take him and please go up to my room where I left my slippers and a couple of censored plays under the bed and send me some posters immediately for God's sake and don't have a fit that I'm not sending you a telegram because I don't have more

than twenty worn-out kopecks from me your friend who
greets you one and all in a most friendly way.

Sholom-Meyer Murovchik

A few days later this Sholom-Meyer Murovchik received an
answer.

Most worthy friend Sholom-Meyer on your head should
be piled up what you deserve to get for borrowing fifteen
rubles from Breyndele Kozak and putting it on my account
what business do I have you bastard with Breyndele Kozak
the whole troupe loves her like a pain in the eye for the
way she scrimps over a *groshen* about the sets I can't tell
whether you're playing dumb or you really are stupid I
think you know very well the sets have long been hocked
where do I get the money to get them out of hock you can't
get an engagement here for love or money and my measly
bit of gold and jewels I refuse to squander on filling strangers' bellies and it wasn't so easy to come by unless they
underwrite binding contracts don't even mention profits or
shares or partners Hotzmach as partner he should live so
long I share half-and-half with him let him threaten me to
form a separate company let him go to hell I'm sending you
playbills and arrange right away for eight spectacles and a
benefit and what are you talking about you thief that all
you have is twenty worn-out kopeks are you too sick to
hock your watch like I did everyone is on my back everyone wants a starring role and when it comes right down to
something no one's home now I'm going to make this my
last try if Bessarabia works out it's fine and if not go knock
your head against the wall I'll take myself to Romania and
put together a troupe that God and man will rejoice in and
finally be rid of that accursed nuisance in the meantime get
everything that's ready but don't run up any big expenses
watch your pocket we're all coming soon God willing on
Shabbes and on *Shabbes* night we'll rehearse and Sunday
we'll put on a performance and you should know your slippers and censored plays are long on the garbage heap with
best wishes and great respect your friend director.

Albert Shchupak

CHAPTER 6
The Holeneshti Public

Drunkards who had not tasted a bitter drop for months, starving people who had not had food for days, would not have thrown themselves upon drink and food with the passion that the Holeneshters threw themselves upon the Yiddish theater.

At the opening performance, not only was Rafalovitch's court-yard packed with people, but the street outside was overflowing. The townspeople were intensely curious to see anything they could of the theater, even from outside. In fact, fewer were enthusiastic about going inside, for several reasons. For one, they were told it cost money, which in Holeneshti was hard to come by. Second, not everyone could allow himself to go to the theater. What is appropriate for young men and women, boys and girls, is not for respectable people, bearded Jews who might have marriageable daughters. But temptation, heaven help us, whispers into one's ear: "What would be the harm, Reb Jew, to take a peek from a distance through a little crack to see how they do Yiddish theater?"

Those who yielded to temptation and peeked through whatever cracks they could find were so many that the theater administration had to hose the crowd with cold water to disperse them. This worked perfectly, a thousand times better than the best police, and it cost little.

It was our acquaintance Sholom-Meyer Murovchik, the "real character," who invented this solution.

What did this Sholom-Meyer Murovchik actually do in the the-ater? He was nobody and yet everybody, a bookkeeper, a cashier, a box office manager, an occasional prompter, and, if need be, a fill-in actor. To say he was a great artist wouldn't be true. But for all that, he was an honest man, devoted to the director, whom he served as loy-ally as a dog. The director, Albert Shchupak (whom we will soon get to know better), knew this very well and consequently used Sholom-Meyer wherever he was needed. And everywhere, wherever you made a move, it was Sholom-Meyer and again Sholom-Meyer. If you didn't have money and needed a complementary ticket, you went to Sholom-Meyer. In Holeneshti there were many such lucky ones. Take Benny Rafalovitch's household, around twenty strong. As we well know, Benny was a wealthy man who could certainly afford to pay. Yet he had a point—why should he have to pay to get into his own stable?

On opening night the Rafalovitches marched in en masse: the cousin who was the family bookkeeper, the nursemaid, and the rest of his large retinue occupied the first two rows of benches. Sholom-Meyer came over to raise the little matter of tickets. At first Benny acted as if he weren't there. Sholom-Meyer let him know in his hoarse voice that they had taken up the best places.

Only then did Benny deign to look at him and respond in his elliptical way: "Remove yourself from here on those short stumps of yours before I smack you on your scraped-off noodle-board of a head and call my boys to work you over and make cornmeal mush out of you."

After that strange diatribe Sholom-Meyer realized that no money would be coming from that quarter. To argue would hardly be worth the trouble, and time wasn't standing still. The theater was open, and the public was streaming in mostly on passes. Yechiel the musician alone used up a good number. Sholom-Meyer had never figured a musician, *kayn eyn horeh*, could have such a big family! And what about the rest of the musicians? The wigmaker? The carpenter? The blacksmith? The tailor? The shoemaker? All of them did work for the theater, and all had, blessed be His name, wives and children who were entitled to passes. And how about his "little *mezuzah*" of a landlady? Was it her fault she had two younger sisters and an old mother, deaf as a doornail? Wasn't it enough that she had to support them—why should she still have to pay for their tickets? Was that fair? And how about Shimen-Dovid the coachman and Chayim-Ber the porter, who had helped move the stage sets from the train station? Were their souls worth any less?

When it came to handing out passes, Sholom-Meyer turned a deaf ear to the director, Albert Shchupak, even if he went crazy, gnashed his teeth, whipped himself into a frenzy, and dropped dead. Whoever needed a pass to get into the theater got one.

You can't argue with the public.

CHAPTER 7

Eyes

Let the reader not mistakenly think that the entire Holeneshti public received passes. Some spent their last hard-earned ruble or

arranged a short-term loan from a good friend to buy tickets for
their children.

Yiddish theater! How could you refuse to take a child to the theater? Were there so many other pleasures in Holeneshti? But what did
you do if money was nowhere to be had and the child was begging,
desperate, almost ready to die for a chance to attend the theater?

Let us take as an example Yisroyeli the cantor's daughter, Reizel.
In what way was she any worse than other girls? You had to have the
heart of a Tartar not to take pity on such a child, especially since she
was an only daughter whose parents would readily go to the ends of
the earth to bring her whatever she needed. But as bad luck would
have it, just when the theater was opening, Yisroyeli the cantor had
not a single kopek, not from his chanting, not from tuition. Try to
squeeze water from a stone! Poor Leah was distraught. She could do
nothing, even though nosy neighbors said she pampered her daughter, spoiling her with sweets and expensive shoes.

Well, it's true, she'd say to herself. *Let them have an only daughter, and one as bright as my Reizel, may no harm befall her, and
we'll see if they still talk about shoes and sweets!*

Then Leah came up with a solution. Her husband was teaching the rich man Rafalovitch's son, Leibel, and the theater production was taking place in Rafalovitch's courtyard. To her mind, it
fit together like having a kosher spoon to stir a kosher pot. Leah
would persuade her husband to tell Leibel to tell his mother to tell
his father to let her daughter into the theater for free.

The cantor was poor, but he was also proud. It was beneath
him, he said, to beg one of his students for favors.

Leah then wiped her lips and cornered Benny Rafalovitch's son,
saying to him, "Leibel, I have a favor to ask of you."

"A favor?" Leibel stood stock still. Of him? Of Leibel? A favor?

After hearing Leah's request, Leibel's always-red cheeks turned
even redder. He immediately replied that he would certainly speak
to his mother, that his mother would certainly speak to his father,
and . . . and that his father would certainly speak to his mother
and . . . and his mother would certainly speak to his father—tphoo!
Leibel was getting all tangled up. In short, he said it would surely
work out.

But at the same time Leibel's large, fine, gentle, mild eyes met
Reizel's black gypsy-eyes, which shone with gratitude and happiness as she looked at him from a modest distance. He imagined her

eyes were speaking, saying to him, *You are a fine young man. If you want me to be at the theater, I will be. I know it.*

He lowered his eyes.

And that very day after supper Leibel brought the good news to the *cheder* that he had spoken to his mother, that his mother had spoken to his father, and that his father had said that Reizel could come to their home that evening and join them at the theater.

Hearing those words, Reizel's charming, dark gypsy-face blushed, and her black gypsy-eyes flashed. She embraced and kissed her mother. Then she began singing and dancing and whirling around, trying to draw her mother into singing and dancing with her.

Leah said to her with a laugh, "Have you gone out of your mind, child? Better go wash, get dressed, and I'll braid your hair. You're going to be among fine people, don't you know?"

That evening Leah escorted Reizel to the Rafalovitch home, delivering her into Beylke Rafalovitch's hands, begging her to look after her. "You must know that she is my only daughter, my one and only!" she said.

Beylke looked at the cantor's daughter with the black gypsy-eyes and liked what she saw. "Don't worry," she said to the cantor's wife. "Rest assured. Like my own child."

And the cantor's wife went home.

Reizel did not feel comfortable in Benny Rafalovitch's grand house among his large household. It didn't help that they all devoured her with their eyes. She liked the house itself and the people too. But all those eyes were staring at her, and each one was wondering: *What is her name? How old is she? Is she grown up enough to pray, to read, to write?*

She had never imagined a house could be so large and beautiful, with so many rooms, beds, tables, chairs, and mirrors and all sorts of bric-a-brac. The dining table was laden with so many glasses, cups, and spoons—and fruit, all kinds of preserves, an endless variety of preserves! And the noise around the table, the shouting, the fun, the laughter! So this was what a wealthy home was like!

Reizel knew that Leibel's parents were the wealthiest in town. But what exactly did "wealthy" mean? What was the definition? She had no idea. That being rich was a good thing and that being poor was a bad thing she had heard from her mother thousands of times. From her childhood on, almost every day, her mother had rehearsed countless folk sayings and brought down countless curses on the heads of the wealthy. But only now, as Reizel sat at that large, abundantly set, happy table, did she realize what her mother had meant. She had never wished to be rich, but she did at that moment. Envy—a new feeling—stole into her heart. Then her black, glowing gypsy-eyes met another pair of eyes, familiar, large, handsome, gentle, mild eyes that gazed at her shyly, yet with warmth and friendliness. She imagined those eyes were saying to her, *Do you like it here? I'm pleased that you do. I'm pleased that you are happy.* She felt her heart stir. She was suddenly hot, and her face was burning.

She lowered her eyes.

CHAPTER 8
The Curtain Rises

For the first performance the Holeneshti public filled the theater, gathering early. They were afraid they might be late, God forbid, you could never tell. People were packed in so tightly that those who did have seats were almost on one another's laps. The luckiest were those who had been the very first to arrive—along with the Rafalovitches, they snatched up the best places right in front. Naturally this irked those who arrived a little later. They had paid good money, hard cash for seats, and now there were none! The ever-ready hose was turned on, and a near riot ensued, almost bringing down the whole theater. Luckily Sholom-Meyer (everywhere Sholom-Meyer!) signaled Yechiel the *klezmer* to strike up a lively tune. Once they heard the music, the crowd thought the play was about to start. Quickly they seated themselves as best they could, and the theater became quiet.

But the crowd was mistaken. The music stopped, and the curtain was still down. From the other side of the curtain loud voices could be heard shouting and cursing, and axes and hammers were banging. Something was going on back there, but no one knew what. The audience was sitting on pins and needles, and the young people were becoming quite restless. They could hardly wait to see what awaited them once the curtain rose.

Among those eager young people were two particularly attractive children, a bar mitzvah lad with large, fine, mild eyes and a dark-skinned girl of fourteen or fifteen with black gypsy-eyes and dimples in her cheeks. They sat very close together, these two who came from such different backgrounds, he the wealthy Rafalovitch's son, she the poor cantor's daughter.

Who had arranged to seat this couple so close together? Perhaps they had managed it themselves. But in such a hubbub who would have noticed them? Who would have paid any attention to them when all eyes were riveted on the curtain and only on the curtain! There sat our happy pair, Leibel and Reizel, side by side, close together for the first time. And truly they *were* seeing each other for the first time. They did see each other daily at Yisroyeli the cantor's *cheder*, but what kind of seeing was that? When Leibel went to *cheder*, it was either to study the Gemorah or to write out texts. There was no time or place to visit with a girl.

Moreover the teacher's wife, long life to her, kept a careful eye on her child. Leah dogged her daughter every step and didn't allow her so much as a peek into the tiny corner where the *cheder* boys were studying: "A girl has no business with boys, because a girl is a girl and boys are boys, don't you know."

That was what Leah the cantor's wife had said, and when Leah said something, it was said and done. Nor was Reizel allowed to sing while the boys were in *cheder*. Reizel had a very sweet voice and really loved to sing. But if she had ever sung during *cheder*, the older boys would have listened with smitten hearts. When they went home, they would have remembered Reizel's voice. While lying in bed, they would have sighed quietly and fallen asleep dreaming of their teacher's daughter.

Perhaps Reizel did not appear in the dreams of every older boy, but for Leibel she appeared more than once. He was often distracted from his studies thinking about her. More than once he held the Gemorah in his hand but saw Reizel's face.

Now she was so near to him that not only did he see her, not only did he hear her, but he felt her, right next to him! He heard a heart beating without knowing whose it was. Was it his or hers, or was it both beating together? When their eyes met, they both lowered them. Both desired to say something, but speech was not possible. Not for him, not for her. Words failed them!

Leibel reminded himself how many times he had sought a pretext to stand close to Reizel, to hear her voice, to speak even a few words to her. But then her mother would materialize, and Reizel would be gone. Reizel reminded herself how she had searched among her father's pupils for the rich man's son, not because he was a rich man's son but because her father thought more highly of him than of all his students. He predicted great things for him. Yisroyeli the cantor was a good judge of people, saying here was "a boy with a future." His wife Leah interpreted this remark in her own way: "Why not? A rich man has luck in everything, even with children, you can be sure!"

Now sitting so close to Reizel, Leibel regretted that he could find nothing to say. Reizel too did not know whether to speak to him. What would she say, and how would she say it? Each was wondering about the other, and both were silent. Suddenly the lamps were turned down and the theater became dark, a signal that soon the play would begin. Cries from the audience were heard:

"Oh, oh, oh, oh!"

"As dark as the plague in Egypt!"

"Ay-ay-ay, my leg!"

"Serves you right—whose fault is it? You have an extra leg, leave it at home!"

"Quiet, the devil with you!"

The audience became lively, happy. Leibel did not know how or when it happened, but Reizel's soft, smooth, warm hand found his own. He held her hand in his awhile, and then he gave it a squeeze, as if to say, *Are you happy?* She responded with her own squeeze, which meant, *Very!*

The curtain rose.

CHAPTER 9

In Paradise

If for the Holeneshti Jews the Yiddish-German theater was a pure pleasure dropped from heaven, for our young pair it was a sheer, God-given paradise, to which not everyone was privileged to gain admittance. For these two it meant infinitely more than for anyone else. Night after night they attended the theater, occupied the best places, and saw and heard wonders of which they had never dreamed.

A new world revealed itself to them, in which strangely costumed people disguised themselves and strode boldly about. They spoke an odd language, half-Yiddish, half-German, as they sang and danced, struck artificial poses that made one burst into laughter or dissolve in tears.

And this was all done by ordinary people? No, these were not ordinary people like you and me. These were imps, spirits, devils, or angels. Their postures and gestures, the way they moved and talked—everything was full of charm, enchantment, magic. From the moment the curtain rose, Leibel and Reizel were enchanted, transported to a world of imps, spirits, devils, and angels. Once the curtain fell, it vanished! Gone were the magic, the imps, the spirits, the devils, the angels. They were again ordinary mortals living in the workaday world. Leibel and Reizel felt as if they had been in seventh heaven and had suddenly been lowered back to earth. They sorely regretted having to return to earth so soon, but they consoled themselves that once the curtain rose again, they would again be in heaven, and so tomorrow and so the day after tomorrow and so every day.

Happy children!

How many boys in Holeneshti envied Leibel because all this excitement was taking place in his father's courtyard! How many girls envied Reizel because, thanks to her mother, she had been able to gain entrance to the higher-ups, the Rafalovitches! What difference did it make to those rich people if another person tagged along with them to the theater?

"My child has really found favor with the rich, *kayn eyn horeh,* may it not turn out badly," the cantor's wife boasted to her neighbors. And lest they think, heaven forbid, that she had begged a favor for her daughter's sake, she added very diplomatically: "How did my Reizel come to these rich people? Well, listen. I was just walking in the market the other day and ran into Beylke Rafalovitch. 'Good morning.' 'Good year.' 'What's new?' 'What's new with you?' 'Don't ask, a big to-do in our courtyard, a theater, a big fuss, a regular holiday for my family. For them it's a rare occasion. And how is your daughter?' 'Thank you, how should she be?' 'They say she's very talented.' 'Thank you, may it not turn out badly.' 'Why don't you send her over to me?' 'Thank you, what will she do there?' 'She'll meet my girls and also go to the theater with them. Don't worry.' 'Thank you, if she wants to, I will certainly send her.'"

By inventing a big lie, Leah cleverly hid how it had really happened. What doesn't a mother do for the sake of a child?

Not that we wish to defame the cantor's wife, but because we thirst for the truth, we must report what actually happened. The cantor's wife would not have agreed to send her daughter to just anybody, but she sent her to the Rafalovitches with the greatest pleasure and respect—and why not? Let the world know with whom her child was hobnobbing.

The morning after the first performance Leah somehow managed to be talking with her daughter quite openly within earshot of other people: "Tell me how you were received yesterday by the rich folks?"

Or: "Reizel! What time are you going to the rich folks today?"

Or: "If the rich folks invite you to supper, don't turn them down again. Why should you be ashamed, of all things?"

Nonsense! It didn't occur to the daughter to turn them down. Reizel felt more and more at home in that opulent house. Visiting there always put her in a festive mood and made her heart beat with excitement, as if she were going to an eagerly anticipated party at a close friend's house.

It was no wonder. Each time Reizel arrived, she was received as a guest. The large, bright, rich Rafalovitch house always welcomed the cantor's daughter with friendliness, happiness, laughter, and excitement. And always they went as a group to the theater, occupying the front rows, and always it worked out that she sat side by side with Leibel. And always when the curtain rose and the theater darkened, her hand was in his. And they were carried upward from the earth as if they had grown wings and were being borne away, away, far away, high up, to the seventh heaven, to paradise.

CHAPTER 10

Home from the Theater

When the cantor's daughter left the theater to return home, she was excited, her cheeks were flushed, and her heart was overflowing. She could still hear the speech of the angel-people blended with the playing of the musicians and the resounding laughter of the Rafalovitches. She recalled what the rich man's son, Leibel, had said to her quietly, almost whispering, as he squeezed her hand: "Are you coming again tomorrow?"

What a question!

She answered, not with words, but with a squeeze of the hand as they departed the theater. The crowd was pushing and shoving to the point of suffocation. Jews love to be the first to arrive and the first to leave. Leibel and Reizel were being squeezed so tightly together that for a moment, as the crowd swept them from the theater, they felt like one person.

Outside it was a starry, pleasant night, one of those warm, bright, summer Bessarabian nights when you have no desire to go home to bed. On such nights sleeping is truly a sin. Your eyes are drawn to gaze at the sky, the moon, the stars. Your soul strives, not knowing toward what. Your heart longs, not knowing for what. You feel an odd yearning, not knowing for whom. It was quiet and calm in Holeneshti. The earth had cooled off after the setting of the Bessarabian sun. The stifling dust had settled, and you could catch your breath. A cool breeze wafted from somewhere, bringing with it a greeting from Bessarabian gardens and fields that smelled not of exotic spices but of bread, melons, apples, and pears. The sound of piping was heard from a shepherd who was driving his flock of sheep to pasture somewhere. You could barely hear the fife as it grew fainter and fainter and finally died out.

The Jews were leaving the theater, the Yiddish theater. When Jews leave the theater, they behave like Jews—they talk, they argue, they wave their hands around. One tells another his opinion of what he saw and heard. Each one imagines that what he has seen and heard, only he has really seen and heard. They sang the songs over and over. The young people were loudest of all. Running ahead of everyone were the children. Holeneshti was fully roused, stirring awake on that peaceful, beautiful, warm, bright summer night. But not for long. The Jews would soon be going home, saying their prayers, extinguishing the lamps, and going to sleep—goodnight!

In the tiny house on God's Street where Yisroyeli the cantor lived, the lamp still burned. The cantor and his wife were preparing for bed, but they were also waiting for their daughter to come home before going to sleep.

Yisroyeli the cantor, still a fine-looking young man with shiny black hair, sat half-dressed in his white fringed prayer shawl and fanned himself with his skullcap as he recited his bedtime prayers. Leah was almost fully undressed. The shadow of her white nightgown—which so suited her swarthy, strong face and her angry black eyes—played on the white wall.

When their daughter arrived safely home, Leah peppered her with questions: What kind of comedy had they put on tonight? Did she see any of their friends? What did the Rafalovitches serve for supper?

After receiving only vague answers, the cantor's wife blurted out, "What is it? I can't understand when you mean yes and when you mean no. Sometimes I think it's yes and sometimes I think it's no. Do you know what I mean?"

But Reizel wasn't really listening. She heard only the sound of her mother's voice ringing in her ears, words pouring out, while her father recited his bedtime prayers and fanned himself against the heat. Ah, what a contrast between here and there! There, brightness, happiness, and congeniality! How crowded and dark and sad it was here, after the evening she had spent, first at the Rafalovitches in their great, beautiful, brightly lit, happy house and afterward at the theater, in paradise, and then, walking home from the theater in that warm, lovely, starry summer night!

Leah prodded her with more questions, but at last she realized she was going on too long. It was getting late. "Look at the time!" she interrupted herself. "Too much talk. Time to go to sleep, and I'm talking her ear off, have you ever heard such a thing! I am blowing out the lamp, daughter. Goodnight! Sleep well."

"Goodnight!" answered Reizel, and snuggled down in her bed, covered herself, and closed her eyes. Her thoughts carried her far away from God's Street, back there, there, to paradise.

CHAPTER 11

Honored Guests

The first to be expelled from paradise was Reizel the cantor's daughter. This is how it happened.

One fine morning the cantor was in *shul,* his wife was at the market, and the students had not yet arrived. Reizel sat at the open window above her bed, half-dressed. Her hair hanging loose, she was sewing the ripped seam of a jacket and singing the beautiful, haunting melody of the song from *Shulamit* that she had heard at the theater:

The little goat has gone off peddling.
That is what you will do,
Rozhinkes mit mandlen.
Sleep, my Yidele, sleep, ay-lyu-lyu.

"Bravo, little kitten, bravo!" a hoarse voice cried from under Reizel's window.

It was none other than our old acquaintance, Sholom-Meyer Murovchik, the right-hand man of the Yiddish-German theater.

Sholom-Meyer Murovchik, who performed a thousand different jobs in the theater, was also a good housekeeper. Early in the morning when everyone else was still asleep, with basket in hand he would go to the market to buy food for the "children" (which is what he called the actors). As he was walking by God's Street, he heard someone singing a familiar song from their musicals, singing so purely and sweetly, so full of feeling, that he was riveted to the spot. Who was it? As he approached the window, he saw a dark-complexioned girl, still a child, deeply involved in her needlework, singing beautifully. It so delighted him that he could not contain himself, and he applauded the young songstress: "Bravo! Bravo!"

Apparently he frightened her, for the little red shawl covering her thin childlike shoulders slid down, exposing for a brief instant her upper body, which was more like a young girl's than a child's. This sight gave our good friend Sholom-Meyer an even greater incentive to stand under her window and, as was his habit, to chat further.

"Little bird, why did you get so scared?" he said. "You have a voice, I tell you, sweet as sugar. Three leading ladies would give anything for your voice, may God grant me luck and prosperity. Wait a minute—if I'm not altogether senile, I could say you look familiar to me. Didn't I see you with Rafalovitch's kid on the bench in the theater? If not, may my eyes fail me. Aha! You're blushing even redder than your little shawl. Laugh, laugh, little girl—when you laugh, you're even prettier. Your dimples become deeper, and your white teeth contrast perfectly with your black hair and your gypsy-eyes, may God grant me as much luck and prosperity."

Reizel was frightened not so much by the man's flirtatious tone and exaggerated praise, which she barely understood, as by the fact that she was half-undressed before a stranger, a man, under her window. *What would Mother say if she saw me?* Reizel thought, and jumped up and shut the window.

* * *

That evening when Reizel arrived at the theater with the Rafalovitches, Sholom-Meyer Murovchik greeted her with devilish eyes,
and Reizel blushed like the Bessarabian setting sun. At the first intermission, as Yechiel the *klezmer* showed off his talent playing Yiddish tunes and the audience cracked nuts, ate pears, and talked and
laughed and repeated word for word what had just been performed
on the stage, Reizel noticed that this same man was pointing her out
to the director of the theater. The director, a tall man wearing a high
top hat and huge jewels on his fingers, was staring at her from a distance with his small red, browless eyes. Reizel's face turned an even
deeper shade of crimson.

The following day Yisroyeli the cantor dismissed the students,
washed, and sat down at the table for the midday meal next to
Leah and Reizel. Just then the door opened and two people entered:
Sholom-Meyer and the director of the Yiddish theater. Both were
freshly shaven and strongly perfumed with patchouli soap and *eau
de cologne de violette*. The director wore a broad necktie pierced
with a diamond stickpin. Every finger sparkled with jewels. A heavy,
massive medallion hung from a large golden watch-chain. The
medallion was artfully inlaid with diamonds, sapphires, rubies, and
emeralds to form a crown of two interwoven letters: *A* and *S*. These
precious stones formed the monogram of that famous name:

ALBERT SHCHUPAK

Those precious stones in the rings and the massive medallion had
many tales of their own, but as we are in a hurry to tell our story, we
will not stop here. We will have more than one opportunity in our
story to get further acquainted with this person. But for now we must
tell you briefly—and it must remain between us—that he was wasting
his time displaying all those expensive baubles. Did he mean to show
off the "artistic trophies" of his theatrical triumphs, the many gifts
bestowed on him by the public? No, he had bought them all himself,
one at a time, with money earned through the toil of the countless
poor, always hungry, but always happy souls of his company. Albert
Shchupak was of the opinion that one cannot trust anyone, not even
one's own wife. So he wore his entire fortune in jewels on his own
person, where it was safe and incidentally served to impress people.

Yisroyeli leaped from his chair to greet such dignified guests.

His wife brought over two stools and asked them to sit. And Reizel? Let her be. Soon she would be consumed with embarrassment!

"B'churim bruchim—how do you say it?" The director Albert Shchupak made a lame effort to be gracious but stumbled over the phrase. Luckily Sholom-Meyer was sitting at his side (he always had to rescue him from his missteps!) and saved the day with his hoarse voice and his flowery speech:

"Bruchim hayeshuvim. Go on eating, chew and swallow, enjoy it. Don't mind us. We are common folks, ordinary Jews like you. This is my superior, the director of the local Yiddish-German theater, and I am his right-hand man. He is called Albert Shchupak, and I am known as Sholom-Meyer Murovchik. Now that we've gotten acquainted, one could almost say intimately, we can have a brandy together, if you have any in the house, and if not—send for it, and it will be brought. As for food, we'll eat whatever you are eating. I see you're grating beets and plums, a fine delicacy I haven't eaten, I tell you no lie, for easily a hundred years, may God grant me as much luck and prosperity!"

CHAPTER 12

Yisroyeli the Cantor Shows Off His Skills

As Sholom-Meyer was holding forth, and as the cantor and his wife and daughter were hearing him out, the director of the Yiddish-German theater, Albert Shchupak, sat at the cantor's table, lips sealed, toying with his medallion, flashing the sparkling jewels and diamonds on his fingers. He never removed his small red, browless eyes from the cantor's daughter.

After the meal, and after Sholom-Meyer's little speech, and after the cantor's wife had cleared the table and the cantor said grace, the director felt it was time to get to the matter for which they had come. First he lifted his top hat, revealing a large bald pate, smoothed his fringe of pomaded hair, and wiped the sweat from his forehead. Then he began speaking. By nature he was a man of few words, but once he got going, it was hard for him to stop himself. His tongue would carry him off God knew where, so that he often ended up saying things he didn't intend. Sholom-Meyer, his right-hand man, knowing his weakness, would try to take over, but the director would persist in speaking in his own style.

"You must understand, dear cantor," Shchupak began, "that this is the way it is. Listen, I myself was once a cantor's chorister. Actually I carried the slop pot. I mean I sang. I had a true soprano voice and caught more than a few slaps—I helped out on the pulpit. Then I went out on my own, sang at weddings, circumcisions, and *pidyon habens* chanting a *kol m'koydesh* that I had actually composed by myself. You should see this book full of my songs with my portrait on the cover. My *kol m'koydesh* goes like this, just listen." He began to warble:

> Kol m'koydesh *[Tzipkele my wife]*,
> Sh'vii *[may the devil take you]*,
> K'rui lo *[this very night!]*

Albert Shchupak was into his role. He was preparing to sing *kol m'koydesh* in another key when Sholom-Meyer signaled him with a kick under the table that the sooner he stopped the better. Then Sholom-Meyer began explaining in plain words to the cantor exactly why they had come.

Even before they decided to go to Bessarabia, they had heard of Yisroyeli the cantor's reputation. Since music was their livelihood as well—actually their livelihood came from the theater, but music and theater went together like brother and sister, or man and wife—wouldn't it be fitting for the cantor to chant something for them?

"Something special in Yiddish, something spicy!" added Albert Shchupak, wagging his fingers and smiling with his pursed lips, making his already grossly wrinkled face even more wrinkled.

Yisroyeli understood immediately what was expected of him. At first he held back, allowing himself to be coaxed, protesting, "What are you saying! That's not so! The world loves to exaggerate!" But he was already preparing himself to perform. (When have you ever heard of a cantor or any artist turning anyone down when he is strongly urged to perform?) He rose from the table, wiped his lips, cleared his throat, ran through a few scales, and asked almost in passing, "What would you like me to chant?"

Without waiting for an answer, he began to chant a passage from the High Holidays service, warbling the high notes and dropping to the low octaves, up and down, with trills and tremolos.

The guests exchanged glances, blinked their eyes, and licked their lips, as after a delicious meal or a good glass of wine. That served only to egg the cantor on, as if they had paid him the highest compliment. The poor cantor's head was turned. They must now be shown what he could really do! And he sang another and yet another chant, and then he was preparing to sing one of his own compositions, when Sholom-Meyer took him by the elbow.

"No offense, my dear cantor," he said, "you sing so sweetly that every cantor in the world and his choristers are not worth your little finger. Believe me, if we didn't have to worry about the theater and auditions, with actors and their nuisances and problems, we wouldn't step out of your house till after *shemini-atzeres* prayers. We would never tire of sitting here with you listening to your chants, may God grant me luck and prosperity. But the problem is making a living! No time, you understand, tomorrow we put on a brand-new play: *Kuni Leml*. Now would it be possible for you to honor us with a little treat before we go?"

The cantor was confused. "What kind of little treat would you like?"

"*That* little treat!"

And Sholom-Meyer Murovchik pointed to the cantor's daughter, who all the while had not taken her eyes off him. Poor Reizel almost fainted. The cantor and his wife perked up their ears. The director was about to launch into one of his orations, but Sholom-Meyer signaled him with a kick under the table and then explained what he meant.

"We want your daughter to sing something for us. They say she has a good voice and sings, I tell you. An opera singer would die to sing like that."

"How do you know my daughter sings?" The cantor's wife could no longer restrain herself. Poor Reizel held her breath—she was terrified that he would tell how he had chatted with her by her window yesterday, and she had not even mentioned it! She would surely get it from her mother!

Sholom-Meyer's shrewd eyes discerned that Reizel had turned all colors and quickly changed course. "That's easy to answer. How does everyone know that your husband, may he live till a hundred and twenty, has a one in a million voice and coloratura style? For fifteen years we've traveled around the world with a Yiddish-German theater, and we never knew that a town called Holeneshti existed. Nevertheless, here we are! What a find! Yisroyeli the Hole-neshter! The whole world resounds with his name! What do you think about that, my dear woman?"

The "dear woman" had nothing to say about it. That her husband's name resounded throughout the whole world was no surprise to her. But that her daughter would suddenly be asked, right then and there, to sing in front of two men, total strangers—you can say what you want, but according to her woman's sixth sense, this made no sense at all!

"Just like that? A girl suddenly starts singing without prepar-ing, right out of the blue? A girl is not a boy. A boy is a boy and a girl is a girl. What an idea!"

CHAPTER 13

The Cantor's Daughter Sings "Reboynu shel oylem"

"A boy is a boy and a girl is a girl" was not the way Yisroyeli the cantor saw it. He took the request at face value. True, his wife might have a point, but still and all, once in a great while, out of respect for such honored guests, what harm would it do if Reizel were to sing something together with her father? Besides, he wanted to sing some more. A cantor, when he starts singing, it's like rain—once it starts, it's hard to stop.

Yisroyeli looked at his wife with a pleading expression, as if to say, *Why should it trouble you if the child sings something?* Leah understood her husband's look. Once the urge to sing had taken hold, there was no fighting it! She responded with a look of her own, which he immediately understood to mean, *You really want to? Well, if you like, that's fine with me, why not?*

Yisroyeli was delighted. He coughed, cleared his throat, and said to his daughter, "If someone requests a song, you cannot be rude and refuse them. The question is, what shall we sing for them? Why don't we sing '*Reboynu shel oylem*'? All right? Let's do that. You sing the melody, and I'll sing the harmony in a lower key. So, Reizel, start: la-la-la-la!"

Reizel, relieved and grateful that yesterday's incident had passed unmentioned, was glad to sing, especially since from childhood she had loved to sing. She would have sung for days without tiring if her mother had not forbidden it. Whenever Reizel started to sing, Leah would scold her, "Be quiet, Reizel, I've told you again and again! Do you think you're a little girl? You're a young lady, *kayn eyn horeh,* don't you know."

"A young lady?" Reizel would laugh, and Leah would laugh with her, but she would allow her to sing only occasionally with her father, and even then as long as no one else heard them.

Reizel stood next to Yisroyeli, her hands folded behind her, her eyes raised to the ceiling. With a smooth, sweet, pure, silvery voice like a violin, she drew out a plaintive, authentic Yiddish melody. She sang it as a prayer in which could be heard lamentation, grief, pleading, tears:

> *Reboynu shel oylem!*
> *Almighty Master of the Universe!*
> *I come before thee with*
> *A beggar's prayers.*
> *Dear God, the truth of exile*
> *Is told in tears.*
> *How long, how long, dear God,*
> *The awful fears*
> *Of being beaten, driven*
> *And no one cares.*
> *When, oh when, dear God, wilt thou*
> *Be He Who Hears?*
> *When, oh when, dear God, wilt thou*
> *Answer our prayers?*

Both guests sat spellbound. When Reizel finished, they stared at each other, mouths gaping, disappointed that the music had ended so soon. They had no words. Sholom-Meyer cried out in his hoarse voice, "Bravo! Bravo! Bis!" But he soon realized that his cries could be taken as mockery. Too sad was the melody, too holy were the words. Too sweet was this young lyrical voice, sweet as a violin, and too beautiful and too heavenly was this young singer who was, in truth, still a child.

What about Albert Shchupak, the director of the Yiddish-German theater?

It was difficult to know what was going on in the soul of this Jew. He removed a strongly perfumed silk handkerchief from a trouser pocket and wiped the tears that stood in his small red, browless eyes.

His shriveled Jewish heart still lived, it appeared—warm blood still coursed through it and a pulse still beat. His eyes could still show compassion, which had apparently not yet entirely died. He could still shed tears for Jewish woes, for an exiled people, and a few simple, heartrending words, sung in a melody so plaintive that it could move a stone to tears, had moved him.

Or perhaps what produced this stunning reaction was this divinely beautiful, dark-complexioned girl with dimples in her cheeks and lovely, black gypsy-eyes. Her sugar-sweet voice tender as a violin poured from her soul directly to his heart and, like balm, soothed every limb. Who could say? Who could ever know?

The reader, who by now is acquainted with our director of the Yiddish-German theater from previous chapters, knows what a master of words this man was. After the "*Reboynu shel oylem*," he leaped up, approached the cantor, took the cantor's hand in both of his, and, with tears in his eyes, barely managed to utter these few words:

"May my name not be Albret!" It must be noted that he really did know his own name—don't be ashamed for him. But he could never pronounce it properly, and Albert always came out Albret!

"Hear me out, may my name not be Albret!"

This expression was the highest compliment anyone could earn from Albert Shchupak, the director of the Yiddish-German theater.

CHAPTER 14

Albert Shchupak Loses His Temper

Had Albert Shchupak been content simply with granting the compliment, all would have ended well, with everyone satisfied. The guests would have been happy that they had heard a beautiful rendition of "*Reboynu shel oylem*," a rarity not heard every day. Reizel would have been happy with her first appearance before an audience. The cantor would have been happy that his daughter had so impressed the guests. (Which father would not be proud of the first success of his child? What more does a father require?)

Even Leah, who should have been offended by the sight of her daughter displaying her voice in front of strange men, was now so moved that a soft sigh unwillingly escaped her, "Still a child, may no harm come to her."

But it was fated that a cloud would darken this bright, clear sky and that the joyous occasion would be marred. And because of whom? Because of the director himself, and because of his tongue, alas, over which he had no control. It is no laughing matter when a person loses his temper.

Whether out of great enthusiasm or because his position demanded it, Albert Shchupak again began to speak, while playing with the jewels on his fingers, "Ay, what a voice! Ay, what a throat, ay—some little mouth, *nu nu*! Listen to me, dear cantor. You are living here in Holeneshti, hear me, a nothing town, a hole. What is it? Where is it? Wallowing in the mud and knowing only about melons and cornmeal and praying night and day, heh heh. A pity, do you hear? Such a gem, what will become of her here, your child, may my name not be Albret!"

The cantor's wife understood that he was speaking of her child's future, and she immediately cut him short. "You cannot count the teeth in someone else's mouth. My child has, thank God, someone to look after her."

Albert Shchupak seemed not to understand the allusion to teeth, or else he pretended not to, and he continued with his spiel, now directing it to the cantor, no longer looking at the wife:

"So, what was I saying, my dear cantor? Yes. About your being blind, forsaken fantasists living in a fool's world—what can I say? There's another world out there, and what a world—imagine it! Hear me out, my children—gold! Girls and more girls! Dolls! We have a leading lady—also a young child. Not as pretty a face as your child, but a voice, do you hear, fit for grand opera! If she were to come with me, your child, who knows? In three or four years, do you hear me, this much gold!" Shchupak demonstrated with both hands what a hatful of gold their daughter could bring in for them if she were to join his theater.

Whether Leah grasped this at all was difficult to say. This man with the tall chimney hat, she did realize, with his coarse, shaven chin, was proposing a reprehensible deal for her daughter and was putting forth possibilities that turned her stomach. The mother in her took over, the mother who was created to protect and shield her child, the mother who had lived to see her stand on her own two feet, the mother who trembled for her safety as for a delicate precious treasure. She refused to be drawn in further and cut him off even more sharply than before.

"May my enemies not live to see the day!" she exclaimed. "What must you think of us? Do we come from tailors, from shoemakers, that we would allow our own flesh and blood to join up with *Purim-shpielers*, actor types, comedians, *shleppers*? How can you imagine such a thing?"

Those few heated words, which Leah spoke in one breath, did not sit well with the director of the Yiddish-German theater, and he was quite offended. His coarse wrinkled face suddenly turned livid, and he broke into a sweat. His pursed lips twitched, and his small, browless eyes became bloodshot. Albert Shchupak was prepared to sail into her, as she deserved. The gall of this mere woman to talk that way to him, the director of the Yiddish-German theater!

God only knows what a scandal a row would have stirred up. Albert Shchupak hated long fights. With him it was plain and simple: either you gave a beating or you got a beating.

Luckily Sholom-Meyer was on hand. He knew what kind of character his boss was and he would try to head off a scandal. In his view, you didn't have to either give or get a beating. It was always better to act with goodwill, he maintained. He pulled his superior over by the elbow, gave him a knavish wink, pulled his cap up and down, and addressed the cantor.

"Your spouse is absolutely right," Sholom-Meyer said. "What a good wife you have, may we all be as blessed. But you know, she does have one fault: she's a little too hot-tempered. She did not understand what the director was saying. He was just saying that there are all kinds of ways to earn a living. Everyone brags about his own business. Every dog is master at his own doorway, and every swine believes his mud is deeper. Nothing more was meant by it, God forbid, not against you, not against your husband, not against your daughter. We came here, as I told you, only to hear the cantor sing, may God grant him luck and prosperity. We would stay on, but we don't wish to disturb you any further. Besides, I see the young scamps coming back to *cheder*. You have to get to work. As they say: Torah is the best merchandise, better than *rozhinkes mit mandlen*. Be well."

After her guests were on the other side of the threshold, the cantor's wife honored them with a blessing: "May your heads be buried deep in the ground and your feet kick in the air!!" And to her daughter she said, "You may as well, daughter, say goodbye to the Yiddish theater. You will not see it again so long as I am not lying in my grave!"

The greatest portion of her rage was reserved for her husband—

and Leah could go into a towering rage! But it was his good luck that the students were already sitting around the table at their open books.

Yisroyeli did not feel happy after the uninvited guests' visit, but he took heart, put on a smile, rubbed his hands together, and sang out a tune from the Gemorah: "Remember now, children, once more, let's see, where were we? Yes, yes, yes . . ."

CHAPTER 15

Introducing Hotzmach

It was a lively scene in Benny Rafalovitch's courtyard. The stable in which the Yiddish theater was playing seemed never to be closed, but came the morning, it sprang to life. People were up and awake and at their jobs—carpenters fixing benches, painters retouching sets, porters carrying crates, hauling lumber, and carrying planks. The sounds of hammers striking nails, of ropes being pulled, were unceasing, and above all the din and clamor people shouted to be heard.

More frequently heard was one cry, one name: "Hotzmach!" louder than any other:

"Hotzmach, may the devil take you!"

"Hotzmach, are you blind?"

"Hotzmach, get a move on!"

Hotzmach, stop! Hotzmach, go! Hotzmach, run! Hotzmach! Hotzmach! Hotzmach!

Who is this Hotzmach? Leibel would wonder after glancing into the stable on his way to *cheder*. It wasn't long before Leibel knew quite well who this Hotzmach was.

Tall, thin, sickly, coughing, and short of breath, with a pale, pockmarked face, a sharp nose, a bullet-shaped head, and pointed ears—even his eyes were piercing, sharp, and hungry-looking—this was the man.

His name was really Holtzman, but from the very first day the theater director, Albert Shchupak, crowned him with the name "Hotzmach"—and so it had remained.

Leibel became fond of Hotzmach from the moment they met. And they had met without any introductions, ceremonies, or pretensions.

One day Hotzmach saw Leibel standing at the door of the stable, and from a distance began talking to the boy. "Dumbbell! What are you doing here?"

"Nothing."

"Who do you want?"

"Nobody."

"Who are you?"

"Benny Rafalovitch's son."

"So why are you standing at the door like a poor man's son? Come over here, youngster! Do you smoke cigarettes? Or not yet?"

"Not yet."

"But your father smokes? Your brothers smoke, the rascals? Good, you can bring me some cigarettes."

The following day Leibel, out of breath and flushed, delivered a full packet of cigarettes, while cautiously looking around.

Hotzmach took the cigarettes with his thin, pointy fingers and pocketed them, as if accepting a gift from a good friend rather than snatching stolen goods, God forbid. With no change of expression or offer of thanks, he lit one up, inhaled, blew the smoke from his sharp nose in a thin wisp, coughed, and said, "Who in your family smokes such expensive cigarettes?"

"My older brother," answered Leibel softly, almost inaudibly.

"The devil take that older brother of yours—he knows a good smoke!" responded Hotzmach especially loudly. "Tell me, my little song-bird, what do they eat at your house in the morning with their coffee?"

"What do they eat? The usual. Sometimes they eat butter, cheese, sometimes eggs, *kichel*, butter rolls."

"Wait, wait, wait," Hotzmach cut him off, "that's all I need to know! Bring me a couple of butter rolls, but fresh. Do you hear me? Fresh!"

He shouted the word *fresh* so loudly that Leibel was startled. He was afraid they might be overheard.

Still he obeyed, and the following morning he slipped two freshly baked butter rolls into his pocket, fearful their aroma would give him away. No sooner did he pull them out than the hungry Hotzmach quickly gulped them down his skinny throat.

"Like pills!" Hotzmach said to him, and licked his lips like a cat after it eats. Then he smoked one of Leibel's brother's cigarettes that were so to his liking he asked for more to be brought.

And Leibel brought him many more, thereby gaining free access, not only at night during performances, but during the daytime auditions and rehearsals. He was even allowed to wander in the wings on the other side of the curtain, where his soul had yearned to see what really went on.

And oh, what Leibel saw! Another world altogether! A world where people literally re-created themselves, disguised themselves, and painted their faces with makeup, so they could step out on the stage as devils, imps, ghosts, and angels. It was paradise, always lively, always lighthearted. This one was singing, that one was dancing, this one was puffing out his cheeks, that one was swigging from a flask—*gulp-gulp-gulp*—and another was smoking a cigarette on the sly, crouched in a corner so the director wouldn't see him and land on him. A tough director! They were all terrified of him, as if he were the Angel of Death—even though they all mocked him, made fun of him, stuck their tongues out at him behind his back, and mimicked how he stood, how he walked, how he sat, how he spoke, and how he flashed his jewels—real mischief-makers!

Best of all the mimics was Hotzmach. He mimicked everyone so perfectly, one's belly ached from laughing. A jolly clown was this Hotzmach! Leibel could not understand where such jollity came from. No one else toiled as hard as Hotzmach, no one ran around as much, no one suffered as much, no one was as hungry, no one coughed as much, or received as many blows and shoves from whoever felt so inclined as Hotzmach, yet no one else was as cheerful and ready to laugh as Hotzmach. Just now the director had grabbed him by the collar and kicked him out of the cloakroom—"Hotzmach, devil take you!"—and there he was, right behind the director's back, slightly bent over, his little head to the side, his small lips pursed, but to look at him from the front, you would see a coarse face with small eyes—*Albert Shchupak to the bone*!

So how could you dislike someone like that?

CHAPTER 16

Hotzmach Writes a Letter

"Hey there, young whippersnapper! You study in *cheder*, so you should know how to write. Bring me some ink and a pen, a sheet of paper, and an envelope—and yes, a seven-kopek stamp!" said Hotzmach to his young friend one fine morning as he was polishing the actors' boots.

In no time at all these items appeared in the stable—or rather in a wing of the stage behind the curtain. On an overturned crate next to a three-legged table Leibel sat down to write a letter. Opposite him Hotzmach lay stretched out on the ground coughing and dictating dramatically, a cigarette clenched between his teeth, the boots he was polishing set aside.

"Write this, my dear heart:

" 'To my dear beloved mother Sora-Brucha, long life! And to my dear beloved uncle Zalman, long life! And to my dear beloved sister Zlatke, long life! And to all my dear and devoted friends, long life!'

"Ready, my pet? Go on.

" 'First I wish to inform you of my well-being and to tell you I am, *boruch hashem*, quite healthy, as I wish for you from the depths of my heart ever and always, hoping to hear from you—Amen!'

"Did you put down, little tomcat, the word *amen*? Then I love you. Scratch on.

" 'And secondly, I wish to inform you, my dear beloved mother, we find ourselves in Bessarabia, a land of melons, cornmeal mush, and fat women. We are putting on plays every night, and I am informing you that I am playing starring roles, and after the holidays we begin to receive a percentage of the ticket sales. For now I am working on salary, which means I get paid every week. Not so much to turn one's head, but, thank God, I'm not working for nothing. I know that I am worth far more, but for a bastard named Sholom—a Sholom-Meyer from hell, may he suffer instead of you and me and Zlatke. This is a dog that eats waste and doesn't let anyone else eat. I am sending you three rubles. I beg you, my dear mother, don't take offense that it isn't three hundred. This is all I have. I give it to you as a little something to buy what you might need for the holidays. Buy Zlatke shoes without fail, for God's sake, and tell Uncle Zalman to stop pestering me about the military conscription officer, to hell with him! I'm safe from conscription, and I have him, my uncle Zalman, to thank for that. And I ask you, my dear mother, if you write me a letter, let Eli the scribe tell me when I have *yahrtzeit*. Last year it came out exactly on the third day of Succos. Write me if you still have the same job, and for sure, buy Zlatke shoes, and that's all the news I have to write, and be well, my dear mother, from me your son who wishes you much good and happiness forever and ever at all times, hoping to hear from you. Amen.'

"Now, my chubby fellow, hand me the pen, and I'll sign it."

Hotzmach rolled up the sleeve of his right arm to the elbow and set to work putting down a few indecipherable smudges. He asked his scribe: "Does this say Hersh Ber Holtzman?"

Leibel peered intently at these hieroglyphs, searched hard, and could find no Hersh, no Ber, nor any other name.

"My dear sprite, stop looking so hard," Hotzmach admonished his young friend, and went back to polishing the boots. "It looks to me as if you must really like my handwriting. I taught myself, little fool, from my own head. Everything I know, I taught myself. Everyone says I would have a very fine handwriting if only I had been taught. But where could I have been taught? I became an orphan at a young age. My mother had to work as a servant, and my uncle Zalman took me off to work for him. He's a tailor, just a patcher-upper, an incompetent, but beatings he delivers like a regular master. Once at the table he threw a hot iron right at my heart, and I've been coughing ever since. My mother took me away from that monster of an uncle and handed me over to another cripple. But I couldn't do the work on account of the iron my uncle had honored me with. So my mother decided to place me as a helper to a teacher of very young children, washing them, reciting their prayers with them, bringing them lunch in *cheder*. Well, bringing food is not a hard job. You can grab a snack, a lick here, a sip there. The problem was you had to carry the children on your back if there was mud, and where do you get the strength for that? God came to the rescue, and a Yiddish theater rode into our town. Yiddish theater—what do you think of that? Everybody was running to the theater, and I'll stay home? I managed to sneak in without a ticket. Just my luck, the director, Shchupak himself, decided he wanted to walk through the benches to check who had tickets. He grabbed me by the ear, twisted it, and threw me out. This wouldn't have been so bad if he hadn't thrown off my cap. How could I go home without a cap? My mother would tell my uncle, and that ogre would murder me! So I waited outside in the frost till the audience had gone home and put myself at the mercy of the direc-tor, Shchupak, that is. I wept, sobbed, kissed his hands, pleaded with him to give me back my cap, told him the whole truth that I was, after all, a poor orphan boy and had a villain of an uncle. He heard me out, looked me over from head to toe with his little eyes, may they come out on the other side of his head, and said to me: 'You're an orphan and don't have where to go? Maybe you would like to join my theater? I will make,' he said, 'an actor of you.'"

CHAPTER 17
The Making of a Comic

Hotzmach was wrenched by a spell of coughing. He paused from the boot-polishing, lit a cigarette, stretched a few times, and continued telling his young friend about the wonders of becoming an actor.

"Do you think my mother was pleased that I had gotten such a job? Not on your life. It's not so much my mother as my uncle Zalman. 'Wait, once he's off with those actors, you can forget about his saying kaddish, this *gonef* of yours!' my uncle warned her. But who cares about an uncle? Who cares about kaddish when I was suddenly raised up so high? Picture it—at first it was no bed of roses. Shchupak began teaching me the hard way. First he honored me with a hefty beating for the way I polished the boots. 'This is the way to polish boots,' he said, and took the brush from my hands and showed me how a boot likes to be polished. Then he began to work me like a dog, making me do so many jobs that you had to have the head of a prime minister to be everywhere and do everything he wanted. If anything was not just so, a beating was on the way. That's the kind of Jew he is, may his hands wither! A month went by, and two and three and four, and I didn't so much as lay an eye on the stage. God, where was this all going? For this I sacrificed myself? To ask him when I would see myself on the stage was to invite a beating. If I complained to the actors, that bastard Sholom-Meyer would deliver everything straight to Shchupak's ears, may a plague afflict them both! In short, there was nothing for it, you had to tighten your belt, may a noose tighten around his neck, Shchupak's I mean! I waited a year, I waited two, and finally my time came. This is what happened. It was a miracle."

Hotzmach had a long coughing fit and swore at the cough with deadly curses, "Blast this cough! To hell with it!"

After cursing out the coughing, he drew in a deep breath, took a few puffs on his cigarette, got back to the shoe brushes, and continued:

"We had an actor in our troupe, a romantic leading man—Uchvatevker they called him, a dear fellow, a rare romantic actor. He played the most demanding roles—charlatans, heroes! He was a handsome young man, healthy, broad-shouldered, strong-boned, with a voice made of iron, a true basso voice. And languages! German included. That was a leading man!

"What does God do? This healthy Uchvatevker lies down sick and dies. No fooling. Well, dead is dead, blessed be God's truth. But what do you do without a leading man? Posters were already up, and out of spite the box office was taking in money hand over fist, tickets were in great demand. My Shchupak was on the verge of a breakdown. 'Hotzmach,' he said to me, 'can you play the romantic lead?' 'Ah,' I said, 'why not?' and I began studying my role. They were putting on a serious piece, *Dora, the Rich Beggar*, by Shakespeare, Improved and Staged by the only Albert Shchupak.' That's what was actually on the posters! When it came to the night of the play, they very nicely prepared me and sent me out on the stage, playing the romantic lead, a freshly pomaded, all decked-out 'Rudolf' with painted cheeks and black whiskers, sporting a new coat and trousers and a pair of boots without holes. Mind you—I tell you, may I be such a Rudolf in real life!

"Why should I go on and on, my dear songbird? Who can figure out an audience! From the first minute I appeared on the scene, even before I had opened my mouth, they started to laugh, and they're still laughing! Of course, I approached the leading lady, Dora, and began playing my part, taking her by the hand and saying in High German, just like Uchvatevker, may he rest in pieces, 'Oh! *Liebes* child, we must marry because after the wedding love is much stronger than before the wedding!' The hilarity lasted maybe half an hour. I thought they would tear the theater apart! The more I played my role, the greater was the laughter. The devil himself had gotten into them!

"Finally, the curtain dropped and I ran off, sweating, unseeing, not knowing where my stumbling feet were carrying me. But I sensed I was at the mercy of Shchupak. I could almost feel the blows raining down on my head. He shouted, 'Bastard! Why didn't you tell me before that you're a comic?' May I know as much about him, and may he know as much about his two and a half wives, Lord in heaven, as I began to know what that meant—a comic!

"And that's how it went for me from then on. I began to play the

greatest comic roles, first Shmendrik, then Tzingitang, then Kuni-
Leml, then Noah the drunkard in *David's Fiddle*, and even Poopoose
in *Bar-Kochba* too. I even tried Zelikel Mangan in Lateiner's little
jewel. When I stand up to offer congratulations, 'Bride and groom,
mazel tov!' it becomes a sensation, people roll on the floor dying
with laughter! So imagine how it was when I stepped out wearing a
torn gabardine, sang, and did a dance to 'I Am a *Chasid'l*':

> *A lusty* chasid'l *am I*
> *Who loves to dance and sing*
> *A lusty* chasid'l *am I*
> *Who loves to have his fling*
> *A lusty* chasid'l *am I:*
> *Hop-chik! Hop-chik! Hop-chik!*

"I had the audience in the palm of my hand. I don't need to
show off for a little squirt like you, but I can brag that Hotzmach
has made a name for himself, thank God. My only complaint is they
don't let me on the stage every night. And who's to blame? Shchupak! A miserable fellow, may he perish! He doesn't give me any
roles, may God give him aches for a whole winter! He takes the best
parts for himself because if they applaud for anyone else, God forbid, he throws a fit. That's the kind of imbecile he is. Let him suffer
before I'll polish boots for him! But don't worry, every dog has his
day. God willing, after the holidays, the actors will each get a percentage of the box office. If not, we'll break with him and start our
own company. We would have done this a long time ago if not for
that bastard, Sholom-Meyer, a plague on him—tphoo!"

So Hotzmach ended his biography, spat on the brush, and began
polishing the boots with all his might.

CHAPTER 18
Leibel Shows What He Can Do

Leibel enjoyed Hotzmach's biography enormously. Not only the
biography but everything connected with the theater was dear and
sacred to our young hero.

Leibel saw Hotzmach often, at least several times a day. While he was going home from *cheder* for supper, Leibel would first nip into the stable to find out what was going on there. He would rise early in the morning to bring Hotzmach something to eat. Hotzmach was always to be found in the stable. That's where he lived, ate, and slept.

"A theater must never be left unattended. Someone must always be in the theater. Just think of it—stage sets, costumes, wigs! Except for me, Shchupak doesn't trust his property to anyone."

So Hotzmach boasted to his young friend. With time, their friendship became closer and stronger. Hotzmach had found someone to whom he could bare his bitter heart. He grew fond of this youngster with his handsome, mild, benevolent, serious eyes. Besides which, he brought frequent supplies of food and cigarettes.

"Life is hard and bitter, my dear songbird," lamented Hotzmach to his young friend, "when you have to earn your daily bread working as a comic actor for the likes of Shchupak, may he sow thick and reap sparse. Our years are shortened by this monster with his big jewels, may they drive him mad, God in heaven!"

Hotzmach coughed as he went on: "But realize we actors blow hot and cold too. Every other day we threaten to leave him and start our own theater. If not for his sidekick, that Sholom-Meyer, may a silent illness afflict him, we would have done it a long time ago. But who cares about them? I am satisfied to know that I am, with God's help, a Yiddish actor, even though a comic."

Hotzmach struck a serious pose, appearing even more comic. Leibel gazed at him with great respect as Hotzmach the comic spoke further: "When evening comes, do you hear me? and I step onto the stage, all my troubles and worries vanish like smoke. On the stage I am an entirely different person. Shchupak—who is he? Sholom-Meyer—never heard of him. May their bones rot in the earth. When I am on the stage, I don't see anyone. I see only lamps and heads, bald pates, caps, little hats and big hats, and nothing else. Who is then my equal—your father with his fat belly? Let him offer me this stable and this courtyard, together with his whole fortune to let him go on the stage in my place for one night—not on your life!"

So Hotzmach bragged to his young friend, who gazed into his eyes, devouring every word. And Hotzmach continued boasting: "Or let's suppose they offer me this stall full of gold and throw in a princess for a wife, in exchange for giving up being a comic actor and becoming a shop clerk or a worker instead. I'd spit them full in the face! Do you hear me, little one? You're still naïve, my little songbird, you have no idea what a crazy passion the theater is, how it draws you, pulls like a magnet, curse it!"

"Exactly the same for me!" Leibel blurted out as Hotzmach smoked a cigarette, admitting to his friend that the theater drew him too and had done so ever since he had begun to appreciate things. Even before he knew that theaters existed, he had put on plays with his friends, *The Sale of Joseph*, *The Exodus from Egypt*, *On Mount Sinai*, and many other biblical pieces that they had actually worked out in *cheder*. And Leibel demonstrated how they would dramatize.

"For example, I would enter the palace of Pharaoh, King of Egypt, stand before him like this and declare to him"—here Leibel laid his hands on his heart and spoke, first quietly, then louder and with more and more fervor—"My name is Moshe ben Amrom. I was sent to you, my Lord King, by the Jewish God, the God of Abraham, Isaac, and Jacob, whose name is Adonoy asher Adonoy, commanding that you free His Jews from your land of Egypt. How long can this go on? Why do you hate them? Why do you punish them? Why do you slaughter their children and bathe in their blood, you most wicked of the wicked! You evil murderer! Do you realize with whom you are playing? I will raise my right arm to heaven"—Leibel raised his arm—"and show you what I can do!"

Leibel's eyes were ignited with fire, his cheeks aflame, face glowing. Astounded, Hotzmach cut him off in the middle:

"A strong performance!" he cried, grabbed his young friend by the shoulders, and shook him, "A strong performance! May I die on the spot if you're not an actor! A true actor, as I am a Jew, an actor born for the stage! Do you know what I'm going to tell you, my little fellow?"

Hotzmach could speak no further. His coughing prevented it. He grabbed a post with both hands till he had finished coughing and cursing. "Curse this cough, God Almighty! May it and my short breath afflict Sholom-Meyer, and the sticking pain in my side I'll bestow on Shchupak for the holidays."

Having caught his breath and calmed down, Hotzmach livened up and resumed his former tone. "Do you know what, my dear chap?"

Leibel looked into his eyes, wondering.

"My dear songbird, if I were in your place, I'd spit on everything. I'd send that father of yours with his fat lips to the *cheder*, better he should warm the bench. I'd throw out that fat Gemorah and tell the cantor to chant '*U'mifnei Chateynu*,' and I'd—"

At this crucial point the actors arrived for rehearsal, and their conversation was interrupted.

CHAPTER 19

A Probing Eye

Never would anyone at the Rafalovitches' house have noticed that cigarettes were disappearing, or that someone was carrying off batches of butter rolls, or that there never was enough sugar in the tin, if not for the old grandmother, the one whose head shook "no no," the one with the sharp eye who could see for a mile. This old lady had noticed for some time that there was a thief in the house. She set her mind to sniffing it out, and by snooping with her sharp eye, she did figure it out. She knew whose work it was. It was that little good-for-nothing, Leibel!

One question arose: why did a boy need butter rolls, cigarettes, and sugar? And where was he taking them? Could it be to the *cheder* for his classmates, or possibly for the *rebbe* himself? And the old lady took to keeping an eye on him. While everyone else slept, he would wake up bright and early, cut short his prayers, and disappear. Where to? Why would a boy need to go *to cheder* so early when even the *rebbe* was still asleep?

The old grandmother decided to play dumb. She pretended to sit over her fat prayer book, praying quietly and shaking her head "no no," but her eye saw everything. As soon as Leibel sneaked out of the house, the old lady was right behind him, watching him from the balcony as he stole into the stable. *What business could he have in the stable, that young scoundrel?*

The next morning it was the same story. The old lady did not rest, her eyes looking, her heart pounding, her head shaking "no no," and her brain calculating. Praised be God, now she knew everything: "The rascal has befriended one of the Purim players who sleeps in the stable—fine company—naked, barefoot, and hungry good-for-nothings, may God not punish me for these words!"

Now but one thing remained—what to do about it? Confront the boy? *What have you got there? Where are you going with that?* Do you think he would answer? Modern children, you can do nothing with them! Do they know you must show respect for an old grandmother of almost eighty? What does one do then? Tell the daughter-in-law? Some mother, that Beylke! She was a good soul but a weakling. What good was her tenderness, what use was her goodness, when the children crawled all over her, did what they pleased, grew wild? No no. *If I have to tell anyone, I'll tell my son, Benny. Benny is a father, and a father is not a mother.* A father yells at a child, scolds him, sometimes beats him, or else he calmly advises the boy to know better next time.

That was how the old lady reasoned, and that was what she did, but with a plan. To tell tales, make accusations—that alone was not enough. She had to catch the thief in the act, red-handed, and then show everyone how a good mother spoiled her children, ruined them, destroyed them.

CHAPTER 20

The Worm Enters the Apple

The old grandmother did her work so quietly and shrewdly that not a soul was aware of it. With the greatest secrecy, she whispered into her son Benny's ear what his youngest son was doing, where he was going, what he was delivering, and with whom he was meeting.

Benny heard her out, turned his hairy face toward her, peered at his old mother with his bulgy calf's-eyes, and responded in his own characteristic way, curt and sharp: "A cow flew over the roof and laid an egg."

That meant he didn't believe her. Benny could not believe that his youngest son would do the things she said. Leibel was the best, the quietest, the most competent of all his boys. Benny was no great scholar, but everybody said his Leibel would amount to something one day. Just the other day Benny had run into Yisroyeli, Leibel's *rebbe*, and had asked him how his son was doing. Yisroyeli launched into paeans of praise that made his head swim. The cantor said that this boy was no ordinary child, that something great would come of him, something special, something, something . . . The rest was demonstrated by the *rebbe*'s hands, and Benny completed the sentence for him: "A doorknob, a wagon hitch, or a who-knows-what?"

Benny's heart swelled with pride. God had blessed him with a fine son, a success to enrich his later years! He looked at Leibel with great pleasure and wondered, *What will he become? Will he become a rabbi, or perhaps even better than a rabbi?* Who knew? Maybe through this son of his it was fated that he, the father, would become renowned. Till now it was known only in Holeneshti how successful he was, but later it would be known everywhere. They would come from everywhere to see him in Holeneshti. *"So you're the famous Leib Rafalovitch's father!"* And he would answer: *"The famous Leib Rafalovitch—that is one of my sons."*

Those were Benny's golden daydreams—when the old grandmother came along and put a worm in his ear. This child, this wonderful child was nothing but a thief, an ordinary thief! Benny became enraged, furious as a bear, and went around all day in a bad temper, letting out his anger at his hired hands or his wife.

Beylke knew her Benny thoroughly and asked, "What's the matter?"

He did not answer.

"The boss has swallowed a cat," his hired hands said.

"Papa woke up on the wrong side of the bed," the children said. In the house everyone went around on tiptoe. They didn't know how or why, but they smelled trouble.

At night in bed Benny tossed and turned, sighed and groaned like a penned-up ox, and could not shut his eyes. "Ay, a worm! *Nu*, a worm! They've gone and punctured my dream!"

He suddenly leaped out of bed. He had the urge to strike, break, take something apart, throw things, wreak havoc! Gradually he calmed down. *Maybe this is just a terrible mistake. Maybe the old lady saw a pear tree and took if for a goat.* And Benny fell soundly asleep, snoring mightily.

CHAPTER 21

The Thief Is Caught

The next morning, while even the Creator Himself was still asleep, Benny Rafalovitch was up and about.

Upon awakening, he put on a large robe and a pair of heavy

hobnailed boots, then went off on his morning inspection of his farmyard to make sure everything was in order. Benny hated if, in his language, he discovered that a "yarmulke had been crumpled" or that he had been "whistled off." In ordinary talk that meant that something was not as it should be, or that his orders had been disobeyed. The lumber had to be accounted for, the courtyard swept, the trash piled. Each cow had to be in her own stall, and each had her own inimitable Benny-style nickname: "Fat butcher-woman! You're visiting the *rebbitzin*'s stall again? A happy holiday to both of you!"

This was Benny's way of scolding the cows, one of which actually was a fat, big-bellied, skittish cow, the other a mild-mannered, easygoing cow with the innocent, pious face of a rabbi's wife.

He took a stick to them, more to the butcher-woman, as Benny gave her to understand his reasoning: "You have your own bowl— use it! Why do you nose around in places you don't belong?"

From the cows he went on to the horses, again honoring them with his particular jargon: "Listen here, you old wiseacre, if you keep bothering the young boys"—he was referring to the colts—I'll give you a lecture you won't forget!"

The horses paid no heed to their master's language but instead turned their soft muzzles to him and looked at him foolishly, as if to say: *Are you talking about oats?*

The master poked one in the side with his elbow, tickled another's neck, and patted a third's mane, then went on to his workers, cursing them out a bit in Moldavian. Who should suddenly appear out of the blue but the old grandmother, her head shaking "no no." With her sharp eye she winked at him, indicating with a nod, *There he is, the brat, with full pockets,* and vanished.

Benny remembered what she had told him about his son, and his heart thumped. He had been hoping the whole thing was a lie. For a moment he wished he could dispel it all with a wave of his hand: "What is it? Wives' tales, women's prattling!" But when he saw his son walking hurriedly toward the stable, a fire ignited in the father's heart against the son. What was this young scamp doing, going so early to the comedians? He called him over in his loud, thundering voice.

Leibel, who had been absorbed in his own thoughts, heard his father's voice and considered whether to stop or keep going. But a father's summons must be obeyed.

"Where are you going so early?" his father asked.

Leibel had not counted on such a meeting. "So early?"

"What? Is it late? Tell me where you are going."

"Where should I be going?"

"How would I know where you should be going? That's what I'm asking you."

Poor Leibel had no time to think of an answer that would make sense. He stared guiltily at his father.

"Why are you shining those lamps of yours at me? Don't you recognize me? Said your prayers already?"

"Yes . . . no . . . I mean, yes." Leibel was tongue-tied.

His father's fury mounted: "Said your prayers or not? Better tell me."

Leibel broke out in a cold sweat. "Yes—not yet. I mean I haven't done it yet. That's what I was actually doing. I was actually going to *shul* to pray."

The father's heart felt a little easier. He hoped it was the truth. But he saw by his son's eyes that it was a lie, a lie! His anger rose again. The best of all the children! He moved closer to him and saw how he was clutching both pockets. So it was really true what the old lady had said—he was carting off the whole house. The father demanded: "Come on, show me what's wobbling around in there. You look very swollen somehow."

For this demand Leibel was in no way prepared. He stood nailed to the spot, unable to move.

"You don't want to show me? Then I'll have to use my own ten fingers to poke into your pockets." The father began rummaging through Leibel's pockets. He shook out a treasure trove of tasty morsels: fresh butter rolls, chunks of egg bread, tea, sugar, half a gizzard of a roasted goose, and a large batch of cigarettes.

CHAPTER 22

A Cruel Punishment

One could not say Benny Rafalovitch was an overly strict father. He rarely interfered in his children's upbringing. The household was run by his wife, Beylke. Benny knew only one thing: you had to "keep the oats pouring." In his language that meant you had to provide.

Benny provided generously, never asking where it all went—that was not his concern. He never bargained, never asked for explanations—that was not his business. The children too could do as they pleased, even bite off each other's noses—that was not his business, unless a child did something that forced him to intercede. A cloud would then darken the household accompanied by thunder, lightning, and hail. Everyone would be terrified and hide in corners. More than anyone, it was Benny's wife, the tiny, frail, quiet Beylke, who bore the brunt of his rage.

In his fury now at his thieving son, Benny bestowed two fiery slaps on his cheeks that made sparks fly, but he was not content. He took Leibel by the hand, led him into the house, called together the whole household, and forced that miscreant to confess before everyone what he had done and on whose behalf he had become a thief. But this too was not enough. Benny sentenced Leibel to be confined and whipped.

However much the poor frail Beylke pleaded with him to punish her rather than inflict such humiliation on the child; however much the household came to Leibel's defense, saying he had not committed a really terrible sin; however much Leibel himself pleaded, promised, and kissed his father's hands—it was no use. Once Benny decreed, "Confine and whip him!" it was over!

CHAPTER 23

After the "Execution"

After administering the punishment that evening, Benny's rage subsided, and his heart softened. (It is always so: after a father punishes a child, his heart relents.) He ordered the household to attend the theater. No one was in any mood to go to the theater after the cruel punishment Leibel had undergone. But a father's orders must be obeyed.

As usual, the theater was packed. As always, the audience was noisy and cheerful, cracking nuts as the musicians played and the artists sang. But poor Leibel sat as a stranger, with dry, unseeing eyes. His head was heavy and leaden, and a shameful fire simmered in his heart. Never had he imagined such humiliation, that someone like himself, a bar mitzvah boy, the best student in *cheder*, the most favored and beloved child at home, should be dealt with so cruelly by his father, and in front of everyone! So unexpectedly had it all happened that he had not time to digest it. Only after the deed was done did a fearsome protest, a great storm rise up in our young hero. But this was the protest of a weak little worm against a powerful giant, a protest that could show itself only in hot tears. And Leibel wept many hot, bitter tears.

Leibel did not weep alone. Crying with him was his mother. Poor Beylke had no words to comfort her beloved youngest son. Instead she spent the entire day at his side, kissing him, caressing him, while she tried to staunch her own tears. That day Leibel did not go to *cheder*. He was allowed to sit at the table, but he could not make himself touch his food. That day the Rafalovitch table was strangely still. All eyes were lowered, staring at their own plates. Only the old grandmother examined everyone with her sharp eye, as if to say, *You should all be punished one at a time.*

"Good morning!" Benny Rafalovitch cried out to his household, noticing that he alone at the table was eating and drinking. "Why are you all standing with the oxen in the mud? Grease the wagon and drive on!"

This time Benny's arcane language did not have its usual effect. They finished eating in silence and then left the table in silence, each going to his corner. At the theater they all wondered what the young Leibel must be nursing in his heart as he sat watching the performance.

But no one knew what was going on in Leibel's heart. As he watched the performance, his thoughts were far away. His young spirit did not rest, his young head was hard at work forming a plan on how to get even with a father who could inflict such unheard-of humiliation. He must have his revenge for the whippings. The welts would heal, thought Leibel, but it would cost his father dearly. Oh, he knew what had to be done! Not for nothing had he become attached to Hotzmach. Just yesterday he had had a serious conversation with him.

Hotzmach had spoken in all frankness, as was his manner— Hotzmach hated to talk in circles: "Fool! Steal into your father's pockets, take out a hefty sum, and come along with us. We leave Saturday night. You'll become an actor. And what an actor, may I die on the spot if I'm wrong!"

What Hotzmach had said out loud, our Leibel had been thinking quietly in his heart. But the idea of stealing into his father's pockets made him feverish. *Wait! That's stealing, becoming a thief!* thought Leibel. Well, and what he had been bringing all this time for Hotzmach's breakfast along with cigarettes to smoke—wasn't that stealing? No, he justified himself, that wasn't stealing. If someone needed food, you shared with them fifty-fifty. If someone wanted to smoke, you brought him cigarettes, and what punishment should you get for that? But money? Stealing money from your father?

Leibel wanted to tell Hotzmach he was afraid to steal money. What would his father say? But he was ashamed and found another excuse. "Do you think my father will let me get away with that?" said Leibel, his teeth chattering.

"How will he know, little fool?" Hotzmach replied.

"He'll figure out I'm gone, and he'll come after me."

"So, what will he do—pour salt on your tail? We're going from here to Bucharest, little fool. Do you know how far Bucharest is from here, my little colt? Do you know anything at all?"

"I know where Bucharest is, in Romania. I even know it's not that far from here," answered Leibel.

"Smart aleck, you don't know what you're talking about. Once you cross the border, your father has no power over you. Not your father, not your mother, nobody. You can kiss them all goodbye! You can walk around Bucharest, your hands in your pockets, and tell the whole world to go hang. You're free as a bird. Do you understand what I'm saying or not?"

Leibel understood very well. Why should he not understand? But then Hotzmach mentioned his mother, and he was struck by a thought. "My mother? My mother! How will she live through it?"

"Well, if that's the case, you must go to your mama, hide under her apron, little one, and let her give you a little cookie."

Leibel twisted and turned, seeking excuses. He wanted desperately to go off with the actors. What would be better than that? But he was hesitant, still wrestling with the idea.

But all that had been earlier, before the whipping, before the cruel "execution." Now, after the humiliation his father had inflicted on him—never mind the pain, the worst was the humiliation! The humiliation! That made a difference. Now Leibel would let nothing stand in his way. No longer was he even troubled by his mother's tears. Let her weep. Looking at her, the whole household would weep and mourn. And even his father would be the better for it. Certainly, at first he would beat himself and blame himself. But after that he would be remorseful. Ay, would he be sorry! He would beat his chest in contrition! And when no one was looking, he would weep silently and would search for him, cry out for him, "Where are you, Leibele, my dear, my dear one? He would not be comforted, like Jacob our Father when he was brought the bloody coat and was told that his son Joseph had been devoured by an animal in the wild. Or like King David, when he was told the news that his beloved son Absalom had died. "Died? Wait! Maybe that's the thing to do! To die! To die! I have to lie down and die!"

CHAPTER 24

Leibel at His Own Funeral

The plan to die appealed greatly to our young hero. He imagined he had already died. How he had died, and of what he had died, he had no idea, he had just died. And there lay Benny Rafalovitch's son, dead, cold, on the bare earth, covered in black. Candles were burning at his head. The entire household surrounded him, wringing their hands and weeping over him. His mother had fainted, and doctors were attempting to revive her. She was revived and fainted again. And his father? Oh! His father was smiting his head with his fists and crying out: "God in Heaven! Jews, this is what I, I, Benny Rafalovitch alone, with my own hands, have done—murdered a child, the most beautiful, best, most beloved child!" And even the grandmother, shaking her head, wept and reproached God for not taking her instead of this young sapling, this innocent lamb, who by right should have been allowed to live and live! The nursemaid who worked for them was weeping and hitting her head against the wall. Women, total strangers, stood over him, tears streaming down their cheeks.

Now began the funeral, and a fine, rich funeral it was! All of Holeneshti gathered for Leibel Rafalovitch's funeral. The wailing of the women, their lamenting and sobbing, was loud enough to reach to the heavens and deafen the mourners. "Be quiet, women! Let there be quiet! Make way! Let the sextons through!"

The sextons, accompanied by the entire burial society, carrying their vessels for washing the dead, pushed their way through the crowd. They laid Leibel out on the stretcher for the dead and bore the young corpse from the house as his mother fainted and his father smote his head with his fists, while the alms box jingled: "Alms for the memory of the dead! Alms for the memory of the dead!"

Silently, heads bowed, the crowd followed Leibel's laid-out corpse. And Leibel was there too! Remarkably! It didn't bother him at all! On the contrary, he was delighted to have died and was pleased to have such a fine funeral. All the people he knew were there, his whole *cheder,* all his friends, Yisroyeli, his *rebbe,* and Leah, his wife, and their daughter, Reizel . . .

Reizel! Where was Reizel? What had happened to her? Why hadn't she come tonight to the theater? Every night she had come to their house and gone to the theater with them. Not tonight. Why?

No more death, no more funeral, no more crying for alms. Once Reizel came into his mind, the thought of her drove away every other thought.

CHAPTER 25

Tears

After the visit from the director and his adjutant, the cantor's wife could not figure out what this Jew with the bald head and bejeweled fingers was after. Upon his departure she blessed him with the prayer that he might break his head. She announced clearly and plainly, "As long as I, Leah, am still on this earth, never again will any daughter go to the theater, even if the world comes to an end!"

"What can you mean by that?" the cantor almost unwillingly interjected.

But his wife cut him off: "You want to know what I mean by that? My reason is simple. A person has to have a sixth sense and has to understand when to say yes and when no, do you hear me?"

What exactly was going on, Reizel did not fully comprehend. But she could surmise from her mother's words that it was over—she could say goodbye to the theater. She knew her mother very well. Her mother's word was law. It was just difficult to get her to that point. But once she gave her word and swore to it, all the power in the world could not budge her! You could get anything you wanted from her mother, but you would not get her to break her word. Reizel felt her heart sink, as if the sun had suddenly set in broad daylight and it had turned dark. Something had been taken from her, ripped by force from her hands, and she choked up with tears.

For the rest of the day she tried to pull herself together, consoling herself with the thought that not going to the theater was not the end of the world. Where was it written one must go to the theater every night? But when evening arrived, and her father let the students out, the cantor's wife lit the smoky lamp, and God's Street wrapped itself in a dim veil, Reizel was filled with restless yearning. With heart and soul she longed to be at the theater—not only at the theater but at the Rafalovitches' bright, happy house with the lighthearted, good, dear people. She reminded herself of those sweet words Leibel had spoken when they were leaving the theater: *"Are you coming again tomorrow?"* She remembered how the next morning, when Leibel came to the *cheder*, fresh, healthy, handsome, and clean as always, she had read from a distance in his fine, mild eyes the same words, *Are you coming again tonight?* Her answering look from across the room replied, *Of course I'm coming again tonight—what a question!* and quickly lowered her eyes so her mother wouldn't see she was looking toward her father's students. Her mother disapproved of her looking toward where the students were studying.

Ach, mama! Did she think Reizel was interested in those boys? Not a chance! But among those boys was Leibel, the wealthy man's son, and oh, what a boy! Not because he was the rich man's son but because he was good as an angel! Ach, what did her mother know about this boy, what kind of house he lived in, what kind of people lived in it?!

These were Reizel's thoughts as she looked forward to the day ending and night coming on, when her father would let the class out and she would put on her one *Shabbes* dress, throw the red shawl over her shoulders, take the little parasol with tassels that her mother had bought her, and leave for that large, rich, happy home, among those carefree people and accompany them to the theater for the whole evening—to paradise! And now suddenly everything had turned upside down! The devil himself had sent those two men, and some evil spirit had made her sing before strangers, leading to her being driven out of paradise!

Reizel threw herself facedown onto her bed and burst into tears, crying bitterly over her miserable luck and the terrible, terrible tragedy that had befallen her. As she wept, she could hear from behind the curtain her parents whispering, quarreling under their breaths, apparently over her. She heard her mother's voice: "If I say no, it is no, do you hear!" Reizel cried even harder. Her father tiptoed to her bed behind the curtain, bent down over her, patted her hair, and spoke quietly so Leah could not hear, calling her sweet names, Reizel and Reizele and Reize'nyu, pleading with her to stop crying, and promising that tomorrow her mother would buy her material for a dress and wool for a jacket, and they would buy shoes for her, new shoes. Reizel cried even harder, until Leah, who had heard everything, grabbed her head and began screaming, "I'll stab myself! I'll hang myself!" Yisroyeli begged her to be quiet, people would come running over!

Hearing the cantor's wife screaming, several neighbors did run over, and for a few minutes there was a commotion: "God be with you, Leah'nyu, what is it?" "Nothing, nothing." "Who was screaming like that?" "Screaming? God forbid! You imagined it. We were just laughing." "Laughing? A fine laughter!" "You don't like it? Then why did you come?" "Out of friendship, Leah'nyu, out of friendship. We heard screaming, and we thought someone was being murdered." "Murdered, here? May God murder my enemies!" As they left, the neighbors slammed the door so hard the windows shook. "Slam your heads against the wall!" Leah called after them, cursing them at length, ending with, "Some good friends!"

Reizel heard all of it lying on her bed behind the curtain, sobbing silently, sorrowfully, over her miserable fate to be born to parents who were too poor to even buy her a pair of decent shoes and who were forced to live in darkness, barely lit by a smoky lamp, having to listen to her mother curse the neighbors with whom she quarreled and made up daily. And over there? Oh! There it was bright. There it was happy. There they laughed. There they knew how to live! Right now they were all at the theater. How far along was the performance? Right in the middle? Maybe at the end? Soon the curtain would fall and the audience would applaud and shout: "Hotzmach! Hotzmach! Dance 'A *Chasid'l*'! Hotzmach!" the crowd would shout until Hotzmach appeared, exhausted, perspiring, smeared with white makeup, and dance for the third time "*A Chasid'l*." The musicians would play, and the audience would clap as Hotzmach sang:

> "A *lusty* chasid'l *am I*
> *Who loves to dance and sing . . .*"

With that lively tune in her ears Reizel fell asleep.

CHAPTER 26

A Fire on God's Street

It was well past midnight when the bells of both churches started ringing out:

BONG! BONG! BONG!
BONG! BONG! BONG!

In Holeneshti when three BONGs in a row are heard, it means a fire. As soon as a fire broke out in Holeneshti, the entire town ran into the streets preparing to go into action, because in Holeneshti there were no firefighters. The streets became thronged with people, and for that reason alone it was worthwhile to be at a fire in Holeneshti. You could see everybody. You heard the latest news. It was quite merry.

In Yisroyeli the cantor's house the first person to hear the bells ringing was his wife. Reizel's tears had kept Leah awake, and even though Reizel herself had long been sleeping that sweet sleep only innocent children know, Leah was not able to shut an eye. Gnawing at her was her vow, which now she regretted. Why had she had to make that vow? Troubling thoughts and frightening images, like burrowing insects, crept into her mind as she tossed and turned, feverish one moment and chilled the next. No sooner did she shut her eyes than she imagined that at any moment Reizel would jump from the window, run to the lake, and, heaven help us, drown herself. The poor distraught mother sat up, listening in the still darkness. *The child is asleep*, she thought, and spat three times to ward off the evil eye. Lying back down to sleep, she groaned as she tormented herself with the thought that she might indeed fall asleep.

Suddenly she heard the three BONGs followed by another three BONGs. Quickly looking to the window, she saw a red streak in the sky. She sprang out of bed and woke her husband gently, so as not to frighten him: "Yisroyeli! Yisroyeli! Wake up, God be with you, it's nothing. There's a fire alarm."

"An alarm? What alarm?" Yisroyeli was frightened.

Leah calmed him: "Don't be scared, it's on our street, on God's Street, but far, far from here. I'm afraid it might be the third house from Ben-Zion the slaughterer," she said, looking out the window.

"Oh my God! Come here, Yisroyeli. What do you say to this! The third house from Ben-Zion, not far from the *shul*, no?"

Yisroyeli peered out the window. "The third house, you say? I'm afraid it's the second."

"This is terrible! Yisroyeli, hurry, get dressed. The *shul* might be lost, God forbid! What will we do then? Faster, Yisroyeli, faster. Put on my shawl so you won't catch cold. Hurry, hurry!"

Leah needn't have rushed him. Yisroyeli was soon ready. He put on his caftan (he refused Leah's shawl, it was warm out) and ran out as fast as he could to rescue Ben-Zion the slaughterer and save the *shul*.

Always among the first in Holeneshti to rescue someone from a fire, Yisroyeli required only someone to provide him with help, a bucket of water, a ladder, an ax, a rope, and whatever else he needed, and he was ready to leap into the fire, heedless of his own life. Normally Yisroyeli had a delicate, spiritual disposition and was as weak as a fly. But when it came to a fire, he became a tower of strength, a hero, the most valiant of men. Breaking out ten window-panes and bloodying his hands was as nothing to him. Clambering onto a roof, a life-risking feat, was as nothing to him. Leah, who knew this, wouldn't let him go without her and meant to follow him closely, especially now when it was so near the *shul*!

But what should we do with the child? Leah said to herself, looking in on Reizel as she slept soundly but uncovered. She listened to see if she was asleep, tucked the blanket around her, and said quietly: "She fell asleep in her clothes, poor thing." She would go out to have no more than a look, one look, half a look, at the fire, and then she would come right back.

Come right back? Just words. How can you leave a fire when it's crackling and leaping from roof to roof? True, it was still some distance from Ben-Zion's house and even farther from the *shul*. In the meantime Asher the baker's house was burning. (What about Asher, and what about the *shul*?) Wasn't Asher the baker a Jew too? True, he himself was to blame. How many times had he been warned to be careful with his kindling and to sweep out the chimney more often because one of these days there could be a tragedy on account of him? Can you expect a baker to listen? Now he was paying for it! Never mind the baker—his house was lost. It was burning on all four sides, burning like a candle. But what could they do for the neighbors? Jewish houses all around, made of straw and shingles, packed closely together. One little wind, and all of God's Street would go up in flames.

The crowd concentrated on the houses around Asher the baker's house. They ran for buckets, brought axes, dragged ropes, hauled ladders. Yisroyeli climbed up Moishe-Ber the butcher's roof and from there gave orders like an able fire chief, demanding assistance, otherwise the butcher's house would burn down next, then Reb Shmuel the rabbi's house, and then Noah the assistant to the rabbi's house, and after his Ben-Zion the slaughterer's, and after that the *shul*. There was good reason for this street to be called God's Street.

The shouting and commotion from the throng below was so great that Yisroyeli's cry from Moishe-Ber the butcher's roof could not be heard.

"Woe is me!" his wife screamed at him from the distance, waving her arms. "What are you doing, you madman? You'll kill yourself, and just before the High Holidays!"

It was just as Yisroyeli had predicted. Before there was time to bring out the meager belongings from the butcher's neighbors' houses, the fire had leaped from Asher the baker's house right to Moishe-Ber the butcher's house.

A cry arose from the crowd: "The cantor! The cantor!"

CHAPTER 27

Sholom-Meyer Talks in Riddles

What did they have against the cantor's daughter? They had taken her and lashed her to wooden beams in Benny Rafalovitch's courtyard. Countless women were whirling around her. They approached the beams where she lay tied down, bent over her, gazed at her, and asked one another: "Is it burning? It's burning, it's burning."

What could this mean? Were they going to burn her alive? Why? She wanted to get up but could not. She was bound hand and foot. She could hear the dry wood crackling under her. A red brightness struck her eyes. She pulled with all her might and broke the ropes and— awoke. She was in her own home and in her own bed fully dressed. She listened, hearing sounds of running and loud shouting: "It's burning, it's burning." She caught a glimpse out the window. The street was suffused in red. The sky was alight with a fiery glow, and people were running onto God's Street from all directions. Reizel called her mother, then her father. No one responded. What was going on?

In a split second Reizel was standing spellbound at the door, shielding her half-awake eyes with her hand. Her little red shawl slid down, freeing her loosening hair. A pair of worn-out shoes poked out below her white dress. From head to toe she was bathed in reddish light from a blazing sky. The girl glowed with a fiery light. Who would dare attempt to paint a portrait of this dark-skinned, exquisite girl, her beautiful hair flowing, her dimpled cheeks aflame in reflected light from the hellish red sky, her half-awake gypsy-eyes igniting and shining forth from her lovely, fire-bathed face like two stars in the dark of night? And where could one find the colors to paint God's Street on this warm, still summer night under a hellish-red sky that lit up the houses and the faces of the people who were running and gathering together, yelling and shouting, waving their arms, looking from a distance like so many dancing demons?

"Good evening, little kitten! All alone, are you? What a mother you have! Probably off to the fire. The whole town is there. When I heard there was a fire on God's Street, I said to myself right away, *I'd better see what's happening at the cantor's, may God grant me luck and prosperity!*"

From his manner of speech, it wasn't difficult to recognize that this was Albert Shchupak's right-hand man, our good friend Sholom-Meyer Murovchik.

This time Reizel was not afraid of him. She was happy to see a familiar person. She asked if he knew whose house was burning.

"I haven't the faintest idea. What's the difference to me if it's Berl's or Shmerl's? I saw people running, so I ran too. Better tell me, little girl, how come you weren't at our theater tonight? I looked for you, little bird, next to that young scamp you always sit with and couldn't find you. I was worried you might, God forbid, be dead, or that some other disaster had befallen you."

Only then did Reizel remember what kind of day she had lived through and the night of despair, disappointment, and tears. She decided to place her trust in this man. She told him what had happened, how her mother was punishing her and she didn't know why. Was it because she had sung *"Reboynu shel oylem"* with her father for them?

"Is that all? Jewish nonsense, ha ha ha!" Sholom-Meyer laughed a dry, hoarse cackle, then quickly changed to an earnest tone and shook his head in regret, sighing: "What a pity that such a jewel has to wallow here in the Holeneshti mud among ignoramuses who don't know how to appreciate her, with fanatic parents who don't realize where their child's happiness lies."

Reizel lifted her eyes to him. What exactly did this man mean?

Sholom-Meyer continued, still talking in riddles. "From the first minute I heard you singing right here at the window—do you remember that morning? You were singing '*Rozhinkes mit mandlen*'—I said, 'That's the one, the true prima donna of prima donnas, may God grant me luck and prosperity.'"

Reizel still did not exactly understand his meaning.

He went on: "And when you sang that '*Reboynu shel oylem*' with your father, I said, 'This girl was created by God for our theater!'"

"Me?" More than that Reizel could not utter at that moment, and she felt all her blood rush to her face.

"I said it at once to our director, 'We must not,' I said to him, 'lose such a priceless prima donna. We must,' I said, 'tear her away from here by force.'"

"By force!?" Now Reizel was taken aback.

Sholom-Meyer Murovchik went on without pausing: "How else? How can you allow such talent to be lost? I picture your first appearance on our stage in the role of Little Blossom, or Blimele, or Shulamit, or in *Holy Sabbath—Shabbes Koydesh*, wearing short dresses and little shoes, and with your sweet voice you sing the lovely songs of Goldfaden, Feinman, or Lateiner, and, I tell you, you will have the whole theater eating out of your hand! Or, let us suppose, you're dressed as a boy with curly black hair, and you look up with your fiery gypsy-eyes and sing 'Hot Rolls' like this."

Sholom-Meyer softly sang "Hot Rolls" in his hoarse voice, all the while looking at Reizel to see what impression it was making on her;

I see a scoundrel in the street
Hands in his pockets, shoes on his feet
Scoffing at me because I try
Through blood and sweat to just get by.
I stand and shout in shoes with holes,
"Hot rolls! Hot rolls! Come buy hot rolls!"

"Obviously when you sing about those rolls with your voice and your looks, the audience will go wild on the spot. Isn't that so, my soul?"

Sholom-Meyer saw that his words had not been wasted. He

approached her closely, patted her hand lightly, and said to her in his hoarse voice: "Listen, my little bird, you can thank God you met me. Our current leading lady is also a cherished child of her parents, also from the lower class, like you. She's from a small town in Poland. She has me to thank that she's an actress in our theater. It was I who helped her escape. It's a nice story, truly, you should hear it. Her father himself is a—"

Too bad Sholom-Meyer Murovchik had to interrupt the story about the leading lady. He saw at a distance, lit by the fiery sky, a figure cutting across the street and running toward the cantor's house. It would be seen as inappropriate for him to be standing with the cantor's daughter on her doorstep. That could damage the plan he had worked out in his head as he was standing with her in the street. He shook Reizel's hand goodbye and tossed in a few words from a song in rhyme:

> Be a smart little girl,
> And your dresses will swirl . . .

The figure that had cut across the street was none other than our young hero, Leibel.

CHAPTER 28

Fifteen-Minute Intermission

We left our young hero going to his funeral. He was in fact sitting in the theater imagining how he had died and how everyone was lamenting his premature death, weeping over him as they accompanied him to his eternal rest. This image was so true to life and so sadly moving that his heart almost broke. He tasted his own salty tears on his lips. Leibel was weeping over Leibel, and as he sat in the theater, he neither heard nor saw what was happening on the stage. He only roused himself when a frightening sound of loud laughter and shouting erupted: "Hotzmach! Hotzmach!"

This clamor woke our young hero from his sorrowful dreams and brought him back to the living world where Jews were enjoying the Yiddish theater.

"Fifteen-minute intermission." That was what it said in the theater program. But everyone knew very well (you can't fool a Jew) what kind of fifteen minutes this was.

"Who are they kidding! More like thirty!" the Holeneshti theatergoers said. They left their recently fought-over seats and went outside to chat, to breathe some fresh air, or to sneak a relative or friend into the theater without a ticket.

Others took advantage of the intermission to steal backstage. Obviously no respectable person did this. Among those who did you would find a musician, a worker, or a transient youth who had nothing to lose.

And always, when Leibel used to enter backstage, he felt he was in another world. Treading on the shaky boards of the stage, he imagined he wasn't so much walking as swimming or floating. As he observed the costumed actors and actresses with their quickly applied makeup rushing about, grabbing something to eat or drink on the run, he imagined himself one of them and unconsciously took on their manner of speaking and gestures. The following day in *cheder* he would demonstrate how the actors carried on to his classmates, who envied him more for that than for being a rich man's son.

This time when Leibel went backstage, he did not have in mind the actors or their tricks. He allowed the leading lady, with her large blue, heavily made-up eyes and heavy bouncing brass earrings, to pass unnoticed. He quickly ran by several actors who were sharing an apple while dissolving in laughter. Leibel wanted only to find Hotzmach.

Hotzmach was difficult to recognize in the costume of Kabtzenzohn. That evening they were performing the famous piece *Kabtzenzohn and Hungerman*. His costume consisted of a torn, ragged dress coat, an old creased, tilted top hat, worn-out, unlaced shabby boots, from which his toes poked out, and a pair of patchwork britches in which the ace of diamonds served as one of the patches.

This ace of diamonds elicited from the Holeneshti audience so much hilarity that, from the first moment Kabtzenzohn appeared until the final scene, they could not stop laughing. To patch up a pair of old britches, please forgive me, with the ace of diamonds is a device no one in Holeneshti would ever have thought of in a thousand years! The audience was positive that it was Hotzmach's idea (naïve people!), and they gave their darling an ovation that turned Shchupak, who was playing Hungerman, green with envy.

But Hotzmach was in seventh heaven. He felt that on this

evening he was acting divinely, that this evening he was being idolized. No one could touch him.

When he saw Leibel wandering backstage, he realized he was
looking for him, probably wishing to congratulate him for his performance and hopefully bringing some goodies. "Hey, little scamp!"
he called out joyfully. "Who are you looking for? How come we
don't see you anymore?"

Leibel went to his friend and asked him to bend over so he could
whisper something important in his ear.

"A secret?" said the tall Hotzmach, bending way down to Leibel, almost folding in half. He listened to the secret, straightened up,
and his sharp eyes lit up. He slapped Leibel on the back.

"When you talk that way, I love you! When you talk that way,
you're one of my people! Of course! My very words! I've been telling
you all along that your place is right here. If not, may I drop dead!"

At that moment Albert Shchupak appeared behind Hotzmach's
back. "What place? Whose place? Go to hell, Hotzmach!"

Hearing the director's voice, Hotzmach turned to him fearfully.
But he quickly collected himself and pointed to Leibel. "He was saying,
this scamp, that someone took a place in the theater without a ticket!"

Those words, "without a ticket," enraged the director. Albert
Shchupak could not abide hearing them any more than a gardener
could abide hearing someone tell him, "There's a pig in the garden."

"Sholom-Meyer! Where the devil is Sholom-Meyer? Damnation!" yelled Shchupak, at the same time looking for Leibel. But Leibel was gone.

CHAPTER 29

Vengeance! Vengeance! Vengeance!

That night our hero slept as if after a long hot bath. He had completely worked out a plan to take revenge, sweet revenge! He had to
avenge himself! He had to teach his father a lesson, to repay him for
the beatings, for the humiliation, for everything, everything!

Leibel did not have to think too hard. What was there to think
about? It all seemed so simple, so natural, and so obvious—nothing
could have been more obvious.

Here is the plan Leibel worked out.

At night when everyone was asleep, he would quietly get up and tiptoe to the bookkeeper's bed. Leibel and he shared a room. Sison v'Simcha was a fellow who loved sleep. Nevertheless he boasted that he slept so lightly that he could hear a fly. But everyone knew that once he fell asleep, you could carry him and his bed outside without waking him, unless you poured a pail of cold water over him.

Still, you could depend on Sison v'Simcha to protect the money. He was, after all, one of the family, a relative of Benny Rafalovitch's, some cousin or nephew. And second of all, he was simply an honest fellow and trustworthy, who guarded the cash box in the drawer where the money was kept like a trusty watchdog. He always carried the keys to the cash drawer in his pants pocket. He would not go to sleep until he had thoroughly examined all the windows and shutters to make sure they were tightly shut and had peeked under the beds in case a thief had stolen in. When he undressed, he laid his trousers under his head. And the master's son slept opposite him. So need he be afraid?

God Himself had sent this bookkeeper to Leibel so he could obtain money. Hotzmach had whispered to him, "You've got to have money. Money! The more money, the better it will be!" And Leibel, working out his famous plan, already pictured in his mind how he would filch the money from the cash drawer. In his plan, Sison v'Simcha was soon asleep like a dead man, snoring like a slaughtered ox, as Leibel stood in the dark behind his bed, wondering how to remove the pants from under his head. Slowly, slowly, he would put his hand under the pillow. He would pull out first one leg, then the other, and remove the ring of keys. Softly he would tiptoe over to the table, stopping after every footstep so as not to be heard, his heart pounding with fright. More than anyone Leibel was fearful of the old grandmother, who slept in the next room. That old lady really did sleep lightly and had a sharp eye that could see through walls as another could see with eyeglasses.

With a beating heart and trembling hands he would open the cash drawer, carefully slide his hand in, and remove a fistful of paper money ("The more paper money, the better," said Hotzmach). He would slowly return the keys and the bookkeeper's trousers back to their place and slip out the door. Waiting for him with a carriage, ready to drive off to the train station, would be his friend Hotzmach. Leibel would arrange to change his usual clothing for other clothes, so that he could lay his own clothes at the edge of the lake. Let them think he had drowned himself. They would surely search for him in the lake and would find nothing. They would sit shiva for him. They would wail and lament until eventually they would forget him.

And time would pass, a year or ten or twenty, by which time Leibel would have become a world-famous artist with a traveling troupe of his own. Out of curiosity he would stop at Holeneshti for a performance. Through an agent he would rent this same stable from his father. He would permit the entire town to enter without tickets. Let them see what real acting was! And when the curtain rose, he would step out on the stage together with the whole troupe, all elegantly dressed, and he, now the director, would stand in their midst, dripping diamonds and jewels, almost as many as Shchupak. And no sooner would he appear on the stage than they would recognize that this was he, Leibel. His mother would surely fall into a faint, and his father would cry out with his thunderous voice: "Leibel!" And from all sides joyous shouts would rise: "Leibel! Leibel! Leibel! Leibel!"

Leibel opened his eyes and saw the bookkeeper standing at his bedside.

"Sison v'Simcha! What is it?"

"What is what? Have you ever seen a person who slept so soundly? You wake him, and you wake him, and you can't wake him up. Wake up! There's a fire."

"What fire? Where?"

"On God's Street. Everyone's at the fire. Get dressed. They've been ringing the bells for an hour. You'd think it would wake the dead."

He himself had just been awakened and had been warned not to leave the house on any account. That was easy enough to say— "Don't leave the house." How can you stay in a house when there's a fire outside? The loyal bookkeeper and Leibel left, agreeing to do so for no more than a second, only to get a quick look. When he saw the fire-illuminated sky and heard the BONGs of the bells, the bookkeeper was instinctively drawn where everyone else was drawn that night. But not Leibel.

Leibel was drawn in another direction. He turned right, intending to look into the cantor's *cheder* and knock on the window to awaken them in case they were still sleeping and didn't know there was a fire on God's Street.

But before he arrived at the cantor's house, he saw from a distance, lit by the hellish-fiery sky, the cantor's daughter Reizel, standing at the door, and next to her some person who suddenly took off, running speedily to the left. Leibel himself broke into a run, but toward the cantor's house, not toward the fire.

CHAPTER 30

A Night of Hidden Magic

If our hero lived to be a hundred, he would never forget that night of the great fire on God's Street.

In the very best as well as the very worst times of his later years, when he would find himself alone, it was pleasurable to lie with closed eyes and to relive again and again that happy, wonderful, unbelievably magical night when he ran, half-asleep, to see what was burning on God's Street.

The sky, as far as the eye could see, was awash in red like blood itself. Where were the stars? The stars had hidden themselves, vanished behind that redness. As he ran toward the fire, he could hear a distant rumble, the hullabaloo of people, the barking of dogs, and the crackling of burning roofs. Black figures played against the red brightness. Wrapped, it seemed, in a red cloud, the cantor's daughter stood before his eyes, appearing like a beautiful, enchanted princess of the night. Never before had her dark-red cheeks flamed so glowingly. Never before had her large gypsy-eyes sparkled as on that dark night. He imagined seeing her rise up and disappear somewhere with the stars into the red brightness of that magical night. He felt himself drawn closer and closer to her.

Reizel had recognized him from the distance. She looked around to make sure no one else would see them. No, no one was nearby. The whole town was at the fire.

She took two steps in his direction. When they met, she told him in a few words how she had awakened, finding herself all alone in the house. "Whose house is burning?" she asked him.

"I don't know. They woke me up and told me there was a fire on God's Street and I ran straight here."

Reizel gazed directly into his eyes. "Straight here? Why straight here?"

"I really don't know, because even if the fire weren't on God's Street, I would have run straight here."

He stood still. He was afraid he had misspoken, and blushed. Reizel never let her gaze leave him. Ah, how handsome he looked at that moment in the midst of the fire! How charmingly did his cheeks flame! How benevolently and lovingly his large, mild eyes gazed at her, as if he were her brother.

Leibel pulled himself together and explained to Reizel why he had come there first despite the fire elsewhere on God's Street. On such a night, what was the fire to him? Houses were burning on God's Street? Let them burn. Let the whole street burn, even the whole town, what did he care? He cared nothing for Holeneshti anymore. Nothing. He was no longer a Holeneshter. In another day, another two days . . .

He clasped her hand. "Will you give me your hand and promise this will remain between us? I must tell you something."

And Leibel pressed her hand into his large, warm hand, as he had often done back in the theater, and said to her quietly, earnestly, with longing in his voice: "I am going away from here."

She looked at him with her gleaming gypsy-eyes. "Where to?"

Where to? He himself did not know. But that he was leaving he was sure, as sure as it was night and it was God's sky above them.

Both of them raised their eyes to the sky, and Reizel felt chilled by this news. She moved closer to him, looked at him, and listened to him speaking such serious words. She imagined he had suddenly grown up. She asked him, and one could hear her voice trembling: "For long?"

"For long? What do you mean, for long? Forever. For always."

"Forever? You mean we'll never see each other again?"

"Never."

In the red glare Leibel saw Reizel's lovely dark-skinned face turn pale, and he again clasped her hand, which had suddenly become cold. He was sorry he was leaving, but there was nothing he could do about it. It had been decided. It was no use. And he resolved to entrust her with his secret, his sacred secret—where he was going and why he was going and because of whom he was going. Reizel looked into his eyes, heard him out, and let out a little sigh.

Leibel looked at her, saying, "You don't want me to? You'll miss me? Tell me. You'll miss me?"

Reizel reddened, "No. Not that. Not that!"

She was envious. He wanted to leave home, and he left. Let her try to pick up and leave. She couldn't. Perhaps she would also like to leave, perhaps as much as he. Did he think he alone had problems with his parents? Oho! It could be that she had the same problems as he and maybe even more.

And she told him everything she had gone through that day and night, the conversation she had had with that person who in Holeneshti was called "a real character," and the words of the director, everything. Everything.

Leibel did not know how it happened. They were both sitting on the threshold of Yisroyeli's house, her small, childlike hand in his hand. He raised it to his warm lips and kissed her fingertips. She did not remove her hand but looked at him frightened, and her large black gypsy-eyes gleamed and twinkled in the red glow of that rare beautiful enchanted night.

What power had seated them so closely, so tightly next to each other, these two young, innocent, childlike souls? What power had made them pour out their hearts to each other? What power had suddenly brought them so close as if they had been friends forever?

It was the marvelous power of that strangely enchanted night.

A night of hidden magic.

CHAPTER 31

Stars Do Not Fall—They Wander

What Reizel told Leibel on that magical night as they both sat together on the cantor's doorstep was news to him—happy, strange, welcome news. Her words soothed his troubled heart. To his ears her voice sounded like the most beautiful music on this remarkable, wondrous, divinely magical night. How he regretted not knowing this sooner. It was good that she had told him, good that he knew. Now he saw it was God's doing. It was fated that they both would have to suffer. Both would go into exile, but they would find salvation in that exile. Both would tear themselves free from cramped, bleak, dark Holeneshti, and both would set out for a new world, a greater, brighter world. Oh! A new life would begin for them, a new kind of existence, a bright, shining life. They would take the same path, each learning the art that suited them, he acting and she singing. And both would become world famous, he with his acting, she with her singing.

Leibel gave her his hand and called on the night and the heavens as witness: "May this night, this red, fire-cloaked sky, be witness that never, never will we part." They took each other's hands, vowing as God was their witness that they would always, always be together, always and forever! Whatever happened to them and wherever life would take them, they would be together, always and everywhere together. And even when they grew to be adults, one would never be without the other. Never. Never! They would work together in the same theater, they would travel the world together. And when the time came, they would return to Holeneshti. Certainly they would return, without fail. They would visit their parents. When the town learned about it, they would all flock to marvel at Benny Rafalovitch's son and Yisroyeli the cantor's daughter. Ah, wouldn't that be wonderful! Everyone would envy them. They would all run after them. They would point them out: "There is the fortunate, fortunate couple!" And by then they would surely be betrothed. What do you mean, betrothed? No, not betrothed, but man and wife, because they had been betrothed ever since that night when they were first seated together at the theater.

"Do you remember that first time at the theater?"

No need to ask. She could sit that way forever. What could be better, lovelier, and sweeter than theater, Yiddish theater?

Leibel was thinking, *God in heaven! How we have been feeding on each other!* Was that not itself a gift from heaven? From that alone it showed how God Himself had taken pity on them. God Himself had looked down on them from above and had sent them each an intercessor, a savior: to her, the *shlimazel* Sholom-Meyer, and to him, Hotzmach.

And Leibel recounted to her the entire interesting story of how he had gotten to know Hotzmach, how he had befriended him and become close, how his father had found him out and severely punished him, and how he had vowed to take revenge for his humiliation. He had no fear of telling her the whole story in the fullest detail. What was there to be afraid of? He could feel that he and she were one from that night on, they had pledged it. Her hand was in his, God was their witness.

They looked up at the sky, now no longer as red. The fire was abating, and the noise and clamor of the crowd were quieting. Stars reappeared in the sky, in that warm, end-of-summer night, first one and soon another and another, then many, many, an infinite number of stars. To Reizel, the stars seemed to be moving in different directions as they showed themselves, one up, the other down. Or perhaps they were falling.

"See how the stars are falling," said Reizel, her voice trembling, her heart beating rapidly.

Leibel laughed. "Don't be afraid," he comforted her like an adult, although in truth she was a year older than he. "What is there to be afraid of? Stars don't fall—stars wander."

Like an older brother, he explained how stars wandered. He knew. He had studied about it in *cheder*. This was his learned explanation: "Every star is a person's soul. Wherever the soul goes, the person goes. That's why we imagine the stars are falling. But stars don't fall—they wander."

Leibel looked deeply into the sky, its redness now fading. In only one corner of the sky was still visible a reddish hue, which gradually dissipated. The shadowy, crowded figures were dispersing in all directions. The pair heard voices nearby. Anytime now someone would see them sitting on the doorstep. It was time to stand, time to go, as reluctant as they were to leave each other.

"Goodnight."

"Goodnight."

Leibel stood up and started walking toward the waning fire. He paused and then turned to look at Reizel one more time, one more time: "Goodnight."

"Goodnight."

A moment later he had vanished.

CHAPTER 32

A Good Week

It was *Shabbes* evening.

But all traces of the gracious, holy *Shabbes* were now gone from Holeneshti.

Gone from the rich neighborhood were the aristocratic-looking youths and the finely dressed girls who once promenaded all day *Shabbes* till late at night, chattering Russian, a badly mutilated Russian, so long as it sounded like Russian.

Gone from God's Street were the poorer men and women, the

men clad in holiday gabardines, their wives with jewels in their ears—
no matter if they were paste, so long as they looked like jewels.

Gone were the children who had been playing that new game,
Yiddish Theater—they had long ago been shooed into their houses.
The sun, with its lush splendor and radiance, had set. The last spark
of the warm Bessarabian summer day was extinguished, and in its
place was the lovely Bessarabian summer evening. Here and there a
star appeared, twinkling and smiling down on the dark, dusty earth.
Pious women finished praying softly in the dark, "God of Abraham, Isaac, and Jacob," and felt a quiet longing for the beloved holy
Shabbes now passing. Tiny yellow flames appeared in the windows.

Observant men finished performing the *havdalah,* the closing
Sabbath ceremony that ushers in the new week. Others finished the
hamavdil and the *eliahu* prayers, and the concluding songs honoring the close of *Shabbes,* while still others were in the midst of their
prayers, singing and swaying *"al tira ivdi yaakov."* A melancholy
pervaded their prayers. A mournful undertone crept into the cheerful singing.

How difficult to part with the beloved Sabbath! How hard to
bid farewell to the beautiful Sabbath Queen!

"Have a good week, a good week!" Yisroyeli the cantor said,
sighing deeply to his wife and daughter, right after the *havdalah*
prayer. He began to chant movingly from memory *"Vayiten lach,"*
snapping his fingers to the rhythm. He looked at Leah and thought:
*Soon she will be complaining about money, about shoes, and about
other daily worries.*

"A good week and a lucky week!" responded Leah, also with a
sigh, but her attention was on her daughter, who was sitting alone,
strangely preoccupied, in a corner of the room.

*What is the child thinking of now, may her troubles fall on my
head?* thought Leah, her heart hurting for her child.

Leah regretted that she had been so angry and severe with her
daughter, an only daughter, a delicate child, a one-and-only. One
mustn't give over to such feelings, she knew very well, but it was too
late. She could not take it back, especially not now—certainly not.
There was to be no more theatergoing. The theater was said to be
leaving this very night, the devil knew where to. She regretted cursing Jews at the beginning of a new week.

Leah was a bit sorry that the theater was leaving Holeneshti
but a bit pleased as well. "One less ruckus in town," she consoled

herself. "Holeneshti has managed to do very well till now without a Yiddish theater. It will manage well enough in the future. The child will surely forget there ever was a theater here. A child remains a child." She would buy her a new pair of shoes, and all her wounds would heal. And of course candies, marmalades, and other good things, which she would bring back, God willing, from the market. "Oy, what's wrong with me! Tomorrow is Sunday, a market day, and I don't have so much as a *zloty*! I must talk to Yisroyeli right away. The new week has begun, did you ever!"

These thoughts carried our cantor's wife into the midst of her daily preoccupations, so that for a while she forgot Reizel's unjust treatment.

And Reizel? Let her be. Reizel was far, far away.

For now, she was still in her own home, but where would she be tomorrow? Tomorrow . . . tomorrow? Only the two of them, she and Leibel, knew. And two others knew their secret as well: the director of the Yiddish theater and his right-hand man, Sholom-Meyer. This Sholom-Meyer had confirmed that very morning, when all were at the synagogue, that at midnight when the clock struck twelve, she would . . . ach, she already knew, she knew what to do! Just she and he, and no one else, no one!

She took pleasure in the fact that she knew something her mother didn't know. It served her right! Served her right! Sholom-Meyer understood—he said she should not have confined a young girl in the house like a caged bird. No freedom, no will of her own! *Don't sing for strangers! Don't go to the theater! Don't look here! Don't stand there!* Was she in bondage to her parents? A slave? That was what Sholom-Meyer said, and he was right. Very right! God willing, tomorrow morning her mother would wake up and see that the bird had flown from its cage. Oh, would she be sorry! Oh, would she cry! But then it would be too late. Then she would really have herself a good week. *A very good and a very lucky week*!

Her heart ached for only one person, her father, whom she did pity. He truly loved her. She had always been very close to him, not like daughter and father but more like sister and brother. Who would spin the *dreydl* with him on Chanukah? Who would steal the *afikomen* matzo from under the Pesach pillow? Who would pick Shevuos greens for him? Who would go to synagogue with him Simchas Torah? And who would sing *Shabbes* songs with him?

Reizel recalled how at a recent *Shabbes* night, she and her father had chanted the *havdalah* prayers together, singing Yiddish songs that he had taught her, while her mother brewed tea in the little samovar.

One song in particular they always sang at that time, especially when the cantor was in high spirits. The song was called "*Moshiach*" and was sung half in Yiddish, half in Russian: the cantor sang to her in Yiddish, and Reizel sang to him in Russian:

> HE: *What will come to pass?*
> SHE: *The end of our exile.*
> HE: *Where will Jews go?*
> SHE: *To the land of Israel.*
> HE: *What will happen there?*
> SHE: *We will meet our savior.*
> HE: *Who will be our savior?*
> SHE: *Our blessed* Moshiach.
> HE: *When will this be?*
> SHE: *In our own time.*
> BOTH (fast): *Day of gladness, day of joy,*
> *Day of friendship, day of deliverance,*
> *Gladness, joy, friendship, deliverance,*
> *Love and devotion!*

And again: *Yom gilah, yom rinah!*

"Enough with this gladness and joy!" her mother would interrupt, carrying over the little samovar. "Better to drink our cups of tea, I say!"

Ah, how pleasant that evening was, how bright, how happy! It seemed like just yesterday, and yet it was so long, so long ago. It would be a long time till it happened again, only God knews when! She fell into a deep, terrifying gloom, and her heart grew heavy, her throat tightened. She did not know what was coming over her, but any moment she would break into tears.

Her father noticed the way she was sitting alone so preoccupied in a corner, and he approached her, still singing, caressed her beautiful black, shiny hair, and bent down to her. "What is it, daughter?"

"Nothing. Have a good week!"

And her fevered head fell upon the cantor's breast as she kissed him and clung to him tightly.

CHAPTER 33

The Temptation of Money

Benny Rafalovitch had also finished performing the *havdalah*.

At Benny's the *havdalah* was executed in style. When Benny chanted it, he was surrounded by his entire household, and all had to respond, "*Boruch-hu u'boruch shemo*," Amen. Blessed be He and blessed be His name—his wife, the children, his ancient mother, the young bookkeeper, the cook—all.

Benny's *havdalah* was impressive. He started off chanting the sorrowful melody loudly, expansively. But at a more difficult passage he became tangled up in the Hebrew and mumbled the whole section under his breath, until he was able to get back on the right track and sing out again, "*Beyn t'hiyah lonu*," stressing the B. Then going down a few tones lower, he drew out: "*Bey-n ko-desh l-cho-l*." With the same melody they all responded, "*A-me-n!*" He blew out the *havdalah* candle, stuffed everyone's pockets with enough for a full week, and announced in his growling lion's voice: "Have a good week, a good week!" They all responded in one voice, "Have a good week, a good year!"

That was how Benny Rafalovitch performed the *havdalah*.

When he was finished, he winked to the bookkeeper to tally the payments for the week and write them down in the account book. Sison v'Simcha rolled up his sleeves, pulled out the key ring from his pants pocket, opened the middle drawer, and sat down to count the remaining money with fervor and zeal.

First to appear on the table was the paper money, packet after packet. The bookkeeper was expert at counting money. As he licked his thumb, the bills fairly flew through his fingers, shimmering before one's eyes. First the "aristocrats," the hundreds, or as Benny called these broad bills, the "bedsheets." Then came the white "delicates," twenty-fives, followed by the red, fiery tenners, and the blue fivers. After them the "small fry," green faded threes and yellow torn ones, endlessly.

All the time the bookkeeper and Benny were counting the money, our Leibel was sitting at a distance. He was reading a little prayer book, seemingly muttering a prayer, rocking back and forth and turning page after page, helping count the money. He counted and counted but could not add it up. When they were counting the

big bills, he could keep up, but when it came to the small bills, he
lost track. So he went back to his little prayer book and chanted
his own soft melody as before. But the packets of money kept floating before his eyes and would not let him be. Where would they
be, these fine packets of money, tonight around midnight? Where?
Why, with *him*, with *him*, only with *him*! A chill came over him; he
rocked back and forth even harder, praying with renewed vigor.

Benny and the bookkeeper were so deeply engrossed in their
work, they took no notice of Leibel. Nor did they hear his praying.
But his mother Beylke, sitting to the side, observed how Leibel was
praying and took great pleasure in it, praising him to herself, *How
lucky we are. How precious this child is.*

The great pain she carried deep within her heart had slowly
begun to heal. She reflected, *What sin has this child actually committed? He gave a poor, sick actor something to eat. For that you have
to punish a child so harshly, humiliate him before the household? If
only Benny could see him with my eyes, bless his bright face!*

But quite otherwise, Benny was neither looking nor hearing. He
was immersed in counting money. After finishing with the paper
money, they turned to the silver. When it came to counting silver,
Simcha was even more of a master. He gathered the coins in piles,
and the number of piles kept growing—first one, then two, three,
five, ten and more, and more, and more. The silver money now
counted, they moved on to the small change, which flew through the
bookkeeper's hands with frightening speed, clinking and vanishing
between his fingers as if by magic.

Leibel was thinking, *I don't need small change, I don't need
silver. What would I do with it? All I need are those packets of
paper money my father is holding in his hands.* Leibel saw his father
delighting in the money. Benny let his gaze linger over each packet,
then felt it, smoothed it, before handing it over to the bookkeeper.
Simcha laid it back into the table drawer, putting each packet in its
place, first the "aristocrats," then the small bills, followed by the
silver and coins.

Leibel shifted his eyes from the little *siddur* to the table where
the packets of money were disappearing into the drawer. It was in
that drawer that his dreams now lay. There all his hopes, his whole
being and soul, now lay.

How many times had Leibel heard from his *rebbe* in *cheder* and
from so many elders that money was a temptation as powerful as it

was evil? But only at that moment did he grasp the full meaning of it. The evil temptation of money was clutching him with its claws, tightly, ever more tightly! Leibel knew it was useless to struggle. He could not free himself from its grasp. He wasn't even trying. On the contrary, he begged God to let his crime be successful, for if he failed, if they caught him, God forbid—it was not to be thought of! That would be his undoing, in both of his worlds. Hotzmach—gone! The theater—gone! And Reizel—also gone? What would become of him? No more theater! No more Reizel! No more golden dreams! All ended . . .

"*Mazel tov!* Here come the in-laws to clean out the stable of its Jewish filth." That was our Benny speaking in his own obscure language as he rose from his seat.

The reader, now well acquainted with our Benny Rafalovitch's language, will realize that by "in-laws" he meant the coachmen, and by "Yiddish filth" he meant the Yiddish theater.

CHAPTER 34

Welcome, Shimen-Dovid the Teamster

Benny could have kicked himself that, for a few rubles, he had given over his clean, tidy courtyard and stable to the Yiddish theater. Had they let loose a herd of swine into his courtyard, they would not have befouled it as badly as they had in only a few weeks. Benny didn't know altogether why, but as a kosher Jew despises pork, so he despised those avaricious demons, by which he meant the actors. And more than anyone, he could not abide that decked-out clown with his scraped-off noodle-board of a head, in other words, the director, Albert Shchupak.

Benny Rafalovitch and Albert Shchupak had hated each other at first sight. Each man looked down his nose at the other. To Benny, Shchupak was no more than a clown, and to Shchupak, Benny was a Bessarabian ass. So it was easy to understand why Benny was happy when he came out into the courtyard and saw Shimen-Dovid the teamster pulling up to the door in a large van, followed by a line of wagons of all sizes, and finally an exceptionally large tall wagon that in Bessarabian was called a *harba*.

Benny began chatting with Shimen-Dovid the teamster in his own language: "Welcome—look who's here, a guest, Shimen-Dovid! Tell me, dear fellow, how much do you charge these tramps for carting off their 'corpses'?"

"Pity the poor teamster!" answered Shimen-Dovid, and (as was his habit) tossed in a quotation from the Psalms as commentary. He complained to Benny how bad business was, counting off on his fingers: "The horse has to eat, drivers have to be paid, oats are expensive, a wagon needs greasing, you need a peasant to help you, and a peasant is a thief . . ."

Running out of fingers, Shimen-Dovid waved his hand in dismissal and came up with a quotation from the Psalms, freely translated as "Go bury yourself."

Shimen-Dovid was more of a businessman than a teamster—he owned a house and three teams of horses. His children studied in *cheder*. He was also a bit of a scholar, knowing all the Psalms by heart and spouting quotations, exploiting the helpless Psalms at every opportunity.

Shimen-Dovid had insisted on signing a contract with Shchupak. What happened after he fulfilled the contract was not his concern. All he had to do was pack up and move the whole theater—artists, sets, everything—to the train station on Saturday night, right after *havdalah*. And without fail, bright and early the next morning, he would put the whole gang, theater and all, on the train for Faleshti, even if stones were to rain from the sky. From then on they were on their own, and as far as he was concerned, they could go by sleigh all the way to Eretz Yisroel.

That's what Shimen-Dovid said, and when Shimen-Dovid spoke, that was the way it was. But come Saturday night, there was no Shimen-Dovid. The stars appeared in the sky, candles twinkled in the windows, but no van was to be seen in the courtyard. Hotzmach was sent to find out what the matter was.

He found Shimen-Dovid loudly praying over his big *siddur*.

"Reb Shimen-Dovid, *nu*?"

Shimen-Dovid pointed to his mouth with one hand and with other indicated the *siddur,* saying, "*Nu nu.*"

That meant no talking and no work until he had finished praying. Hotzmach sat down to smoke a cigarette, while back at the theater Shchupak was jumping out of his skin. Never before had Albert Shchupak been as nervous as on that Saturday night. He kept whispering in private to Sholom-Meyer, pacing up and down, quarreling with the actors and actresses. More than anyone, as usual, it was the scapegoat Hotzmach who really caught it. Shchupak loudly commanded that the accursed Hotzmach appear immediately with teamsters and vans, or his name was not Albret.

"What is it with our director?" said the artists among themselves in the stable backstage.

"Don't bother him. He's crazy. His wife is coming tomorrow morning."

"How do you know?"

"There was a wire."

"Shchupak has a wife?"

"*Mazel tov!* Where have you been?"

"I wouldn't be surprised if a man like Shchupak has three wives."

"But I heard that he divorced this one."

"No truth to it at all."

"So why is he going after the leading lady?"

"Leave the leading lady out of it. The leading lady couldn't care less about him, or any of us."

"Why are you protecting Breyndele Kozak?"

"How's about shutting up?"

"Or maybe drop dead?"

"Where? Here in Bessarabia? Or there, in Romania?"

"Enough of wagging your tongues."

"Where were we, with Shchupak's wives?"

"Quiet, kids—I think we're leaving!"

"We're leaving! We're leaving!"

At these words the troupe sprang up as one and burst into a high-spirited song, entirely meaningless:

"Rom-tarerom! Terararom! Hertzum-pertzum perel-virel-vertzum! Ribe zshi, pootz zshi, pootz zshi, pootz getrie!"

Marching to this tune they exited the stable for the courtyard where, as if arriving at a wedding, they "welcomed the bridegroom," the finally arrived teamster, with song and dance.

CHAPTER 35

Shimen-Dovid the Teamster Takes Charge

In order to move the Yiddish theater, Shimen-Dovid brought with him a gang of teamsters and a squad of horsewhippers, young and old. All wore oversize, well-oiled boots, and all carried long whips in their hands.

They were: Noach Brimze, a teamster with a torn smock and a felt vest. Nachmen Kokosh, an angry Jew who looked like a hare. Yenkel Mometlive, a sleepy-eyed lad with red lips. Getzi Galagan, a tall youth with only one eye. Henich Kusti, a short but sturdy teamster. And Karpe Munjiuk, a Moldavian peasant with a fur hat. Karpe the Moldavian shoved his hat back, stuffed the hems of his tunic into his boots, and began to grease the wheels as the other teamsters set to their tasks with gusto, packing up sets, carrying boxes from the stable, box after box, bundle after bundle, loading the vans and ignoring the actors and actresses running behind, pleading with them to be careful.

Like a general, Shimen-Dovid stood over the teamsters and barked orders, spitting out phrases from the Psalms, mixed with choice Moldavian phrases:

"Listen carefully, you horse's ass. Hold on to that van, or I'll deliver a fist in your craw." "You, over there—may the Lord show you the right path, or I'll send you packing."

The gang of teamsters and horsewhippers were apparently not very frightened of Shimen-Dovid's orders or his Psalm-quoting, because as they were working and loading the crates, they were trading quips and insults, teasing, laughing, and mostly talking in their teamster argot about food, which they too often lacked:

"Tell me, you liver-loving jerk, aren't you in the mood for a bellyful of thick black bread smeared with goose fat?"

"Get out of here, you blind idiot, with your black bread! What I want is a little *tsimmes* and chickpeas."

"And you'll probably down it with a quart of vodka, ah-ha!"

"Or better still, a flask of brandy!"

Overhearing, Shimen-Dovid shouted: "Why are you talking about food, you bastards? I'll give you a vodka, with a wagon-shaft through your throats!"

The laughter and uproar of the teamsters and horsewhippers,

the bossing and cursing of Shimen-Dovid, blended with the din of the actors and actresses, who tore around madly, screaming and shouting at one another and all of them at Hotzmach:

"Hotzmach, may the devil take you!"

"Hotzmach, go! Hotzmach, stay! Hotzmach, stop! Hotzmach, here! Hotzmach, there!"

Poor Hotzmach carried upon his gaunt frame and bony shoulders the entire imminent departure of the theater. He absorbed everyone's insults, toted and dragged everything, while coughing and coughing without stop. Looming over him, dripping jewels, was the director of the Yiddish theater, Albert Shchupak, who drove him mercilessly, cursing and humiliating him to the point that the agitated Hotzmach could hardly hold on to whatever he was carrying.

But what did Hotzmach care about the director now? To hell with him! Just let this new plan that he had concocted work. Just let the kid get there tonight, and his fortune would be made!

By the kid he meant Leibel, whom he was even now searching for but could not locate. Everyone was in the courtyard, all of Rafalovitch's family, the sons and daughters, the sons- and daughters-in-law, the nursemaid, and the bookkeeper whom Leibel had dubbed Sison v'Simcha. Even the old grandmother had come out to keep her sharp eye on the movers—in the wink of an eye between yes and no they could "accidentally" stow away something that wasn't part of the theater. Only Leibel was not present. Hotzmach was beside himself. *What could have happened?* he thought. *Maybe the little squirt changed his mind about the plan?* Then Hotzmach would look like a real sucker. He would be polishing Shchupak's boots forever and would probably have to marry that witch Etel Dvoyra, may a pestilence afflict them all, *reboynu shel oylem,* this very night! May they not live to get out of here! And if they did get out, may they break every bone in their bodies along the way and not live to get where they're going!

"Hotzmach, what the devil are you muttering about?"

"I'm not muttering, I'm studying my lines."

"A fine time to study lines, may you roast alive, idiot! Come here!"

"Amen, the same to you. I'm coming! I'm coming!" said Hotzmach under his breath, and coughed, his eyes roaming everywhere, looking for Leibel.

CHAPTER 36

Sholom-Meyer Murovchik Gives a Speech

A crowd of Holeneshters gathered Saturday night at the Rafalovitches' courtyard to give the Yiddish theater a proper send-off.
Sholom-Meyer harshly scolded them. They were wasting their time,
he informed them, and threw in a few curse words directed at their
ancestors. Their waiting was in vain. Much more packing had to
be done. But the Holeneshti theater-lovers were not persuaded by
Sholom-Meyer's explanation. Everything has to come to an end—
the packing too had to end sometime. The theater had to leave the
courtyard sometime. That was certain. So it was nonsense not to
wait. How could a Yiddish theater leave Holeneshti as if it were an
everyday occurrence without the town giving it a proper send-off?

     This stubbornness the director of the Yiddish theater and his
right-hand man had not foreseen. For the grand plan that they had
cooked up, the very opposite was required. No onlookers must witness their departure. What was to be done? What could the director
tell them? Hadn't Sholom-Meyer tried to drive them off already? But
you can't argue with a whole town. A scandal could come of that.
What they needed now was secrecy, absolute secrecy. A delicate task
lay ahead of them on God's Street, a good piece of work!

     An idea occurred to Sholom-Meyer (who was a diplomat, after
all). He clambered onto a tall wagon and stepped up before the
crowd, clearing his throat to give a speech, a real oration.

     "Respected public! Ladies and gentlemen! In the name of the
director of the Yiddish-German theater and in the name of the whole
troupe, I have the honor to convey to you, respected public, our deepest gratitude for the appreciation you have shown our theater. The
entire time we found ourselves in your town, the theater—I can say
this proudly—was never empty. Not only were people seated in the
theater, but many were standing outside. That alone shows me how
much you appreciate art and how much you value Yiddish theater.
I take it upon myself right now standing before you to ask for your
pardon for my previous ungentlemanly behavior. I beg a hundred
pardons of you if I ever treated any one of you impolitely, cursed you
out, threw you out of the theater, or sprayed you with cold water.
A man is not an angel. I assure you our theater will never forget
your Holeneshti. Respected public! Our theater is about to leave

here, perhaps for a long time. It would be very flattering to us if you would honor us by seeing us off. But I deeply regret to tell you that we will not be ready to move from this place until daybreak. If you really wish to please us, go home to sleep, and, God willing, tomorrow morning you can come here and you will all be *Willkommen*."

The effect of Sholom-Meyer's speech and his German *Willkommen* was beyond description. The "respected public" gave the speaker a thunderous ovation, shouting "Bravo" over and over, but *bravo* was not enough. They began shouting "Hoorah," but *hoorah* proved insufficient. So finally they began to shout for Hotzmach. "Hotzmach! 'A *Chasid'l*'! Hotzmach! Hotzmach!"

Sholom-Meyer climbed back up on the wagon and excused himself before the "respected public," saying that their shouting and clamor were in vain. Hotzmach would not be performing any more or singing "A *Chasid'l*." The theater was closed.

The clamor did not abate, but rather the cries of "Hotzmach" and "*A Chasid'l*" grew even louder.

Sholom-Meyer Murovchik realized that the gentle approach wasn't going to work. He would have to resort to his old remedy that had always stood him in good stead, the cold water spray. So they unpacked the sets and removed the hoses and sprayed the "respected public." A good solution! In a few minutes the place was cleaned out of everyone.

Sholom-Meyer waited a few hours until the town quieted down. The director gathered the troupe and took Yechiel the *klezmer* and the whole company off to a wine cellar for a glass of wine, some dessert, and some chickpeas, and to live it up a little, as God in his wisdom commanded us.

The troupe could hardly believe their director had suddenly become so kind. Some whispered, "There's something fishy going on here!" He ordered round after round, drinking and inviting the group to drink with him; "Let me tell you, *this* is a wine! Children, drink! Pour it down your gullets!"

In the midst of all the heavy drinking our Sholom-Meyer Murovchik slipped away from the company, as silent as a shadow, and stole off to God's Street.

CHAPTER 37

Needless Fears

When Isaac was led to be sacrificed by our ancestor Abraham, he was surely not as terrified as was our poor hero Leibel, sitting that Saturday night in a wagon with his friend Hotzmach. They were on their way to the train that would take them to Potcheshti and from there to Ungeni on the Romanian border. He was frightened lest anything happen before they were on the train. Someone might chase after him, grab him, and take him back to Holeneshti, and his father would demand to know about the missing money. Oh! Leibel was afraid to allow himself to think of what would happen then. It would be better not to live to see it—better to throw himself into the lake.

Leibel listened intently to the horses galloping, to the wheels clattering, to the wagon shaking. He imagined someone was really coming after him. Every fiber of his being trembled with fright. Poor Leibel and Hotzmach! This old wagon was capable of shaking the very soul out of a person. It had been Sholom-Meyer's idea to seat Hotzmach on top of the coach with the baggage, to make sure no harm came to the stage sets.

But Hotzmach no longer needed to listen to Sholom-Meyer and the director. Now Hotzmach, sitting atop the wagon, was the director with his own troupe and had his own stage sets. In Hotzmach's bosom pocket, you must understand, lay a little packet that warmed him and spread balm through all his limbs, filling his heart with the greatest happiness.

That welcome packet had been surreptitiously handed over to him, right there on the wagon, by his young friend, his hands cold and trembling, his teeth chattering, his body shaking as if he were convulsing.

"How much have we here, dear boy?" Hotzmach asked softly, leaning closer so their driver wouldn't hear. He could tell by the size of the packet that it had to be a small fortune.

"I have no idea," answered Leibel, also very softly, and Hotzmach could feel that Leibel's breath was hot.

"Why are you shivering, poor boy? Are you cold?" Hotzmach asked with the tenderness of an older brother.

"I am wa-wa-warm!" Leibel replied, his teeth knocking together.

"Really? You're wa-wa-warm?" Hotzmach mimicked him.

"You've got a fever. Here, let me wrap you in my cape, and you'll feel much better. My cape will warm you like it was your own mother."

Hotzmach turned to unwrap a package of clothes and drew out an old cape, a real *shmatte*, a rag. Why did he call this *shmatte* a cape? Once long ago, when it had belonged to Shchupak, it actually may have been a garment that could be called a cape. It had to have been long ago, surely in the days before Albert Shchupak became the director, when he was simply one of the actors. It might even have gone back to when our Shchupak used to perform at weddings, circumcisions, and *pidyon habens* and sang *kol m'koydesh*. In any case, when Shchupak had presented this old garment to the comic Hotzmach, he had said repeatedly that he was giving it to him as a gift. He took the trouble to call together all the artists to show them what a gift he, Shchupak, was capable of giving away.

He turned poor Hotzmach around, praising him, showing him off, and boasting all in the same breath: "I want you to know that this was once a special cape of real expensive velvet with an expensive collar of real velvet, do you hear, a bargain I bought ready-made from a thief. It was a pleasure to look at, even if it didn't have sleeves, heh-heh, may my name not be ALBRET!"

In Shchupak's red, browless eyes a tear had actually appeared. Hotzmach donned this valuable garment, and on the spot, behind Shchupak's back, he mimicked Shchupak with his weird, creased, pity-me face, with his puckered little mouth and his small teary eyes—but so ingeniously there was no knowing which of the two was Shchupak and which was Hotzmach.

Nevertheless, this cape had gone on to serve Hotzmach like a devoted mother. It had served as a raincoat, a sheet, a blanket, and a robe, whatever he needed. And now it was coming in handy to wrap this youngster who was shivering like a newborn lamb.

Hotzmach bent down to the youngster and whispered in his ear, as one comforts a child: "What are you afraid of, little silly? We're almost in Potcheshti, where we'll get on a train, and by morning we'll be at the border in Ungeni. From Ungeni to Yas is no more than half an hour's ride, so that when they realize at home what's happened, we'll be long gone!"

This happy thought made Hotzmach chuckle quietly. He coughed and then cursed the cough.

But Leibel did not hear what Hotzmach was saying. He was trembling. He could swear he heard someone running after the wagon and panting: "Ha-eh! Ha-eh! Ha-eh!" As terrified as he was, he poked his head out of the cape, glanced back, and saw—their old dog, Terkush! How did Terkush get there? Probably Terkush was running ahead of someone from back home. Leibel broke into a cold sweat. And before he had time to glance back again, he heard a whoop and a whistle and the crack of a whip of someone chasing behind them. *Too late—all is lost!* thought our young hero, preparing for the worst.

But it turned out to be Shimen-Dovid in his covered wagon, pulling up to speak to their driver, half in Moldavian, half in Yiddish, sprinkled with Hebrew: "What's going on here? Why are you lagging behind, you lazy lummox? I thought you'd be more than halfway to Potcheshti by now. Damn! Give that old nag a poke in the ribs or a lash across the legs. He's moving like a snail."

Shimen-Dovid didn't wait for the driver to act but himself delivered the blows to the old nag's legs, saying, "Damn! When you get to Potcheshti, better tell the others that I decided to switch horses and drive back home. Don't wait for me. Do you hear what I'm saying or are you asleep? Giddyap, boys, giddyap, giddyap!" Shimen-Dovid shouted to his horses, pulling the wagon sharply to the right.

Our young hero wiped the sweat from his brow in relief and thanked God that he had been spared. He slowly poked his head out of the cape and with one eye glanced back. A pair of very familiar black gypsy-eyes were shining in Shimen-Dovid's covered wagon.

Leibel rose from his seat, tore off the cape, and screamed: "Reizel!" But before that word could reach Shimen-Dovid's covered wagon, it had turned around, and with a whoop and a whistle and a crack of the whip, it was off in the opposite direction, almost as if it were turning back. The wagon vanished, leaving behind a thick cloud of dust and the strong mixed smells of horses and tar.

CHAPTER 38

Questions! Questions! Questions!

When a person is gripped by fright, he can imagine things that don't exist, thought our young hero, sitting with Hotzmach atop the wagon, perched on the stage sets. Where did he get the idea

that Reizel had been sitting in Shimen-Dovid's wagon? If that were
Reizel, why had they turned off in another direction? Weren't they
going to the same place?

Those questions were disturbing Leibel as he swung around
again to see where Shimen-Dovid's wagon had disappeared to. But
his eyes met those of his friend Terkush, who was still chasing the
wagon, his tongue hanging out. "What a foolish dog!" mused Leibel,
his heart aching with pity for that old faithful creature that would
now be lonesome and all alone. *And my poor pony,* he thought.
Isn't he going to be lonesome and all alone too?

"A plague on both of them!" Hotzmach cried out suddenly.

"A plague on whom?" Leibel asked, puzzled.

"Whom? I mean Shchupak, together with that bastard Sholom-
Meyer. Did you see the way they were sprawled out in Shimen-
Dovid's wagon? Made themselves right at home."

Leibel stared at Hotzmach, even more puzzled. He had not seen
anyone else in Shimen-Dovid's wagon besides Reizel. What was
going on?

Hotzmach was preoccupied only with his own concerns, Shchupak and Sholom-Meyer. He muttered to himself: "One thing I can't
understand, even if you chop my head off. Why on earth did they
turn back? I have to ask this sleepy driver. Eh, Uncle! Wake up, it's
time to pray!" Hotzmach said to him. "I'm sorry to interrupt you in
the middle of your sleep. Can you tell me where that road leads to,
the one Shimen-Dovid suddenly took off on?"

"Heh? That dirt road?" the driver replied, turning his drowsy
face to him. "That dirt road takes you to Novoselitz—that is, if you
want to go there."

"To Novoselitz?"

"Heh? To Novoselitz."

"How does Novoselitz come into this? We're supposed to be
going to Ungeni."

"Heh? We're going to Potcheshti, that's where."

"I know," said Hotzmach, "to the train station at Potcheshti.
From there the train goes to Ungeni on the Romanian border.
Novoselitz is on an altogether different border."

The driver woke up again with a start. "Heh? A different border, you say? Right, a different border."

"So what's this talk about Novoselitz?" Hotzmach asked, getting angry.

"Heh? The dirt road, I said, goes to Novoselitz. With that dirt road, you can go, if you want to go, I said, to Novoselitz."

"Again with Novoselitz! How does Novoselitz come into this? We're not going to Novoselitz. We're supposed to be going to Ungeni!" shouted Hotzmach with all his might.

"Heh? We're going to Potcheshti, that's where."

"Ah, may a rock strike you dead! I tell him Ungeni, he tells me Potcheshti! Try and reason with a wagon driver!"

Hotzmach spat at the driver and whispered to Leibel, "What a simpleton!"

But Leibel paid no attention. Leibel's brain was working, posing questions and still more questions, but the main question was: *What's happening to Reizel?*

"Do you know what I think, my dear songbird?" Hotzmach said to him. "I'm afraid my Shchupak and that bastard Sholom-Meyer forgot something at the train station and had to go back to Holeneshti. But you have to ask"—here Hotzmach shoved his cap back and spoke as if to himself—"why did Shimen-Dovid tell the other teamsters not to wait for him? Something fishy is going on." Hotzmach stroked his chin, as if he had a beard. "What does this mean? The driver tells us they drove off, may the devil take them, on the dirt road to Novoselitz. But why? That's what we need to get to the bottom of, if this driver is right about their driving off, the devil knows why, on that dirt road to Novoselitz. Ay, the question is"—this Hotzmach said in the singsong of the Gemorah, gesturing with his thumb—"ay, what is the question? Why did they send off the whole troupe and the stage sets to the Romanian border while they themselves went crazy, may it not be catching, and went off, God knows where, to Novoselitz?"

Hotzmach remained speechless, thumb in the air, and then answered himself in the same Talmudic singsong:

"Leave it be—it must remain a question!"

CHAPTER 39

Holeneshti Doesn't Sleep

Of all the Holeneshti Jews who were agitated and upset, their heads spinning over the extraordinary disappearance of the rich man's son and the cantor's daughter, only one person remained calm, did not cry, did not groan, did not sigh, but immediately threw himself into what had to be done.

That person was the rich man himself—Benny Rafalovitch.

The first thing Benny Rafalovitch did, when he was informed of the unfortunate incident, was to demand quiet. And it became quiet. Then he ordered that horses be harnessed and that the Russian police commissioner, with whom Benny was on a first-name basis, be brought to him.

"Take as much as you want," Benny told him, "whatever I own down to my last shirt. Just bring me back my child."

It was hard to believe how a person could change in one day. Benny's usually red cheeks had turned pale and drawn. His eyes seemed to wander, as if he were looking for someone. Even his paunch, always plump and round as a drum, seemed to sag. This was no longer the same Benny as before. He paced the house, dark as a shadow, avoiding the courtyard, never stepping into the light of day. Beylke lay seriously ill, suffering from heart failure. Her doctor said she must be kept calm. Calm? How could Benny keep her calm when he had been destroyed by this crushing blow? His best, most beloved, most precious child had been taken from him.

"You can have as much as you want," he said again to the police commissioner, "whatever I own, down to my last shirt. Just bring me back my child."

The police commissioner looked at Benny. He had never seen him so upset. He felt sorry for him and laid a sympathetic hand on his shoulders. "*Budyet charasho*—everything will be all right. Let someone give him something to drink."

With great dispatch, the authorities began their investigation, thoroughly exploring every possible clue. They came to the conclusion that the guilty party was that "scoundrel," the cantor. He knew very well where the couple had gone but was playing dumb. If they could, they would put him in jail for a few hours and let him get acquainted with the mice and bedbugs—then he'd stop playing dumb. Yes, they'd cart Yisroyeli off to prison—if not for Leah his wife, with her clever, mannish way of thinking.

As soon as the first wave of anguish passed over her, Leah's eyes were opened. All this, she surmised, had to be connected to the Yiddish theater, and she said so to the authorities. All the evidence pointed in that direction. Her maternal instinct, sharpened by her grief and misery, confirmed it. Her mother's heart affirmed what her instinct grasped. From the instant those two *shlimazels* had first crossed her threshold, the thought came like a thunderbolt—They were after her offspring! God in heaven! God in heaven! Where were her eyes? She had been bedazzled—God's punishment for her great, great sins! Now everything was clear, clear as day. So many people in town had played a part in her tragedy.

The first was that holier-than-thou Necha, the owner of the inn, and her two wanton younger sisters, who were always ha-ha-ha and ha-ha-ha with everyone. Those two *shlimazels* had lodged in her inn and were so cozy with her and her sisters. They must know everything, everything. And what about Yechiel the *klezmer*? Didn't that charlatan get drunk all night with the troupe in Henich the winemaker's cellar? And Henich the winemaker himself—another wolf in sheep's clothing! Hadn't his older daughter run off with a writer from Stanovoi three years ago? She could swear up and down that they all had contributed to her tragedy! Why didn't they arrest Yechiel and Henich and Necha instead of wasting their time on her husband, innocent as a lamb?

With these words, she opened the officials' eyes and showed them how to proceed and where to look.

Yechiel and Henich and Necha were quickly arrested and inter-rogated. Terrified of being falsely accused, God forbid, they were more than ready to answer the officials' questions about the actors of the Yiddish theater and the runaway pair. And luckily they had much, much to tell.

The officials required no more of them. Once the arrestees told them what they knew, the officials would release them.

CHAPTER 40

Witnesses and More Witnesses

The first to be questioned was Henich the winemaker, a man in his later years, white as a dove, but with red, puffy cheeks like those of a younger man, and with a substantial Bessarabian paunch. Henich was not clever, but he did have one virtue—he was a truthful man and would never say something he didn't know to be so and would invent no tales. He began telling the truth, as if standing before God. This is what he recounted:

Shabbes night, as he had done for all the years he had been a winemaker, he took a candle and went down to his wine cellar to check on the wine—which wine needed more aging and which still needed to be filtered, which needed more sugar and which was sweet enough. Some wines needed to be decanted into bottles and corked to prevent mold, he explained. And weren't there wines that needed to be left alone in order to achieve their full taste, the right sweetness and strength? And doesn't a winemaker have to keep this all in mind?

The officials had to interrupt the winemaker because they were interested in something besides how you make wine. They had heard that the actors had spent a whole night in his wine cellar getting drunk.

Hearing the word *drunk*, Henich laughed: "Ha ha ha, getting drunk? They call everything getting drunk!" This is the way it had happened. He had been working in the wine cellar when the Yiddish theater came in for some wine. He set aside his work, expecting that the wine would flow. But it turned out they drank altogether only two and a half bottles of red wine and one bottle of white wine. They only talked about wine. Henich had a maxim: He who talks about wine does not drink wine, and he who drinks wine does not talk about wine.

"That's all very true," the officials interrupted the winemaker, and urged him to tell what he knew of the runaway pair. It turned out the winemaker knew as much about the runaway pair as they did. This was the story: He woke up in the morning and first went down to the cellar to check on the wine . . .

"Enough with the wine!" they said to Henich, and turned their attention to Yechiel the *klezmer*.

Yechiel the *klezmer* was a Jew with a fine head of hair. He wore a silver signet ring on his finger and sported a tall hat and a cape. Although he was ordinarily fairly healthy, he went around with his throat wrapped up, speaking in a hoarse voice, dreading that some awful disease would soon afflict him. Yechiel wanted people to believe that the source of his fears was his fiddle, but his colleagues said that was untrue. His fears were caused by his inclination to do what he shouldn't do. He had "assignations" with all the young wives in town. He was a charlatan, they said, may God protect us!

His wife, Chana-Perel, you must imagine, was well acquainted with all his tricks. But Chana-Perel was not someone to let on. She hated scandals and was not made of iron—everyone has a limit. But she settled her accounts with him so that no one heard about it. Chana-Perel really hated scandals.

So when Yechiel was arrested, it was no surprise that he became frightened and realized he had to tell what he knew of the Yiddish theater. He cleared his throat, combed his luxuriant hair, and stood up, ready to talk. But this time he told a different story. Maybe it was because Chana-Perel was standing nearby? He couldn't get the words out straight as he babbled on about auditions and rehearsals, rehearsals and auditions, orchestrations and musical scores, musical scores and orchestrations. He had had no time for anything else, just notes, rehearsals, orchestrations, orchestrations, rehearsals, notes. And if his *klezmer* buddies said he was fooling around with the leading lady, he would spit them full in the face, it was an utter falsehood, not a word of it true, pure lies, never happened, nothing to it . . .

"*Charasho!* All right!" they interrupted his rant. "All right, enough!" They would speak to him later about his fooling around with the leading lady. There was time. Perhaps he would be so kind as to tell them what he knew about the couple who had vanished the night before with the actors of the Yiddish theater?

Yechiel the *klezmer* swore up and down that he did not know the first thing about it. "Nothing?" "Not a thing." "Absolutely nothing?" "Absolutely nothing." "Not even this much?" "Not even this much." "Perhaps you're lying?" "May I suffer a horrible death! May I be buried alive! May there grow from my body a—"

"*Sha,* enough! Enough!"

Yechiel the *klezmer* thought he was through, but they led him into a separate room where they locked him up and told him to sit till he was called again if he was needed. In the meantime they turned to Necha the innkeeper and her two younger sisters, and from this interrogation there arose a frightful scandal.

As our readers will remember from the start of our novel, Necha was, to quote Sholom-Meyer Murovchik, "a little *mezuzah* of a landlady." It is hard to say why she became so upset when she was asked to testify. Was she such a pure kosher soul that she couldn't abide the thought of having some stain besmirch her, heaven forbid? Or was it something else? But when they asked her what she knew of the runaway pair, she poured out such a torrent of curses and raised such a ruckus it was impossible to silence her. She poured ash and tar over her enemies who begrudged her a crumb of bread, she said, and all those who wanted to see only the bad in her! "May their mouths, *reboynu shel oylem*, twist to the side of their faces! May their tongues drop off! May their eyes fall out! May they walk on crutches! May their arms and legs wither! May they lose their mothers and fathers! May they never be buried in a Jewish cemetery! May they go begging from house to house with their children's children through all generations, dear God, our Father, sweet Father, beloved, benevolent, devoted Father!"

CHAPTER 41

Like Oil on Water

Necha's nonstop cursing did her no good. The officials reminded her in the sternest language, and with finality, that she had better start talking about what she knew. If not, she would sit with the *klezmer*. Necha became frightened and started talking, some in Russian, some in Yiddish:

"I am just a widow who owns an inn, ha ha, if that's what you want to call it. Some inn—a stable, a stall, a nothing really. I would have sold it long ago, but that was out of the question, if you saw what kind of bomb my husband, of blessed memory, left me."

The officials perked up their ears in alarm: "What bomb?"

"I mean the house, a ruin that nobody would buy, unless I gave it away. Everyone who came to look at the house complained that it wouldn't be so bad if only it were at least located near the market. Should I take the house on my back and move it over to the market?"

"No, don't go on with that. Leave the house for another time. Better tell us, my dear, what you know about the Jewish actors who stayed at your inn."

Necha was not terribly insulted that they had cut her off right at the beginning of her story and began talking about the actors.

"That *Shabbes* night I had just finished my 'God of Abraham' prayer and had put on the samovar for those *shlimazels*, the actors, when that old pain in the neck they call Sholom-Meyer came up and said to me: 'What do you want for your woolly cloak and your winter shawl?' I looked at him as if he were crazy: '*Shlimazel*,' I said, 'why do you need a woman's shawl and a woolly cloak in the summer?' He said, 'Let your *bubbe* worry about that. If I'm asking for them, I probably need them.' I tell you, he pestered me and pestered me till I brought him the old woolly cloak and the winter shawl. He asked what I wanted for those *shmattes,* and I said, 'Make up your mind. Since they're *shmattes,* why are you buying them?' And again he said, 'Let your *bubbe* worry about that.' So I gave him a price and he got angry: 'Are you crazy or just out of your mind?' I told him he was the crazy one. We argued and bargained. He said to me 'old *shmattes*,' I said 'so don't buy,' he called me '*mezuzah'le*', I called him 'pain in the neck.' The long and the short of it was, we settled on a price. I took the money and thought to myself, *God in heaven, what can this man need an old woman's cloak and a winter shawl for? And just now, right before leaving?* I wondered what was going on. In the meantime the other *shlimazels* came from the theater, drank tea, and paid for their rooms, may they have as many boils as they gave me false coins, and they left for Henich's cellar to drink wine.

"Why wine suddenly, right before leaving? Let them worry about it. It was no business of mine. Let them drink to their good health. I wasn't paying for it. But I was curious about something else: I was dying to know why that *shlimazel* was buying a woman's winter shawl and a warm cape when it was summer. Had he packed them with the rest into the wagon, I would have figured he was bringing someone a gift from Holeneshti. I now regretted asking such a low price, the cheapskate. So what do you think finally happened? He took the shawl and the cape and said: 'Let these hang on a hook here on your wall till just before we leave.' Can you believe that?

"Around midnight along came the *shlimazel,* took the shawl and cape, and was leaving. I asked him: 'Where are you going?' And he said: 'Let your *bubbe* worry about that.' So I said: 'Go to hell!' I wanted to go to sleep but couldn't. How could I go to sleep when the *shlimazels* were still off somewhere drinking? How could guests who had stayed as long as they had leave without saying goodbye? And so it was. It was long past midnight. I looked out the window— aha! One van, another, a third. Who? It was the *shlimazels,* the whole company, returning to say goodbye.

"I peered into the third van, Shimen-Dovid the teamster's van, and inside on the front seat sat their director—and right next to him some woman, wrapped in my old woolly cape and winter shawl. No face was visible, only eyes, familiar eyes! *Reboynu shel oylem!* Who could this be? I know every woman's face in town—funny-looking, ugly ones, tphoo! One uglier than the next. But this one appeared to be pretty, even though I couldn't make out anything but eyes— black gypsy-eyes, familiar, familiar eyes. Who could she be? If those *shlimazels* would at least slow down, I would find out who it was, but they pulled up near me for a moment, said their farewells, and were gone in a split second. All night I tossed and turned, unable to sleep: 'For God's sake! Who was that girl with the familiar gypsy-eyes?' Not till morning, when I heard the whole story about what was going on in town, did I grab my head and called out to my two younger sisters: 'What an idiot I am!'

"Well, I swore to you up and down that I would not hide a thing. The truth has to rise like oil on water. As God is my witness, I knew it would turn out like this. But why didn't it happen to my little sisters? Didn't my little sisters also go to the theater every night? Why didn't my little sisters make eyes at the *shlimazels* like the cantor's daughter?"

"Shut your mouth, you slut!!" suddenly someone cried out like an enraged wild animal. The cantor's wife leaped at Necha. The poor mother was ready to tear her apart for what she had just said. Fortunately they separated the two women in time or an ugly scene might have taken place.

CHAPTER 42

In Pursuit of the Runaways

As a result of the interrogations, the officials firmly established one thing and issued an official statement stating that "the son of Benny Rafalovitch, Leib, fourteen years old, and the daughter of the cantor, Reizel Spivak, fifteen years old, ran away Saturday night with a company of Jewish actors to the Romanian border, and the above-mentioned son of Benny Rafalovitch, Leib, stole from his above-mentioned father, Benny Rafalovitch, a sum of so much and so much from his cash box . . ."

That being the case, they must posthaste pursue the thief in order to retrieve the money. They decided to send a party after them, the sooner the better. The search party consisted of Rafalovitch's bookkeeper, Sison v'Simcha, and one of Rafalovitch's other sons, Anshel.

Anshel was an attractive young man of twenty-two, well bred, pale, and smooth-skinned, with puckered red lips, a trimmed little rounded beard, and shiny, curly black hair. One couldn't say that Anshel didn't have a good head on his shoulders; he simply didn't want to apply himself.

"Peasant! What will become of you?" his father would berate him. "A dogcatcher? Or a bear-trainer? At least learn to say kaddish for your parents. Here, repeat after me, go ahead: *yiskadal v'yiskadash* . . ."

The tiny Beylke could not restrain herself any longer.

"Are you out of your mind? Why are you saying kaddish now? We're still living, aren't we?"

"You're a fool!" retorted Benny. "You'll wait a long time till this brat knows how to say kaddish."

The outcome was that Anshel was taken out of *cheder,* with his father's admonition: "You don't want to study, you can't say kaddish, go herd swine."

In Benny's eccentric language that meant he was going to make a businessman of him. Anshel was cut out for the job. He was a good horseman, he learned to speak Wallachian like a true Moldavian, he gave advice about corn, and with one look he could tell which tree would yield the best lumber or firewood. In a word, Anshel displayed all the qualities of an excellent businessman.

Recently Benny had arranged a match for him with a mild-mannered, not-too-pretty girl from an upper-class Beltz family who had promised a sizable dowry. When Anshel saw the bride-to-be, he was crushed but was afraid to reveal his feelings to his father. Benny was most eager to buy into high society, and if Benny wanted something, who would deny him?

His spirit broken, Anshel returned home from Beltz. But he quickly recovered, consoling himself with the nursemaid, a sturdy woman and quite handsome. True, the nursemaid protested strongly and swore she would stir up the greatest scandal all over town. But what did a rich man's son care about the town, especially a young man like Anshel? There was hardly a girl in town who had not slapped his face. If Benny had known of this, all hell would have broken loose. But who would tell him such tales? If someone did threaten to talk, Anshel made sure to silence that person.

One person in the Rafalovitch household did know of all Anshel's escapades, but she kept her anguish to herself. That was the tiny, silent Beylke, who carried on her frail shoulders the burden of the household. Her face burned with shame for her Anshel. She felt like hiding from everyone, knowing she could do nothing. She prayed to God on her son's behalf, that He would send him the right match. At fifteen he had sprouted a beard, and from eighteen on it was nothing but problems and more problems.

That was Benny Rafalovitch's son Anshel, whom his father sent to hunt down and bring back the runaway son. He sent along with him the bookkeeper with a good deal of money.

"Get going! Bring him back, the little scoundrel!" Benny told the bookkeeper not to scrimp on money but to spend whatever it took, and if they needed more, he should write, and more would be sent.

He also gave them signed documents that allowed them to bring the runaway home in chains if necessary.

"But better to rely on a gentle approach," Benny warned Anshel several times.

When the search party was seated in the coach and the horses were starting on their way, Benny shouted after them, "Remember now, gently, gently!"

CHAPTER 43

The Search Party in Hot Pursuit

Anshel Rafalovitch and Sison v'Simcha reached Yas without finding a trace of the acting company. They were told that some young people with ill-fitting shoes and shaven faces had straggled through—presumably the Jewish actors—but where they had gone, no one knew. The search party realized they had to drive on farther. Without wasting any time, they drove till they reached Bucharest.

Once they were in Bucharest, Anshel told the bookkeeper that it made sense to stay at a decent hotel.

"What's the difference?" he reasoned. "It's already costing so much money, let it cost more, especially since Father said a hundred times over not to spare the cash and, if we needed more, he'd send more."

This was Anshel's first journey away from home and his first visit to a large city like Bucharest. He had long felt a deep desire to see the great wide world beyond Holeneshti and would often dream of beautiful cities. Ever since his betrothal to the plain girl from the Beltz elite, he had promised himself that after the wedding, when he would have more freedom, he would occasionally pop down to Bucharest, see the world, and live it up a bit, as God commanded.

Now, as it turned out, here he was in beautiful Bucharest even before the wedding. He had money to spend and was as free as a bird. It was, as they say, on the up-and-up and entirely kosher.

There could be one snag: the bookkeeper. But who had to listen to him? And wasn't Sison v'Simcha also a young man, single and a servant besides? Whatever the boss's son wanted should be fine with him.

They stopped at the renowned hotel Datshyo, located on one of the nicest streets in Bucharest, Strada Podemogashoi. The hotel had achieved its fame during the Russo-Turkish War, when it was rumored that the famous Pasha Osman stayed there. Furthermore, the hotel was noted for its nightclub, Paradiso, which featured the famous Romanian singer Marinesco-Milanesco, known for her popular Russian songs.

To stay at a hotel with a well-known nightclub named Parad-iso—wasn't that in itself a paradise? True, a paradise costs money. When the bookkeeper heard what they were asking for a room, he grabbed his head. But Anshel reassured him, "Don't be foolish. When you travel with this kind of responsibility, you can't live like pigs."

The bookkeeper thought it over. *If the boss's son wants it, that's fine with me.* He was no more than a servant. And the two of them did live it up, as God had commanded. The people at the hotel, see-ing these two young Russians changing one hundred-kopek bill after another, regarded them as scions of a wealthy family who had just come into a large inheritance and had come to enjoy themselves. The hotel honored them the first week with a bill that almost gave the bookkeeper apoplexy. But again Anshel reassured him. "You fool!" he said. "Why are you worried about money? Here money doesn't count, here the spirit counts. I only hope we find what we're looking for."

And they fell to their task with gusto. They hired a coach by the hour and drove through all the streets, passing gardens, museums, galleries, theaters, circuses, nightclubs, and cabarets. Anshel was of the opinion that artists could be found only in such places. "Nightclubs and theaters are closely related," he pointed out. Anshel was not old, but he was clever, thought Sison v'Simcha, who could not get over how his young boss, *kayn eyn horeh,* knew so much "like a grown man." Anshel was at ease and felt at home everywhere, as if he were in Holeneshti.

More than any other place, our Anshel enjoyed the nightclub Paradiso. He said to the bookkeeper, "May my name not be Anshel if we don't nab them here, in this very place. Let's sit down at that corner table. It's a perfect spot. You can see everything from there."

Anshel was right. It was perfect, and you could see everything from there: the stage, the all-girl orchestra dressed in short red dresses trimmed with gold fringes, high black boots laced to the top, and little red hats tilted to the side stitched with gold. Anshel ordered food and drink. As they ate and drank with relish, their spirits took on a festive verve. They began to feel lighthearted and lively. This was the good life! Everything sparkled. Everything was gay.

A sweet, soothing song wafted across the hall, from what sounded like a chorus of women's voices. It was so beautiful, it was hard to tell whether these sweet sounds were women singing or harps playing, whether they issued from human throats or arose from the metal strings of wooden harps. Anshel stared at the harps and greatly enjoyed the all-girl orchestra playing their instruments, strumming the metal strings with their slender fingers, nodding to the rhythm and smiling. At whom were they smiling? At him, at Anshel.

"Look how they're smiling. Look, just look!" Anshel said to the bookkeeper, poking him in the arm.

But that had not entered the bookkeeper's mind at all. Sison v'Simcha could barely sit still. He would rather be in his bed asleep. This all-girl orchestra was giving him a headache.

Now the famous Marinesco-Milanesco, sparkling with diamonds, appeared on the stage and launched into her popular Russian repertoire. To Anshel, the hall brightened as the crowd sang along with mounting pleasure. A delight! A paradise!

CHAPTER 44

They Are on the Track

In this way our search party night after night devotedly did its work—until something did happen.

It was a lovely evening at the Paradiso. Our two travelers were seated at their little table drinking *dulshatza*, a sweet drink made of water and preserves, listening to the music.

Anshel was especially cheerful and in high spirits. Sison v'Simcha, on the contrary, was his usual worried self. It broke his heart to see the money going down the drain for no reason that he could fathom. Here they were searching throughout Bucharest, and nothing was turning up. The money was disappearing. How would it all end?

Sison v'Simcha, as we all know, had been given that nickname out of sheer spite. His real character was one of deep melancholy. For him life was bleak, sorrowful, and cloaked in black. But here he found himself in the midst of foot-tapping music, people enjoying themselves, out for a good time. They too gobbled, guzzled, and tossed money to the wind.

Brooding on these melancholy thoughts, our melancholy bookkeeper sat, taking in the scene with his sleepy, bulging eyes. The allgirl orchestra made its entrance, followed by other oddly costumed women, and then came women who had hardly anything on, and finally some without any clothes at all. For the finale, like a fruit dessert, the famous Marinesco-Milanesco appeared. With eyes and jewels sparkling, she sang her signature song, and the crowd grew even livelier. Anshel joined the crowd in singing along with her. From the stage she winked at him. Anshel was thrilled and winked back.

Right after her number she walked past their table, and Anshel rose to his feet. She came over, and he made room for her to sit between himself and the bookkeeper. Suddenly she was so close, Sison v'Simcha could hear the rustle of her costume and smell her strong perfume, which penetrated even his chronically stuffed nose. And that nose, unaccustomed to such aromas, involuntarily sneezed. Anshel gave him a dirty look. Sison v'Simcha did not know where to hide himself and his nose that had suddenly erupted in sneezing.

"Such a handsome man!" said Marinesco-Milanesco, slapping

Anshel's wrist with her fan, her gems gleaming. "How come a handsome man like you is just drinking sweetened water?"

How did one resist such temptation? How could Anshel's heart not melt at such a compliment? Anshel called the waiter over and gazed at Marinesco-Milanesco, as if to say, *What is your desire, beautiful princess*? The beautiful princess desired champagne, which Anshel ordered, all the while gazing at her, as if to say, *What else do you desire, beautiful princess*? The beautiful princess desired roasted pheasant. It was ordered. *And what else do you desire*? She desired liqueur, and she herself ordered it, the best chartreuse. Anshel repeated the order, adding that pineapple be served as well. The waiter said they were out of pineapple. Anshel was angered. "That's no excuse. If I order pineapple, bring pineapple—or else!" Sison v'Simcha tugged at his elbow and stared at him with his bulging eyes: "God in heaven, it will cost a fortune!" Anshel laughed, "Idiot! Do you see the jewels she's wearing? Do you realize how much those jewels are worth?"

No, Sison v'Simcha did not know how much they were worth. But he did know something—their money was running out. He had mentioned it to Anshel that morning, but Anshel had turned on him: "Idiot! Why aren't you doing something about it? Write home, tell them we need more. They'll send more."

Sison v'Simcha was always willing to oblige. "What should I write?" he asked.

"Write that we're on the right track. We're working very hard. We're doing everything. We're not sleeping nights. We're looking everywhere. Good people are helping us. But it costs money. Lots of money! No one does anything for free. So you have to send more money, the sooner the better. Be well and send regards, and so on . . ."

Sending the letter lifted a great weight from his shoulders, but the melancholy bookkeeper became even more melancholy: '*Vey vey, where will this all end*?' Meanwhile Anshel was ordering more wine. He poured three goblets full, toasted Marinesco-Milanesco, and saw to it that the bookkeeper also toasted her: "It's not polite to sit there like a dummy." Anshel did everything he could think of to liven him up and finally succeeded. Sison v'Simcha's brow began to perspire. His fat hairy upper lip lifted a bit, and something like a little smile appeared. His sleepy, bulging eyes began to droop, and he licked his lips, a sign he was quite tipsy.

One could almost say that this was the first time Sison v'Simcha behaved more in keeping with the real meaning of his name, joy and gladness. Both men suddenly felt giddy with joy and good feeling. Out of sheer happiness Anshel embraced Marinesco-Milanesco, while Sison v'Simcha, in a state of exhilaration, lifted the empty goblet and roared with laughter, almost choking. All at once he stopped laughing. His sleepy, bulging eyes became alert and were riveted to the door. And still holding his goblet in the air, he sat frozen in his seat.

What was it? At that moment he saw coming through the door two people, one larger, one smaller. As soon as the newcomers caught sight of him and Anshel, they withdrew. Sison v'Simcha pursued them madly, but in vain. He swore with every oath he could muster that with his own eyes he had seen their Leibel at the door! Anshel didn't believe him. He maintained he had imagined it. Responsible for it was the champagne, ha ha!

CHAPTER 45

The Birds Change Their Plumage

No, Sison v'Simcha had not been mistaken. The two people who had entered the nightclub Paradiso and quickly turned and ran out were the very ones the search party had been sent to find. It was the runaway Leibel Rafalovitch and our good friend Hotzmach. That's how we know them.

Our two heroes had done nothing upon arrival but walk around and take in the sights of beautiful Bucharest. They too were only human, and in Bucharest there was a great deal to see. For one who had an artistic soul and an artistic eye and who planned to become a theater director, Bucharest offered much to learn, much to study.

"We must study stagecraft, my dear songbird," Hotzmach insisted to his young friend. "We must search out a theater somewhere and get down to the business of opening it. You can't live on what you have in your wallet. There's no future in wasting pennies—you have to figure out how to earn big money."

To our young hero, Hotzmach's words sounded too vulgar, too money-grubbing. His heart also yearned for the stage, but not for money alone. His soul was drawn to something higher, of which he himself was as yet unaware. For him every day, every minute, was precious. He was eager to be on the stage, putting on makeup and acting, acting, acting. But if Hotzmach said they must study stagecraft, he knew what he was talking about. And so both began studying stagecraft from A to Z.

They began in a very practical way. They investigated the poorest slum neighborhoods, where they found the cheapest coffee-houses, after which they moved higher and attended all the leading theaters, variety shows, and nightclubs. In each place Hotzmach picked up something valuable and learned something different.

"Now, little songbird, pay attention to how they set a stage! Look at those costumes! Look at those clothes! Those shoes! Those stockings! To hell with money!"

Hotzmach patted his side pocket. "It's a good thing we found this city. It will be useful to us. You'll soon see what an acting school I'll put together, God willing. People and even God will envy me—even that thief, Shchupak!"

What Leibel was learning was quite different. Voraciously he absorbed every gesture, every word of every artist he saw on the stage, as if he himself were on that stage. He was carried away, drawn as if by a magnet, his face and eyes burning, his throat tickling. Still, he could summon little more than a sigh.

"What is it with you, my boy?" Hotzmach asked him. "Are you still afraid they'll recognize you? Take it from me—no one will know who you are!"

So Hotzmach comforted his young friend, and he was right. Leibel was difficult to recognize. In fact, it was almost impossible to recognize either of them, so much had they changed. The birds had cast off their old feathers and refurbished themselves from head to toe.

As soon as they arrived in Bucharest, Hotzmach had his face completely shaven, leaving but two short sideburns that added, according to his mirror, a great deal of charm. At a large clothing store he outfitted himself in the latest fashion. He bought a tall stovepipe hat, a fine cane with an ivory handle, and lacquered shoes with yellow buckles.

"Eh? What do you say now, my dear little songbird? Would anyone say that this is Hotzmach?"

"No one in the world would!" Leibel told him, quite enjoying the new look of his made-over friend.

If Leibel enjoyed the new Hotzmach, Hotzmach's joy was no less great in seeing the new Leibel after he removed his little Holeneshter gabardine and Holeneshter cap and donned a suit jacket, new hat, and yellow buckled shoes and sported a cane, all of which Hotzmach bought him.

"May Shchupak suffer pains and pangs if you look like you!" said Hotzmach, examining his young friend as he turned him around. "God bless me, what a handsome little lad you are. You're not a little boy anymore, but a lad, as I am a Jew!"

And that day they both felt almost weightless, floating on air.

CHAPTER 46

Holtzman–Rafalesco

One morning when they were lying in bed, yawning and stretching, oblivious to the fact that it was quite late in the day, Hotzmach exclaimed to Leibel, "I think it's high time, my dear boy, that we stopped lying around. Let's get up and have an aromatic Turkish coffee with fresh warm buns, and to hell with the money!"

They got up, washed, put on their new clothes, and prepared to go to work, which meant strolling around Bucharest and admiring all the fine goods displayed in shop windows. But they did no more than admire. Buying would have been a waste of money. They would tuck into a restaurant for something to eat. With lively anticipation, Hotzmach pictured all the dishes they would be served. Never in his life had he been so constantly hungry. No matter how much he ate, he felt as if he hadn't eaten at all. After eating they would rest up a bit. Hotzmach had worked hard all his life, but only now did he feel that no matter how much he rested, it was as if he hadn't rested at all. When night fell, they would make the rounds of the theaters and from there go to a nightclub to "learn about music, art, and theater."

Leibel said he could swear that just yesterday he had seen a carriage drive by with his older brother Anshel and their bookkeeper, Sison v'Simcha.

"Go on now, you imp!" Hotzmach laughed. "You're dreaming of brothers and bookkeepers. Nonsense! Even if they came here, they would need to have eighteen brains to pick you out, and certainly me! Now, do you know what else we lack, my dear boy?"

"What?"

"Different names."

"Really?"

"Really. I was lying awake all night wondering what is going to happen to us. We can't go on forever like this, idlers, no work, living off the money we have. Sooner or later we have to decide on something, establish a school, go into a small town and put on plays. Think about what names we should give ourselves so people won't know who we really are. Well, I would like to propose as my real name Holtzman. Bernard Holtzman. You can be sure no one will know who this Bernard Holtzman is, when everybody has always known me as Hotzmach."

"You're absolutely right!" Leibel agreed. "Holtzman is much nicer than Hotzmach."

"Well, then. But what do we do with you, dear soul? Picture it, we go out into the world, and we arrive in some town where they know your old name. Do you see what I mean? It will do no good to still be a Rafalovitch."

"What should I be called?"

"What should you be called? That's what's been keeping me awake. All night I was lying there thinking and thinking. And this thought came to me. Why shouldn't you have a Romanian name, ending with *esco*, like they all do here in Romania? For instance: Margolis—Margolesco. Chazanovitch—Chazanesco. Rafalovitch—Rafalesco. Do you get it, dearie? We arrive in a town and I have them print up big posters: THE FIRST YIDDISH-ROMANIAN THEATER OF BERNARD HOLTZMAN AND THE FIRST YIDDISH-ROMANIAN ARTIST RAFALESCO STRAIGHT FROM BUCHAREST. How do you like that idea, my dear little songbird? Yes indeed, Hotzmach is full of good ideas. What do you say?"

His new name greatly appealed to Leibel, as did everything else his friend Hotzmach thought up. Hotzmach himself was so pleased with his idea that he grabbed his young friend's hand and did a little jig.

For as long as Leibel had known Hotzmach, he had always been a lively soul who never seemed sad, was always happy, having a wonderful time, even in the most difficult, dire, and bitter times, but he was never as cheerful as he was now. Life itself radiated from him. He had almost stopped coughing and cursing himself, a rare thing for him unless he mentioned the name Shchupak or Sholom-Meyer Murovchik. At those times he tacked on a few choice curses.

"Remember now, my little songbird, I am no longer called Hotzmach. I am now Holtzman. And you, what are we calling you?"

"Rafalesco," said Leibel.

"That's the way I love you, my dear boy."

CHAPTER 47

"Change Your Place—Change Your Luck"

That same night our heroes Holtzman and Rafalesco, as they now called themselves, strolled aimlessly around Bucharest, no longer studying art, music, and theater but simply out for a stroll. They had studied enough of this city. They had already been to every place where art and music flowered, it seemed. Strolling along, they wandered onto an attractive street called Strade Podemogashoi and saw before them an enormous sign with large neon letters: PARADISO.

"Paradiso? Doesn't that mean Garden of Eden? Maybe we can stop for a minute in paradise, eh?" said Holtzman to his young friend, without waiting for an answer because he always made the decisions. To Leibel, Holtzman was a god, and Holtzman's word was Torah. And so they both went down to paradise.

We say "went down," because entering paradise wasn't that easy. You first had to pass through the Seven Gates of Hell. And for that you needed an entry card—that's how it is with all the world's paradises. Then our two heroes had to turn left and go up a few steps, where they gave the guard their overcoats and canes, for which they had to pay. Only then were they allowed to go up a few more steps and enter a wide, well-lit corridor. There they showed the entry cards that they had obtained from the guard, and the doors finally opened for them to the real paradise.

Upon walking in, they were greeted by a hellish blast of light from many electric, multicolored little fires. Before them an elegant crowd of men and women sat around small white marble tables, eating, drinking, laughing, and generally enjoying themselves, as one should do in paradise.

Our heroes quickly became accustomed to the bright lights of this cheerful nightclub, but they were hesitant to make their way directly to a table, take seats, and call out "Wai-ter!" like real gentlemen, steady local customers. Neither their new clothes nor their changed names could prevent them from being identified as provincials. "Small town" was still written all over their faces and could be spotted with every step they took. Not surprisingly, they remained standing for a time at the door of paradise, not knowing what to make of it all, staring at the brightly lit walls, the beautifully painted ceiling, the red velvet loges, the white marble tables, and, above all, the festive, lively, elegant crowd.

"To hell with the money!" Holtzman cried, eager to find a seat.

Suddenly Leibel grabbed his friend by the hand and, terrified, was barely able to utter, "It's them!"

"Who?"

"My brother Anshel and our—"

"Go on!"

Holtzman raised his eyes to where Leibel indicated. There he saw in a corner, seated at a table laden with food and drink, the two men whom we know well. Just at that interesting moment Anshel had embraced the famous singer Marinesco-Milanesco, and a fellow with full lips was holding his sides with laughter.

Quickly, more quickly than one can imagine, our heroes sped out of paradise. For two or three minutes they could not speak. All their effort went into their legs, which carried them swiftly along as if they were on wheels.

Not till they were three streets away, where they slowed down to mingle with the dense crowd and realized they were out of any danger, did our Holtzman speak, quite magnanimously, as was his style. "Your brother is, I see, a rich customer," he said. "Wait till his father finds out! And who is that fellow with the fat lips?"

"You didn't recognize him?" said Leibel, his teeth chattering. "That's our bookkeeper, Sison v'Simcha."

Here Holtzman instinctively touched his pocket and picked up his pace. "May he be struck dead by lightning! Do you know what I think, my dear songbird? I have no intention of running into them here, and I'm sure you don't either. That being the case, let's leave them here in Bucharest. Let them rest in paradise, and we'll travel on."

"Where to?"

"Wherever our eyes take us. We have to get out of here, and the sooner the better. It's not that I'm so worried about what they might do. I just don't want to run into them. I don't go for your Holeneshter crowd, may God not punish me for these words. Listen to me, my boy, let's go a little faster, or—wait! Here comes a carriage. Let's jump in and tell him to whip the horse to full speed, to hell with the money!"

* * *

A few hours later our brave heroes were seated in an express train from Bucharest to Budapest. As it was a chilly night and they were still dressed for summer, Holtzman drew out his old garment, the large cape, and threw it around his young friend.

"Wrap it around yourself, little bird—that's the way. Good, good, or you'll catch a chill. How is it said in the Bible, 'Change your place, change your luck'? A clever saying, as I am a Jew!" said Holtzman, clasping his bosom pocket while coughing and cursing Shchupak and Sholom-Meyer with deadly curses.

CHAPTER 48

In Galitzia

Our heroes were now named Bernard Holtzman and Leo Rafalesco and had changed so completely in appearance that they were almost unrecognizable, but they still were wary of being too close to Holeneshti.

They left Romania for Bukovina, and from Bukovina they went to Galitzia, traveling with an acting troupe that Holtzman had put together. It put on performances as they went. Posters printed in large letters announced THE FAMOUS BERNARD HOLTZMAN AND CO. ITINERANT ACTING TROUPE. And in even larger letters appeared the name of the renowned young artist LEO RAFALESCO STRAIGHT FROM BUCHAREST.

Who was this Rafalesco? Where did he come from? Not too many knew, but all had heard that arriving in town that night was a Yiddish troupe with this Rafalesco, whom the newspapers were raving about. It might be worthwhile seeing him. According to the reviews, he was a phenomenon. Not only Jews but Christians as well could not praise him enough. (And if Christians are praising, what more can be said!) The word was out that he was a second

Sonnenthal, a Barnay, a Possart, an Irving, a Rossi, and other great names. People flocked to see this famous young phenomenon and were astounded by the new star shining so brilliantly in the firmament of the Yiddish theater.

What was it about him that so enchanted everyone? Reviewers were impressed that he had demonstrated "throughout and at all times a simple earnestness, a humble naïveté, as honest as truth itself, as natural as nature itself."

"This whole itinerant Yiddish troupe," another critic wrote, "isn't worth a blown egg. Without Rafalesco it is, like all Yiddish theaters, a wasteland, a *Purim-shpiel*, a gloomy wilderness, dead as a cemetery. But from the moment Rafalesco appears on the stage, it lights up, and everything becomes warm and familiar, alive and exciting. It is no longer a stage, a theater. It is life itself."

Everywhere they performed, the reviewers and critics all described him in this laudatory fashion. And what did the Galitzian public have to say? The Jewish public, never enamored of theater, neither with good plays nor with famous artists, at first came out of curiosity to see this rising star, this phenomenon Rafalesco. But after seeing him once, they would besiege the theater, fight over tickets, and applaud tumultuously, shouting "Bravo" to the heavens. Much of the public went, not because they were great connoisseurs, but because they thought "the experts can't be wrong," but once there almost everyone felt he was witnessing something unique, a sensational force, an extraordinary power. A human being steps before you who speaks simple words so directly, so naturally, so without artifice, that they resonate with one's most profound feelings, and awaken one's hidden thoughts, and a light shiver ripples over one's skin. You feel with him, you live with him, you cannot tear your eyes away from him. And when he exits the stage, a cry of "Bravo!" involuntarily issues from your throat.

Not surprisingly, the public was eager to learn who this phenomenon was. Where did he come from? Where had he studied? Where did he get this towering talent? How did he look in real life, away from the stage? What was his real name? There is no limit to Jewish curiosity. But no matter how much these devotees probed and speculated, they could find out no more than that this wonderful artist was named Leo Rafalesco, that he came from Bucharest, and that he was still a young man, only eighteen or nineteen years old. That was as much as they could glean. More than anywhere else, the young artist, the rising star Rafalesco, was a sensation in Lemberg, the capital of Galitzia.

In Lemberg there had long been a Yiddish theater. The owner of this theater, the director, was a certain personality with whom we must become acquainted. He had a peculiar name, Getzel ben Getzel.

Getzel ben Getzel, like all directors of Yiddish theater, fed the public heartrending dramas and potboiler tragedies that had unusual titles like *Shminder Begetz on the Auto-da-fe*, *The Bloody Inquisition in Sobyeski's Times*, *Isabella, Tear Off Your Blouse for Me*, and other such dramatic pearls, written overnight by hacks like Shchupak and his right-hand man, Sholom-Meyer Murovchik.

Getzel ben Getzel was not pleased with this state of affairs. He had recently begun putting on occasional literary pieces like *Hinke-Pinke*, *Shloyme Adam's Apple*, *Leap in Bed*, and *Velvele Eats Compote*. But you can't always put on literary pieces. You mustn't pamper a Jewish audience. Whatever you offer Jewish theatergoers, they will lick their fingers as if it were a delicious treat, applaud loudly, and tear down the house.

Soon after his first meeting with Getzel ben Getzel, Holtzman came to the conclusion that this Yuckel ben Fleckel—that was the name he gave him—wasn't worth even Shchupak's fingernail. In his whole life, he confessed, he had never met such a clod. Carrying Lemberg in another direction himself would be much easier than trying to work something out with this incompetent.

Holtzman was a stubborn, determined man. He wasn't so much interested in making money as he was consumed with ambition. In order for his troupe to have a chance in Lemberg, he allowed this clod, this exploiter, to pressure him to agree to conditions that he otherwise would never have accepted.

After both sides signed the contract for the first three performances, they went to a restaurant for a bite to eat, and Holtzman asked Getzel ben Getzel, in all seriousness, "Tell me, my dear Yuckel ben Fleckel, has it ever happened in Lemberg that the cholera should find its way here?"

"Till now God has spared us. Why do you ask?"

"Too bad. There would still be a ray of hope that we might get rid of you . . ."

But Getzel ben Getzel overlooked this comment. They had come to a Jewish restaurant to celebrate the contract, drink glasses of good wine, smoke cheap cigars, and dine very well on goose liver and other delicacies. Both directors behaved in a very friendly way—until it came time to pay for the meal.

Getzel ben Getzel suddenly pretended he hadn't so much as a coin and tried to sneak out of the restaurant. Holtzman stopped him, reproaching him, "*Pani* d'rector! Why are you going to all this trouble? It doesn't befit a d'rector who has a Yiddish theater in a German city to steal out the back door."

Soon Holtzman was needling him with more than words. He knew that Rafalesco's first performance would deliver a death blow that would be long remembered. And he was not mistaken.

As everywhere, so in Lemberg, his Rafalesco secured the audience from his first entrance. The Lemberg theatergoers, who were not that different from the Holeneshti public, could not figure out exactly why this Rafalesco so enchanted them. He was direct, plain, and ordinary, without songs, without dances, nothing beyond words, yet so calm, so quietly graceful—not at all like other actors. His every step, every movement, every word was naturally simple. He spoke not like an actor but like you and me, and yet something strange happened! You wanted to watch only him and hear only him, because compared to him all the others were like dolls, mannequins, live stick figures.

"Who is he?" the audience murmured.

"No one knows. Some Rafalesco from Bucharest."

That was the first night. The second night the theater was packed. And by the third performance it was sold out, standing room only. Getzel ben Getzel was dogging Holtzman's footsteps, trying to persuade him to remain with his troupe for at least three more guest performances.

You can be sure that each director wanted to be rid of the other, the sooner the better. But like duplicitous diplomats, they were devising different ways to deceive, swindle, and do each other dirt.

CHAPTER 49

Henrietta Schwalb

Getzel ben Getzel had to be stronger than iron to tolerate how the foolish public walked mindlessly like sheep into his theater, paying good money to see this "ordinary youth" perform. Though three-quarters of every ticket price went to him, he resented how hard he had to work for it. Distraught and angry as a demon, he sat near the cash box and watched the crowd going crazy fighting over tickets. Once all the seats and reserved places were sold out, and the little theater was overly full, and the audience was packed in to the point of suffocation like too many birds in a cage, only then did our Getzel ben Getzel out of curiosity decide to see what "these foolish Jews were going so insane about."

Peeking out from behind the curtain, he saw these "foolish Jews" smacking their lips with pleasure, thoroughly enjoying every minute and shouting "Bravo!" again and again. It all made his head spin—not the acting, which he couldn't see, but how packed the house was. It took his breath away. For as long as he had been a director, he had never had such a full house. If the young man from Bucharest was the reason, then he simply had to get him away from Holtzman. But how? If he approached Rafalesco directly and offered him a price he couldn't refuse, the scamp might tell his director, and a scandal might ensue. That Holtzman was a shrewd one. Getzel ben Getzel did not want him to open his mouth at him. No, Getzel ben Getzel had a plan. He would work through someone else, his new leading lady, Henrietta Schwalb.

Who Henrietta Schwalb was and how she became a leading lady can be told in a few short words.

Getzel ben Getzel once happened to notice a young, simply dressed working girl who had, as he later described it, "a stunning figure and a majestic bearing." And he set about finding out who she was. Whether she was a seamstress or a chambermaid, she was absolutely spectacular.

"If I could get this girl into my theater, I could make a leading lady out of her," Getzel remarked to one of his toadies. "Maybe you can find out for me where she works."

"That beauty?" the toady answered. "I don't know where she works, but I do know her brother. His name is Schwalb, Chaim-Itzik Schwalb. He goes around selling cigars and cigarettes from a large tray strapped to his waist."

"You mean that oaf with the red kisser? Just last week I slapped him around and threw him out of the theater for stealing backstage and treating the actresses to cigarettes when they should be thinking about the show."

"So what? Think of it this way—you're already old friends. If you want, I can have a word with him."

"Say whatever you want, but don't let on I want something from him. Get it?"

"Of course I get it. What am I, a blockhead?"

The talk with her brother succeeded, and soon Chaim-Itzik brought his sister to the director. He waited outside, reluctant to risk another beating. That was at midday, right after the director's nap, and he received his guest barefooted.

He asked her to sit down, but she refused, saying she would rather stand. "Where do you work?" he asked her. She boasted that she had a very good job, an easy job. "How much do you make?" She was making fifteen gulden a month plus a laundry allowance of ten gulden. Sometimes she made an extra six or seven.

"How much does that add up to?"

"You figure it out."

The barefoot director stood up to look for a pencil and piece of paper. He asked her what she would say if she were offered fifty a month to begin with. She replied, "Fifty is good, but it depends on what kind of work."

"No work at all, just acting in the theater. What's your name?"

"They call me Yentl, and my family name is Schwalb."

"Yentl? Feh! What kind of name is Yentl? Henrietta is much prettier. Henrietta Schwalb. They say you have a brother? Where is he?"

"He's right outside, by the door."

"Oh? Send him in. Tell him I would like to see him. We'll come to an understanding."

CHAPTER 50

Chaim-Itzik Schwalb

If Getzel ben Getzel thought he and Yentl's brother would quickly come to an understanding, he was sadly mistaken. Chaim-Itzik proved to be a tough nut to crack. Another entirely unforeseen problem arose—be a prophet! In this fat-bellied, short-legged Chaim-Itzik dwelled an artist! Who would have guessed that from behind this red face there shone a refined soul who adored the theater,

music, and all that was beautiful! That explained why this cigarette vendor was always slipping backstage, giving away his last few
cigarettes—so they would allow him to watch them act onstage. A
person's soul is a mystery. You cannot appreciate a person by his
appearance alone.

When Chaim-Itzik heard what the director was offering his sister,
he said to himself: *Now my time has come.* He took heart and made
a bold counteroffer. He would let the director turn his sister into an
actress on the condition that he took him on as an actor as well.

"What kind of actor can you be with that face?" said Getzel.

This question hurt Chaim-Itzik deeply. It wasn't the first time
someone had commented on his face. He had been told he had a face
like a vagabond and eyes like a highwayman.

He lowered his eyes and asked quietly: "What kind of face do I
have then?"

"The face of a . . . I don't know what."

Chaim-Itzik sighed. "Would I be going out onstage like this?
They'd surely put makeup on me." The cigarette vendor raised his
eyes to the director. "Do you think I don't know about these things?
I used to do some acting."

"Where did you act?"

"Where? I acted with the *Purim-shpielers*. I still do when Purim
comes. I dare anyone play Haman better than I do!" Chaim-Itzik's
knavish eyes lit up.

But the director quickly cut him off. "It's possible. It's very possible. But what will we do with your big belly?"

Chaim-Itzik glanced down at his fat belly and short legs. "I'll
wear a tight corset. Do you think I don't know about these things?
Our *Purim-shpielers* had the very same things I've seen backstage in
your theater."

The director was not too pleased that his theater was being
compared to *Purim-shpielers* and again cut him off, "And what will
you do about the way you speak?"

"I imagine I speak the same as everybody."

"You *are* imagining it. Just be careful not to whistle."

"Who's whistling? Am I whistling?"

"Who then is whistling? Me?"

"I think you're picking on me." The cigarette vendor rose with
a frightfully red face. "Be well and happy. Since I do not meet your
requirements as an actor, then my sister is no actress either."

There was nothing for it. Getzel ben Getzel was determined to have the sister as an actress, even if he had to accept her brother too and pay through the nose. Henrietta had displayed no particular ability for the stage, nor had she as yet a trained voice, but at least she had a magnificent figure and a majestic bearing. But what could one do with a block of wood like this cigarette vendor? If he were willing to play bit parts without lines, then to hell with it, the director would have paid ten gulden a week for the sake of having his sister. But Chaim-Itzik insisted on being center stage and playing the best, most serious roles.

What won't one do for money? Getzel ben Getzel's business was lately going downhill. The people weren't coming to the theater, no matter what show he offered. And if an actress like Henrietta Schwalb, with her magnificent figure and majestic bearing, did not bring in business, then there must be no God in heaven.

Getzel ben Getzel printed up posters announcing COMING SOON! THE FAMOUS SINGER FROM BUENOS AIRES. HER FIGURE HAS ENCHANTED THE WORLD. He did not see fit as yet to put her name above her brother's, who just the other day was still selling cigars. Getzel had thought of Buenos Aires only because there was no city farther away.

Then they began making an actress and a singer out of Henrietta, teaching her roles, a few stock songs, and perfecting a few double entendres. But primarily they taught her the art of dressing so that it would be revealing without being obscene. When she finally stepped out on the stage, she created a furor. They were shouting from the gallery: "Schwalbele!" and "Little Bird!" and "Ketzele!" and off-color names not fit to print. The director was thrilled, in seventh heaven.

But her brother shortened Getzel ben Getzel's life. "It's a travesty to put him on the stage," he said to his troupe, and they all agreed. It must be noted, however, that they were not entirely correct. Chaim-Itzik sweated till he knew his lines by heart, but he spoke them as if he had cotton in his mouth. Was it his fault? They were picking on him for the way he stood and the way he walked. Was that his fault? He had walked like that since childhood. Still and all he felt confident doing even the most difficult roles. He was a terror when he played a villain, a tyrant, or a bandit. His devilish eyes became bloodshot like a real highwayman's, and his red vagabond face became fearsome. No wonder that he had had great success as Haman when he had been acting with the *Purim-shpielers* so long ago.

CHAPTER 51

The Leading Lady Has Many Admirers

For everything you must have luck. In fact, Chaim-Itzik Schwalb was not a bad tragedian. There are many far worse than he. There are comic actors who believe they are fine tragedians and tragedians who believe they are outstanding comic actors, and it seems to work out. "Listen, without luck you shouldn't bother to be born," said Chaim-Itzik. He knew his fellow actors were his blood enemies who would just as soon drown him in a spoonful of water. They laughed at him and called him demeaning names.

No one liked him, and the director of the Lemberg Yiddish Theater hated him more than anyone. Once the director unwittingly spoke out against him within earshot: "Amazing! How do you account for it? Brother and sister, from one mother, and yet I adore Henrietta with all my heart, and him, that vagabond, I cannot bear to look at!"

That was not what Chaim-Itzik needed to hear. He knew that the director, like all the other actors, thought a great deal more of his sister than of him. But he still kept a careful eye on her, making sure Henrietta was behaving properly. On the stage she could appear naked before the public, she could dance and leap and throw herself about wildly, but nowhere else! That was his responsibility as a loyal, devoted brother—perhaps a bit too devoted.

The actors would say among themselves, "Watch out for this bone-crusher of a brother, may his arms wither this very day!" But from the lowliest actor to the director, they still leered at Henrietta Schwalb, the leading lady.

Yes, Henrietta Schwalb was now a leading lady. The poor former leading lady, with shame and heartache, had to step down from her place. Even though she could, without a doubt, sing and act better, Henrietta Schwalb was prettier. A pretty face is appealing anywhere. That's the kind of world it's become. You can't argue with it.

Our Henrietta was now the leading lady of the Yiddish theater in Lemberg. There was no recognizing the old Yentl. You would do well to have a look at Henrietta. The hat she was wearing was a real Panama hat with real ostrich feathers—not imitation, heaven forbid. And her bearing was like that of a stately princess. After her performances she no longer received mere oranges, as at first—no, she received real gifts worth twenty gulden, twenty-five gulden, and why not thirty? Henrietta now had her own maid who served her and brought her wardrobe to the theater.

True, if no one was looking, she would join her maid in washing and ironing the laundry. Once Henrietta could not find a little collar and blouse. Together they were worth no more than half a crown, but our leading lady still raised a fuss with her maid, claiming she was stealing from her. A squabble ensued in which neither cast any glory on the other.

Henrietta also accused the maid of being much too close to Chaim-Itzik. The maid's feelings were quite hurt by this accusation. Henrietta, you understand, accused her of even worse things. It almost came to blows, but luckily the brother came along. It turned out the lost items were among his scripts and notes. How did they get there? Who knows!

The maid burst into tears. Schwalb asked her why she was blubbering. The maid told him what his sister had said about their being too close. This awakened the old Chaim-Itzik, and he . . .

No! We will pass by this scene in silence. Who cares how artists carry on among themselves?

CHAPTER 52

Backstage Politics

If you need a thief, hire him straight from the gallows, thought Getzel ben Getzel as he prepared to welcome Chaim-Itzik Schwalb into his office for a private meeting. He locked the door before sitting down with the "vagabond." Schwalb had that very day highly praised the young artist from Bucharest to his sister. He convinced her to try to become closer and warmer to this Rafalesco, even though he was a mere kid.

"Do you understand, Henrietta? You have to turn his head, this kid, so he won't think of leaving, which will be good for us all. What's good about it you can figure out for yourself if you have any brain at all."

But Schwalb's wisdom was superfluous. Our leading lady had already taken to that youth with the innocent, thoughtful eyes and the beautiful blond hair, not because she was charmed by his acting but simply out of chagrin. Accustomed to having men desire her, Henrietta was hurt that Rafalesco kept his distance from her. She employed all the wiles that every beautiful woman possesses to entice those they wish to seduce. She made sure to be near him, showing off her dancing and her singing. She batted her eyes, flashed her dimples, and smiled flirtatiously. Whether appropriate or not, she laughed constantly in order to show off her small white teeth. Like a bee around honey, like a fly around a candle, like a bat on a warm summer evening, she flitted and floated before his eyes. But it was all wasted. The story of Potiphar and Joseph was being repeated, but not as it was in the Bible, because Henrietta was no Potiphar, and Rafalesco was no Joseph.

Everyone except Rafalesco was hoping a romance would develop between this pair, and everyone had a different reason.

Getzel ben Getzel, as we know, had only one reason. With the help of his leading lady, he wanted to trick "the youth from Bucharest" into staying with his theater because it would benefit the box office.

Henrietta set to work, one could say, more for sport, to show off what a beautiful leading lady was capable of doing. Look how many oafs were wild over her—why shouldn't she be able to vanquish this mere kid? In the end, however, neither she herself, nor her large eyes, nor her silken eyebrows, nor her thick head of hair, nor her figure or bearing, nor her hat, nor her feathers, nothing at all had any effect on him. This, she thought, was unthinkable. The world might as well come to an end! With even greater zeal, she went to work on him.

Her brother Chaim-Itzik had his reasons. The idea of this match appealed to him. It was time for all those oafs to stop dancing around his sister and for him to stop being a constant bodyguard and bone-crusher. It was time for Henrietta to make a respectable match. An article with a pretty face like her could easily fall into the wrong hands. Schwalb made a deliberate effort to gain the favor of the other director, Holtzman, playing up to him with both flattery and a free dinner. They became close friends.

As clever as all of them put together and maybe even cleverer, Holtzman saw quite clearly what was going on and laughed at the whole intrigue. He undoubtedly had a longer view than any of them. He planned not only to keep Rafalesco but to steal away from Getzel ben Getzel his beautiful leading lady and her brother plus a couple of other company members. Why not? Why should this Yuckel ben Fleckel hold on to his troupe? To tell the truth, our Holtzman had his eye on Henrietta for himself. If she could get used to him, who knew what could happen? He was not going to remain a bachelor forever. Well, if she was rather cool to him now, he would find a solution—a little special treatment, a little present, some other little token of appreciation. To hell with the money, as long as it worked! He was extremely happy that this beauty was flirting with his Rafalesco, but one thing he could not figure out. Why was this foolish kid running away from her? And why, ever since arriving in Lemberg, had he become so self-absorbed and more preoccupied than ever?

CHAPTER 53

Breyndele Kozak

The night of the troupe's first performance in Lemberg, Holtzman thought he spotted a familiar figure of small stature backstage. As the Lemberg backstage was then, and is still to this day, not illuminated by electric lights except for one small smoky lamp that emitted dangerous fumes, he did not realize immediately who it was. For a moment he thought he knew her and the next moment he thought he was imagining it. But as the familiar figure drew nearer and laughed, a sign that she had recognized him, he took a closer look and sprang back:

"Breyndele Kozak?!"

"Hotzmach?!"

"Sh-sh-sh—don't let on we know each other. God help me, what's happened to you? You're much wider than before! You're working here, for this Yuckel ben Fleckel? How long? And where is our Shchupak? And that bastard Sholom-Meyer Murovchik? May a plague afflict them both on the same day!"

"Amen!" replied Breyndele Kozak, laughing. At that moment the two had to separate because the call bell was ringing, the artists were gathering, and the stage manager was rushing them onstage. The curtain had to go up, otherwise the audience would take the place apart. They would meet after the first act, agreeing that not a soul must know they knew each other.

Holtzman immediately went off to Rafalesco in his dressing room and whispered that he had just run into one of Shchupak's actresses, Breyndele Kozak, who once used to act with him. He must remember her from Holeneshti—short and chubby.

He told Rafalesco several times over that when he met her backstage, he should act as if he were seeing her for the first time.

The dressing room where the young visiting actor was changing his clothes was no better lit than backstage. Rafalesco was in the midst of making up his face in front of a smoky, cracked mirror. So Holtzman's eye did not at first notice that for a moment Rafalesco could not breathe or utter a word.

Almost indifferently Rafalesco asked Holtzman, while making himself up before the cracked mirror, "What did you say her name was?"

"Breyndele Kozak."

"Breyndele Kozak? Hmm . . . I don't remember her. You'll have to introduce me. How do you like my new makeup?"

"Your makeup is excellent. Right after the first act you'll meet all the other artists and probably her as well. I want you to act as if you're seeing her for the first time, understand? What good will it be for people to know too much about us? Do you understand?"

He understood. Why shouldn't he? What time was it? Was it time to go on? Whose entrance was it? His? And he quickly got up to go.

"With the right foot first!" said Holtzman, straightening Rafalesco's wig.

Rafalesco performed poorly that night. The audience, however, thought he had performed brilliantly. He received enthusiastic ovations and loud bravos. But Rafalesco knew that tonight he had performed like a shoemaker. He deserved to be beaten and sent off to the army. He had missed lines and added new ones. He had not listened to the prompter, had made up entire speeches, and had barely managed to get through the first act. At last he tore himself away from the audience, which in spite of everything was going wild, refusing to stop shouting "Ra-fa-les-co! Ra-fa-les-co!" Back in his dressing room, he grabbed the cracked mirror. His eyes were burning and he felt his whole body on fire. The dressing room was frightfully small and was soon crowded. Getzel ben Getzel's entire theater company squeezed in to congratulate the guest star, some with barely disguised envy, others with sincere praise. One by one they introduced themselves to him. He imagined their faces were those not of people but of animals and birds. One strongly resembled a goat, another a rooster. He could have sworn another was a cat with green catlike eyes, licking herself.

Rafalesco immediately recognized Breyndele Kozak and she him, though he had grown up and was wearing makeup. She had seen him countless times with Hotzmach back in the stable in Holeneshti, where she and Hotzmach had performed with Shchupak. *Can this really be he? Ah-ah-ah!??* Like lightning a thought flashed through her mind, and like lightning she put two and two together. Amid the noise she called Holtzman to the side: "So that's your Rafalesco from Bucharest? That's the owner's kid from Holeneshti."

"Sh-sh-sh," Holtzman signaled to her and stepped on her foot. "Not a word more! Let's talk of something else."

"Of what, for instance?" she said, looking into his keen eyes, thinking, *Look how a person can change! Who would guess this is the same Hotzmach who once polished Shchupak's boots and was beaten like a butcher's dog?*

"So where the devil is Shchupak? And Sholom-Meyer Murovchik? And the rest of the crew?" he asked. She did not know which to answer first. Before she could answer, he followed in one breath with a dozen other questions. All he wanted to know about was Shchupak, while all she wanted to know about was "the kid." As they whispered together, their eyes were riveted on Rafalesco. *Too many people crowding him*, thought Holtzman. *It's dangerous leaving him alone among those wolves.*

Holtzman never let his eyes stray from Rafalesco. In the dim light he could make out that everyone was pressing to get closer to the guest, to the "young sensation from Bucharest." They all wanted to shake his hand and hear him speak. But the guest was not inclined to speak. His eyes were searching for the small, chubby woman named Breyndele Kozak. He spotted her speaking with Holtzman in a corner and wanted to go up to her but restrained himself. For a moment he pictured himself removing his makeup and running over to her, asking, *Have you heard or seen anyone named Reizel? You must know who I mean—the cantor's daughter from Holeneshti.* He would not speak quietly but would shout it loudly for all to hear. He could feel the words sticking in his throat, tickling, choking him. Swimming before his eyes were the faces of animals and birds that he did not want to see, and rushing in his ears were compliments he did not want to hear.

Pushing his way through the crowd toward him was a small man with gold-rimmed glasses, a triangular-shaped skull, and strange-looking, large, white overlapping teeth. His face shone, as did his eyes behind his spectacles. He pushed his way through the crowd with all his might.

As soon as the actors and actresses realized who it was, they cried out. "Kids! Make way! It's Dr. Levyus!" As he approached, they stepped back, making way for him, calling out loud, "Oafs! Let Dr. Levyus through!"

CHAPTER 54

Dr. Levyus-Levyusn

Holtzman never allowed his attention to wander too far from Rafalesco, keeping an eye on the kid as he spoke to Breyndele Kozak. But when he noticed some stranger aggressively elbowing through the crowd toward Rafalesco, he pushed Breyndele Kozak aside and planted himself between the stranger and Rafalesco, examining the newcomer with his keen eyes. "Who and what do you want?" he asked.

The stranger, appraising the director with his elegant mutton-chops, presented a calling card: "Dr. Levyus."

Holtzman glanced at the card and studied Dr. Julius Levyus with his triangular-shaped head and his large, white overlapping teeth and thought to himself: *Who is this character?* One of the artists called him aside and whispered into his ear that this was Dr. Levyus, whom the actors had nicknamed Dr. Levyusn. (The word means "leviathan.") He was a famous doctor, a learned man, a noted patron, and fanatical devotee of Yiddish theater, in addition to being a wealthy man with perhaps a half-million.

Neither the title "Dr." nor the nickname "Levyusn" nor the fact that he was learned and a patron and devotee of Yiddish theater impressed our Holtzman as much as the last virtue, that the doctor was a wealthy man with perhaps a half-million. The moment he heard that, he turned to the doctor and welcomed him so warmly that the doctor as well as all those standing nearby were embarrassed. Dr. Levyus, or Levyusn, politely addressed Holtzman in

German, inquiring if he were the impresario of the famous guest artist.

Holtzman (may no shame come to him) may have been hearing the word *impresario* applied to himself for the first time and apparently did not fully digest its significance; in any case, he did not directly respond to the doctor's question. He commenced trying to speak to him in German more than in Yiddish, drawling the German *ah*'s more than stressing the Yiddish *ay*'s. He told the doctor that he himself was a Russian, from *Rusahya*, but the boy hailed from Bucharest—not from Bucharest itself, but half an hour away from Bucharest.

Realizing that the impresario's German was really more Yiddish, Dr. Levyus began speaking to him in Yiddish. And what Yiddish it was. Many Yiddish-speaking Jews would wish that they could speak such elegant Yiddish. But the problem with German Jews is that they soon trot out their German and kill any possibility of being understood.

When he heard that Dr. "Levyusn" spoke Yiddish as a person should, our Holtzman was delighted and no longer tongue-tied. Now unloosed, he carried on, boasting at length of his accomplishments to the doctor. He, Holtzman, had made the youth what he was today. How had that happened? In Bucharest he had spotted the son of a poor workingman and liked him from the start. He'd told the father, "This boy of yours I will make into an artist." The worker had stared at him: "What does that mean—an artist? What kind of work is that?"

Holtzman accompanied his account with such genuine and hearty laughter that Dr. Levyus believed every word. A German remains a German! He swallowed every word as if it were holy writ.

Our poor Holtzman got so carried away that he was about to boast that he had been presented to King Karl of Romania. How he would have gotten out of that, only God in heaven knew. Luckily at that moment the house manager ran in, perspiring and agitated.

"Of all the worst nightmares!" he said. "The audience is tearing down the house out there, and here you are licking your chops like *Shabbes* after dinner!"

Holtzman was eternally grateful to him for the interruption. He breathed a sigh of relief. It was over—he had averted a disaster. How had he ever come up with King Karl of Romania! What was he thinking!

CHAPTER 55

Some Ride in Style and Some Go on Foot

The first guest performance of the itinerant troupe ended at the Lemberg Yiddish Theater in the same way it had everywhere. The curtain had to be lowered many times, raised, and again lowered. The ovations did not let up: "Ra-fa-les-co! Ra-fa-les-co!" The actors removed their glued-on flax beards and were changing their clothes—this one searching for a collar, that one for spats—as they sang snatches of songs while exchanging barbed comments. In the theater the chanting could still be heard: "Ra-fa-les-co! Ra-fa-les-co!"

"Shout-your-selves-hoarse!" mimicked a pimply faced actor who was struggling, unable to put on his coat because of a torn sleeve lining.

"Should I pull it open again?" the stage manager with the sweaty red face asked Holtzman, holding the curtain pulley with both hands.

"Haven't we given them enough for their kosher money?" said Holtzman. But there was no satisfying the crowd. The guest actor from Bucharest had to make at least one more appearance. The curtain rose one last time. Rafalesco appeared and bowed, but the audience clamored for more: "Ra-fa-les-co! Ra-fa-les-co!"

"That's it. I'm not going out again!" said Rafalesco like a capricious child, throwing off his wig and ungluing his mustache. Wiping off his makeup revealed his young, handsome face framed by long blond hair falling loosely down his pale white neck.

Nearby the other actors looked at him with curious, wistful eyes and envied everything about him: his extraordinary success, his calm demeanor, and the loud, enthusiastic audience going wild over him, as well as his physical beauty. They envied him yet could not understand exactly how this young actor had achieved so much, or what the hue and cry, "Ra-fa-les-co! Ra-fa-les-co!" was about. Before the guest from Bucharest stepped out onto the stage for the first time, the public had had no idea what to expect. They anticipated witnessing God-knew-what charismatic presence. They thought they would be witnessing acting that would shake the walls. His voice and language would be beyond the ordinary. But in the end it was nothing like that at all! He stepped out onstage like an ordinary person, stood like an ordinary person, and conducted himself on the stage calmly, relaxed, plain, as plain as an ordinary person. Did you call that acting? He wasn't even speaking like an actor but like a plain, ordinary person! Why was the audience so thrilled, for God's sake? What were they making such a fuss about, those idiots? Sheep! Cattle! Jackasses!

Everything on earth must come to an end. Even calling an artist back out onto the stage of the Yiddish theater must come to an end. Realizing that the curtain was no longer going to rise, the audience finally began to exit the theater. The lights were shutting down. In a few minutes the theater was empty.

Only one person remained waiting for the artists—Dr. Levyus. He had invited both troupes to join him right after the performance at a coffeehouse to enjoy some food and drink at his expense.

The Lemberg artists knew this patron well. They knew that Dr. "Levyusn" was not so open-handed as to actually lavish money on Yiddish actors. He was generous, but only with kind words and compliments. His purse was shut tight.

Dr. Levyus outdid himself in heaping compliments on our young hero. Like the true patron he was, he ran backstage to Rafalesco's dressing room after each act. He rubbed his hands together, per-spired, displayed all his strange, overlapping teeth, and thanked the young guest star and his impresario, Holtzman, almost with tears in his eyes. After the third act our patron was in such a state of rapture that he embraced the young artist and kissed him. Then he called the director Holtzman over to one side and discussed something with him with great intensity, placing his hand on his heart, as if to say, *I want to sponsor him.*

Realizing that the German was smitten with the kid, Holtzman thought to himself, *If only this German would make a proper gift . . . cough up a few thousand crowns . . . or—wait!—maybe he could be approached to become a partner, to rent a proper theater together, with a leading lady and the whole shebang. He might say: "Here, Holtzman, God has given you a treasure—Rafalesco. Me, He has given money. Let us be partners." Why not? Who could tell what a doctor might decide to do when he was a patron and devo-tee of Yiddish theater and had maybe half a million?*

But such thoughts were not on Rafalesco's mind. The resound-ing applause of the audience and the compliments of Dr. Levyus in no way turned our young hero's head for so much as a moment. He could think of no one else but Breyndele Kozak—the only one who could tell him about the cantor's daughter, Reizel.

Reizel! Reizel! No matter where he was, or what he was doing—Reizel stood before his eyes, today more clearly than ever. His heart pounded even before he sought out the petite, plump Breyndele Kozak. He saw her in the crowd, looking steadily at him, taking him in with her eyes, as if she knew something. She was wearing an odd red, round, broad-brimmed hat and looked like someone about to break into a dance. She was shaped like a little barrel—round and chubby, short-legged, with hands like small puffy pancakes. Her eyes were small and slanted, with very thick eyebrows, and her face was round and white like a platter or a moon. She was always smiling, displaying healthy white teeth in a large mouth. Anyone who looked at her, no matter how heavy their heart, would have to smile. A strange comical figure was this Breyndele Kozak!

And yet at that moment she appeared in Rafalesco's eyes as rather imposing. How our hero craved, right then and there, for all the artists from both troupes to vanish into thin air, leaving him alone with this charming, comical figure! He could then talk to her about Reizel, and only about Reizel. But as luck would have it, the actors remained standing around him, as if they had been hired for the purpose, waiting for him to join them and Dr. Levyus at a café. Meanwhile they chatted, gossiped, and laughed, a cheerful bunch.

"What's taking you so long?" Holtzman said to Rafalesco, helping him dress, wrapping his neck in a scarf so he wouldn't catch cold. As they headed outside, the whole crowd followed them, laughing, teasing, and shouting like schoolboys just let out of class.

Outdoors it was a still, starry night. At the door of the theater a horse and carriage stood waiting, not a usual sight for the Lemberg Yiddish Theater. The actors stopped in their tracks: "Whose carriage? Whose horses?" Dr. Levyus had ordered his carriage and horses for himself for his guest star Rafalesco, and naturally for his impresario Holtzman. All three seated themselves in the carriage. Holtzman could not contain himself and had to say: "To the devil with money!" Dr. Levyus announced to all, *"Also, meine Herren, zum* Café Monopol?"

The group stared, envying the lucky Rafalesco. They said to one another with a little laugh, "Some ride in style, some go on foot."

CHAPTER 56

He Drinks to the Wandering Stars

The actors made a raucous entrance into the Café Monopol, taking over the tables as if they intended to drink and eat up everything in sight. Materializing out of thin air, two waiters with sizable noses, uniformed in short jackets, silently placed themselves on either side of the newly arrived guests, as if to say, "*What do the* Herren *desire?*" It turned out the *Herren* wanted nothing for the time being. They were waiting for a few people. In the meantime they made fun of those they were waiting for, most of all Dr. "Levyusn." One actor expertly mimicked the way he held his hands in his pockets, peered over his eyeglasses, and sprayed spittle while speaking. Another mocked how he had applauded Rafalesco, stomping his feet, and jumping up and down. Another imitated how he had embraced and kissed the kid, scaring the poor boy to death. And the group broke out laughing.

Actors are a happy breed. They are ready to laugh, even if there is nothing to laugh at. They will laugh at something silly as hard as at a clever witticism.

Someone commented that "our 'Levyusn' must be giving those two a lecture on the fine arts."

They were not far from wrong. Dr. Levyus had told the coachman beforehand not to take them directly to the Café Monopol but first to make a small circuit around the town for some fresh air. A moneyed patron doesn't stand for nonsense from lowly actors, who are Jewish to boot. Dr. Levyus was accustomed to receiving special treatment. Money talks. When he finally entered the café, the crowd rose as one person, respectfully making way for him to sit at the head of the table. He accepted with the attitude of a person who knows what is due him. He seated the guest artist Rafalesco to his right and the impresario Holtzman to his left.

The earlier raucous mood settled into a quiet attentiveness. Dr. Levyus rang, and the two waiters with short jackets and long noses again materialized and hurried straight to his side. Standing at attention, they fixed their eyes on him and awaited his orders with such heightened eagerness and expectation, and with such great adulation, that one would have thought that Dr. Levyus's words would have a momentous impact on them, the café, and the entire world.

Both waiters bowed almost down to the floor, their hands behind their backs, and held their breath as long as humanly possible.

But Dr. Levyus was not quick to speak. Leisurely he smoothed his triangular-shaped head, furrowed his brow, half-shut his eyes, and gazed deep in thought over his eyeglasses at a distant point like a person who is about to solve a universal problem. This was what he finally said: Dr. Levyus desired that the waiters be so kind as to bring steins of beer for everyone to drink and kosher *Wurst* to eat.

The waiters straightened up and took off, their faces aglow, as if to broadcast to the world that a close friend of theirs had discovered the North Pole or, at the very least, freed someone from long captivity.

The beer was served, and a special place was cleared on a table for the kosher *Wurst*. Dr. Levyus rose like a presiding officer, and a sweet smile spread across his fat lips and his large, white, strangely overlapping teeth. In a lengthy, splendid speech, he proposed a toast.

He spoke, of course, in High German. For Dr. Levyus, anything official had to be delivered in German. We summarize his remarks in a few words.

First Dr. Levyus gave a brief overview of the Yiddish theater, of how the theatrical arts had evolved among all peoples in different countries, from the great Shakespeare's times to this day. He displayed vast erudition. The names of the countless books and writers he cited fell like hail on the heads of the starved actors, who gazed longingly at the foamy, appetizing beer before them and smiled wistfully at the kosher *Wurst,* whose smoky aroma of German garlic wafted toward them. Some sipped from their beer steins slowly, because they could tell from this "short overview" that they could have polished off the beer and the kosher *Wurst* three times over before Dr. Levyus finished with Shakespeare.

Dr. Levyus apparently realized he had gotten carried away with his "short overview" and artfully jumped from Shakespeare right to the father of the Yiddish stage, Goldfaden, and then to his followers, until he finally reached the artists of the Lemberg Yiddish Theater and the other troupes that wandered from city to city, raising the flag of Yiddish art. One of the most significant wandering artists, the speaker said, was the young guest on his right, the already famous maestro from Bucharest, that most talented of performers whom they had the honor to welcome into their small circle of dedicated artists.

"This young artist, *meine Damen und Herren*," Dr. Levyus pointed to Rafalesco, "this young artist has appeared unexpectedly among us, like an astronomic manifestation, a brilliant phenomenon in the starry firmament, a bright, shining, wandering star. This star has wandered into our midst and has illuminated the full range of our Yiddish stage. He will not be here for long, *meine Damen und Herren*, but sadly only for a short time, like all great wandering stars that vanish as quickly as they appear. I raise my glass and drink to our Yiddish wandering star. *Hoch!*"

The artists of both troupes repeated *Hoch* three times and thanked the speaker with a resounding round of applause and then fell to the beer and kosher *Wurst*.

"To our wandering star!" Dr. Levyus again toasted him with his last quaff of beer, signaled the waiters, paid the bill, and bade the crowd farewell until the second performance the following day.

"*Auf Wiedersehen.*"

"*Boruch sheptarni!* Thank God *that's* over," cried one of the actors, once Dr. Levyus was on the other side of the door.

"Everything in its time," another added. " 'Nothing under the sun lasts forever,' as Don Pedro says."

"Stupid! What Don Pedro? It was our own Moses who said that."

"Don't you mean King Solomon?"

"Let it be King Solomon. Children, let's get to work! Time doesn't stand still."

The crowd rose from the tables and sauntered into the adjacent game room, where they could enjoy a game of cards.

CHAPTER 57

At Cards

Time flies when actors gather in the small game room of the Café Monopol. Someone must always be the scapegoat, on whose head most of the insults fall and at whom the jibes are directed. Usually that scapegoat was our friend, the tragedian Chaim-Itzik Schwalb, who was playing the cards with passionate intensity, as if a seductive woman were sitting at his side. But nothing was going his way.

He and his sister kept exchanging money for chips, and both were breathing fire.

He was worried about his sister. In front of the crowd he reprimanded her for "burning up money." She retorted that it was her own money, not his. "Go back to washing laundry," he snickered. "Go back to rolling those cigarettes of yours," She came back hotly. He said, she said—one word led to another, and soon things became interesting. The crowd joined in. Many sided with the leading lady, but some sided with the brother. Inflamed, he maintained he didn't need any help and was not asking any favors. The mood became lively as the laughter grew.

Little by little the two directors were drawn into the game. As befits directors, they had at first sat by, looking on as the others played. They were finding it interesting to see who would win and who would lose. At one point they put some money into the pot, not so much to win as for the fun of it, curious as to whose hand would be lucky. But as the game went on, they both began losing. Trying to recoup their losses, they ended up losing even more. Hotly engrossed in the game, they concentrated on three things only: the banker, the stakes, and the cards.

The cards flew. Faces blazed. Eyes burned. Coins clinked. The shouting grew. They tore the cards from one another's hands. The winners laughed. The losers groaned. The winners were exhilarated. The losers despaired. All were ready to kill one another.

Only two people did not partake in the gambling bacchanalia. They were our young hero, Rafalesco, and Breyndele Kozak, or as she was sometimes called, Breyne Cherniak.

Not that these two were strangers to cards. On the contrary, Breyndele Kozak could beat three men at once. Winning from her, those who knew her said, was like getting water out of a stone. When she was winning, she grabbed your skullcap and emptied your pockets; she hid her winnings deep in her own. If she saw that the cards weren't going her way, she stopped playing immediately. That's the kind of player Breyndele Kozak was.

Nor did Rafalesco dislike playing cards. Quite otherwise, one could say, he really loved it. But his playing was of an entirely different sort. The winning or losing interested him less than the playing itself. It was the game that was of the greatest interest to him.

He might exclaim, "It's the sixth time I've played away the king of spades, and you wonder why I didn't win once with him?"

Or: "What do you say to that? I've lost again!"

Breyndele and Rafalesco waited until the noise was loud enough and the players were wrapped up in the game, and then they moved off to one side. Was he mistaken, or hadn't he once seen her in Holeneshti? No, he was not mistaken. Madame Cherniak's round face turned red, and her upper lip perspired. She had immediately recognized him, though he had grown up since she had last seen him. Perhaps they could sit down for a while?

They sat at opposite ends of a table and engaged in a tête-à-tête. The conversation wound back and forth: "Holeneshti . . . theater . . . troupe . . . Shchupak . . ."

He asked in passing: "Where is he now, this Shchupak?"

"Shchupak? He's gone. May he rest in pieces!" She gestured with both hands.

Rafalesco sat up suddenly: "Dead?"

Madame Cherniak had a good laugh, displaying her teeth:

"Ha ha ha! Shchupak dead! Shchupak would not do something so foolish. He's quite healthy and strong, but he's in big trouble. For one thing he has troubles with his wives—that jack-of-all-trades doesn't begrudge himself three wives, may he have three boils on his neck. But besides that he now has an added disaster he will long remember and, God willing, he will not get out of this one."

Madame Cherniak moved closer and told him with great animation that Shchupak was in trouble, deep trouble. "No small matter—a person who has always been a spendthrift now has to pawn everything, has to sell every last piece of jewelry he owns! Whoever knows Shchupak and his jewels will appreciate this. And for what? For a mere girl who he dreamed would become his inspiration, his gem, his protégée, his answer to everything. She was to be the leading lady who would make him a fortune, may it make him a curse. In the end, there really is a God in heaven. It so happened that the world-renowned singer Marcella Embrich heard the girl sing. And when she did, she went wild over her, took her away to Vienna, and placed her in a conservatory. Well, you can see why Shchupak would have apoplexy after losing a leading lady who could have been his meal ticket. Ay, what a little leading lady! A golden girl, still a child, as beautiful as the day is long, and her singing—to die for. Rosa is her name. Rosa Spivak."

"Reizel!"

CHAPTER 58

Let Others Be Beautiful

When Rafalesco cried out, "Reizel," Madame Cherniak could no longer control herself. She clapped her hands and complimented herself:

"Oy! Oy! *Nu!* Let others be beautiful—I am clever!"

Yes, she might very well boast. She did have an eye for such things. From the very moment when, standing in the wings, she had spotted Leo Rafalesco, the Bucharest star, she knew he was the one she had seen together with Rosa Spivak, not once but many times. And she quickly sorted through her memories. God in heaven! Where had she seen them? Of course, at the Holeneshti theater! Now it was all clear to her. It explained many things. First of all, she could understand why Rosa had been so ecstatic about him. Ah! A wonderful young man like that—no wonder she longed to see him. Oh, if only he knew how much Rosa missed him!

"She really misses me?"

Rafalesco caught his breath, and Madame Cherniak slapped his hand. "Look at you, playing dumb! Poor boy! Poor boy! So young, and he can still pull one over on you! Miss you, you ask! Can the word *miss* describe it? She went crazy, was dying for you, do you hear? The girl was inconsolable." How did Madame Cherniak know? Ha ha, what a question! She and Rosa were close, like sisters. Was there anything Rosa would not confide in her? It happened one time . . . Wait! Where did it happen? She didn't remember exactly. Where had they not been? Like gypsies they had roamed with Shchupak from country to country, from city to city, may he roam forever, God Almighty. Wherever they spent the day, they never spent the night. He could never stay long in one place, on account of his wives, who pursued him and persecuted him. Every day a different wife came after him, may Pharaoh's plagues descend on him. And he had a troupe at the time, what a troupe—one crisis after another. If not for her, Madame Cherniak, with her acting, and Rosa Spivak, with her singing, he might as well have taken a sack and gone begging from house to house, or thrown the whole thing over. The survival of that little theater depended on the two of them, especially on Rosa's singing. And what a voice that was! What singing! Madame Cherniak was the first to predict that the girl would one day be great and famous, because she, Madame Cherniak, was a true connoisseur of such things.

What had she not witnessed in her lifetime! She had told Rosa many times that this was not the life for her. No one else would have been as honest with her, and Rosa would not have bared her soul to anyone else as fully, because no one, no one, knew Shchupak, may his name be eradicated, as she knew him, and so she knew where he was heading. Rosa was all alone, still a mere child, mother's milk still on her lips. People supposed she was Shchupak's own child or a niece whom he had brought from Warsaw. A niece from Warsaw? Ha ha! That's what he might tell someone else—not her! Breyndele immediately sniffed out that Rosa was as much a niece as she was a czarina. But if he wanted a niece, the devil with him, let it be a niece. And she kept an eye on them, sniffing around and feeling out Shchupak's assistant, Sholem-Meyer. Surely Rafalesco remembered him?

"Oh! I remember him quite well, why shouldn't I? He was a short, comical fellow, a real character."

"A real character?" Breyndele questioned, "A vagabond, a thief, an outcast, an even greater rascal than his boss. He is devoted to this Shchupak like a loyal dog. Only the devil knows what keeps those two together. They pop up where you least expect them."

As she poured fire and brimstone on their heads, our young hero took in every word. He was eager to hear anything about Reizel, but Breyndele kept hammering away at Shchupak. Then she realized she was going on too much and interrupted herself: "Yes, where was I? I was talking about Rosa Spivak. She once came to me and asked me if I read cards. Why so suddenly? I told her I didn't but that I knew someone who was an excellent fortune-teller. Rosa threw her arms around me, 'Dear heart, my soul, my love,' and begged me to take her there immediately. 'Why the rush, little bird?' But that's what she really wanted. What a capricious child this Spivak was, what a spirited, passionate child. She could suddenly burst into tears, hide her head in a pillow, and refuse to eat or drink—nothing would do. Other times she would grab you and dance around the room in the middle of the day. 'What's this about? Are you crazy?' Other times she would break into song and sing like a nightingale. What a capricious child this Spivak could be.

"Anyhow, where was I? Yes. We went to the fortune-teller. Good. We arrived there—a clever witch, very experienced. She looked into Spivak's eyes and spread out the cards. The ace of hearts came up—for romance. Then a jack of diamonds—a blond cavalier. And sixes, always a different six, which meant travel. Romance, a blond cavalier, and travel—good. Keeping her eyes steadily on Spivak, the fortune-teller said the "blond cavalier" was always thinking of her, always. Day and night he was thinking only of her. He was seeking her with all his might, with body and soul. He wanted to find her, she said. He was dying, desperate, not knowing how, because they were both traveling, always traveling, always always traveling, she here, he there, he here, she there. 'You love each other,' she said, 'you love each other and you seek each other, want more than anything to rush toward each other, but you wander, you are always wandering, like stars,' she said, 'like stars in the sky.' "

The witch had gone on and on, but Breyndele Kozak didn't remember it all. She recalled only that when they left the fortune-teller, Rosa had thrown her arms around her, kissed her, and wept for joy. *A capricious girl*, she had thought, *a capricious girl.*

"Now many questions are answered for me," Breyndele Kozak ended in a Talmudic singsong. A satisfied smile spread over her round face.

CHAPTER 59
He Feels Like Singing

Well after midnight the actors of both companies finally finished their card-playing and dispersed, all with their own feelings—some full of regret, others disappointed, one happy as a lark, another worried, and one really angry at himself and at the whole world.

As if out of spite, there was not a single *droshky* to be found on the street. Holtzman and Rafalesco had to trudge along with everyone else over the Lemberg streets to their lodgings.

It was one of those autumn nights that was neither winter nor summer, neither warm nor cold. Why, one might wonder, was our young hero so affectionate and happy? Why did the sky seem to be smiling at him? Why were the stars twinkling at him so? Why were the streets singing? Why did the night smell so sweet? Why was he floating on air? Why did he so desire to sing? Why did he so wish to embrace his friend, his dear, beloved friend, and kiss him right then and there in the middle of the street?

"No, I must embrace you, Holtzman, I love you, I really love you!"

Holtzman looked at him as if he were a madman. "What's come over you, my dear songbird?"

Holtzman had no patience—that night he had incurred great losses at cards, gambling as he had never before. What devil had made him get into the game, what evil spirit? Seeing a full pot, he had been tempted—curse the money! At first he had been winning, but instead of grabbing his hat and going home, he wanted more and more. A person has big eyes. And on top of that, he couldn't refuse the director, Getzel.

"May a curse descend on that Getzel, together with my cough."

A bad sign. When Holtzman started coughing and cursing the cough, it was a sign he wasn't in high spirits. But Rafalesco *was* in high spirits. High spirits? That was an understatement. "Blessed above all other nights be this night. Blessed be this world, this beautiful, lovely, sweet world!" Their journey from the Café Monopol to their lodging consisted only of his talking, laughing, and singing. *What is it with this kid?* Holtzman puzzled, examining Rafalesco's shining face and glowing eyes. *Obviously Dr. Levyusn's compliments have gone to his head.*

Arriving at their lodgings as daylight broke, they prepared to go to bed, Rafalesco all the while babbling and laughing. It struck Holtzman that his young friend was talking strangely. The words weren't making sense: "I really like Lemberg. A pleasant city, Lemberg. A pleasant name. Lem-berg. And the people? Fine people. And I like the theater too. And the artists—outstanding people all."

"And the director, Getzel ben Getzel?" Holtzman interrupted.

"Why not? A very fine person, this Getzel."

"May he go to hell!" Holtzman added, and wanted to shut the light—it was time to sleep.

But Rafalesco wouldn't let him. He wanted to talk on.

"Are you crazy? It's almost morning."

"Just a little bit more," Rafalesco pleaded, and laughed.

"What do you want to talk about?" Holtzman asked him.

"I want to talk first about Dr. Levyus."

"What is there to say about Dr. Levyus? He's a German art patron who can go on talking forever."

"No, I want to hear what you think about Vienna, about us going to Vienna. Ach, to go to Vienna!"

Vienna? How could they shut down all their business dealings in Lemberg and suddenly take off for Vienna? Did the kid think they had money to throw away? Let Dr. Levyus pay their travel expenses—he was up to it! He had almost half a million—he could afford to foot the bill, Holtzman said.

Rafalesco became thoughtful: "Pay the expenses? He would certainly pay the expenses, why shouldn't he? An exceptional man, that doctor, exceptional. Not just any old doctor, but a jewel of a doctor."

"Everyone is an exceptional person to you. All gems. Meanwhile we have to sleep! Sleep! Sleep!"

Holtzman stuck out his long neck from the blankets, blew his nose, shut the light, and closed his eyes.

But Rafalesco still would not allow him to sleep. "That little one, the chubby one, that Breyndele Kozak. She's a good one, isn't she?"

Holtzman leaned on his thin, emaciated elbow and peered with his sharp eyes into the darkness, which was pierced by a thin blue ray of morning light.

Until that moment Holtzman had almost forgotten Breyndele Kozak. Now he remembered that she had spent that whole evening with Rafalesco. What could they have been talking about? Who knew? There were enough gossipy bastards in the world. He could not forgive himself for losing so badly at cards that he forgot to keep an eye on the kid. Next time he would not allow that to happen.

Now Holtzman couldn't sleep—he had a coughing fit. Drowsily he asked Rafalesco what he had talked about with Breyndele Kozak.

Rafalesco's voice calmed him: "What should we talk about? About nothing. Absolutely nothing. Just chatted. Gabbed, jabbered about anything at all."

"So?"

Rafalesco made up some white lies. It amused him that he could come up with lies so easily, so simply, as smooth as oil. And the more he lied, the more it made sense.

But then Rafalesco felt he wasn't saying what he really had in mind and interrupted himself. "This Breyndele Kozak," he said, "believe me, she's a fine person, a good soul, a person without guile. And a good actress—she must be really good at it. All the artists here are outstanding. What? Isn't that so?"

There was no answer. Was Holtzman asleep? Yes, he was.

Our poor Holtzman slept a troubled sleep. Something inside his chest was always wheezing, rumbling, and rattling, working its way up through his throat, something he could never get rid of, keeping him from staying asleep. He would cough and then choke on the cough, cursing it in his sleep, "Damnation!" as he turned over, fell asleep, and wheezed until the cough woke him up again. Again he would curse it and fall back asleep.

Rafalesco did not understand how anyone could sleep on that magical, wintry, yet pleasant night. "Blessed be this night!" He sprang out of bed, opened the window, leaned out, and breathed in as much fresh air as possible. His eyes scanned the sky. The stars were gone, and a high pale moon was about to set. Soon, soon, it would vanish. The midnight blue was turning into an early morning gray. Before his eyes the boisterous day would awaken. To our hero it was all one and the same. Let it be morning, let it be day. God created a wonderful world, a beloved, benevolent, sweet world! Blessed be this world! How could he sleep when his heart was so full and he felt like singing?

He wanted to sing and sing.

CHAPTER 60

Diplomats

Holtzman had sniffed out with his sharp nose the fact that the director of the Lemberg theater, that "Yuckel ben Fleckel," had his eye on his kid. Everyone was dancing around his Rafalesco, eyeing him as a cat eyes cream, but Holtzman pretended not to notice. *Dance, children, dance. You're dancing at your own funeral*, he thought, as he proceeded to strike one sneaky deal after another.

First he joined up with Henrietta Schwalb's brother. Picture those two together—the potbellied Schwalb could have stuffed ten Holtzmans under his belt. Henrietta, Holtzman noticed, somehow managed always to be hanging around the kid, mooning over him. It was time, he thought, to invite the tragedian to a restaurant. Over a glass of beer and a kosher sausage, Holtzman praised Chaim-Itzik Schwalb to the skies, swearing on his life that Schwalb was a better actor than all his colleagues. His director, Yuckel ben Fleckel, in no way deserved a tragedian of Schwalb's caliber. And with such praise Holtzman won him over. He had touched him exactly where he was most sensitive. Schwalb admitted, in confidence of course, that he had long wanted to be rid of that exploiter, but he was tied to him with a contract for another three years, and besides he had no alternative, nowhere else to go. "If I only had the chance, I would know what to do. I would go with a leading lady like my kid sister to London. It's a bit bigger than Lemberg, right?"

"A bit," conceded Holtzman, taking a gulp of beer.

"Well, they say their theater is a bit nicer, isn't that so?"

"I believe so," Holtzman added, taking another gulp.

"No. Much nicer," said Schwalb. "I have a brother there, he's also a tobacconist. Well, he used to peddle cigarettes like I did but now he's a real businessman living in London. He recently sent a picture of himself—a young fellow with a gold watch-chain across his big belly and a diamond ring. I could hardly recognize him. He wrote me to come to London with our sister, and we'd discover what real living was like!"

Holtzman heard him out. "What a clever fellow your brother is!" he said. "Haven't I too had the thought of hopping over to London with the kid? I've always wanted to go there. A fine city, they say, that London. I believe you can really make a killing there. But first you have to set up a real company. And I know what my company is missing. It needs a great tragic actor to play the powerful roles and a beautiful leading lady. If I could get those two, nothing would stop me!"

A half-hour later the two of them left the restaurant with fat, strong-smelling cigars stuck in their mouths, having awkwardly shaken hands and smiled at each other congenially like people who have tacitly understood each other and established a close bond.

As soon as the actors saw those two teamed up, they ran to their director: "Listen to this. Our Itzikl has suddenly become pals with the big shot from Bucharest."

Getzel ben Getzel listened dumbfounded, turning colors, and got himself worked up over that Bucharest vagabond and that cigarette peddler. He called Schwalb in.

The director shut the door behind Schwalb when he entered, and checked the windows. Only then did he sit down to have, as he said, a long talk just between the two of them, a calm, quiet talk, "We have to be careful in case someone is listening at the door. The world is full of hypocrites, schemers, idlers," he said.

By the time Schwalb left his director's office, his face was aflame, and he was sweating profusely.

Looks like he really got it! thought his colleagues, but they were greatly mistaken.

CHAPTER 61

Holtzman Makes Still Another Deal

The artists of the Lemberg theater had before them a new bit of work: the Bucharest director had suddenly become tight with their Breyndele Kozak. Why? They were breaking their heads trying to figure it out. And as was their way, they began to poke fun at the pair and their sudden intimacy, sharpening their tongues and trying to outdo one another with cutting remarks and crude wordplay.

"Look at them, like two besotted lovebirds."

"Doesn't it strike you as a mismatch made in heaven?"

"*Mazel tov*, they'll be so sappy together."

"May God bless them with lots of muck."

Who would have suspected that Holtzman was using Breyndele as a way to win over Henrietta Schwalb? One would have needed Holtzman's own keen nose to sniff out that Breyndele Kozak was the best means to achieve that end. And he went at it with intelligence, energy, guile, and persistence, as one would expect of him.

It started with a little talk, a stroll, and ended with his dropping by Breyndele's place. They were, after all, old friends. But the longer it went on, the friendlier they became. Holtzman told her he enjoyed being with her. Too bad Shchupak couldn't see them.

"What would happen if he did?" she asked him, puzzled, looking at him with her small Oriental eyes.

"He would have a fit."

"Amen! From your mouth to God's ears!" Breyndele gazed at Holtzman admiringly and thought that if Shchupak were here and could see his "Hotzmach," he would *really* have a fit. She listened to him speak and could not get over it. He simply wasn't the same person. That wasn't at all the way he once spoke. He was talking now about "results," about "business," about "capital." Hotzmach talking about capital? What, a joke! And boasting that he was making, thank

God, a good bit of money. He said he wasn't a big capitalist, but he would soon catch up with Shchupak. That one had jewels, but he had cash. Ready cash, he said, was worth more than all the jewels.

"Don't bother yourself about Shchupak!" Breyndele interjected. "He has more aggravation now than he ever had jewels."

"I won't believe it till I see it with my own eyes, and I won't rest till Shchupak cleans *my* boots. May he be cursed, together with my cough!"

Speaking of Shchupak made him upset, and when he became upset, he coughed. Once his coughing fit was over, he hooked his fingers into his vest and paced back and forth over Madame Cherniak's small room on his long, thin legs, while looking down at his feet, all the time boasting how much money he had and how much he was worth. He suddenly stopped pacing and felt he should explain why his new affluence was no surprise. It was simply a matter of earning and saving, of scrimping and putting away, till he had finally seen a bit of success, may God help him, made a little bundle, and now had something to show for it.

"Amen, why not?" added Madame Cherniak. "I don't see what there is to explain. Is it a shame to have money? It's a shame to be a pauper, a bum, like all those oafs who go around without a shirt on their backs, who only know gambling, fooling around with women, and cadging loans whenever they can to cover their losses! I can't stand those people, and to them money is like water, it just runs through their fingers. Is it a crime to be a good actor and also hang on to a *groshen*? What's a person without money, after all? What?"

"Like a body without a soul," he answered, matching her tone. He remembered that when they were still with Shchupak, she had always had a nest egg. The troupe used to say that Breyndele Kozak was as stuffed with money as she was with years. The problem, they complained, was that God did not perform a miracle and kill her off, so that they could lay their hands on it.

Gradually Holtzman and Breyndele's talk came to important matters. He raised questions about their future: "How long can we be wanderers, sold to a nothing like this Yuckel ben Fleckel? Wouldn't it be a thousand times better for you to go hand in hand with me? Two people like us could really make things happen, could accomplish something worthwhile, eh? Two people like us, who've led a dog's life, we know suffering and don't need to be taught how to make money or how to hold on to it. To earn a *groshen* isn't as hard as holding on to a *groshen*. You have to look after a *groshen*. Too many people are after that *groshen*, no?"

"Too many," Breyndele chimed in.

And so their conversation flowed, on both personal and practical subjects, until Holtzman arrived at the point that was urgently on his mind—the leading lady.

"We have to snatch away that pretty heifer from Yuckel ben Fleckel."

"The pretty heifer, ha ha," Breyndele repeated, and a wide smile spread over her chubby, round moon-face. She was pleased that she had guessed whom he meant and that he had called Henrietta what she really was. And she was quite satisfied with the direction of their talk.

Holtzman took her in with his sharp eyes and explained, half in earnest, half in jest, the logic behind snatching away the pretty heifer: "A pretty little leading lady, you understand, even if she is a calf, is good for business."

"Good for business, ha ha!" Breyndele echoed.

"Just what the doctor ordered," Holtzman continued in the same half-earnest, half-jesting tone.

"Just what the doctor ordered," she repeated, coquettishly giving him a slap with her chubby hand, as her fat moon-face perspired with excitement. And her small Oriental eyes became even smaller, so small that one could hardly see them.

CHAPTER 62

Breyndele Kozak's Romances

What could Holtzman's proposal to "go hand in hand with me" have meant to Breyndele Kozak? And why shouldn't she have been happy about it? She was a lonely, rootless soul who had been wandering for years from city to city, from country to country, from theater to theater. Back when Holtzman had been with Shchupak and was still called Hotzmach, it had been a different story. But now Hotzmach was Holtzman, and was the director of his own company, and had laid his hands on that rare kid Rafalesco, whom everyone was fighting over, and in addition was bringing in a little capital—now it really *was* a different story. Were they to go "hand in hand" and snatch away the "pretty little heifer" and the "kid," the four of them would be able to travel the world. Then she would certainly have a new life.

Pondering those sweet thoughts, our Breyndele Kozak took to her task like a true diplomat, cleverly and adroitly. She succeeded magnificently. The naïve, pretty-faced Henrietta let herself be persuaded, and she agreed to all the benefits and privileges offered her. In particular, Madame Cherniak impressed her with the fact she could then be much closer to Rafalesco.

Henrietta gazed at her with her lovely blue eyes and turned red as a beet. Breyndele noticed and anticipated her: "There's nothing to be concerned about. This kind of thing happens to everyone. You don't need to be coy. It's obvious you're crazy about him and that he is about you."

Henrietta Schwalb blushed furiously. "He's crazy about me? How do you know that?"

"Oh, I know. I know everything. There is nothing I don't know. Just ask me, and I'll tell you in the blink of an eye. One two three— and they'll be breaking dishes at the engagement party."

"Breyndele! Dear heart! Darling!" Henrietta threw her arms around her and hid her pretty, flushed face in Madame Cherniak's cloak.

It was no surprise that the leading lady had earned such fine nicknames as "pretty heifer" and "little fool." Henrietta had apparently undertaken to show everybody that you could have a pretty face and no brain at all. Breyndele Kozak was capable of putting her in her pocket, buying and selling a dozen pretty foolish girls like that leading lady from the Lemberg theater. And oh! Breyndele Kozak had never been happier in her life. Each human being has his star in heaven, and for every creature there must come a time. That time had come for Breyndele Kozak, for her heart would now awaken from its long sleep and beat and tremble with the warm feeling of true happiness.

But this was not her first romance, nor sadly her last.

How many times had she been burned in her life! How much abuse had she suffered at the hands of "false, corrupt, depraved men"—and yet she had never learned.

Once upon a time Shchupak had needed her favor; he had proposed marriage, and she had accepted, but later she was ready to tear her hair over him. To that very day she could not bear to hear his name spoken, and yet she invoked it often.

After Shchupak, his assistant, our old acquaintance Sholom-Meyer Murovchik, had made a pass at her. He came after her with heart and soul, to the point where she was imagining standing under the wedding canopy with him. But then Sholom-Meyer Murovchik would have none of it. As a rule, actors avoid getting married. A girlfriend, a fiancée, a stroll, a gift, a dinner, a joke, a dance—anything. But marriage was out: "Better dead than married."

Breyndele Kozak's romance with Sholom-Meyer Murovchik, like all her romances before and after, fell apart. It began when she made him a little loan, then another and another, and it ended with a scandal, with a pain in her heart, and with hatred for all "false, corrupt men."

But what wound does not heal with time? Sholom-Meyer never repaid the money he'd borrowed from her, and Madame Cherniak remained Madame Cherniak. (The title *Madame* she gave herself on account of her imposing figure and her years.)

But she had not lost hope. Sooner or later someone would reveal himself, someone who would understand her and appreciate her worth. He must, he must come! She would take him to her heart. She would offer her wealth to him, and he would see her treasures. He would see her linens, her clothing, her jewelry, her welcoming body. It was all ready for his sake, *for his sake*, and he didn't even know it! She would lay open her soul to him. Ach, perhaps she was not as beautiful as others. Perhaps she was not as young as others. But how much devotion, how much passion filled her heart to bursting! How much true, pure love and loyalty lay dormant in her soul!

Holtzman was now the one upon whom Madame Cherniak's fate hung. He now took possession of her heart, dominated it like a king, and would rule her as long as it served his purpose. They had not really understood each other about the meaning of "go hand in hand." To him, it meant she would have a share in the business, be a partner in the troupe. Why not? With the greatest pleasure he would take her money!

Take her money? A share in the theater company? That was not what "hand in hand" meant to Madame Cherniak.

Poor Breyndele Kozak!

CHAPTER 63

They Pay a Visit

Once, between acts of a performance, Dr. Levyus-Levyusn approached Holtzman and politely invited him, along with the young maestro Rafalesco, to his home for lunch. "I hope," he said with a friendly smile, "you won't turn me down."

"Turn down an invitation like that?" Holtzman was quick to reply, winking to Rafalesco, which meant: *What do you say to this German?* "Of course, ach! With the greatest honor."

To our Holtzman, the visit would be like a celebration—he had to prepare: "Whatever you say," he told Rafalesco, "you have to go to a patron's house for lunch like a *mensch*."

And he was off to the shops, where he bought himself a brand-new suit, exchanged insults with Lemberg's German salesmen, bargained shrewdly, and succeeded in getting a big discount for paying cash.

"What do you say to this bargain, my dear boy?"

"It's a steal," said Rafalesco.

"You mean it?"

"Why not? Sure."

"Then why are you laughing?"

"Do you want me to cry?"

"Who said cry?" said Holtzman. They both enjoyed a good laugh as they prepared for the special visit. Holtzman sat down to shave his dry, sallow face. He left two black muttonchops, which suited his gaunt, hollow cheeks and his scrawny neck, which stuck out from a stiff, snow-white collar and a smartly knotted necktie. A new pair of polished shoes with broad straps and a shiny black top hat on his head gave his slender figure even more charm. His young friend could barely contain himself and complimented him, saying he was growing handsomer and younger every day. "Handsomer, maybe, but younger—God knows," Holtzman said soberly, bowing.

"Do you see these gray hairs?" he said. "Cursed be Shchupak—I have *him* to thank for them."

Rafalesco also dressed for the visit according to the latest fashion. His large, white, unusually beautiful hands extended from a smoking jacket that was a bit too short and too tight on him because he was still growing. His attractive white shirt under the vest vied with his graceful, white throat. His entire appearance conveyed so much youth and freshness that it was truly a joy to look at him. It was easy to see why Henrietta Schwalb had thrown over all her other suitors and set out to "conquer this young puppy" who "either had the heart of a Tatar, couldn't see, or else he was simply still wet behind the ears." Henrietta, accustomed to having men go wild over her, could not understand what was wrong with him. After all, she made sure always to be where he could see her and dressed herself to impress him—she recently had a silk dress made just for that purpose. She did everything in her power to win him over, but he—nothing! "He's an odd young man. It's all very strange! One minute he's happy, dancing, singing, and the next he becomes sad, goes around lost in a dream. We have to take this young man in hand!" she would say.

But Rafalesco was oblivious to her charms. His head and heart were only in one place—Vienna. In his dreams at night and in his daytime fantasies he saw before him only Vienna, the paradise where his soul yearned to be. In Vienna were two people who drew him like a magnet. "To be with these two and then die . . ."

That Reizel was in Vienna, he knew from Breyndele Kozak. That he would find her there he had no doubt. But would she recognize him? And how did she look now? And how would their first meeting go? And what would be the first thing he said to her? He would not reveal himself to her. No, let her recognize him herself.

And he imagined she would recognize him immediately. They would fall into each other's arms. Not a word would be spoken. They would be speechless, but for two single words: "Reizel!" "Leibel!"

But he now had a second dream—Sonnenthal! In fact, it was difficult to tell which enthralled him more, which captured more of his heart: Reizel, his goddess, or Sonnenthal, the God himself? He imagined himself in Vienna. Do you have any idea what Vienna was like? What made Vienna so great? Vienna was the city where Sonnenthal lived. And what was Vienna without Sonnenthal! He dreamed of the scene of his arrival.

His heart pounding, he crosses Sonnenthal's threshold. With an angelic face and a smile like the sun on a beautiful summer morning, the god of artists and actors, the great Sonnenthal, stands before him. He takes him by the arm and leads him into the interior rooms of his magnificent palace and seats him opposite himself on a chair. He observes him acting and praises him so highly, it makes his head spin: "No, you mustn't be playing those roles," Sonnenthal warns him, in the same words and the same tone that Dr. Levyus had used that first evening they had met. "No, such a God-given talent must be displayed in more serious, classical roles." Again, exactly what Dr. Levyus had said, word for word.

DR. JULIUS LEVYUS, our two heroes read. The small plaque hung on a large, high portal, in a magnificent courtyard with iron gates and tall poplars. Behind the trees they spied a substantial white wall and an opulent, elegant mansion that seemed to be saying, *Here is wealth. Here is luxury. Here is peace.*

"To the devil with money!" Holtzman could not help saying; he blew his nose thoroughly into a brand-new handkerchief and rang the bell.

CHAPTER 64

The Lemberg Patron

When our invited guests entered Dr. Levyus's mansion and met their host, they barely recognized him. Where was the broad smile on his friendly face? Where had his endless talk without pause gone? In his own home he seemed to be more staid and restrained. He also appeared smaller, not like the patron at the theater, nothing like the Dr. Levyus they had known before.

Certainly he welcomed them warmly. He helped them with their coats and then escorted them into his richly appointed office, lined with books from floor to ceiling. He seated them in two tall, soft armchairs and politely chatted about ordinary matters. How did they like Lemberg? What did they think about the weather? And other such insignificant, dull topics that are discussed for the sake of appearances in almost every aristocratic home where one is officially invited for lunch. The meal is not yet ready, and one must sit and starve while there is nothing much to talk about. The host looks at you as if you were the eleventh plague in Egypt, thinking, *What a tedious guest this is. You have to nurse him along.* And you look at the host and wonder, *Why on earth am I here—to starve? Don't I have lunch at home, God help me?* Finally your host will stand up, invite you to the table, and introduce you to the finely dressed, friendly, smiling hostess. Your mood will be softened somewhat. They will seat you at the head of the table, to the hostess's right, and they will pour you a glass of wine. You will move your chair to the table, while the food peers up at you from the platter, smiles at you, and gives off delicious aromas. At last you will play your role . . .

After another half-hour of dull chitchat in the office, Dr. Levyus stood and led his guests through a series of wide, high-ceilinged salons, appointed with the most expensive furniture, heavy doors, and high, shiny mirrors, to a sumptuously set table. But at the head of the table, instead of a friendly, smiling hostess, sat a gray-haired old crone with a wrinkled, sallow face that reminded one of a sour prune.

"My *Mütterchen*," Dr. Levyus told them, after going up to her and kissing her hand.

The *Mütterchen*, a Jewish woman wearing a wig, a silk dress, jeweled earrings, and large pearls, favored them with a glance that chilled their innards. *An old witch*, Holtzman's keen eyes signaled to his young friend. Both of them, famished, sat at the table, did not wait to be asked, and began to satisfy their hunger. All the while they regarded Dr. Levyus, unable to reconcile this man with the man they had met at the theater. And now as he sat at the table he became yet another person. The slightest hint of a smile played on his face, although it looked like the grimace of a person about to have a tooth extracted. At any moment, one imagined, he might throw his head back, squeeze his eyes shut, and, using all his courage, open his mouth wide: *"Here, pull, yank. Do what you have to do . . ."*

The *Mütterchen* was thinking, *Why did he bring these dull oafs here? Everything they talk about is pointless.* If not for the clatter of the forks and knives on the plates, one could have heard our guests almost choking on every swallow. The time passed in that stultified silence. It was an utter relief when the doctor rose from the table, kissed his *Mütterchen*'s hand, and returned with them to his office.

There the host unlocked a drawer of the handsome desk and removed three different cigars from three different humidors. Holtzman's sharp eyes discerned that the three cigars were of three qualities: better, worse, and awful. The better one the host took for himself, the worse one he gave to Rafalesco, and the awful one he handed to Holtzman.

It became apparent that Holtzman was a cigar fancier, because no sooner did he take one puff than he began sputtering and coughing.

Had Holtzman not made this visit with a specific purpose in mind, he would not have suffered such an indignity at the hands of the patron. He would have asked the man where he had laid his hands on such a stinking cigar, one of those that are sold on the street and are used to poison flies. But as the visit had an important aim, Holtzman, with great effort, smoked this terrible cigar and coughed to the point of choking, while listening to the doctor deliver an entire lecture on acting, about which he had recently read up with Rafalesco in mind.

Again the same old story—it makes me sick to my stomach, thought Holtzman. *Acting, and again acting, and classical roles, and Vienna. By US in Vienna . . . and Sonnenthal . . . OUR Sonnenthal . . . All this German has to do is mention Sonnenthal, and the foolish kid acted as if it were the word of God. I need to have a talk with him.*

"Don't be offended, Reb German. I'm just a simple, ordinary fellow and don't understand what you mean. You're saying the kid mustn't continue playing the serious roles he has spent so much time studying? You say he has to go to Vienna? Who knows, maybe you're right. But then again, how do we get there?" And Holtzman winked at his young friend, indicating he should help him out.

But Rafalesco, whether he understood him or not, did not come to his aid. Holtzman's hopes for financial support from the patron vanished. The patron suddenly sprang to his feet as if singed. "Pardon! You must mean the letter for my friend Sonnenthal that I promised to give you. One moment."

In vain Holtzman tried to reassure him that the letter could wait for later. In vain he broadly hinted that they could not pay for the journey. But Dr. Levyus was deaf to Holtzman's hints, deaf as a doornail.

Realizing that the situation was critical, Holtzman made a last effort to speak frankly. But he made no more than an effort, because before could even open his mouth to speak about money, Dr. Levyus gave him the handwritten letter, shook his hand, rang for the servant and indicated that the *Herren* wished to leave, rose, and very politely escorted them to the door:

"Tonight is your final performance. Tonight we shall see one another at the theater. Certainly we shall see one another. Then we will speak of everything, of everything. *Adieu. Auf Wiedersehen.* I thank you heartily for your visit. *Adieu. Adieu. Auf Wiedersehen.*"

CHAPTER 65

The Final Guest Performance in Lemberg

The renowned Bucharest troupe's final performance in Lemberg ended with greater *éclat,* more beauty, and more luster than any of their other performances. It was a resounding success, a rare spectacle. The actors were in their proper places. The stage manager needn't have sweated. The director needn't have worried. The prompter had nothing to do. Everything went as smoothly as butter. Both troupes seemed to mingle harmoniously that evening, and above all of them hovered the masterful spirit of the young artist.

Rafalesco felt himself to be more in his element that evening than ever before. As flimsy, foolish, and clumsy as the play was, the performance nevertheless gave a feeling of rare ensemble acting. True aesthetes enjoyed it. Even lesser connoisseurs were ecstatic. And the greater audience went wild intoning: "Ra-fa-les-co! Ra-fa-les-co!"

Rafalesco took curtain call after curtain call, not alone but with the famous Lemberg leading lady, who shared with him the triumph of that evening. Whenever Rafalesco took her hand for a bow, Henrietta felt a shiver pass over her body. *That young man is mine!* she thought as she smiled broadly, flashing her white teeth and the fake jewels she had recently bought.

Her brother beamed with joy. A gold mine had opened before his eyes, and from it his fortune was about to be made. He would get rid of that bloodsucker Getzel ben Getzel. The new director, Holtzman, had finalized a deal with him to become partners. They would open their own business together, a theater under both their names: Holtzman, Schwalb & Co. And he would be rid of the weight of looking after his sister, who seemed to have really turned the kid's head. Not a bad match, he mused, wiping his red face with both hands. The rest of the troupe would die of envy and, with luck, Yuckel ben Fleckel would suffer a well-deserved apoplectic fit.

"Why do you keep peeking around the curtain, and who are you looking for?" Schwalb asked his new partner. Holtzman was restlessly pacing in the wings, apparently waiting for someone to show up in the house.

"None of your business," Holtzman said, continuing to search the orchestra.

It was Dr. Julius Levyus he was searching for. He had promised to come to the theater for the final performance, but he had not come. This so aggravated our Holtzman that he ceaselessly cursed with bloody curses all doctors and all Germans and all patrons all over the world.

"Whom are you blessing so deliciously?" the curious actors wanted to know.

"Something reminded me of an uncle, a tailor, who was so poor he could only sew with remnants. He's long dead."

To the actors this explanation did not hold water. Something was not right with Holtzman, they informed their director. What could be upsetting the big shot from Bucharest?

Getzel ben Getzel heard them out with lowered eyes. He could barely hold back a little smile. *Upset?* he thought. *You are all big fools. He'll really be upset tomorrow when he has to leave here. Just wait till tomorrow, and then he'll really be surprised.*

But the following morning it was Getzel who was surprised. Something had occurred during the night, something that had never before happened since Lemberg was a city, since a Yiddish theater had existed there, and since Getzel ben Getzel had been its director. Holtzman & Co. had undone him. First they had tricked him out of his leading lady—and what a leading lady! And then, in another maneuver, they had snatched away her brother, the tragedian, as well as another actor, Benny Gorgel, who was also a superb prompter. Even Madame Cherniak had vanished.

"What shall we do now?" poor Getzel ben Getzel lamented, weeping before the remaining actors. "We might as well lock up the theater, lie down, and die!"

"There's no other way!" the deserted actors comforted him, and out of great heartache they went off to the Café Monopol for a game of cards. But the director of the Lemberg Theater vowed to pursue the runaways to Vienna, to Bucharest, and, if necessary, to the ends of the earth. "May my name not be Getzel if I don't catch them! Unless there is no God in heaven!"

CHAPTER 66

The Schwalbs' Life Story

Our noted companions, Holtzman and Schwalb, propitiously sealed their partnership in the beautiful, festive city of Vienna, and in the most congenial manner.

In one of those Viennese coffeehouses that are far from first class, one could sit in a side room with a glass of Pilsener beer and little tasty sausages and relax with a friend. That was where our two partners met and worked out all the particulars, point for point:

Holtzman and Schwalb will open a theater under the name of "Holtzman, Schwalb & Co."

1) The directors of the theater are Holtzman and Schwalb.
2) The directors are contributing to the partnership as follows: Schwalb, his sister Henrietta as leading lady, and Holtzman, the famous artist Leo Rafalesco as leading man.
3) All earnings, after expenses, will be split evenly between both directors.
    a. The directors are not obliged to act onstage unless it happens that one of the actors becomes sick and cannot go onstage. The sick actor's pay will go to the directors.
    b. All actors work for them on the basis of shares, meaning that however much net profit remains from an evening performance, the directors take off the first half, and the other half is shared among the actors, each according to his worth, except for Rafalesco and the leading lady, who each receive two shares.
    c. None of the actors must know how much the directors earn or how much, God forbid, they lose.
4) The treasurer of the company will be . . .

At this point a bit of a quarrel arose between the directors. Each naturally wanted to be closer to the till. The spat was quickly settled when Holtzman offered a solution. Schwalb was to sit at the box office, because he was a heavy person and needed to be seated. But all expenses, money, and accounts would go through Holtzman.

Other less important considerations were worked out amicably and sensibly. Holtzman would put the finishing touches on these additional matters. He had had a good master—Shchupak was his name, may it be erased!

When he was finished working out all the points, Holtzman asked for a pen, ink, and a sheet of paper, apparently preparing to write down what they had just agreed on verbally. He said to his partner in the friendliest manner: "All right now, scratch down your mark right here!"

"I?" Schwalb responded in embarrassment, pushing away the pen and ink. "I am, as you see me, a simple Jew who has never in his life held a pen in his hand."

"Is that true?" Holtzman asked in astonishment. "How can a person not be able to write at least a few words in plain Yiddish?"

"How would I know?" Schwalb protested, and having by this time finished his third beer, his tongue loosened, and he put before Holtzman his life story, which we relate here briefly:

He was born he didn't know where, and grew up an orphan, he didn't know whose. In fact, they were three orphans: he and an older brother, Nissel, the one in London, and the little sister, Yentl, who was now the leading lady Henrietta. The three of them had wandered homeless until kind people took pity on them and took them in, one here, another there. He and Nissel were handed over to a baker to deliver egg bagels. The work wasn't to their liking, and they took to selling cigars instead. You earned a bit more money from cigars. Still, selling cigars came with plenty of heartache. Luckily Chaim-Itzik Schwalb always had a talent for acting. Came Purim, he would earn a bundle.

In short, the two brothers were able to scrounge out a meager living so they could stick their tongues out at the world, even if they still went naked, barefoot, and hungry. But their worst problem was the little sister. What did you do with a girl? To rid themselves of the burden, they hired her out as a servant, for little more than a crust of bread. But this led to one trouble after another. Every other week she switched jobs because most of her employers could not resist a pretty girl. Their bad luck—ever since childhood she had been a charmer, more for her beauty than for her intelligence. Had Nissel been at home, he would have known how to deal with these employers. "Compared to my brother, I'm no more than a puppy," Chaim-Itzik said. "But he got it into his head to take off for London, and on foot. He promised to write letters every week, but nothing came of it. He left without a goodbye. And when did he remind himself to write? Only when I became an actor of great tragic roles and our sister a leading lady for Yuckel ben Fleckel. Is it any wonder that I never had time to learn how to write?"

Our Holtzman heard out his partner's interesting and candid biography and had to confess that he was absolutely right. He himself could write only when no one was looking. But then again, why did one need to write? With those words Holtzman tore the sheet of paper in half and said to his partner:

"To hell with writing things down! Documents don't matter, people matter! Let's shake hands on the deal. Everything we agreed on here should be holy and pure, and let us have more beer, and let us embrace with a *l'chayim!* May God grant us luck and good fortune!"

"*L'chayim! L'chayim!* May God grant us success and all that is good!"

"Amen."

"Amen. Amen."

CHAPTER 67

The First Visit to the Great Sonnenthal

Arriving home a bit under the influence, our partners told no one about the important agreement they had concluded. They scoured the city of Vienna, looking for a place to locate a Yiddish theater, but they soon realized they were wasting their time. Vienna was not really a Jewish city, and the Viennese Jews were not really Jews. "Jews," said Holtzman, "who can get along without any real Yiddish theater, Jews who run to hear Sonnenthal or are satisfied with a cabaret or some little tavern where people gather for a beer, smoke cigars, and listen to someone singing such ordinary songs as 'Chava' or 'Every Friday Night,' and then clap their hands and lick their fingers—such Jews ought to be hanged from a tree or shot."

Holtzman was complaining in his accustomed way. He and his new partner decided to spit on that fancy Vienna and return to the provinces, to the small towns in blessed Galitzia, Bukovina, and Romania, where Jews had as yet not tasted of the Tree of Knowledge, and where the public still gathered to see Jewish actors the way they run to see a bear, an elephant, or a monkey.

Only the prospect of visiting Sonnenthal was keeping Holtzman in Vienna. "An artist who makes a million is entitled to have people spend an extra day in Vienna for his sake," he reasoned. Not because he was so impressed with millions, heaven forbid! Did Holtzman say a million? He had seen millionaires in his lifetime. He had spoken with them, driven in their carriages, and eaten at their tables. (Here he was thinking of Dr. Levyus-Levyusn.) Holtzman, you understand, was of the opinion that an actor like Sonnenthal was worth a visit because he could earn a million and not waste it, or drink or gamble it away.

Holtzman refreshed his attire, smoothed out his top hat, bought himself a pair of new gloves and a half-silk umbrella, brought along the letter Dr. Levyus had given them, and summoned the kid. "So, my dear songbird, here we go, right foot first . . ."

Here Schwalb could not help but remark that he would love to go along to see Sonnenthal: "Since we are partners, it seems only fitting."

But Holtzman clipped his wings. "What nerve!" he said. "Business is not the same as friendship. A partnership is a partnership, but you have to know who is best suited for what."

Schwalb could not understand why his request was being rejected: "Why not? Will it cost you for three of us to go? Will I bite off his head?"

Holtzman explained, "A person has to know his place. Let a pig into your house, and he'll climb on your table."

Now Schwalb let him know that Henrietta Schwalb was his sister, and that he was her brother. This infuriated Holtzman, who began coughing and cursed him out in Hebrew. That ended the matter.

Neither Rafalesco nor Holtzman could understand why the great Sonnenthal lived not in his own home but in a hotel. "All right, ordinary fellows like us—we live in garbage dumps, get acquainted with chickens, ducks, landladies, and bedbugs," Holtzman mused as he drove with Rafalesco in a fine carriage to Sonnenthal. "We are, after all, wretched Yiddish actors. But Sonnenthal? In Vienna? Not to be believed!"

They drove up to the first-class hotel where Sonnenthal was staying, and a man in livery with gold buttons greeted them. Holtzman instantly changed his opinion and commented to Rafalesco: "To hell with money!" They wished to see Sonnenthal, he informed the man in livery and gold buttons. Gold Buttons looked our two people over from head to foot and told them they would not be able to see Sonnenthal. "Why not?" "Because Sonnenthal is not receiving visitors." "What do you mean, he's not receiving visitors?" Gold Buttons left that question unanswered as he turned around to leave. Holtzman called out firmly that they had a letter for Sonnenthal from a very important person who probably made as much as his employer. He was not to think they were just anyone; they were themselves artists.

Holtzman grabbed his top hat, removed a glove, put the hat back on, and honored Gold Buttons with a clap on the shoulder. Gold Buttons, taken aback by this behavior, took the letter from him and left our visitors cooling their heels for some time. He finally returned with the message that Sonnenthal was deeply regretful. He was in the middle of studying a new role. If they insisted on speaking with him, they could come backstage tonight at the theater during intermission.

Not a single word more could they draw from that gold-buttoned emissary. Before our visitors could open their mouths to speak, he had shown them that he boasted the same gold buttons on his back as on his front.

"Not exactly what we hoped for, my dear songbird, but what can we do? We must accept the situation," Holtzman lamented to Rafalesco as they rode home, their faces burning with shame.

CHAPTER 68

Dashed Hopes

Returning from the visit as if beaten, our visitors received a warm welcome from the acting company, who greeted them with a broad *sholom aleichem*. Then: "So?"

"So what?"

"What happened with the great Sonnenthal?"

"What did you expect?" Holtzman said casually, feigning indifference. "You can imagine that he's really something, that Sonnenthal!"

With great verve, Holtzman spun a fanciful tale about their visit. Sonnenthal lived in great opulence, he said, and was a priceless person. He had welcomed them expansively and honored them with tea, beer, and cigars. "Each cigar this long!" Holtzman demonstrated how long, extending his hands until one of them smacked Schwalb's red face. Schwalb, as we all know, was a specialist in cigars and could not contain himself. Cigars of the size Holtzman was describing did not exist anywhere in the world, he said. And who should know better than himself, who had dealt all his life in cigars?

"What a waste you didn't stick with your trade," Holtzman cut him off. "I wish you had stayed with your cigars, and the Yiddish stage would have had one less *nudnik* to worry about."

That response was a little too sharp for an artist like Schwalb; his red face turned redder, and he perspired. But Schwalb was not the sort of person to be deeply insulted or bear a grudge. So good feelings were quickly reestablished, and then and there they agreed that all of them would go see Sonnenthal that very evening, and they reserved a box at the local theater. This did not really mean that the entire troupe would sit in a box, only the two directors, Rafalesco, Henrietta, and Breyndele Kozak.

And what of the rest of the company?

The rest of the company, Holtzman decided, could just as well stay home and mutter their prayers. If they really wanted to, they could clamber up to the highest gallery where seats cost much less and in the meantime they would be closer to God.

In a word, our Holtzman showed no sign of unhappiness. On the contrary, that morning he was as lively and talkative as ever, gesticulating dramatically, hopping and skipping and singing under his breath, like a person who had just found a fortune.

Quite otherwise was the demeanor of our other visitor, Leo Rafalesco. Where Holtzman was lively and happy, Rafalesco was worried and sad, going around in a state of utter dismay. All his fantasies and dreams had come to naught.

His first dream was of meeting the cantor's daughter in Vienna, a dream that cost him many a sleepless night. The second dream was of receiving a welcome from the great Sonnenthal.

But his hopes of finding Reizel had been dashed. After he made many inquiries and investigations, one thing became clear: neither Marcella Embrich nor Rosa was in Vienna. Madame Cherniak had assured him that Rosa was in Vienna and had promised to arrange a meeting without fail. But once in Vienna she began singing another tune. She came up with one story after another. First she said that Rosa and Marcella had suddenly taken off for Berlin. Then she brought news that Rosa was in Paris at the Conservatory, study-ing at the expense of a wealthy patron, Jacques Reszko, a Christian who had fallen deeply in love with the Jewish songstress. Another time, arriving in her red cape, she called Rafalesco over to the side and whispered in his ear that she knew for certain that Rosa Spivak was now in London giving concerts with a famous violinist, a Jew-ish boy, Grisha Stelmach, who was a great sensation. And likely this Grisha would marry Rosa if he had not already done so.

"Lies, falsehoods!" Rafalesco cried uncontrollably.

"What do you mean, lies?" Madame Cherniak retorted, glaring at him with her little Oriental eyes, and on her round moon-face a little smile appeared that spread over her large mouth.

Ah! If Rafalesco had not been ashamed, he would have raised his hand to this witch, so ugly did she at that moment appear to him with her fat round face, her tiny Oriental eyes, and her chubby figure attired in that red robe, when not long ago she had held such favor in his eyes! No, she was not the same Breyndele Kozak as before, absolutely not!

CHAPTER 69

He Is Out of His Mind

Five very different people were seated in the box at the Vienna State Theater. They each reacted to the play and to the great Sonnenthal's first entrance according to his or her own perspective.

Holtzman's mind was focused solely on the audience and the sets. *Now that's what I call a theater!* he thought. With God's help, if he were to have a little theater like that in around three years, he would show the world who he was. They would go out of their minds! Let's not fool ourselves. Holtzman was no less competent than these Germans. Some money was available, and energy wasn't lacking, thank God. Only one thing was lacking—where did you find an audience like that?

Holtzman looked down at the sea of faces. He had to concede it was truly an elegant audience filling that splendid theater. The customary curses issued softly from his mouth. Was he cursing the Germans who packed the theater or the fact that these same Jews would hardly prefer the Yiddish theater he planned to establish in that accursed city? No one could know exactly. "Feh!" Holtzman muttered to himself. "Vienna—some city! I have to put this city behind me and take off for a real Jewish town, the sooner the better. Who would give a fig for this dressed-up crowd with their bare, smooth, uncovered heads, or trade them for one Holeneshti Jew?"

Madame Cherniak was thinking almost the same thing, but from a different point of view. Despite the short time she had known Holtzman, she had come to share his vision. She was looking forward to that happy moment when Holtzman would declare his love for her and say that he was prepared to go "hand in hand" with her, meaning to marry her. Then, ah, then they together would truly establish a theater, and what a theater!

Her thoughts took hold of her and carried her far, far from Vienna, to a Jewish town in Galitzia or Bukovina. There she pictured herself as Madame Holtzman, the wife of the director Holtzman. With God's help, they would own their own company, their own sets, and their own troupe of the most renowned players, among them the young Rafalesco and the leading lady Henrietta, who would by then be Henrietta Rafalesco. Yes, Henrietta Rafalesco! She, Madame Cherniak, would see to it that the match would be made. And if that happened, Holtzman would quit ogling the leading lady like a cat after sour cream and would stop lusting for young actresses, damn him!

Breyndele Kozak's eyes followed Holtzman's every move. She saw very keenly how he danced favors around the leading lady, not at all as he should behave. *I have to hurry and get this foolish girl with the pretty face to marry that curious young man*, she thought, and began to work on a plan. First she had to knock that Rosa Spivak out of his head and make him forget her. Then she would persuade Schwalb to realize that his foolish sister with the pretty face should marry her equal—Rafalesco—and to stop considering entirely unsuitable matches well above her, such as Holtzman.

Breyndele Kozak glanced at Schwalb. He was looking at the stage while imagining a nice glass of beer and some sausage, which was what he really wanted. His thoughts carried him to the buffet, to the white-covered little tables, to the bottles and glasses, the plates and forks, and all the good food. But on the outside he looked as if he were deeply engrossed in the acting, pretending to be charmed by the great Sonnenthal, may the devil carry him off!

Henrietta was also gazing at the stage, but she was entirely pre-occupied. It was a joy to look at her. She was wearing a wig in the latest fashion, was showing off her fanciest clothes, and was decked out in all her jewelry. It was not for the great Sonnenthal that she had put on her best, however, but for the young Rafalesco. He was not yet altogether hers—but there was hope. Ah, leave it to her! Henrietta was an expert at these things. This young man must first be worn down. Let him run off elsewhere for a while, and when he came back to her, ready to lick her boots as they all did, then she would be able to handle him.

But what was going on with him now? Henrietta looked at Rafalesco—he was utterly unrecognizable. Leaning halfway out of the box, he was totally on the stage, so absorbed in the acting that he neither heard nor saw anyone else. No one existed for him except Sonnenthal, the great Sonnenthal. Trembling all over, his face burning, his eyes intense, he wrung his hands, and frequent sighs escaped from deep inside him. Henrietta could not figure out what was happening to him. How could he not tear his eyes from the stage even for a minute, how could he be sitting next to her in the same box without saying a word, without granting her half a glance? Just let the act end, and she would tell him a thing or two. Quiet! The first act had just ended. Rafalesco was simply out of his mind. With tears in his eyes, he pressed everyone's hands. When it came to Schwalb, he embraced and kissed him:

"Now that was acting! That's the way one must act!"

Henrietta stood to the side watching all this and thought to herself, No. *This fellow is out of his mind.*

CHAPTER 70

Still the Dreamer

As soon as the first act ended, Holtzman negotiated with the ushers to go backstage to seek out Sonnenthal. But it turned out Sonnenthal would receive only one of them, the younger one, about whom Dr. Levyus from Lemberg had written him.

"This is a fine how-do-you-do! Do I smell of garlic or something?" Holtzman ranted, but he stopped himself when he saw that his partner, the leading lady, and Breyndele Kozak were listening. Had a hole opened up, he would have jumped in. He was embarrassed before the group, who were exchanging glances. And his partner Schwalb was squinting at him with shrewd eyes, as if to say: *How come? After all those cigars?*

Meanwhile the usher was waiting. Holtzman took Rafalesco off to the side and whispered to him some news he had just learned that night. "This Sonnenthal has a son, a spoiled brat, may he have many problems and short years, a real rascal. That son keeps signing promissory notes, and the father keeps paying out. So you have to be careful that the same won't happen as with the Lemberg magnate, may he croak," Holtzman advised him, leaning over him with his angular frame. "Don't mince words with him, and don't let him spoil things for you. Remember, if you're dining with the devil, you must use a long spoon. Do you understand?"

But at this point our young hero did something that Holtzman could not believe. It is difficult to say why it happened. Was it because Holtzman had so pestered him with all his advice about devils and long spoons? Was Rafalesco still upset from that morning, when Sonnenthal had refused to see them at his hotel? Or was it because he was simply excited?

But just when Rafalesco seemed ready to go backstage with the usher, he suddenly turned to Holtzman and said curtly: "No, I'm not going."

"Huh? What?"

"I'm not going."

"What do you mean, you're not going?"

"That's what I mean."

Holtzman stared at his young protégé's face. In the glare of the bright electric lights, he tried to figure out what was going on with him. How was it possible that the kid wouldn't obey him, Holtzman? That was the first *no* he had ever heard from him. That *no*, and especially the tone in which it was spoken, bore such decisiveness and resolution that Holtzman did not question him further. He simply looked into his eyes again and was stunned. Holtzman must have felt like Balaam, when his ass suddenly began speaking like a human being.

"No is no," he said to Rafalesco, with a slight smile that did not match his expression.

In that moment Holtzman aged by several years. His pointy

nose seemed to lengthen, and his cheeks seemed to become more deeply sunken. His bony shoulders slumped, and he choked and coughed. In the meantime the bell sounded, indicating the end of the intermission. The audience took their seats. In silence our two heroes returned to their box.

As they left the theater, the artists of the newly formed Holtzman, Schwalb & Co. gathered to take a walk through the streets of Vienna, the five from the box and the rest from the gallery, all speaking at the same time and gesticulating, as was their manner. They shared their impressions of the Viennese theater, expressed expert opinions, and interrupted one another with outbursts of loud, noisy laughter. The words *fool* and *blockhead* were tossed about, words often heard among actors. Whom these epithets were aimed at was hard to say, but the talk surely was lively. The shouting could be heard far off, and the laughter even farther. A fresh current of new people with a new language had insinuated itself into the old, elegant Viennese life, and more than one German stopped and stared in amazement at this extraordinary group of people whose remarkable behavior had stirred up more than one street in that quiet, friendly, welcoming city.

But two people did not participate in that fun fest: the director Holtzman and the star of the troupe, Rafalesco. Each was preoccupied with his own thoughts and feelings. Holtzman, walking hand in hand with Breyndele Kozak, was barely listening to her chatter while thinking about the kid, who had for the first time said no to him. The kid was walking arm in arm with the leading lady, Schwalb. She was talking to him and laughing, batting her eyes and flashing her white teeth as he pretended to listen, responding with one word to her ten, but his heart was far away. He pictured himself on the stage in the same role as Sonnenthal, and he vowed to himself, *May my name not be Rafalesco if I am not someday able to act like Sonnenthal!*

And our young dreamer began to dream of a new paradise, an entirely new one. He would throw himself into studying new roles, the same roles that Sonnenthal played. The world would be enchanted by him and would say in one voice that he would soon surpass Sonnenthal. He would be invited to Vienna as a guest artist in the State Theater. Sonnenthal, the great Sonnenthal, would sit in the orchestra and observe his acting, and would be overwhelmed by his performance, leap up onto the stage, throw his arms around him, and kiss him. He would admit loudly for all the world to hear that he had been surpassed by this young artist—Rafalesco.

CHAPTER 71

Both Laugh

That night was difficult for our Holtzman. He could not fall asleep for a long time. His heart felt as heavy as a stone. His unhappy thoughts were going in all directions at once: *What's happened to the kid?* he thought, coughing and tossing. *It's this city's fault, may it burn to the ground. Ever since we arrived in Vienna, the kid's become a different person—as spoiled as an only child. We have to get away from here as soon as possible.*

Now that Holtzman had hit upon this beautiful, lively city as the cause of the kid's newfound independence, it seemed dismal and depressing to him, and the people, ugly, false, and wicked. Everything he felt during that night he then imagined was worse, much worse. All his wonderful plans had gone up in smoke. The people on whom he depended had abandoned and betrayed him in the ugliest way. The worst he feared had happened: he was besieged from all sides; they were after his soul, wanting to rob him of everything he had. They wanted to steal his precious Rafalesco from under his nose.

I must keep an eye on Rafalesco, Holtzman thought. *I have to watch him like a hawk . . . too many suspicious characters . . . who knows who might lead him astray? Who knows what ideas Schwalb and his sister might have? What kind of snake could Breyndele Kozak turn into? One man surrounded by a pack of wolves!*

Holtzman sat up in bed, leaned on his pointy elbow, had a good cough, and called to his young friend, who was lying in the opposite bed, "Rafalesco, are you asleep?"

"No. What is it?"

"I have an idea."

"Which is?"

"Do you hear how I'm coughing?"

"So?"

"I think it's the end of me. We have to be prepared to forget the few gulden and go where my father of blessed memory—"

Rafalesco sat bolt upright in bed and stared at Holtzman with large, frightened eyes.

"Are you crazy? Out of your mind? Or are you talking out of fever?"

Holtzman was pleased that Rafalesco was so frightened. Amid coughing and cursing, he laughed:

"What a little fool you are! May Shchupak have as many miserable years ahead of him as I will live, God willing! I'm just thinking about what *might* happen. I'm considering writing to my mother who is suffering with my little sister in that desolate land. Maybe they'll be able to look after me and help me with my cough."

Holtzman coughed long and hard, drew a deep breath, turned his face to the wall, and fell asleep. And he dreamed he wasn't in Vienna but in Lemberg. While strolling down Karl-Ludwig Strasse, he saw from afar the director of the Lemberg theater, Getzel ben Getzel, with the kid in tow. They walked right past him, without giving Holtzman so much as a glance. This burned him up. His feet propelled him toward them, and he cried out to the kid, at first softly: "Rafalesco!" Nothing. He didn't seem to hear. Again: "Rafa-lesco!" Again and again, louder and louder: "Ra-fa-les-co! Ra-fa-les-co!" But the kid didn't even turn around, acting as if he didn't know him at all! Holtzman couldn't stand it. The strongest person could not withstand such a rebuff. "Eh, whatever happens, will happen! I'll grab that bastard of a Yuckel ben Fleckel by his piggish neck with one hand, and with the other hand I'll punch him in the mouth, one two three, like this—*trach-tarerach!*"

Frightened to death, Rafalesco leaped out of bed and ran over to Holtzman. He saw before him this scene: the night table at Holtzman's head was upside down on the floor amid a broken carafe of water, a shattered glass, a bent candlestick. The watch—Holtzman's gold watch, which he had recently bought himself in Vienna—was smashed in the debris.

"What happened?" Rafalesco exclaimed.

Gazing confusedly with blank eyes at Rafalesco, Holtzman saw the destruction he had caused. He could barely contain himself from laughing.

Happy that the dream was no more than a dream, he said to his young friend:

"I must have been dreaming of bandits, to the devil with it! Look at the damage! God curse me this night!"

And both burst out laughing. They laughed hard for a long time until a knocking on the wall from the next room silenced them.

Although both were laughing, their laughter was not the same. One laughed heartily, spontaneously, while the other's laughter was forced, as he thought: *No, this is not the same kid as before. Even his laughter is not the same as it used to be. I have to keep an eye on him. I have to write my mother and little sister. We have to get as far as we can from Vienna.*

CHAPTER 72

A *"Person of Education"*

The only educated artist in the troupe Holtzman, Schwalb & Co. was the prompter, Benny Gorgel, whom Holtzman had stolen from the Lemberg Theater. Getzel ben Getzel had more than once boasted that no one possessed a better prompter because Benny Gorgel was a "person of education." And for that very reason our Holtzman, along with the leading lady, had spirited him away. Holtzman justified his action: "I myself don't know why I need this person—to look at him, he isn't worth a *groshen*. But you can be sure a person of education will always earn his bread."

Holtzman was right. To look at him, you also wouldn't give a *groshen* for him. He was a dark-skinned young man, almost emaciated, with a nose to be reckoned with, a scrawny neck, and a large Adam's apple that rose and fell when he spoke, as if he were swallowing. He wore shabby, threadbare clothes and a worn-out cap atop unkempt hair that looked more like a load of hay. If he had put some pomade on it or combed it every day, it would at least be presentable. But our prompter did not spend his time on such foolishness. A person of education has better things to do. He should be forgiven for wearing a soiled collar and a peculiar tie. Once you put this all together, you can more easily imagine this odd individual, of whom Holtzman said, "It's disagreeable to see this *shlimazel* even eat a piece of bread. But you have to keep in mind that he is a person of education." Holtzman crowned him with a series of nicknames: first *shlimazel*, then *creature*, and finally *nebbish*.

As a rule, the more education a person has, the more humble

he is about himself, and that is why our prompter was not insulted and allowed himself to be ordered about by everyone and why he did Holtzman's bidding. Holtzman, of course, was of the opinion that a person who worked for someone and needed to eat, no matter how educated, had to earn his bread. Wasn't he, Holtzman, himself a human being? Hadn't he at one time, God preserve us, done the work of three, worked like a slave, eaten slop, and polished Shchupak's boots, may his name be obliterated wherever he is?

That was how Holtzman justified his treatment of our poor prompter, the person of education, who bore his burden quietly, never complaining, never saying a word against anyone, fully accepting that that was the way things were supposed to be.

But for every person a time comes when luck smiles on him and his star shines. That time arrived for our "person of education," and his star suddenly began to shine, and he too was raised up in people's eyes, even those of his boss, Holtzman.

It happened at the time when the troupe Holtzman, Schwalb & Co. departed that "wasteland" Vienna to go out in the world performing theater in the old way: operettas, melodramas, and traditional hackneyed pieces.

One day during a rehearsal it was time for Rafalesco to make his entrance, but the hero was nowhere to be found. Where was the young man? They searched for over an hour—no Rafalesco. Nor was the prompter to be found anywhere.

Holtzman was on the verge of apoplexy. His blood ran cold as he considered all kinds of possibilities, each one more frightening than the next. Ever since he'd heard that no from the kid in the Vienna State Theater, anything was possible. Seized with panic, he began to turn the theater upside down. Madame Cherniak became alarmed that his face had become drawn and pale as death; his pointed nose seemed longer and more prominent, and his keen, alert eyes seemed extinguished. She hovered over him, trying to comfort him, pleading with him to lie down while she prepared a compress of vinegar and water. With violent anger he rejected her compress. Whatever came to his mind, he said to her. Who was asking her to push herself in where she didn't belong? he demanded. He called her names that lately she had become accustomed to hearing from him, but she remained silent. She could do no more than what other poor women had done who had fallen in love unfortunately. She wiped away the tears and kept mum.

Meanwhile people came running with the news: "*Mazel tov,*

they found him!" "Where? Where?" "At the inn, Rafalesco and the prompter, holed up in a room, reading a book."

Holtzman grabbed his top hat and cane. Half dead, he ran to the inn, pale and out of breath. "What happened?" he demanded.

"We've found it, a treasure!" Rafalesco threw his arms around Holtzman, hugged and kissed him. "A treasure! A treasure!"

Holtzman looked at him as if he were a madman: "What treasure? What are you talking about?"

"*Uriel Acosta*, the play we saw the great Sonnenthal acting in Vienna. The prompter found it translated word for word into Yiddish!" That was it. From now on Rafalesco would play no other role except Uriel Acosta. That was final. No more operettas. No more melodramas. No more Purim plays. No more! No more!

Holtzman, clutching his top hat and cane, dropped down onto a broken bench in a cold sweat. What kind of talk was this? What was he saying? What had happened to the kid? What did he mean, he wouldn't play any more operettas? And where did that leave him, Holtzman the director? Had he no more influence? And what would happen with the sets? Costumes? Roles? Plays? Notes? Posters? What was going on here? Was it the end of the world?

Holtzman was ready then and there to tear the prompter to bits. What a nuisance—a "person of education"!

CHAPTER 73

Which Cat Gets to Lick the Plate

From then on, the troupe had a new order of performances. In whatever city they played, they first presented two or three pieces from their regular repertory. Then they put on *Uriel Acosta*. The response to *Uriel Acosta* would be so positive that they had to put it on again and again. In some places the repertory operettas were not even requested, only *Uriel Acosta*. For example, in Paris, where the company did twelve performances, only *Uriel Acosta* was presented. It was, in Holtzman's words, "a smash hit." The reviews compared Rafalesco to the greatest actors and predicted that he would surpass Sonnenthal and all the other famous glittering stars.

Certainly our Holtzman was proud, even puffed up with satisfaction, that a piece of dramatic junk like *Uriel Acosta*, may God not punish him for those words, was bringing as much money into the cash box as the finest operetta, even though it contained no dancing, no singing, no happy lyrics. "What a strange world it is," he would mutter. "They prefer morality tales to happy lyrics. They prefer a half-crazed Acosta on the stage to a beautiful leading lady! But as they say, 'Better junk, so long as you make a living.'"

"He deserved a blessing, that *shlimazel*, the prompter, for digging up that little book," Holtzman said to himself. "When it comes to a 'person of education,' ha ha, you don't know what to expect. You have to dress him up in a secondhand suit, make sure that dunce puts on a white collar and a new necktie, and trim his hair a bit so he won't look altogether like a small-town hick."

He raised the prompter's salary, gave him his well-earned respect, and stopped referring to him as a *shlimazel*, *creature*, *nebbish*, and other choice names. "If it is God's will, a broom handle can become a gun," he said. He began twirling his mustache in the style of Kaiser Wilhelm II, and he went around with his hands in his pockets in order to better display the gold double watch-chain on his white vest. And he thanked God that He, blessed be His name, had given him this success without benefit of magnates or famous artists, let them lie in purgatory together with Shchupak, may his name be cursed and erased.

All our Holtzman now lacked was a woman to look after things. You might think he already had one, and one free of charge at that—Madame Cherniak. She oversaw all his affairs, guarded every *groshen*, took care of his rooms, and was as loyal as a dog. She mended his clothes, darned his socks, sometimes cooked him a favorite dish, and gave him hot honey and milk *gogl-mogls* to soothe his coughing. The actors ceased calling her Madame Cherniak and Breyndele Kozak and, behind her back, referred to her as Madame Hotzmach. Luckily Holtzman knew nothing of this, otherwise he would have been upset on two counts: that they used his former name, and that they made a terrible match for him. Holtzman had in mind a different match for himself, a younger woman and pretty; for example, a ripe citron like the leading lady, Henrietta. Why not? What was the matter with that? Maybe she didn't have much in the way of brains, but she made up for it by being so pretty it took his breath away. The problem was that she was a bit too lively. But it was still too soon. Let him put a ring on her finger, and aha! he would teach her lessons in propriety and respect, as God commanded for a proper wife.

Once on a Saturday afternoon, Holtzman dressed himself rather like a dandy. Lately he had begun to dress quite stylishly. "Dressed up like a corpse in a casket," the actors said of him. He shaved himself, brushed his mustache upward, perfumed himself heavily, took his walking cane—and invited the leading lady to go for a stroll. She looked him over from top to bottom and cut him dead: "If I miss you, I'll send for you." Holtzman, wiping his lips, looked as if he had been whipped.

Another time he brought up the subject of marriage with her quite directly. It was time, he had said, for her to stop flitting around, fi-fu-fa, and to think about becoming serious. But Henrietta's reply was coarse, not the way you answer a director. "Why should you worry your head about me?" she said to him. "Better worry about your own ass and keep it off my grass." Holtzman got the rhyme and asked her, "How do you know I'm not worrying about myself? Maybe I was thinking about getting married pretty soon." "Really?" she responded with an impudent little laugh. "To whom, tell me— the Angel of Death?"

Our Holtzman wondered about her reasons for this abrupt rejection, until he fell upon the answer with Breyndele Kozak's help. She opened his mind to the fact that he was a big fool. She said, "If your eyes weren't in the back of your head, you would see which cat is licking the plate."

With those words Madame Cherniak was able to calm herself. She needed no longer fear a rival, spend sleepless nights, or shed countless tears. To her it was as clear as day that the match between the leading lady and Rafalesco was all set—whether today or tomorrow, it would happen. And then Bernard Holtzman would be hers. There was nothing more to be said.

CHAPTER 74

Holtzman Has Guests

When Breyndele Kozak informed our Holtzman about the romance between the leading lady Schwalb and Rafalesco, he felt it like a blow to the head. Not only would he be losing a fine little *esrog*,

but their marriage would mean the destruction of one of his glowing dreams, the magnificent plan on which he had hoped to build a
grand edifice.

He had conceived this plan after he received a letter from his
widowed mother, Sora-Brucha. We relate the letter in its entirety,
word for word, as written:

To my dear devoted son, Hershber Holtzman, Long Life. I
write you, my dear devoted Hershber, a letter written down
by Alter, the teacher's young son, Itzik, that first of all, praise
God, I am in the best of health, grant God we hear the same
from you and no worse, amen. And second of all, I am writing you, my dear devoted Hershber, that I haven't received a
letter from you in a long time, and I don't know what in the
world is happening to you. And I beg you, my dear devoted
Hershber, write me of your health and how you are, and your
sister, Zlatke, *kayn eyn horeh*, long life to her, already grown
up, sends regards, you should see her, you wouldn't recognize
her so grown up and pretty, *kayn eyn horeh,* as the day is
long. I'm not saying this because I am her mother but because
everyone says so, and when I look at her my heart aches.
What is the use of her sitting day and night with the needle
mending other people's jackets, we have to begin thinking of a
match for her. Bridegrooms are around by the thousands, but
they are all only worth throwing into the fire. One is Yossel
the carpenter's youngest boy, Fishl; another one is a butcher
boy, Reuben is his name. But she isn't interested in him, she
says he smells of hide, and Yossel the carpenter's boy really
wants her, but he's some sort of a ne'er-do-well, a charlatan,
the devil only knows what, without a proper pair of boots to
his name. I warned him a couple of times to forget my daughter's name or else I'll show him the door. But today's boys are
worse than swine—chase them out the door, and they crawl
in through the window. I know that if your uncle Zalman of
blessed memory were here, he would know how to deal with
this boor. What can I do, in God's name, an old widow and
a poor one at that? If I could give her a big dowry to stop up
a bridegroom's greedy mouth, she would have been a bride
long ago! When it comes to bridegrooms, there's no lack of
them. I'm not worried because she is getting prettier by the

day, you should see this girl, you wouldn't recognize her. She sends her love, and I beg you, my dear devoted Hershber, in the name of God, write me as soon as possible, how you are and especially about your health, because I don't know what to think. Be well, and your mother hopes to see much happiness from you,

Sora-Brucha Holtzman

This letter worked its way into Holtzman's mind, especially the words "*kayn eyn horeh*, a girl you won't recognize." And the great plan was born: "If she really is as my mother describes, maybe it would be a good idea for her to come here with her, let her get acquainted with the kid, maybe he'll be to her liking, and one thing would lead to another, the wedding platters will be broken, they get engaged, and soon, one two three, four sticks are holding up a canopy—and you have a *chuppa*! And then he could stick out his tongue at the whole world—and let us say amen!"

Holtzman reached an understanding with the prompter that he would take down a reply to his mother and keep it secret.

"I want you to write to her in these words," he said:

> *To my dear mother, the respected Sora-Brucha and her beloved daughter, Zlatke,*
>
> Know that I am, thank God, in the best of health and am no longer, thank God, acting in the theater. I now have my own theater and my own troupe and am earning, thank God, good money and am living like a person, and have a bit of a name for myself. Only one thing is lacking—I have no proper place to call a home, and that is why I have decided, my dear mother, you are not to delay any longer, take Zlatke and come here to me where you can be a respected head of my household and have comfort in your old age. Enough working for others, it's time for you to rest your old bones and know a bit of the good life. About Zlatke you are not to worry at all. I have for her a much better match than Yossel the carpenter's son, and even better than the butcher boy, Reuben. So see to it, my dear mother, in the name of God, as soon as you get this letter, do not delay, take Zlatke and come here to me,
>
> *Your son, Bernard Holtzman, director of the theater Holtzman, Schwalb & Co.*

Once he sent off the letter, Holtzman anticipated his guests' arrival any day. But his anticipation was wasted. Instead of seeing them, he received a letter from his mother saying she had received his letter, she was, thank God, in the best of health, and so was Zlatke, *kayn eyn horeh,* he wouldn't recognize her if he saw what a beauty she was, and about her coming to him—if she had wings she would surely fly to him, but how can she come when it costs so much money, two people's fares, crossing the border. If she had what the train alone cost, she would long ago have married Zlatke off, she had no worries about a bridegroom, a thousand if there is one, *kayn eyn horeh,* a girl you should see her, and so forth.

This response so aggravated Holtzman that he sent her money and wrote her a stern letter to come that minute, not to dare think for a second about a match, but to take Zlatke, in the name of God, and come immediately!

That letter was followed by another and another, till God helped, and one end-of-summer evening in a small town in Galitzia a ruckus broke out in the street in front of the theater as they were about to raise the curtain. Some poor old woman with a girl were demanding to see Holtzman. They weren't being allowed entry and so were pushing their way into the theater without money or tickets.

"A curse on your fathers' graves! Bastards, those are my guests!" Holtzman shouted as he arrived at the scene.

"Your guests? Then *mazel tov.* God love you and your guests!" the theater crew cried out, and looked to see who his guests were.

CHAPTER 75

Poor Breyndele Kozak

It was a clear, cool night in the month of Elul. The moon hadn't yet stepped out from her tent to light the earth. But the stars, appearing one at a time, were sufficient to drive away the darkness so that one was able to make out Holtzman's guests.

The eye first discerned a tall, bony, dried-out, emaciated old woman who resembled a spavined, starving nag. Threadbare and shabby, laden down with bedding—featherbeds, pillows, blankets, and plain old rags—she examined everyone carefully, seeking her son among the crowd. Close by her, like a little colt, clinging to her apron, was a young girl, barely out of childhood, with bright rosy fresh cheeks, a slightly upturned child's nose, and thick eyebrows above eyes shyly lowered to the ground. She was clad in a simple cotton dress with a light jacket, over which she wore a yellowish, poorly fastened cloak revealing a full figure, evidence that she was not a child but a maturing girl.

The company of actors gathered around to look at Holtzman's guests. They ignored the older woman, but as soon as she recognized her son, she flung herself on him, blurting out in a deep man's voice, "Oy, a thunderbolt has struck me! Is that really you, Hershber? My darling son!"

The actors preferred to look more closely at the young girl, who was standing to the side in the tight-fitting cloak, waiting for her brother.

She looked oddly charming, that young, innocent, simply dressed creature. She had rosy cheeks like cherries, and thick eyebrows above her lowered eyes. Her whole figure bespoke youth, freshness, and innocence. Not one of the group spoke so much as a word, but Schwalb chortled under his breath from somewhere deep in his big belly, "That's some little apple—wish it were mine!"

That comment slipped by unnoted. The rest stood gaping and speechless in amazement. With their painted faces, false teeth, penciled eyebrows, fake hair, and corseted, unnaturally high breasts, wearing false, provocative smiles on their painted lips, they remembered that they too had once been young, fresh, and as natural as the day their mothers bore them.

Despite the good impression his little sister had made, Holtzman was feeling none too happy. It did not reflect well on him, the director of the troupe, prosperous and well dressed, that his mother and sister should look so bedraggled and poverty-stricken. And look at how the whole troupe was gaping at his miserable-looking relatives. Angrily he shouted at the actors, excoriating them so that his two guests would see that he, Holtzman, was the boss, the director of a theater, and that he was due fear and respect.

Not only could he scold and revile the actors, but if he so desired, he could make mincemeat of his partner, Schwalb. He lit into Schwalb: "Listen, you fat ox, you beer belly, you unkosher pig, you're just as bad as all the other fools here!"

In a split second the crowd dispersed. The management of the evening performance was given over to Schwalb, while Holtzman took over the handling of his guests' bundles, quilts, pillows, blankets, and *shmattes*, bringing the whole lot over to his lodgings.

The morning after the performance Holtzman gathered the company together and served beer in honor of the guests, who were now more presentably dressed. The old woman, in her *Shabbes* woolen headcovering, looked like an old horse with a veil, and Zlatke, now washed and combed, enchanted everyone, not so much with her attire as with her fresh cheeks, thick eyebrows, small teeth, and shy eyes.

"A little apple!" Chaim-Itzik Schwalb exclaimed once more and this time the crowd exploded in laughter. But there were two who were not in a laughing mood—Henrietta Schwalb and Madame Cherniak. All that morning they had been standoffish, in fact quite huffy. Henrietta was unhappy that there was another pretty girl around, and she was angry at Rafalesco for casting his eyes at that small-town little thing with the rough hands and turned-up nose. Henrietta perceived in this little girl a competitor, and however many faults she tried to find, beyond the raw hands and turned-up nose she found none, which upset her all the more.

But if Henrietta Schwalb was unhappy with Holtzman's guests, Madame Cherniak was pitiable. Red spots had appeared on her round moon-face, and her small Oriental eyes welled with tears, though she held herself proudly and tried to smile.

Poor Madame Cherniak felt that her biblical good seven years had come to an end, that soon they would take away her keys and give them to that old witch, whom she wished with all her heart a speedy and easy death.

Madame Cherniak had known the taste of exile. In the past she had been cast aside like an old pot that wasn't needed anymore, or like an old dress that had gone out of style or that one simply had gotten tired of. *That traitor Holtzman*, she thought, *will soon be acting as if things between us were dead and gone. He'll forget everything we once spoke about, and if I remind him, he'll have a half-hour coughing fit.*

Poor Breyndele Kozak! As her heart had foreseen, so it happened. Holtzman was a person for whom things had to proceed quickly and without complications, one two three. In the morning, when she tried to speak to him, he clutched his heart and started to cough so hard he almost passed out. He didn't even thank her for taking good care of him, for looking after his health and well-being.

At midday, quietly, without saying goodbye or shedding a tear, Madame Cherniak moved to new quarters. She packed her bags and, taking heart, put on her red cape. With a broad-toothed smile and a little prancing step, as was her manner, she departed Holtzman's lodgings forever.

Long before I lie in the ground and grass grows over me, I will avenge myself on this Hotzmach, Breyndele Kozak comforted herself, wrapped in her red cape, following all alone behind the wagon carting her belongings.

CHAPTER 76
He Teaches His Guests Proper Behavior

For the first few days Holtzman treated his mother and sister as guests. He saw to it that they ate and drank well and were comfortable. He was always at their side and sat with them every night at the theater in the front row. Zlatke was in seventh heaven as she watched the performances. It all made her head spin. Even old Sora-Brucha, who usually hated theater as much as a kosher Jew hates pork, to please her son gazed with one eye at the stage and with the other at the audience, laughed out loud, and with good humor ridiculed the comedians for all to hear: "What a bunch of *shlimazels*!" Or: "May my pains fall on their heads!" Holtzman had to signal her with his eyes and hands to hush her. In a word, mother and daughter were simply delighted with it all.

But after the warmth of the reunion wore out for our Holtzman, he had to teach them a bit of proper behavior: how to walk, stand, and sit in the theater, and how to behave among people. He had his little sister wear gloves to hide her red hands. He bought her a hat with a large feather, almost like the leading lady's, and dressed her like a princess.

Those high-class clothes did not please Zlatke greatly. On the contrary, she felt cramped and confined in them. Her head ached, her eyes blurred, and she imagined that her nose wasn't right somehow and that everyone could see that. She would happily have worn her old cotton dress with the little jacket. She wished she could once again put on her comfortable, old, worn-out shoes rather than hobble around in the new, tight, pointy ones with the high heels that made her feel like she was walking on stilts. But what could she do when her brother demanded it?

Holtzman looked at his little sister in her new attire, compared her to the leading lady Schwalb, and discovered she was not a bad-looking girl. There was still something unsophisticated about her—she was shy and too quiet. She needed to be polished and refined, taught to converse, be more flirtatious. In a word, she needed to become a *mam'selle*. In the meantime the kid was chatting with Zlatke as she lowered her eyes and turned red as a beet. Holtzman signaled her with his eyebrows to lower her hands and raise her eyes. This only caused her to blush all the more, making Holtzman furious. When he was alone with his sister, he upbraided her, "Why are you afraid of looking him right in the eyes? Have you stolen something?" Or: "Look at those hands of yours!"

He took to giving his old mother a few lessons in proper behavior too, trying to dress her up a bit so that she would look more presentable. "It doesn't look right," he explained to her, "for the director's mother to be dressed like a charwoman." That did it for Sora-Brucha, a plain but outspoken woman—what was on her mind was on her tongue. If her clothes did not meet with his approval and he wasn't happy with his poor mother, she retorted in her masculine voice, she would do him the favor of turning around and going back home with her daughter that very day.

In a trice the old woman was packing up her bundles, quilts, pillows, and blankets. She called to Zlatke, "Come, daughter! Why should we 'charwomen' stay around here among such grand men and women? We might dirty their fancy clothes, God forbid."

Holtzman backtracked and swore on holy oaths to his mother, dropping to one knee, until he convinced the old woman that he hadn't meant what he had said.

But more trouble followed for our Holtzman when he decided to make an actress of his sister. Like a stubborn mule, the old Sora-Brucha stood her ground: "Absolutely not! I'd rather she died than carry on with those comedians on the stage. Not while I'm still alive!" In short, nothing would convince her. It threw Holtzman into a cold sweat, and he was consumed by a chest-wracking cough that finally brought up blood.

The sight of her son's blood frightened the old woman: "God in heaven! Dear God!" And she gave her approval—but only on condition that he saw to it that Zlatke was first married. He swore in the presence of two witnesses that within six months she would have a bridegroom and would be standing under the wedding canopy fulfilling God's commandment.

CHAPTER 77

Tertle-Mertle

Czernowitz—the capital of Bukovina. Dominating the market square, its windows looking out on the shops below, stood a proud grand hotel named the Black Rooster ready to receive guests. Here the itinerant theater Holtzman, Schwalb & Co. was staying, but the Black Rooster would need God's help before it would turn a profit from them. The troupe occupied only three or four rooms, and they ate at nearby kosher kitchens—or some of them did, as not every artist had the money. Especially during the monthly break in performances, the so-called unclean days, they lived on what they earned from studying their roles, rehearsing, and playing Tertle-Mertle.

This was a card game anyone could play: you didn't need to be too clever, you didn't need a certain number of people, and you could play any way you wished, even standing up. It appealed to actors, musicians, merchants, and anyone who had no time to waste and wanted to play a hand on the run.

The room where the crowd played Tertle-Mertle was so thick with smoke that one could barely make out who was there, even at midday when the sun was shining. Chaim-Itzik Schwalb was the banker, and his face was redder than ever, almost as if his skin had peeled away. He was angry and in a very bad temper. Having spread out his cards, one card after another, he was in misery. Almost every card was for him a loser. Not only had he been forced to pay off many times over, but the winners were needling him mercilessly. From all sides they were reaching out for their cards, as insults and curses flew over his head.

"Schwelbele! For me, three kings and two boils for your red face!"

"Here, Schwelbele—for a high spade and four curses for you!

"Schwalb, I'm going to take you to the cleaners today!"

"Schwalb, I'm going to drain you dry!"

"You'll be a dead man, Schwelbele, when I'm through with you!"

"Aha, *momzer*! I beat you! Hand over the money!"

The more they needled Schwalb, the more he seethed, and the more he seethed, the more he lost and fumed and burned like a straw roof going up in flames.

"Damnation! Quit! Give the bank to someone else. Don't you see, you fool? It isn't going your way!" Holtzman advised him as a partner and a good friend. For that he earned an ugly retort from the infuriated Schwalb.

"Get out of here, you Yadashviler dog. Who asked for your advice?"

And the banker boiled and dealt cards and glared with red, fiery eyes into the pot, seeing his money rapidly diminishing. With a deep sigh, he reached into his bosom pocket and with trembling fingers withdrew a fat wad of money. At the sight the crowd grew livelier.

"Going for broke, eh Itzikl? Go, go—dig yourself a deep hole," taunted one of the emaciated actors with a prominent Adam's apple, and the director's sister, Zlatke Holtzman, erupted with laughter. Everyone turned to stare at her, which made her turn red with shame to the tip of her nose.

Rafalesco felt sorry for her and suggested they bet together on an ace of clubs. "Today the ace of clubs is lucky," he promised. She turned even redder and looked at him with grateful eyes, and her heart almost burst. *Ach, if he would only keep on speaking to me, standing close to me,* Zlatke was hoping. As if guessing her desire, Rafalesco went over and stood close to her.

The smell of his long blond hair almost drove her mad. *My God! How can there be on earth an angel like this boy with the long, blond, sweet-smelling hair and the fine, mild eyes? No, there never was and there will not be another!* Whenever she stood close to him, her heart would pound, and she felt faint, losing track of where on earth she was. Whatever she was holding would fall from her hands. Her mother, noticing it, would comment loudly: "What's the matter, my daughter?" and she would blush even more and reprimand herself. She was thrilled to be standing in the aura of this angel. When he happened to grant her a glance, even one glance, with his gentle, bright, shining eyes, it was as if he were the sun, shining for her alone. What did it matter to poor Zlatke that those eyes were looking at her just as they looked at others?

Chaim-Itzik Schwalb had dealt out more than half the deck of cards and gathered the money into the pot. Slowly, very slowly, he began to deal from the second half, one card after another. The crowd eyed the cards greedily as he slapped them down on the table—the noise grew, and curses flew, as did the laughter—while Schwalb became more upset and kept on paying out money. The ace of clubs showed up in the fourth deal, and the crowd shouted: "Who has the ace of clubs?" "Rafalesco! Why don't you say something? Take the money!"

"We won," Rafalesco whispered to Zlatke, and she was in seventh heaven, not because they had won, but because Rafalesco was speaking to her. Rafalesco showed the banker his card, and the group envied him: "It always goes his way. How about that! What a lucky guy! Somebody up there is looking after him."

And the actors let out their bitter hearts to Schwalb the banker: "Schwelbele! The ace of clubs. Four to one odds. Pay up, Itzikl, pay, pay!"

"I'm paying, I'm paying!" the banker said, and counted out the money, and handed it to Rafalesco with a smile. Rafalesco was not the same as the others. He didn't act triumphant when he won, and he didn't make a fuss or curse himself when he lost. Rafalesco was a rare bird, in no way like the others. He was beloved by all the actors and actresses. More than anyone, the director's sister, poor Zlatke Holtzman, loved him to distraction.

CHAPTER 78

A Telegram from London

Zlatke did not welcome her new acting career. When she shared the stage with Rafalesco, her hands and feet turned numb. The mere sight of him, or the sound of his voice, would rattle her to the point that she feared they might have to lead her off the stage. She did not know what came over her. More than once she was rebuked by her brother. (Holtzman was a strict director, even with his own sister.) He said in front of all the other actors:

"So, Zlatke, today you acted like a real dumb cow! You should have your hands and feet lopped off for such a performance!"

Zlatke knew this was true. But was it her fault that she had fallen in love with Rafalesco at first sight? Really, had it been that bad for her at home, back in that small town? Hadn't she learned to sew jackets, and wasn't she beginning to earn some money? But no, her brother had besieged them with letters, one after another, and had sent money for them to come, the sooner the better! And so they came. And the troupe had immediately put her to work as a soubrette, dressing her up in a short dress and tight little shoes that made her eyes pop. They painted her cheeks with rouge, drew black lines under her eyes, and taught her how to stand, how to walk, how to turn, and how to bat her eyes. And who had taught her all this? Her brother, her own brother! When she complained to her mother, Sora-Brucha said: "Think, if you were working for a stranger and they asked you to climb up on the roof, would you be better off?" Then her brother wanted to make her into a leading lady, but she had no singing voice. He grew furious at her, mimicking her singing: "You are screeching, little sister, like a cat whose tail has been stepped on."

Only when her brother gave her the role of Yehudit in *Uriel Acosta* to learn did Zlatke feel lighter of heart, not only because she liked the role but also because playing opposite her, in the role of Acosta, was Rafalesco. Ach! What a beautiful name, *Rafalesco, Rafalesco.* For his sake alone it was worth toiling, learning roles, repeating like a parrot strange words that she didn't begin to understand, and treading out nightly onto the stage that God alone knew she hated. Oh, how she hated the stage, the theater, the artists—the whole company!

And more than anyone else she hated her brother's partner, Chaim-Itzik Schwalb. She couldn't bear to look at his red face, because he was always rubbing up against her in the wings when no one was looking. He pestered her, pinched her, asked her if she loved him: "My little apple! Do you love me, little apple?" Zlatke thought to herself, *May God love him as much as I do, that swollen beet-face!* and fled. She would have run to the ends of the earth, but she was afraid of her brother. She would spit at the theater in a minute but would regret leaving Rafalesco.

Ach, Rafalesco! Rafalesco! That dear, sweet name was always on her lips. That dear, sweet name was in all her dreams, and more than once, lying in bed at night, she would clasp the little pillow at her head, and recall her role of Yehudit and say to herself: *What harm can it do if I press him to my breast?* And she drew the little pillow to her warm girlish breast and lavished passionate kisses on it in the dark while whispering the dear, sweet name: "Rafalesco! Rafalesco!"

In the morning when her mother woke her, the first thing that came to her mind was sweet, dear Rafalesco. Soon she would be

seeing him again. Soon she would be together with him at rehearsals. Soon she would again be standing with him on the stage. And
with a feeling that only she could know, she would be standing
close, close to him. She would drink in his every word, his sweet
words: "Yehudit! Yehudit! You are the flower on whose every petal
are inscribed the hot tears that have made us one." Before long her
heart would pound, *Rafalesco! Rafalesco!*

Whenever she set eyes on him, she almost swooned. Her limbs
would become cold as ice, and she would turn all colors. She would
blush and hide her face so no one would see.

No one in the company noticed a thing—they were too involved
in their card games. Only Holtzman—who saw things even when
he wasn't looking, and heard things even when no one was speaking—saw everything, heard everything, and thought in his heart,
*Good, good, may no evil come of it. The kid is in the trap. If we are
worthy of God, we will, in short order, be sticking our tongues out
at the world—and let us say amen.*

"Water ox! Why aren't you moving? Deal the cards!" Holtzman
scolded his partner.

"I'm dealing! I'm dealing!" Schwalb answered and dealt the
cards, his face always red as fire. At that moment there was a knock
at the door. "Come in," cried several voices at the same time. And the
door opened—a telegram. "Who is the telegram for?" "For Chaim-
Itzik Schwalb." "Who is it from?" "From someone in London."
"What kind of telegram?" "Take it easy. Let him read it." "Schwalb
can't read! He should be ashamed of himself!"

First Schwalb distributed the money from the bank, which took
him a little time because you had to have the head of a treasurer
to remember what everyone was due. A fine shower of curses fell
on the banker's head and, as was customary, sharp words flew in the
air.

Having distributed the money, Schwalb stole out to the hotel
owner for him to read his telegram. The crowd grew impatient.
What secret was Schwalb keeping from his partner? Most impatient
of all was Holtzman himself. He could not abide that he was left
sitting with everyone else, as if he were of no account. He raged at
himself for having tied himself to that obnoxious nobody: *The devil
take that cigar-maker!* But in came Schwalb with a glowing face,
proclaiming to the group:

"Kids, we're going to London!"

Unimaginable bedlam broke out among the actors when they heard that news. One of them leaped up onto the table and raised his right arm: "Whee! London? London! London! London! Long live London!"

Another slapped himself on the calves: "As God is my witness, I've always wanted to go to London!"

A third—a tall, skinny actor with checkered trousers—drew himself up to his full height, stuck his hands into his pants pockets, stared with big bulging eyes, and began speaking English in a singsong: "Oh, yes yes, my dear my beer my cake my steak my ring my king!"

A fourth slapped a fifth on the back and did a dance step, singing along in a hoarse voice a Russian song, God knows how he learned it: "Eh, *buav tay nema, tay poaychav do mlina!*"

"Pipe down, you bastards!" Holtzman shouted, in order to show who was still boss, and pounded the table with his fist. "Look how they've gotten excited. Big deal! Not an ounce of respect for your boss! Curses on you! May boils break out on your bodies!"

And to Schwalb he bellowed, "So show me the telegram, Schwelbele!"

"Show you the telegram?" said Schwalb, stalling. "Show you the telegram? Yes, sure. You think I won't show it to you? I will show it to you, but not right now, a little later. First I have to tell you something. Come on down to the Cellar—I'll show it to you there."

And Schwalb turned his face to the company. "Who's coming down to the Cellar with me?"

"What do you mean, who? All of us!"

"To the Cellar! To the Cellar!"

Pushing and shoving one another, the crowd left the Black Rooster and headed for the Cellar.

CHAPTER 79

In the Cellar

The Cellar was little more than a small room, really more like an alcove in which wine was served. But in Czernowitz they called it the Cellar. If you say "Let's go to the Cellar" to someone, he knows you mean Meyer Beshel's, the owner of the Cellar, named after his father, Beshel, who had also been a winekeeper.

When they arrived at the Cellar, our artists ordered whatever they pleased—a little *tsimmes,* a plate of beef stew with cucumbers, or just plain cucumbers, each according to the state of his purse after playing Tertle-Mertle. Schwalb announced he would pick up the tab.

"Today the wine is on me!" he said.

From the first glass of muscat that Schwalb downed, his tongue loosened, and he began telling his partner the story, as he promised. He would tell it from beginning to end, he said, the whole truth. May God be his witness, he would hold nothing back. Why should he lie when the truth was straightforward and as plain as day? In his heart he had long been aware that Holtzman considered him superfluous, absolutely superfluous, and yet he had pretended that it wasn't so and had stayed on. And for whose sake? For the sake of his sister.

But for some time now the leading lady had been feeling that she too had dropped out of favor. Since they had discarded all the best operettas to perform *Uriel Acosta* and other such empty pieces, the theater had become Rafalesco and more Rafalesco and yet again Rafalesco. Well, that in itself didn't bother him. *Uriel Acosta* was, after all, *Uriel Acosta.* But what about his sister? She also wanted applause. So he had thought it over and sent off a letter to his brother Nissel in London, telling him the whole story, every last detail. That was the way Schwalb always did things.

And his brother Nissel wrote back: "Blockhead! How long are you going to drag yourself from place to place? Why don't you and our sister come here to London? I have a gem of a theater. It's called the Pavilion. What a theater! But the artists are oafs, blockheads, idiots, each one worse than the one before. They rake in the money by the handful because the public is not very particular. Whatever you put before them, they gobble up and lick their fingers. I've already spoken with the right people, and they assure me, 'Just let your brother come here with your sister, the little leading lady, and we'll make the pot sweet enough.' They say they've heard about her and read about her in the newspapers. Good news travels fast."

Chaim-Itzik sent back a letter saying that going there was easy, but he had to know under what circumstances they would be going: conditions, guarantees, contracts. A reply quickly arrived: "Idiot that you are! If I tell you come, you can be sure everything you mention is all set." Chaim-Itzik's reply was: "I have enough money, and our sister has enough money. Send a telegram, and we'll be on our way." That was what this telegram was about.

"So? Now what do you have to say about my brother?" Schwalb said to his partner, sticking his red face up close.

"What should I say?" Holtzman answered almost cold-bloodedly, staring down at his fingertips. "I've always told you that your little brother was a worthy person and that you're not worth the soles of his shoes. Of course it's bearable being in Czernowitz if you have a rich brother in London—what is there to talk about? But still, I'd like to see that telegram."

Schwalb took a gulp from his glass. "Can you read?"

"I don't need to read. I just want to have a look at it."

"Haven't you ever seen a telegram? It's a telegram like all telegrams!" said Schwalb, and showed it to him by the light of the window. And before Schwalb knew it, the telegram was in Holtzman's hand.

A minute later Holtzman's prompter and newly appointed secretary, the "man of education," was called in. This was what he read in the telegram: YOU CAN COME ONLY IF YOU BRING RAFALESCO.

The director said nothing to his partner, not a word. He simply slapped Schwalb with the telegram on both sides of his red face.

CHAPTER 80

Who Is That Person?

The acclaimed itinerant troupe Holtzman, Schwalb & Co. was preparing to depart from Czernowitz and take to the road. Nissel Schwalb had sent them a Yiddish newspaper from London—on the first page was printed a large advertisement in screaming headlines:

!!A SENSATION!!
!!!AMAZING NEWS!!!
Leo Rafalesco, the Renowned Yiddish Star
Who Has Astounded the World—Soon Coming to
London, to the Pavilion Theater!!!

They had already begun packing for the journey. Only one performance remained in Czernowitz, in honor of Rafalesco. Eagerly

awaiting the performance were the Czernowitz youth and the intelligentsia, who had snapped up almost all the tickets. The young
people arrived from all the surrounding little towns, in which Yiddish theater had not been seen since the days of Adam.

For an artist a full house was a guarantee of success, so Rafalesco
desired intensely to show the public what he was capable of achieving.
With each performance he had lit up the stage with the same passion
as he had with his first. It had been a long time since Rafalesco had
felt as good as he did that evening. He mustered all his powers and
succeeded in portraying Uriel Acosta as a reserved, solitary, profound
philosopher, a veritable Spinoza. He did not consciously intend to do
so; it came from within himself instinctively. He was able to achieve
this considerable artistic triumph because of his extraordinary natu-
ralness, the hard-won fruit of a war he waged heroically not against
another but within himself.

Perhaps the triumph could not have been greater anywhere than
in Czernowitz, which had its own tragedies, because that performance movingly portrayed those who wage war silently against
darkness. Such unknown heroes rarely win, as Uriel Acosta does.
At the end the theater exploded with loud applause and roaring ovations. The young students carried the sensational Rafalesco out on
their shoulders, strew him with flowers, and laid gifts at his feet—
since the other actors hankered after them, Holtzman hid them
away. Some young people read speeches, but no one listened except
a few other students. The evening was a rare triumph even for so
beloved and acclaimed an artist as Rafalesco.

After the first act Holtzman, as usual keeping an eye on things,
noticed an odd-looking person, somehow familiar, among the students. He had a sleepy face and bulging eyes, and Holtzman did not
like him from the moment he saw him. Somehow he managed to
sneak into the wings at the intermissions and kept trying to force
himself into the wings, heading straight for Rafalesco. Holtzman,
offended, asked him to go back. "Uncle!" he said curtly. "Don't go
where you're not supposed to, and don't make a fuss about it."

After the second act the sleepy-eyed man with the bulging eyes
was again pushing himself toward Rafalesco. Holtzman shoved him
out with a few sharp words—"A pig of a Jew. You ask what he's
doing here, and he acts deaf." After the third act Holtzman again
caught him at the door, a mere two steps away from Rafalesco. He
grabbed him by the collar and unceremoniously threw him out,

blessing him and all other intruders with "May you have an agonizing pain on the left side of your belly, devil take you!"

Much later, at the very end of the performance, when the artists were changing their clothes, Holtzman noticed from afar that the sleepy-eyed man had managed to steal into Rafalesco's dressing room. Like an enraged tiger, Holtzman sprang at him—but before he could grab him by the throat, this person was embracing the kid, and they were hugging and kissing like two brothers.

Holtzman's jaw dropped, his eyes widened, and he stood dumbstruck. If his father from the Other World had come back, he could not have been more astounded. At that moment Holtzman looked like a block of clay, like an unfinished statue in which the sculptor had wanted to portray horror but failed. His odd, long, pimply face looked somehow comical and his sharp eyes seemed to say:

Jews! Cut me to pieces! Throw my flesh to the dogs! But tell me, who is that person kissing the kid?

CHAPTER 81

His Mother Is Dead

Who remembers Benny Rafalovitch's bookkeeper, the gloomy fellow with the bulging eyes from Holeneshti called by the fine name Sison v'Simcha? That was the man embracing Rafalesco.

What was he doing in Czernowitz? Why had he come? What was new in Holeneshti? How were Benny Rafalovitch and his family? How were Yisroyeli the cantor, his wife, Leah, and their young daughter, Reizel? About all this Sison v'Simcha would spend the night telling Rafalesco.

When the two left the theater for the Black Rooster, they went to Rafalesco's room, asking Holtzman to be left to themselves.

"Ach! With the greatest pleasure!" Holtzman said, winking a sharp eye at the gloomy man with the bulging eyes, and left them together, announcing loudly that no one was to disturb them. May no shame come to him, but our director stationed himself in the adjacent room with his ear glued to the wall. And so he heard every word of the conversation between the kid and the gloomy man from Holeneshti.

"Listen, my dear soul, to what I have to tell you," Sison v'Simcha began in his monotonous voice, which was a bit more animated than usual. "I have much to tell you. Three nights and three days wouldn't be enough. First Holeneshti—it isn't the same as before. It's more like Odessa, Warsaw, Paris! And the people—not the same. And what do we have to thank for that? The Yiddish theater. Remember?

"From that time on everything changed for us, altogether changed, do you hear? How changed, I myself don't know, but changed. Never mind about your family. Your family was totally turned upside down! First, your father. When you absconded that Friday night—do you remember?—he declared that no matter what, you should be found and brought back dead or alive, but brought back! And your brother Anshel and I—are you listening?—rode out into the wide world looking for you. The truth surfaced like oil on water. According to the police and witnesses, your disappearance could only be the work of Shchupak, and he had no other place to go but Romania.

"So we also made our way to Romania. We arrived—are you listening?—in Yas and began asking everybody if they had seen two *shlimazel* Yiddish actors, one with an ugly wrinkled face, the other one a slight fellow with devilish eyes and a spring in his step. They had seen many Yiddish *shlimazel* actors, and they all had ugly faces and devilish eyes, but whether they had a spring in their step, they had not noticed. The next time they would pay better attention. What do you say to those Moldavian jokers? Listen, we realized Yas was a lost cause. That was bad, bad—what to do? We kept traveling on farther and farther till we arrived in Bucharest. On the way your brother Anshel vowed to me that his name would not be Anshel if he did not find you! I said that I hoped it would be so, 'From your mouth to God's ears.'

"Once we arrived in Bucharest, your brother began to live it up, may the One Above protect all Jews! We had been given a hatful of money, so what did he care? Any theater, any café, any wine cellar, we were there. I begged him, 'Anshel, what are you doing? You are burning up money!' He said, 'It's none of your business. Shut up!' Bad, bad, what to do? I shut up. One day, two days, and three went by, money was melting like snow, hardly anything was left. So he said, 'Write to my father to send money.' I begged him, 'Anshel! In God's name, where is this all leading?' And he said: 'It's none of your business. If I tell you to write—write!' Bad, bad, what to do? We were once sitting in a nightclub called Paradise. Girls were dancing and singing, and one in particular. Marinesco-Milanesco was her name, quite a good-looking woman, and a cunning gypsy for knowing how to get money out of you.

"I happened to look toward the door—are you listening?—and right there at the door were standing two familiar-looking people, both dressed up. I looked more carefully, and I could swear it was you, Leibel. *Yes, it's him, it's him,* I thought, *as I am a Jew!* I stood up and called out to your brother, 'Anshel, look, he's here, he's here!' 'Who?' he said. 'Leibel.' 'You're dreaming, you're asleep,' he laughed. Back and forth this went until I decided to run to the door, but by that time they had gone. Bad, bad, what else to do?

"Meanwhile a letter arrived from Holeneshti with the news that your mother was seriously ill and that Anshel should come home as soon as possible. I said to Anshel, 'Are we going?' He told me to write a letter saying we had picked up the trail, and to please send more money. I said, 'Anshel, in God's name, let us either go home or go on farther. Make up your mind.' He said to me, 'None of your business. If I tell you to write, write!' Bad, bad, what to do? I wrote a letter to your father: 'This is the way it is. You have to know that our journey is a waste of time, money has been thrown away, and we are accomplishing nothing. And what I've written to you before about leaving no stone unturned—I wrote it only because Anshel told me to write it.' What could I do? I wrote—I am no more than a human being! I am told to write, I write. So I wrote, 'Don't send any more money because if you stop sending money, we'll finally have to come home.' That's how I wrote, hiding it from Anshel. What else could I do? Tell me if I did wrong. Just listen. Barely eight days went by—are you listening?—when a telegram arrived, short and to the point, only four words: 'Come home. Mother died.'"

As soon as Sison v'Simcha uttered those words, Rafalesco grabbed him by the hands:

"What? What did you say? My mother?"

"May she rest in peace. How could it have ended otherwise? It's a miracle she lasted that long. She was already, please forgive me, skin and bone, her body could barely contain her soul, and she had great sorrow because of your father, surely you must remember, and then one shock after another. I don't know which of you she loved more, you or Anshel. As long as Anshel was in Bucharest, she still had hope that you and he would return together. But once she heard that—are you listening?"

No, Rafalesco no longer heard him. He buried his head in his hands and began weeping and sobbing like a small child. Sison v'Simcha was at a loss. To give solace, to let another pour out his heart, to speak a comforting word—that he was not made for. He wrung his hands and muttered, "Bad, bad! What to do?" Meanwhile Rafalesco's weeping was heard in the other rooms, and people came to see what was happening, first Holtzman, then old Sora-Brucha, and after her Zlatke, all wondering what the trouble was.

"What has happened? What's going on?" all three questioned as they barged into the room.

"My mother died," said Rafalesco, his voice breaking, and he fell onto Holtzman's neck in tears. Holtzman could not control himself, and his face screwed up like that of a woman about to cry. Both Zlatke and old Sora-Brucha wrung their hands and lamented and keened:

"Woe is me! A thunderbolt has struck me! A poor mother of children, tiny, helpless little birds! Who will feed them? Who will take care of them? Who will worry about these abandoned orphans who are left without anyone? As long as a mother is a mother, the father is a father, but once the mother is gone, better not to live to see it—"

"Be quiet! You're running off at the mouth!" Holtzman assailed his mother, and he upbraided the sleepy-eyed bookkeeper for the news he had brought the kid.

"Who asked you? Who forced you to say anything? You should have had someone else bring the news."

Sison v'Simcha sat as if he had been whipped, but Rafalesco came to his defense. He let it be known that Sison v'Simcha was his guest and that they should all leave the two of them alone tonight. Holtzman understood, and though he was reluctant to leave the kid alone with this bearer of bad tidings, he had no choice. Things had changed; if Rafalesco wanted something done, that was how it would be. Holtzman turned and poured out his wrath on his mother and sister:

"Why did you two come here, for God's sake? Who sent for you? What's all this wailing and lamenting about? Who asked you to be the hired mourners?" he shouted, and shoved them out of the room. Then he slipped back into his room, seated himself at his previous spot, and placed his ear against the wall. Rafalesco, alone with Sison v'Simcha once again, asked the bookkeeper to give him all the details of how and when his mother had died. Had they viewed her body before the burial? What was the funeral like? All this Sison v'Simcha had to tell him, not once, not twice, but many times. Many times!

CHAPTER 82

News from Holeneshti

That night no sleep came to their eyes. As Rafalesco listened, Sison v'Simcha related news from Holeneshti in a monotonous voice that droned on and on, rising and falling like a broken bell drawn out like thick honey. He neither paused nor stopped and interlaced everything with "just listen" and "are you listening?" and "bad, bad, what to do?" Nor did poor Holtzman sleep. Unable to tear himself from the wall, he could not even get up from his chair lest they heard it scrape against the floor. At some moments Holtzman cursed his cough, which he had to suppress several times. Always on the brink of coughing, holding it in with all his might, he sat miserably listening to the news from Holeneshti.

That night he and Rafalesco both learned more about Holeneshti than in all the years they had been away on the road.

First, Benny Rafalovitch. Alas, what had became of Rafalovitch's household! It was a ruination. A catastrophe. It had started with Rafalovitch's wife, Beylke. Tiny, quiet, frail Beylke had expired like a candle. Quietly, without complaint, she left this world where she had suffered so much for her children, never having known a good day. She wished to die as she had lived, quietly, and so she told no one what ailed her, but when things became visibly worse, Benny sent for the best doctors. He ordered them to do everything at any cost, down to the last shirt on his back, if only Beylke would recover. But it was too late. Curled up in a ball like a very small child, Beylke lay alone in her large bed in an alcove with tightly shut lips and deeply sunken white cheeks. No one, no one was at her bedside. Benny was preoccupied with the doctors. The eldest sons were tied up in the business, and the daughters were in the kitchen. Anshel and Leibel were gone. Only Bat-Sheva, the youngest daughter, sat in a far corner, weeping silently so as not to wake her mother. But she could no longer wake her mother. Her mother was now deeply asleep. Her closed eyes were like two black holes in her too-white face. Her blond, once very beautiful brows were still visible under her white forehead, shaded by a white headcovering, lending her small face a childlike, thoughtful, dreamy appearance. One small hand, a bit too white, hung down from the quilt. She looked as if she were in a deep sleep. It was quiet. A heart that had loved so much, and that had suffered so much because of her love, had ceased loving, suffering, and struggling. The quiet was a frightful, holy stillness. It was the stillness of death. Beylke had died.

Beylke had died, and the old grandmother, Benny's mother, the one whose head always shook "no no," lived on! She was now senile and blind in both eyes, yet she lived on. Who knows the answer to the riddle of why!

After Beylke's death her sons and daughters, some married with their own families, went their separate ways. Benny had never gotten along with his children, but once Beylke died, their relations became worse. He married off Anshel to that ugly but rich girl from Beltz and forbade him to come into his father's presence. Benny never forgave him for that journey to Bucharest. So Anshel lived in Beltz, where he owned a tobacco shop and became so stout as to be unrecognizable. One daughter, the middle one, Perel was her name, was divorced from her husband. Another one, Yocheved, to spite her father, married Yechiel the *klezmer*'s brother, also a musician.

And the very youngest, Bat-Sheva, was going to become a midwife, but Benny, again out of spite, married her off to Sison v'Simcha the bookkeeper. Here Sison v'Simcha lowered his eyes and defended himself. He had long cast an eye on Bat-Sheva, he admitted, even though he had never done anything about it. Then again, did Yechiel the *klezmer* really have a better family? In any case, Simcha was one of the Rafalovitches' own, a distant relative but a relative nevertheless. Bat-Sheva was not too enthusiastic about the match—in fact, she raised a fuss, threw tantrums, protested loudly, wept, and upset everyone around her, threatening to do something awful to herself. It made even Simcha feel ill at ease. Bat-Sheva was really a fine girl, one might say the best of all of them, but he was unwilling to force himself on her. Benny Rafalovitch was stubborn. Once he decided something, it had to be.

In the end they were married—and nothing bad happened. Thank God, they already had two little children and another one on the way. Things would have gone well for them if not for the new misfortune that had befallen them.

"What misfortune?" Rafalesco asked, frightened. Sison v'Simcha hurried to reassure him, "Nothing. Nothing. Not really a misfortune. Your father, my father-in-law, long life to him, in his old age became intensely religious, apparently out of despair. And in what way religious! Fanatically! He involved himself deeply in

Yiddishkeit, are you listening? Day and night all he did was pray and recite the psalms. All right, that alone wouldn't be so bad, but there was a bigger problem. What bigger problem? The *rebbe*! Your father, my father-in-law, long life to him, overnight became a Chasid, a zealous, fiery Chasid, and began visiting the *rebbe,* and not just visiting but staying there, not taking so much as a step away from the *rebbe*'s courtyard. First it was the Stefaneshter *rebbe,* Reb Matityahu. Now it's the Boyaner *rebbe.* It's now been more than a half year since he's attached himself to the Boyaner and refuses to come home. He went to Boyan for the High Holidays, and he's stayed on there since.

"I realized it was a problem, so I wrote him, one letter after another, 'For God's sake, beloved father-in-law, when will this all end? Your little bit of remaining business is going to ruin!' Does the wall answer? He had in mind only that I should send him money, are you listening? What do I have, a well? Even a well runs dry! It was bad, bad—what to do? I thought it over carefully and made my way to Boyan to have a talk with my father-in-law. I couldn't just let him stay there. But go talk to the wall. When someone has dug himself into something like that, it's only *rebbe, rebbe,* and again *rebbe.* Speaking to him of home, of Holeneshti, was impossible—he wouldn't hear of it. To remind him of the children was forbidden. And never mind the names of Leibel and Anshel—they were not to be remembered, not to be mentioned. For him, Anshel was the Angel of Death who had murdered his own mother. If not for Anshel and his fine journey to Bucharest, my father-in-law said, he would not now be a widower. That was as certain as the day was long.

"Listen further. I arrived in Boyan and found him—may my sorrow befall my enemies . . . Listen to me, I can't say it, my heart hurts too much. You should see him, half the size he once was. His belly hangs down. His cheeks are sunken. He's old and gray. I broke down in tears. And he—he did not so much as ask about the children. Nothing, absolutely nothing. He only wanted me to go with him to the *rebbe,* right that minute, nothing else would do. I tell you he was stronger than iron. You can draw a moral from this person. I tried to speak to him, to talk about home and ask where this was all leading, but he wouldn't allow it. Tomorrow, he said, tomorrow. Today he had to be with the *rebbe.* And it went on like that day after day.

"In the meantime, while I was staying at the inn, I heard some young folks chatting about Czernowitz, about Yiddish theater, and about a benefit that was being put on by a famous actor from Bucha-rest, still a boy, named Rafalesco. The name Rafalesco, the city Bucharest, and the words *an actor, a young boy*, immediately rang a bell, are you listening? *Can this be our Leibel*? I thought. There had to be a connection: Bucharest . . . Rafalesco . . . Yiddish theater . . .

"I decided that I was already paying for travel expenses—let it cost a little more, I had to see this young actor from Bucharest for myself. First I had to talk it over with your father, to hear what *he* had to say about it. But where would I begin? When he heard the words *Yiddish theater* he became—what can I tell you? A corpse looked better than your father. He shook, grabbed his cane, are you listen-ing? and said he would split my head open if I spoke another word! Bad, bad, what to do? I left, hired a carriage to take me straight to Czernowitz, and paid through the nose. If I had known how much it would cost, I would have gone on foot, no matter how far, just to see you alive, thank God. And the acclaim you received in the theater tonight, will you believe me? When I heard the shouting and clap-ping and cries of "Rafalesco!" and when the young people carried you off on their shoulders, tears came to my eyes, as I am a Jew! I had to remind myself, God help me, that this was actually our Lei-bel, the very one who slept in the bed next to mine in the alcove!"

Here Sison v'Simcha wiped away a tear, and suddenly his voice changed and he said to Rafalesco endearingly yet slyly:

"Do you remember, my dear, how we used to sleep side by side in that alcove? I always used to keep my trousers with the keys at my head. Do you think I didn't hear someone standing by my bed, searching through the trousers, and rummaging through the bed-side table drawer? I did hear, may I hear only as much good news. But I couldn't, are you listening? pry my eyes open. What became of the money from the bedside table drawer? I mean, who did you give it to? To the crazy one with the wrinkled face? Or to the one with the devilish eyes who was always dancing around him? Or to that pimple-faced character whose name used to be Hotzmach and is now called Holtzman?"

CHAPTER 83

The Dissolution of Rafalesco's House

Day was breaking. The Czernowitz market across from the Black Rooster was showing signs of life; the stalls were being set up. Our two old friends were still talking. In truth, Sison v'Simcha was talking, and Rafalesco was listening most attentively, occasionally interrupting with a surprised jolt or an outcry: "Is that really true?" Or: "You don't say!" Or: "Can that be possible?" Sison v'Simcha swore on his *Yiddishkeit* that everything he had told him was God's truth, may he live to come home to his wife and little children and other such vows, as if Rafalesco wouldn't have believed him if he had not sworn. So comical was it that Holtzman, still sitting on the other side of the wall in the adjacent room, listening intently to every word, had to stifle his laughter.

And when Sison v'Simcha asked Rafalesco about the money that had gone missing from the drawer back in Holeneshti, our Holtzman pressed his ear hard against the wall, eager to hear what the kid would answer; but as he did so the chair scraped on the floor, making a squeaking sound. Rafalesco and Sison v'Simcha were simply startled by the squeak, which in the stillness of the night sounded much louder than it actually was. Holtzman was afraid they might find out he had been eavesdropping on their conversation, but the fright lasted only a few minutes. The two returned to their talk, and Holtzman remained undisturbed at his post. Unfortunately he thought he had missed the most interesting part of the story, not because his hearing was bad— on the contrary, he could hear every word through the wall.

There was another reason: Rafalesco had simply refused to answer the question about the money. He stood up, paced about the room several times, and stopped. Instead of answering his recently acquired brother-in-law's question, he responded with one of his own: "So! And how is my old rabbi, the cantor?"

The kid is no fool, thought Holtzman. *He asks him one thing, he answers another, cuts him off, brings up a rabbi and a cantor. If that's the case, I can go to sleep. It's almost morning. Who cares about that sleepy-looking character?*

Our Holtzman went quietly to his bed, undressed, pulled a blanket over his head, and fell right asleep. And our brothers-in-law kept on with their conversation:

SISON V'SIMCHA: "You're asking about Yisroyeli the cantor? Ha ha!
    Happy! Happy as a lark!"
RAFALESCO: "In what way?"
SISON V'SIMCHA: "In that he's become a rich man."
RAFALESCO: "A rich man? Yisroyeli the cantor is a rich man?"
SISON V'SIMCHA: "A powerful man! He's no longer a teacher, and no
    longer a cantor. Teh teh teh! He's nothing like the Yisroyeli we
    used to know. And Leah his wife, do you remember her? She's
    wearing pearls on weekdays, and she dresses, listen to this, like a
    rich man's wife and brags to everyone about her daughter.
    Wherever she goes and whoever she talks to, it's 'my Reizel' and
    'my Reizel.' She's already Reizeled everyone to death. Quite a girl,
    her Reizel! She's no longer called Reizel, but Rosa, and is a famous
    singer. She's in London now. Do you remember her? She recently
    visited us in Holeneshti with a big group of singers and actors
    from London, who ran around town dangerously in carriages.
    What that trip cost them, we can only wish for ourselves.

    "Want to hear something? They say she has a fiancé. He makes
    a million, a whole million! Anyway Holeneshti went wild over her.
    They ran after her in the streets. She's become very beautiful, and
    she's tall and the picture of health. They say her singing is beyond
    belief. She is rich, stuffed with money, yet is still only a cantor's
    daughter. So she wants to buy our house, listen to this, your own
    father's house. For whom, do you think? For herself? Not a chance!
    It's for the cantor. The cantor wanted nothing to do with it, nor did
    his wife. What did they need such a big place for? They preferred to
    buy Necha the widow's place. But Reizel insisted that it had to be
    Rafalovitch's house! And she wanted to buy not just the house itself
    but the whole courtyard, together with the stable and the business.
    What more do you want? She also wanted the dog Terkush,
    remember him? If she's buying, she said, she wanted the whole
    package. She's a crazy girl, that cantor's daughter, heh heh!"

That was the second time Sison v'Simcha had laughed that
night. But then he saw that Rafalesco wasn't laughing with him—on
the contrary, the youth was oddly deep in thought and was looking
worried. So the bookkeeper tried to explain how it happened:

"I myself would never have sold that house, but if God sends us
a buyer like that! I thought it over and decided, let her at least pay
a good price. Don't you agree? What's the trouble, Leibele? What's

happening to you suddenly? Are you sorry we sold the house? Believe me, my dear, it pained my heart no less than yours, maybe even more so. But what could we do? The business was going into the ground, and my father-in-law, long life to him, was stuck with his *rebbe*. The children were all scattered, one in Lisi, another in Strisi, scattered over the seven seas, are you listening? Who remained at home? Just one old senile grandmother, my Bat-Sheva, and the children. I'm not counting myself. What do I need? I, as you see me, need nothing. I live as I always lived. Another in my place—eheh heh!"

That *eheh heh* was drawn out in a singsong by Sison v'Simcha, accompanied by a gesture of the hand. The meaning of that *eheh heh* and the hand gesture was hard to figure out.

CHAPTER 84

They Pack for the Journey

Sison v'Simcha's efforts to explain himself to his young brother-in-law were in vain. Rafalesco's befogged mind and aching heart were far, far away. A confusion of feelings was churning within him: guilt, longing, regret, anxiety, love. Never had our hero lived through as much as he had that night. In one night, one could say, he had lost his father and his mother, his sisters and his brothers, his entire household, and the house in which he had been born, and the city in which he had grown up. All, all that had once been dear to him, was lost that night, lost forever! Everything he once felt so close to was now gone forever. It all seemed like an obscure dream wrapped in a thick veil and enveloped in a night sky heavy with secrets. Only a single star shone down at him from that dark sky, shone and illuminated, twinkling, beckoning him—Reizel.

As Rafalesco reflected on all he had heard, he wanted to know but one thing: Why had Reizel bought their house? Why *their* house and not another? What could she have been thinking? Could it be on account of him? Was the house where he had been born and raised so precious to her? Had she not forgotten him? Had she not forgotten the vow they had made in Holeneshti on that night of the great fire on God's Street, when they had called on the red, fire-illuminated sky to be God's witness to their vow that forever and ever they would be together, that whatever might happen to them and however they might change, their souls would always be as one, always and everywhere one?

He remembered that night of the fire, that magical night, that beauteous, joyous, unforgettably magical night, when Reizel stood before him, as if wrapped in a red cloud, looking like a beautiful, enchanted princess.

Knock knock knock! "Who's there?" Rafalesco awakened as if from sleep.

"It's me, Bernard." The door opened, and in came Holtzman, together with a gust of fresh early-morning air. His sharp eyes took in the kid spread out fully dressed on the sofa, disheveled and distracted, and his sleepy-eyed guest. Holtzman had an unholy urge to grab this Bessarabian gnome by his neck, slap him around, give him a few swift kicks in the rear, and throw him down the stairs, but he knew better. You can't always do what you wish with people. He controlled himself, glanced sideways at the unmade beds, and, putting on a little smile, said, "Look at this—no one slept?"

"No one slept," both answered.

Holtzman felt he shouldn't have said that and with the same put-on smile said, "Didn't even lie down?"

"Didn't even lie down."

"All night sat and just gabbed?"

"All night."

"Hmm . . . time to get ready for the trip," said Holtzman to Rafalesco and looked searchingly into his eyes.

"I'm ready," Rafalesco replied, getting up from the sofa, his face glowing in the light of the rising sun that smiled kindly through the window.

A kid remains a kid, thought Holtzman. Thank God he didn't decide to sit shiva for his dead mother right there and then. What would Holtzman have done if Rafalesco had wanted to make a quick trip to the Boyan *rebbe* to visit his newly religious father? Supposing he turned melancholy and wanted to visit Holeneshti? Who could tell what the kid would do?

All morning Holtzman did not let either Rafalesco or his guest out of sight. Cleverly he always managed to be a third party wherever the two were together—he always had some reason for his presence. But his effort was unnecessary. Rafalesco was feeling lighter at heart now. His new brother-in-law was sitting in the carriage, and the youth had kissed him and bade him farewell, sending fond regards to all.

"Send regards from me too!" shouted Holtzman.

"I certainly will!" said Sison v'Simcha, turning his sleepy face back into the carriage, which was packed tightly with passengers. Those "lovers of culture" were going home with heavy hearts. Only God knew when they might again have the rare privilege of seeing and hearing a true artist such as this Rafalesco!

As the carriage pulled away, Holtzman cursed them out roundly and called to the actors, "Let's get to work, gang!"

The actors packed for the journey, supervised by Holtzman. With his top hat pushed back, wiping the sweat from his pimply face, he bossed them around, just as Shchupak, heaven preserve us, used to do to him:

"Not this way—that way—first the small box, then the big box—I mean the other way around: first the big box, then the small box . . . like that . . . Stupid idiot, why are you just standing there? You take the right side, he'll take the left—I mean the other way around: you take the left side, he'll take the right . . . that's the way . . . Listen you, why are you looking at me like that? Better look at how you're carrying King Solomon's throne—they should carry you out feet first! Careful with Napoleon Bonaparte's crown! *Momzer,* if you break my Napoleon Bonaparte's crown, I'll break your head!"

So Holtzman ordered everyone around, driving them, heaping deadly curses on their heads. For every word that someone said, he found a curse. Someone would tell him they had run out of rope, and he would reply: "Rope ran out? May your brains run out!" "Where should I lay this?" "Lay yourself in the grave!" "He's asking for us to give him more money." "May God give him hot coals in his greedy hand!"

He honored someone with a brand-new curse, long but to the point: "However many holes were stamped in all the matzos in the world since the Jews left Egypt until this Pesach, may that many pimples erupt on your tongue, you bastard!"

As if to spite him, who should show up but the old mother, Sora-Brucha, with her bedding.

"Again? You're here again with your old *shmattes*? You're going to force me to rip up those worn-out quilts and spill out all their feathers!"

"May God grant you a son like yourself!" retorted the old mother, the only being who had not a drop of respect for our angry director.

Holtzman spat, and the old woman stalked away, but she came right back. What more? Nothing. She wanted her son to go have something to eat, to put something in his stomach. She said, "You look like death warmed over, a starved ghost. That's the way ghosts look, with only the cheekbones showing, their teeth knocking." Strength, she said, came only from eating. Eating is not a luxury . . .

Old Sora-Brucha was imparting all her folk wisdom on eating, but Holtzman was in no mood to hear it and cut her off.

"Look at her! That yakker is running off at the mouth. Will you never stop?"

Holtzman coughed out of anger, while the company almost choked trying to contain their laughter. They were afraid to laugh too hard. For such laughter Holtzman would give them something to remember.

No, Holtzman was not in a good mood, not at all. For him, the journey to London was like a bone stuck in the throat: "You can't swallow it, you can't spit it out." He didn't know why, but his heart felt strangely heavy. At night he dreamed about old women—*May my worries fall on their heads!*

PART II

WANDERING STARS

CHAPTER 1

Mr. Klammer

London Whitechapel was a Berdichev, or a Vilna, or a Brod, or all three rolled into one, and perhaps even Jerusalem itself. Nowhere else did the Yiddish pulse beat as strongly as in this English Whitechapel. Nowhere else did a Jew feel more at home. Its atmosphere was our atmosphere, its language our language, the hustle and bustle, the chasing, the shouting, the hand gestures—all ours. Even the trades, and all the other ways of making a living, were the same. What I mean to say is that the Jews there were no different from anywhere else. They lived off one another, tore the food out of one another's hands—what am I saying, hands? They tore the last morsel from one another's mouths. In a word, when you arrived in Whitechapel, you had come home. You had no trouble finding a Jewish night's lodging, a synagogue, or a good Jewish meal.

Speaking of meals, I must recommend a Jewish restaurant right in the center of Whitechapel called Café National. In fact, it was more like a Jewish club than a restaurant. No matter what time of day or night you went there, you would find a collection of Jews of every type that your heart desired: stockbrokers, doctors of philosophy, traveling salesmen, missionaries, peddlers, actors, diamond merchants, office workers, journalists, chess players, clerks, Zionists, Territorialists looking for a piece of land even in Africa where Jews could settle, and young people from who knew where, shouting and blustering, laughing and smoking, taking up most of the chairs and tables. And smoking, shouting, and blustering more than anybody was the proprietor himself, Mr. Klammer, whom we now have the honor of presenting to you.

Mr. Klammer was a Galitzianer Jew, a man of intelligence, with a stately appearance and a Herzl beard, who considered himself a cultured person and a Zionist. He was a Territorialist but not altogether so. Nor did he belong to any political party or social group because, you understand, Mr. Klammer was by nature a heretic. He believed in no one but himself, but if you told him he had a beard exactly like Dr. Herzl, he would call himself a Zionist, and should it happen that Mr. Zangwill managed to find a territory suitable for Jews, he would not oppose it. Dr. Herzl was certainly a great man, a gentleman, but Mr. Zangwill was no slouch either. "Live and let live" was Mr. Klammer's principle. He was at bottom a man of principle. He often showed off his English, which he believed he spoke like a true Englishman, by choosing English sayings to illustrate his principles. In addition, he considered himself something of a scholar, a well-read man. He was convinced there was not a thing on earth he didn't know. His restaurant business was as hateful to him as a pig is to a kosher Jew. He never bothered to look over the cashier's shoulder, but when it came to customers paying, he did you a favor and took your money, however you gave it to him. But if you didn't, it made no difference. He had a principle: Jews came in, filled their bellies, drank up, and sailed off to America—go find them. He was alone in his belief that you didn't go after deadbeats. Still Mr. Klammer talked too much about his worldly knowledge and his generosity. In general, he talked too much. But why shouldn't he talk when he had nothing else to do? The hard worker in the business was his wife, Mrs. Klammer, who labored over a hot oven, ravaged and embittered, never free to see the smoky, weepy London sky except on *Shabbes*. Came *Shabbes*, she put on her hat and a fine dress and became a lady. Nonetheless, she made sure her husband had his breakfast and dinner on time. After eating, he had to lie down for a nap, and only afterward could you see him walking among his guests and patting his Herzl beard, or sitting like a guest with someone at a table with a glass of beer and a cigar, bemoaning his miserable luck. "Woe is me, to think that I, Mr. Klammer, have to sell noodles! But what can one do? As the Englishman says, 'You must work for a living.'"

No, Mr. Klammer detested the restaurant, couldn't abide that business. He much preferred being out among people, mixing with London philanthropists and giving advice on how to deal with Russian immigrants, who to him were nothing more than *shnorrers*. According to him, all Russian Jews ought to be taken out and hanged on one rope. You might believe that Mr. Klammer was, heaven forfend, a bad person? Or perhaps the English Jews were more attractive to him? You would be mistaken. When Mr. Klammer felt something very strongly, he thoroughly cursed out all of London's wealthy men and the Jewish lords and made mud of them. For all that, Mr. Klammer was himself an ambitious man. Pick a quarrel with him, and you would never have a moment's peace as long as you lived. Those who knew him were careful during conversations; otherwise he might suddenly spring in and declare: "Jews, allow me! I will tell you most sincerely that you all are mistaken. Talking doesn't cost any money, or as the Englishman says: 'Talk is cheap.'" So saying, Mr. Klammer would stroke his Herzl beard and demand of you, "Exactly what are you talking about?"

One time an odd character was having lunch at his place and left him with a packet of writings. We now quote the words of Mr. Klammer as he described this character, how he met him, and how this treasure unexpectedly fell into his hands.

"This packet that you see here was inherited by me from some *shnorrer,* a Jewish artist, a small fellow with a hoarse voice and mischievous eyes. I don't know, nor do I care to know, who he is or what he is or where he comes from! I have a principle: If someone doesn't tell me, I don't need to know. Everyone carries his own burden, or as the Englishman says, 'Stick to your guns.'

"Anyhow, two weeks on end he gorged himself and guzzled at my place, saying he had a friend, a performer who made millions. He said he was a close intimate of hers. He said it was difficult to get to see her. But as soon as he saw her, he would be showered with money like a bridegroom with rice. All right! I have a principle: If a person says it's so, you have to believe him, or as the Englishman says, 'Seeing is believing.'

"One time he came to me, this *shlimazel,* asking me to lend him a few shillings. He said he needed to go for a day, not far from here, to Brighton, a place where all the London lords and wealthiest magnates go. There, he said, he'd find his famous performer singing. He handed me a packet, or as they call it in English, a handbag, for me to put away for him under lock and key, because in it, he said, were important papers that were worth who knew how much. All right! I have a principle: If a person says something, you can believe him, or as the Englishman says, 'Seeing is believing.'

"So I gave him a few shillings and took the packet, the handbag, and locked it away upstairs in my desk. And I waited for the *shnorrer* to return, one day and two and three and a week and a month and a year. Have you seen him? That's how I've seen him. Go find him, or as the Englishman says, 'Catch me if you can.'

"One day I reminded myself of the *shlimazel*'s handbag and took it from my desk to find out what treasure might be in there. I took a look—letters written in Yiddish! I thought to myself, *May he have nightmares! What do I need these for? What will I do with them? What value do they have?*"

That was what Mr. Klammer recounted about the treasure God had sent him, which consisted entirely of a packet of Yiddish letters. And since those letters have a strong bearing on our story, we present here a true copy of them, in the hope that the reader will guess by whom they were written and to whom.

CHAPTER 2

A Packet of Letters

FIRST LETTER

I am writing you a letter, my dearest, and am asking myself *why?* Do I know where you are or what you have become or what is happening to you? I live for the day, the hour, the minute when I will at last find out where you are. Let me at least describe everything that has happened to me from the moment I left Holeneshti until this day. As I sit and write, I picture you sitting next to me as I tell you all the many things I have gone through. I won't be able to write it as well or as clearly as I could if you were really sitting next to me. What do I know about writing? The little Yiddish I know, I must thank my father for. He always used to say: "All the boys write—you write too. Why shouldn't you also know how? Remember, daughter, it will come in handy one day!" Today I see how right he was.

Where shall I begin, my dearest? From that *Shabbes* night—do you remember? Oh, that *Shabbes* night, if I didn't die of fright, it was a sign I would live a long time. Till I heard the clock strike twelve, my heart almost leaped out. Every minute was like an hour for me. Did I say an hour? A day, a year. And when the clock struck twelve, I cautiously got out of bed, then opened the window and peered out onto the street—nothing, absolute darkness, not a soul there! What didn't I think of in that minute?

Above all I was afraid for you, my dearest. What if something had happened to you? God forbid. But then I heard a whistle, and then another whistle, as we had arranged with the man with the hoarse voice (the one they call Sholom-Meyer Murovchik). My heart beat like a watch—*tik tik tik*. My hands and feet were trembling, and a chill came over me. *Reizel, shut the window! Reizel, cover yourself with the blanket! Reizel, good night!* I was remembering my mother's voice for a split second, but I soon remembered what we had arranged, and I remembered the vow we had taken and the agreement we had made on the night of the fire. Do you remember that night of the fire?

And I quickly got up: "Goodbye, mother and father! Goodbye, Holeneshti! The cantor's daughter now bids you farewell for good. No more Reizel. The little bird has flown its cage." That was how I parted from my little room and kissed my little pillow. It made my heart ache, and I felt pity for my poor father. What would he say in the morning? But that feeling lasted no more than a minute, perhaps even less, and I was out the window and on the street. God's Street was dead. Like two shadows we walked, the hoarse fellow and I, I running ahead and he running behind me barely able to catch his breath. Not till we reached Asher the baker's burned house, at the end of the street, did we stop. We looked at each other, and he laughed quietly in his hoarse voice: "Little girl, you're running so fast I can't keep up with you." He untied a bundle containing a torn cape and an old shawl. "What's that?" I asked. "That's for you, little kitten, to cover yourself so they won't catch you. They must not recognize you. Wrap yourself tightly in the shawl, that's the way, and keep your mouth shut. Till we're on the train, you mustn't speak a word, do you hear? Not a peep!"

Just then a wagon with three horses pulled up. Murovchik stopped the wagon. On the coach box sat Shimen-Dovid the driver—I recognized him in the dark—and from inside the wagon the director sprang out, quite distraught. He called the hoarse man over to the side, and they began whispering to each other, about what I do not know. I only heard the hoarse fellow insult the director: "I-di-ot!" I sat there in dread, wrapped in my cape and shawl, while the two of them kept on. Then they had the driver come down from his seat, led him aside quietly, and soon all three were whispering. God Almighty! What was going on with all this whispering? I heard the driver complaining in his Moldavian accent. I caught a few words: "It's too far! Where is Potcheshti and where is Novoselitz?" I was thinking, *Should I throw off this old cape and make a dash for it back home while there's still time?* Then a hoarse voice called: "Madame Katz! Madame Katz!" Who were they calling? They must mean me. He had bestowed on me a new name, Madame Katz. "Why are you standing there?" he said to me, adding, "Please, Madame Katz, get in the wagon."

The three of us seated ourselves in the wagon, I next to the director, and the hoarse one opposite us. The director was terribly gloomy. He sighed, and one could hear him crying. The hoarse one commanded the driver to get going. Shimen-Dovid cracked his whip, and we were on our way.

How long we rode I do not know, but suddenly the driver stopped the horses, and we pulled up in front of Necha the widow's house. I was terrified! Necha would surely recognize me by my silk dress. Before I could turn around, she was at the door with her two little sisters, half-dressed, and Shimen-Dovid was deep in conversation with her about the actors, asking whether they had all left for Potcheshti and when had they left. He was also scolding her because he had brought her a few clients from the train just the other day and she hadn't so much as spit in his hand. To this Necha retorted that customers the likes of the ones he had brought her were easy to come by but hard to get to pay up. As she said this, she looked into the wagon, right at me. I could swear she recognized me. My heart sank. I wrapped myself tighter and tighter in the cape and shawl—another minute, and I would have smothered myself. Long live the hoarse one. He shouted at the driver, ordering him to get the horses going lickety-split, *"Yazdeh! Yazdeh!"* He said goodbye to Necha, and she wished him Godspeed.

Shimen-Dovid cracked the whip and pushed the horses so fast, I imagined we would soon be thrown from the wagon. "Why are you going so fast? What demon is after us?" demanded the director, his teeth chattering. But Shimen-Dovid did not reply. He whipped the horses harder, and the thought occurred to me: *Maybe someone is chasing after us? Maybe that's what the three of them were whispering about.* Then I saw, running right alongside the horses, your dog, Terkush. I knew him right away. It was a bad sign. What was Terkush doing here? Probably they were coming after you and would catch me as well. All was lost! We were both lost! I even imagined that they would capture us, that they would lead us back in disgrace to the town, bound together. Maybe, I thought, it would be a good idea to throw myself from the wagon and be killed, rather than suffer such shame. "Stop!" I heard Shimen-Dovid shout. The wagon came to a halt in the middle of a field, and he conversed with another driver. I looked into the other wagon, packed with boxes, and on top of the boxes sat two people. One, it seemed to me, was Hotzmach, the other one—YOU! I recognized you immediately, my dearest, even though you were wrapped up like me in some old coat. For a minute I imagined you were looking at me, that you were standing up, waving to me, and calling me by name. I almost sprang down from the wagon. But I had only imagined it in the split second before Shimen-Dovid turned the wagon around, cracked the whip, and we were heading back toward where we had just come!

Thank God, I survived the fright of that sudden turn-around. Now, I wondered, where were we going? Where were the others going? Why was the director so gloomy? What was the secret? And why did the hoarse man call the director "idiot"? All of this I will write you, my dearest, in my second letter. Now it's late, time to sleep, goodnight.

SECOND LETTER

My only friend!

The calamities I described in my first letter, and all the fears and terrors that I went through that night, were as nothing compared to what I lived through afterward—woes and calamities worse than the suffering in hell. Picture it, my dear—only after we crossed the border did I learn that we weren't in Romania after all, as we had arranged earlier. Do I need to tell you how I felt and what came to my mind? Had a river been nearby, I would surely have thrown myself into it. I beat my head with my fists, tore my hair, and sobbed as I had never sobbed in my life. Both the hoarse one and the director became quite frightened and took turns trying to calm me with soothing words, but the more they talked, the more I wailed. I tore my clothes and my shirt and tried to smash the windows. In fright, the director fled. Perhaps the hoarse one sent him off, realizing that I was afraid of the director's grizzled, wrinkled face and his disgusting red browless eyes. Remaining alone with the hoarse one, the one they called Sholom-Meyer Murovchik, I really began weeping. He tried to console me, swearing by his life and by heaven and by God Himself that no harm would come to me. I flung myself at him, kissed his hands, and begged him to tell the truth, the absolute truth. Again he swore to tell me everything, every detail. And this is what he told me:

We were supposed to have gone to Romania, but at the last minute the plan was changed on account of the director. It turned out the director had two wives. He claimed to have divorced his first wife long ago. He could, he said, supply witnesses. But his second wife said it was all lies. The first wife really wanted a divorce, but he wouldn't give her one. Why? He was demanding that she return all the jewels, clothes, and all the money he had spent on her—a fortune. She claimed the opposite—she had spent much more on him. Which one was right was hard to tell. Murovchik said all three were right, and if that were so, they mustn't be allowed to come near one another, because there would be an explosion.

In the last days before leaving Holeneshti, the director received a letter from a friend reporting that his first wife had found out where he was and was preparing to visit him in Holeneshti. He became thoroughly dejected and had to flee because whenever she found him she caused a scandal. He had long wanted to go to Romania, to Bucharest, so when he received this news, he began preparing to leave with the whole gang. The fool should have gone and been quiet about it! But no, the director had to write to his second wife before leaving: "I want you to know that I am about to leave for Romania. It's time we made an end of it, one way or the other. If you want to be with me, you can come directly to me in Bucharest." What did the second wife do? She answered him: "My dear husband! End it with your first wife. Then you can talk to me." And to the first wife she also wrote a letter: "You should know that if you want to end it with Shchupak, you had better go as quickly as you can to Bucharest." The first wife got on the next train to Bucharest. The director found out about it from some actor who had received a letter from an actor acquaintance. When did the actor show him the letter? It was just half an hour before departure, in Henich the winemaker's wine cellar.

That is the whole story, and that was the secret that *Shabbes* night, and that was why the hoarse fellow called him an idiot. "This story you've told me," I said to him, "explains a lot, but what's going to happen now?" "It'll all work out," he said. "The wives will tear each other's hair out in Bucharest, and we will rent a theater. We will write to the gang and tell them that whenever they get to Yas, anyone who has the wherewithal should come to Bucharest, and whoever has nothing should stay there or go wherever he likes." I asked, "And what about Hotzmach?" He replied: "What do you care about Hotzmach? Do you miss him?" "No, I was just asking. I was remembering how Hotzmach used to dance a 'A Chasid'l.'" "Let him dance with the Angel of Death, that Hotzmach," he said. "Why do we need that beanpole with the long legs? We can find a comedian like him anywhere."

You can see, my dear, that that information chilled my blood, but I controlled myself as best I could and put on a friendly face. My heart told me I would fare better by smiling and getting along with this hoarse character. And I pleaded with him, explaining that until the whole troupe arrived, I wouldn't be able to calm down. If he really wished to do me a favor, he should see to it that they all came and especially that beanpole Hotzmach. "Only then will I feel as if I were at home in Holeneshti." He looked at me and laughed. "Good," he said. "I'll write a letter saying they should all come, including that beanpole Hotzmach, damn him!" He told me that if I needed anything at any time, I should come to him, and he would take care of it for me. He ran off to the shops and brought back a bundle of new clothes and shoes for me to choose from. I washed and then dressed myself in the new clothes from head to toe. When I looked in the mirror, I didn't recognize myself. Where had the tears gone? My appetite returned, and I had the urge to sing! And I began singing like a nightingale, as if I didn't have a care in the world.

THIRD LETTER

From all that I have written in my first two letters, you must think my worst problems were over. No, my dear, they were just beginning. Many more tears followed, homesickness, humiliation, regret, and heartache. A year has three hundred sixty-five days, a day has twenty-four hours, an hour sixty minutes, and every minute brought new misery, new pain and suffering. I had been living with the mistaken idea that becoming an actress was child's play; you changed your clothes and walked out onstage, and that was it. It turns out that the way is hard till you hear laughter. You must first go through a long period of schooling and through all seven circles of hell. Artists are not born. Patti, the famous singer, they say, as a young girl went around singing with an organ-grinder under people's windows. The director and my Murovchik explained that to prepare me for the stage, they would first give me songs to sing and teach me dancing.

I will never forget my first appearance on the stage as long as I live. I performed but one song. Shchupak boasted that it was his song, he himself had composed. The hoarse one said: "Spit in his face, the liar!" Who did write it I don't know. It begins with these words:

> Every Friday night
> Every Jew's a king
> The darkest nook is bright,
> Joyous with laughter's ring.

More important than the words was the singing, and not so much the singing as the makeup, the costumes. They dressed me as a young Chasid boy, glued sidelocks on me, and put a pair of satin trousers on me, a silk caftan, and a black cap on my head. The music played, and I sang out "Every Friday Night" while dancing along with a merry step, a *fraylichs*. And what followed—what can I say? Pandemonium, clapping, and cries of bravo! God save us! I thought the ceiling was going to fall on me any moment. The shouting rose to the heavens: "Spivak! Rosa Spivak!" (That's what I was called in the program.) The ground seemed to split under my feet. I imagined the walls and lamps were swaying, and I didn't know what to do. In the wings the director on one side and Murovchik on the other urged me to go out before the audience again, which I did. The cheering grew even louder. I had to repeat the performance singing "Every Friday Night" and dancing the *fraylichs* again and again. I danced, and everything danced with me: the ceiling, the walls, the lamps, the audience. And when I finished, I collapsed in the wings and burst into tears. "Little kitten, you're crying? You should be happy! Do you realize, little bird, what a success, what a furor, what a triumph this is?" That was Murovchik praising me. "Patti is a dog compared to you, may God grant me as much luck and success." The director stood at a distance (I never let him closer than half a yard to me). He stood beaming at me with pride, with moist eyes and a little laugh that sounded more like crying than laughing. "Oy, those songs, do you hear? sweet as sugar, may my name not be Albret," he babbled, and flashed his jewelry.

From then on it was simply "Rosa Spivak" night after night. After the theater performance, like a kind of compote or dessert, the audience expected to be served Rosa Spivak's "Every Friday Night," followed by a little dance. That little compote caught the public's fancy more than anything else served up at the theater that night. Two dignified men chatted loudly enough for me to hear in the hall: "When will that miserable Purim play come to an end so we can hear Rosa Spivak?" At first I wanted to sink into the ground when I heard such compliments. But no, one must accept that. Men tried to look through the sides of my vest and ogled me in my men's trousers, they commented to one another, their wives looked angrily at them, God save us! Whatever illnesses or plagues existed on earth, I wished upon them. I cursed the men and their wives and the Yiddish theater and myself and the day I was born! But as you see, I overcame everything, and thank God, I can now happily tell it to you. Do you know whom I have to thank? Only you, my dear, my only friend, because all that time I never for a moment lost hope that you would soon be coming to me, that I would soon see your bright face, that we would join hands and go out together into the world as we planned, as we vowed. Murovchik told me every day that the rest of the troupe would be arriving soon and with them would come "your Hotzmach" (that's the way he used to tease me). But days and weeks passed and nothing happened. We didn't see them or hear from them.

The only one who did show up was Madame Cherniak, an odd-looking actress, a comic figure who was called Breyndele Kozak. You must remember her from Holeneshti—a short, chubby woman with large white teeth. From her I learned that Murovchik had lied to me in the worst way. He had written no letters to the troupe in Yas telling them to come back. It had been lies from beginning to end! This Breyndele Kozak filled my ear with things that made my hair stand on end. The scenery, she said, had been sold, but the actors and actresses were marooned in a strange country, without knowing the language and without a *groshen* to their names. If not for her, they would have died of hunger. As much as she could, she supported them. Afterward they sold everything they owned and went their own ways, melted away, she said, like salt in water. "So, and how about Hotzmach?" I asked her. No answer. Hotzmach seemed to have sunk into the earth. She said they would have gone under if she had not come to their rescue. I repeated my question but again received no answer.

But one time Breyndele let it out that a Yiddish actor had seen Hotzmach driving around Bucharest with a very young fellow. You can imagine how my heart was pounding when I heard those words. I wanted to hug and kiss her, and from that time on we were like two sisters. I have her to thank for many, many things. She opened my eyes to what sort the director Shchupak really was, and what Murovchik was really up to. She educated me and made clear what I had to do. She acquainted me with things that would not, perhaps, have been a disaster had I learned them later, but thanks to her I was able to save myself from that sinkhole. She convinced me that my place was not there among comedians. Had it not been for her, I might to this day be dragging myself around with Shchupak's troupe to every hick town. If not for her, I might now still be performing in wine cellars and cabarets, dressed in men's trousers, singing "Every Friday Night" and dancing *fraylichs*.

Dearest! Dearest! When I remind myself of that time, my face burns with shame even now. Anger rises up in me, but not so much at my director and Murovchik—they only wanted to make money off me as every entrepreneur does these days. No, I was furious at those fat rich men with their fat bellies who used to come hear me sing and watch me dance, and then would lick their lips like a cat after lapping up cream, cheer and shout, tear the theater apart: "Spivak! Spivak! Rosa Spivak!" Yiddish theater lovers, they called themselves, and went night after night to Shchupak's theater, peeking into the wings. "When will that girl in men's trousers be coming out?" Ah, those Yiddish theater lovers! I must acquaint you with one of them, and since there is a lot to tell about him, and it's quite late, we'll put it off for another time. Goodnight, my dearest—sleep well!

FOURTH LETTER

Once—it was a hot summer day—we were all rehearsing. I was studying leading roles. Someone came and told the director that a man was asking for him. Every time Shchupak heard that someone was asking for him, he froze in his tracks, obviously having to do with the wives. Madame Cherniak, or Breyndele Kozak, told me Shchupak had not two but *three* wives. So he immediately looked rattled and searched for his adviser, Sholom-Meyer. "Where is he, that scoundrel!" The man apparently could not wait and came backstage where, upon seeing each other, they fell into each other's arms: "Stelmach!" "Shchupak!" At this point Sholom-Meyer came running in, and all three began joyously hugging and kissing. Blood brothers who have not seen one another for twenty years would not have been as happy as those three were, especially the visitor, Stelmach. He almost melted like snow in the sun, apparently out of delight that he had lived to be reunited with Shchupak and his right-hand man, Sholom-Meyer.

He was a man of short stature, dark-complected and hirsute, up in years but solid and well built, with a small belly, a lined face, and small, moist eyes. An especially sweet smile seemed always to be present on his face. This man was apparently satisfied with himself, with God, with everybody, and with the world. Stelmach's great virtue is that he is not boastful, and though he himself admits that he has everything a man could want, including wealth, nevertheless he sees himself as simple, modest, and ordinary. He hates, he says, how others praise themselves, and he hates to display his stature. Then again he enjoys telling anyone at any time the story of his life, of which he never tires. He speaks quietly, almost inaudibly, with an occasional soft sigh and a little smile on his lips, while patting your hand and holding on to your lapel so you won't leave. And the words pour out as smoothly as oil, artfully linked together as he creates wondrous tales worthy of a thousand and one nights. I don't know if I will succeed, but I will try to convey to you his life story in his manner.

"I was—may it not happen to anyone, not to you, not to me—a poor Jew, a pauper with many mouths to feed, without as much as a crumb of bread," he began with a sigh and a little smile, his face shining. "I lived, who knows where, in a tiny village, a desert, a nothing, in the sticks not far from Berdichev called Machnevka or Yachnevka (I already forgot the name) and subsisted by sewing lambskin hats for the Gentiles. I walked three miles to sell the merchandise at the markets in order to earn something. My boots were tied with string to hold the soles on, and my coat was as full of holes as a sieve. The frost burned, the snow blew, the wind whipped my face, and I was ready to faint. At home, may it not happen to anyone, lay a sick wife with little children. The oldest one was then barely six. His name was Hershele, from birth a wonderful child, a jewel. All day long he would go about playing with two sticks. 'Hershele, what are you doing?' 'I'm playing on the fiddle,' he would answer. For fun one day I brought home a plain fiddle that cost three gulden. When the child saw the fiddle, he broke down in tears. Where had he seen a fiddle? Who had shown him how to play one? The child learned by himself! On his own he began fiddling and fiddling until he could play tunes. With God's help, it happened that a wealthy landowner in my village, a count, I don't remember exactly, learned that a Jewish hatter's son in his village was incredibly talented on the fiddle. He asked that the Jew be brought to him with his boy and fiddle. And when the landowner asks, you can't refuse, you must go."

This is what happened. When Stelmach and his son arrived, they stood the boy on a table, and he immediately began playing. The landowner was instantly captivated, and his wife grabbed the boy and hugged and kissed him. Tea and coffee and food appeared on the table: rolls, eggs, jam— everything a Jew is allowed to eat. The landowner said, "Sit, sit, why are you standing? Do you have any idea what you possess here? You possess a precious jewel. You are a million-aire. But you are only a simple man, a blind man. You would be worse than the worst father if you let him grow up here and didn't take him to the city to study music!" The father declared, "My lord! It's easy for you to say—study music. I am a poor Jew, a pauper, a man burdened with children." "Don't let that bother you. You just put him in my hands and I will make something of him," said the rich man, his wife nodding in agreement. But this Stelmach was not like others and was thinking: *Unless the landowner makes something of the child, I will have one child less and Israel one less Jew.* "No, my lord, this is not a good plan," he said aloud. "You would do better to ask me to harness some horses and lend me a few coins for expenses, and I will go with the child to Berdichev, a big city, a lot of Jews, rich people."

And that was what happened. Arriving in Berdichev,

Stelmach and Hershele wandered around the city, a big city, seething like a kettle. Jews were running about, this one here, that one there, preoccupied, excited. No one was paying attention to them. The poor child wanted to eat, and wouldn't you know it was summertime, apples and pears were half price, and the child was dying for plums. Stelmach stopped one person, then another, asking for information, just information: "What am I to do, my fellow Jews? I possess here a precious jewel, do you see? worth a million." They looked at him as if he were crazy. Here was a Jew in rags and tatters, dragging a little boy around, naked and barefoot, saying he possessed a million. So he began to explain, to tell them what the landowner had said; he wanted to show them what the boy could do. They laughed and flung curses at his head! This hurt his feelings. He walked over to some young folks, to one, to another, telling them what the landowner had said and begged them to allow the child to play something, show them what he could do. They said, "Very well, what do you want, Reb Jew?" "What do I want? I need a few coins so I can go back home." One of them said to him: "Wait, do you know what? We'll arrange a concert." The father thought: *To hell with him! Ask him if he knows what a concert is. But if they say a concert, let it be a concert.*

It turned out that they liked him. The fellows hired a hall, printed posters, and went around selling tickets. No one bought any. Bad—what would happen? "Don't worry," they said. "There's still time before the concert." The night of the concert, it was already eight o'clock, nine o'clock, ten-thirty—no one there. At about eleven a few young people gathered, barely a *minyan*. They suddenly realized: Where was the boy? The boy was asleep. They woke him and stood him on a chair. The boy started to play—well, well! That was some concert! They surrounded the child, squeezed him, kissed him, nearly smothered him. But what was the good of it when they didn't even have enough money to pay for the hall? They arrived back at their inn, tired, discouraged, and hungry. The landlady said it was too late to eat. For a bed to sleep in, she asked to be paid in advance. Bitter! They spread out the coat on the ground and lay down. The child fell asleep—a child remains a child—and the father lay deep in thought, his mind racing: *How can we get ourselves out of this place?* His heart told him that next to him, right there on the torn coat, was lying a fortune, a million. But who knew it? With that thought he fell asleep.

He had a strange dream. In the middle of the city there was plum tree. At the very top his son was standing and shaking the tree so that falling down upon him were not plums but millions, one million after another. He bent down, looked around on all sides, picked up the millions, and shoved them into his pockets. The son, on top, asked him: "*Tateh*, more?" "More, more!" the father answered him, and never tired of gathering up the millions. Suddenly he heard a noise, a tumult from afar: "Enough shaking!" he said to his son, and woke up, realizing he was lying with the child on the ground. The room was full of people. The owner was standing there deathly pale. The landlady was wringing her hands and weeping: "My pearls! My pearls!" He got up and wanted to go to the door but was stopped: "If you please, Reb Jew, first we want to search you." "What do you mean, you want to search me?" "We'll strip you naked, you and your boy, and search you and see if by mistake the landlady's pearls crept into your possession during the night."

(A few pages of the letters seem to be missing here, because when we pick up the story again Stelmach and his wonder child are already in St. Petersburg and the child is no longer called Hershele but Grisha and is receiving a state stipend.)

Stelmach and Grisha arrived in St. Petersburg—the city was full of excitement: parties everywhere, going from one to the next, here a lunch, there a dinner, here a supper. The child was carried on people's shoulders. Everywhere, wherever there was a ball, a concert, an evening affair, all you heard was "Grisha Stelmach" and "Grisha Stelmach." Students, professors, elegant women—together in one voice: "Grisha Stelmach!" Things were stirring! About money nothing needed to be said. As there was a stipend, money was eliminated as a problem. True, the stipend was difficult to negotiate, with blood and humiliation and running from one person to another. They finally achieved success, on account of a Gentile, an evil man, a Jew-hater—so much to tell! And in this way one year after another passed.

The boy grew, and his fame became even greater. He had outstripped all his teachers. Thank God that was behind them. He went through all the professors in St. Petersburg and outdistanced them all. What was next? It was time to think of future prospects. They wouldn't keep giving him stipends forever. He had to start earning money, to go out into the world, the sooner the better, because so long as the wonder child was a child, he was a wonder that everyone wanted to see. But as soon as he grew out of his short pants, he would no longer be a child, and no longer a wonder. Only God knew what would become of him and into whose hands he might fall. So it was necessary to get going right now. That was how Stelmach reasoned, and that's the way it happened.

But it was not a matter of "no sooner said than done." Going out into the world costs money, and there was none. What was he to do? He had to find a partner—his money, Stelmach's merchandise. And God helped him, he found an interested party, a German named Schultz, who took them on at his expense. Whatever they made would be split fifty-fifty. But there was a catch, one small detail: Schultz wanted a ten-year contract. "German! Are you out of your mind? What kind of ten years? One year is enough. Two years, three years are more than enough!" There was nothing Stelmach could do, Schultz was a stubborn German!

Meanwhile time wasn't standing still. They had expenses. They tried writing home for money. Back and forth, he finally settled on five years with the German, wrote out a proper contract, and set out into the world. He signed up for concerts, one after the other, and, thank God, they were very successful. Grisha Stelmach met with acclaim everywhere. When people heard he was coming, they took off as if to a fire. The people at his concerts were as many as grains of sand in the ocean, as many as stars in the sky—rich people, powerful people, Christians, rulers—they swarmed around like flies, and money poured in from all sides. It was just a pity that they had to share it with that German.

Why should he get so much money? What had he put in, his father's inheritance? Or was it his great knowledge? Luckily, by now Stelmach knew the business end of concerts. It was not a big deal! You came into a city, you first informed all the newspapers, you paid for ads, and they trumpeted and banged the drum: "Grisha Stelmach is coming! Grisha Stelmach has come! Grisha Stelmach is here!" You hired a hall or a theater, you put up posters, you printed tickets— and that was it. He was just a pain, the German! It was a sin before God. But an agreement was an agreement. Forget it! One silver lining was that the five years would soon be over, the contract would lapse, and to hell with the German. Then who would be his equal? *My merchandise, my money.*"

So Stelmach ended his biography with a radiant face. He patted his belly and asked Shchupak what was new with him and what was going on in the Yiddish theater, because the Yiddish theater was for him, he said, his only pleasure. His son's concerts were merely business, but if he wished to be entertained, he went to the Yiddish theater. He thought well of the Yiddish theater and knew all the Jewish artists. That was the basis of his friendship with Shchupak. Whenever he arrived in a new city, he said, the first thing he did was to ask where to get a kosher meal and was there a Yiddish theater? Jewish fish and Yiddish theater—what could be better than that?

Before coming to this town, he had already heard, he said, that his friend Shchupak had someone noteworthy, one Rosa Spivak, who was winning great acclaim. "There she is," said Shchupak, indicating me with his browless red eyes. Stelmach offered me his hand, a warm, soft hand like a cushion, with short, stubby, hairy fingers. His face utterly glowed with delight. "Can this be true?" he said. "Who is she, and where is she from?" "She's actually a niece of mine from Warsaw, an orphan, without a mother or father." Shchupak had fashioned a bald-faced lie and pursed his lips so as not to sneer. "Poor thing!" said Stelmach with a little smile and a pity-face. He pressed my hand and made his farewells, promising to return that night without fail to hear me sing.

"With the kid?" Sholom-Meyer Murovchik asked him. "God forbid!" Stelmach replied, almost jerking back as if singed. "Do you think my Grisha would go to the Yiddish theater, ha ha ha? Let him show up just once where Jews gather, and that would be the end of it. Not, God forbid, that he's not a Jew. On the contrary, you must understand, it's a delicate matter." Here Stelmach demonstrated with his short, stubby fingers what a delicate matter it was. "My Grisha, when he travels, it's only first class, where no Jews travel. And we stay only at the best and finest hotels. And when it's time to go to the concert, even if it's three steps away, we are driven, and in a covered carriage. No one can simply see him just like that, without paying, ha ha. If you want to see him, you first have to arrange it with the German. And for a German, you must have respect, even though the German—let it remain between us—is really a Jew, even though his name is Schultz, but he doesn't want people to know. It wouldn't be fitting. As for me, if someone wants to see my Grisha as a favor or just get acquainted, I send him off to the German, ha ha ha, to the German."

That is Stelmach. And that is the man I have to thank for my entire career and perhaps for my life itself. And as this letter is already a bit too long, in fact far too long, I will put off the rest for another time. Be well, my dear!

FIFTH LETTER

My dearest friend,

Meyer Stelmach, that "Yiddish theater lover," hardly ever left our theater. Night after night he soaked up every play three times over, never becoming bored. He always sat up front, spread out in the first row, naturally for free—how can you expect a "theater lover" to buy a ticket! But in return he always started the applause and kept at it louder and longer than anyone else. He was delighted with almost every single actor, let alone me and my songs. The first time he saw my "Every Friday Night," he was so enthusiastic he ran backstage and, with tears in his eyes, embraced and kissed my director.

My director mentioned several times that he would love to hear Grisha play, but Stelmach pretended not to hear and changed the subject. But Shchupak's hints were so blunt that he had to give in, and one Sunday he came bearing three tickets for the director, Murovchik, and me for an afternoon concert. All the while he was going on about what a brilliant concert it would be. "This will be a concert to remember. My Grisha will perform, the German will accompany him, and Marcella Embrich will sing. Do you know who Marcella Embrich is? She is the second Adelina Patti. Did I say second to Patti? She's ten times, a hundred times, a thousand times greater than Patti! The first time Patti heard her sing, she fell on her neck, embraced her, and said, 'We are two stars. I am the star that is setting and you are the star that is rising,' and broke into tears. Naturally, with no one but my Grisha would Embrich perform for any amount of money. When it came to my Grisha, it was another story. And that's how it has been—'Grisha-Grisha! Grisha-Grisha!'" *May I only live to see and hear what this Grisha can do,* I thought.

God was good, I did live to see and hear him, and I must tell you, my dear friend, that I saw before me two Grishas. I saw one Grisha and heard another. The first Grisha who stepped on the stage was a young lad, almost fully grown, although he was still in short pants, a chubby kid with full cheeks and freckles and eyes you could barely see, really a rather ordinary boy. If you met him on the street, you would let him pass by like a thousand others. The only thing that grabbed your attention were the highly polished shoes with large straps, which seemed a bit too large for his rather oversized feet, and the broad, round white collar, tied with a too-large bow hanging down in two points. Otherwise there was nothing special about him. But once he began playing, bowing the first notes on the strings, the lad with the chubby cheeks and freckled face quickly vanished, and in his place suddenly stood a new person with an entirely different appearance, a different expression, different eyes—large, blue, heavenly eyes. A strange phenomenon—where had those eyes been earlier? Had I imagined it? When he stopped playing, the audience thundered madly—and again he was that same chubby lad with the broad collar and the long points of the bow tie. He stood calmly before the audience, which was raising the roof, calm and cold as ice. He barely bowed when he was called back perhaps ten times. When he left the stage, he strode out confidently, cold and calm, like a person who was certain he was entitled to this homage.

Soon after he finished playing, the famous singer Marcella Embrich stepped out. I cannot possibly describe her singing. When she creates a sound, it enters directly into your heart and suffuses every limb of your body. You hear it and become enchanted, wondering where such fluidity, such sweetness, such strength could come from. She sang effortlessly. You sit and listen and believe that this is not a voice singing but a violin playing. When Marcella Embrich sings, she seems to absorb everything around her. You forget where you are, or even that there is a world beyond this beautiful, fluid, sweet, heavenly singing. That's how Marcella Embrich sings! On that day I was as if in a cloud, in a dream, on another planet. Right after her the young lad with the chubby cheeks and freckled face came out again. Again the bow swept back and forth. Again his violin began speaking eloquently, singing, weeping like a human being, and suddenly he was gone. In his place stood the other Grisha Stelmach. A sorcerer stood on the stage who had enchanted and drawn toward himself the entire theater. No, I cannot possibly describe so much as a tenth of what I experienced that afternoon and what a concert that was! It is difficult to say which of the two was more triumphant, Grisha Stelmach or Marcella Embrich. Picture it—the audience did not spare its applause for either of them, though I imagined Grisha was more warmly received and cheered more. He played the final piece on the program, and the audience, as one person, simply went out of its mind. How can a human being be so idolized? And what he played as an encore was truly divine. More than divine.

SIXTH LETTER

Most beloved, dearest friend,

In my previous letter I started to tell you about my friendship with the renowned Marcella Embrich and got carried away talking about the concert. That was the first serious concert I had heard in my life. I've heard many great concerts since, but that one I will never, ever forget, perhaps because it completely changed me, altered my life, as you will see.

I left the theater newborn, filled with new ideas and hopes. Still ringing in my ears were the sweet notes, the sacred musical chords, the heavenly singing. I saw no one except those two, Marcella Embrich and Grisha Stelmach. I heard nothing but her singing and his playing. Much of the audience remained standing outside the theater waiting for them to come out. I was among them. An automobile drove up into which stepped Marcella, Grisha, and the German. Grisha's father stood nearby, bowing deeply and smiling broadly. The public followed them with loud applause as the three pulled away. It was like a dream, and I remained spellbound, looking toward where they had vanished. I confess that at that moment a foolish thought stole into my mind: *Will I ever be a Marcella Embrich? Will they ever follow me with applause?* No matter what, I decided I must approach this Embrich. I wanted her to hear me sing. Perhaps she would tell me what I needed to do to become a Marcella Embrich.

At that point Sholom-Meyer arrived. "We're all going to eat something," he said. "What do you mean 'all'?" I asked. "You and I and the director and the elder Stelmach are going with us. Shchupak invited him to a Jewish restaurant for gefilte fish with horseradish. The Yiddish theater lover is fond of gefilte fish, especially when someone else is paying!" I was thinking, *I must ask the Yiddish theater lover to introduce me to Embrich, but how can I manage it so that my director won't know?*

So absorbed in demolishing the gefilte fish and the horseradish that he broke into a sweat, the Yiddish theater lover did not stop talking about the wonders of his Grisha and Marcella. "Oh, that Marcella Embrich! She is the only singer who sings for the Kaiser Franz-Josef. She will not give concerts with anyone else but my Grisha, not even for a million. She herself proposed that they should perform together." And once again he began his little song: *Grisha, Grisha* and again *Grisha!* This man is either drunk or obsessed, and his obsession is—Grisha!

I found a moment when the director and Murovchik were occupied with paying the bill to interrupt his continuing praise and said, "*Pani* Stelmach, I have a favor to ask of you." Hearing the word *favor*, he became a changed man, no more smile on his face, his eyes dry, cold, and glazed over, his face drained of blood. It was a sorry sight. "A small favor," I hurried to say, "a tiny favor. I want you to introduce me to this Embrich so she can hear me sing." Hearing those words, he was greatly relieved. His face again changed, the smile returned, and his cheeks became rosy again. "Ach," he said with a sigh, "why not? With the greatest pleasure!" "Only one thing I must ask," I said to him quietly. "It has to be a secret. None of the people here must know. Do you understand?" "I understand, my dear, of course I do. I understand very well," he said. "But how can this be worked out?" He thought awhile and slapped his forehead: "Wait! Tomorrow morning, we should live and be well, around eleven o'clock, meet me at the inn. Not a soul will know."

To meet Stelmach at the inn without my director finding out was no easy task. Did Shchupak ever lose sight of me? Didn't his right-hand man follow me like a faithful dog? I had an idea: If you need a thief, go to the gallows. Sholom-Meyer himself once promised me that whenever I needed anything, I should turn to him and only to him, and he would do it. I thought it over and put my trust in him. I told him I wanted no more than one thing—to hear what a famous singer thought of my voice. And it went as I had hoped. "Little kitten!" he said, "is there anything in the world that would be difficult to do for your sake? I would go through fire and water, may God grant me luck and success."

A strange man, this Murovchik! He was as faithful to his boss as a loyal dog, would let him chop his fingers off, but for my sake he was ready to buy and sell him three times over. A strange man!

The following morning about eleven o'clock Murovchik announced to the director that he needed to go shopping with me for a few trifles. "What trifles, in the middle of everything?" Shchupak asked, and looked at me with his small, red browless eyes. "Just trinkets, foolishness, nothing at all," Murovchik answered, then Murovchik raised his voice angrily, "What is it to you if we need to go?"

A strange business between these two! The director could curse him out, drive him like a slave, treat him like a choirboy, but if Murovchik raised his voice, he pursed his wrinkled lips and shut up. Otherwise Murovchik would give him a hard time and yell at him, "Id-i-ot!" till the windows shook. The two of us got up and left to meet our "Yiddish theater lover."

Stelmach welcomed us warmly and asked us to sit. As usual, he told us first about his Grisha and then about himself, his whole life story, again from the beginning, a story from the thousand and one nights that could last till three o'clock. But Murovchik came to my rescue and cut him off in the middle, saying we had only a little time. We wished to see Embrich. Stelmach stood up and paced a bit, muttering: "How can that be worked out? How can that be worked out?" Visiting her right now were the German and his Grisha. He couldn't go in now. He wanted to, but he shouldn't. At that moment he seemed to have shrunk. Then Murovchik came up with a suggestion: "*Pani* Stelmach, listen to me. Stop this foolishness. Don't be afraid for your Grisha—we won't, God forbid, bite his head off. And as for your so-called German from Berdichev, let him go to hell. If you want to go in with us, good. If not, we'll go in ourselves this very second, may God grant us luck and success."

When he heard those strong words, Stelmach's expression changed. His lips became dry, and he sat down, stood up, buttoned all his buttons, and tried to smile but couldn't. The three of us entered a beautifully appointed salon, furnished with many soft divans. There the mild-mannered Stelmach told us to be seated while he tiptoed to the door leading to a second room. First he laid his ear to it, and then with his short, chubby fingers he knocked: "It's me, me, Stelmach" . . .

Here the letter cuts off. Unfortunately this unfinished letter was the last in the packet that had fallen into the hands of Mr. Klammer from London, and we really do not know how the renowned singer, Marcella Embrich, received our heroine.

In truth, we know very little about what happened to her. But some time from now we will see the name ROSA SPIVAK printed in large letters on huge posters together with the name GRISHA STEL-MACH. The posters will be displayed in that most fashionable part of London, the West End. At the same time, in the lowliest part of the city, the East End in Whitechapel, one could see huge posters, printed in frightfully large letters, announcing: "Coming to the Jewish Pavilion Theater for the First Time in London—the Famous Guest Star LEO RAFALESCO from Bucharest and the Beloved Actress HENRIETTA SCHWALB from Buenos Aires."

Our young wanderers, the rich man's son and the cantor's daughter, had traveled, like wandering stars, over the wide world, performing in the theater. Finally, for the first time since they had left their birthplace, Holeneshti, they were both in the same city.

CHAPTER 3
Not the Best of Times

When our wandering troupe Holtzman, Schwalb & Co. arrived in London, Bernard Holtzman felt as if he had fallen into a dark hole, or perhaps a boiling cauldron from which it was not easy to crawl. Everything in the city seemed to him dark, bleak, and foreboding. The people spoke a language that struck him as simply crazy. The rush and tumult and bustle made him dizzy. He developed an antipathy for this noisy city with its foggy, weepy sky. From the minute he set foot on English soil, the entire country revolted him, until his nose sniffed the familiar fragrance of Whitechapel squalor.

Upon arriving in London at midday, they were greeted with a frightening darkness, like the plague in Egypt, thick enough to touch. It was not enough that God had cursed this city by taking the sun away from it—Holtzman added his own curse that it should sink into the sea. He wished what Heinrich Heine had once wished, that the sea should swallow it up and spit it back out. And he added a wrinkle of his own—that it turn to salt like Lot's wife.

No, our Holtzman was miserable in London, much more so than in Holeneshti. He had reason to be distraught and unhappy.

The first encounter in London had turned out badly. At the

railway station to greet the troupe were Schwalb's brother Nissel and another person whom he introduced as Mr. Hetchkins. Nissel told them in Yiddish that he was a Gentile and the owner and manager of the large London Yiddish Pavilion Theater. To Holtzman Hetchkins looked more like someone who should be selling oranges or ice water during intermission. *A blank-faced shaygetz*, thought Holtzman, *with an ill-fitting hat and a bare face.*

He was wearing, this manager, a strange, checkered, ill-fitting coat; turned-up trousers that were wide on top and too small on the bottom; and shiny shoes with elevated heels. From his scrawny red neck protruded a pointy Adam's apple that neither his fancy tie nor his jeweled tie-pin could mask. When he was introduced to the newly arrived guests, this Mr. Hetchkins extended two fingers, flashed three gold teeth, and languidly uttered two words: "All right!" Then he turned his back to the guests. Someone signaled with a finger, and to the amazement of our whole troupe, an expensive automobile drove up. Mr. Hetchkins ducked into it and disappeared into the thick, gray London fog.

Nissel Schwalb was an entirely different sort. He projected a greater sense of self-importance than the vanished manager, and he had the air of an owner, not just of a London theater, but of all of London and all its surroundings. Broad and barrel-chested, he seemed twice as tall as his brother. He had a shaven face and always clenched a cigar between his teeth. He wore a hat to the side and exuded an air of supreme satisfaction with himself and with the whole world. Laughing loudly, he ordered the guests around as if they had come especially to see him.

First he embraced and kissed each and every one of them, as if they had been his close friends for ages. Then single-handedly he unloaded all the bags from the wagon. He then hired a carriage and arranged the seating: "You, Itzik, sit down alongside Rafalesco right here on top. Henrietta, you squeeze in between them, that's the way, and your partner and I will sit opposite."

All the while he rested a large pudgy hand on Holtzman's bony shoulder. Holtzman looked at his partner's brother and then at his partner's brother's hand: *Some paw! May it wither and fall off this very night! What's with all this bossing around telling us where to sit? I'll tell that partner of mine that I can't tolerate such carrying on. We have to clip this bird's wings and teach him some respect. You have to give it to these boors right across the mouth!*

That was what our Holtzman wanted to tell him, but instead he called to his partner, "Listen, Itzikl. Your little brother, *kayn eyn horeh*, has grown up pretty big and tall."

Gazing with pride and affection at his brother, his face glistening with sweat, his partner replied, "Grew up, you say? Hah, may we all grow up that big."

"So what?" said Holtzman, thinking: *Where was he when we were going through hell?*

In a flash our newly arrived guests were whisked through the busy streets of the city. Holtzman continued feeling very uncomfortable. He had no time to catch his breath since this "water ox"—the name he gave Nissel—kept pushing everyone around, even after they arrived at their place in Whitechapel. There Nissel helped everyone down, accompanied by a *huplya* and a little laugh that made Holtzman sick to his stomach.

No, the arrival in London did not bode well for Holtzman. His heart told him that here, on the crowded horizon of London's gray sky, his star, which till now had shone so brightly, would descend. He took out his bitterness, as always, on his poor mother and his innocent sister. Running wild among the actors and actresses, he provoked quarrels, vented his fury, and summoned every curse imaginable. Had Holtzman the time and the ability to write, he could have put together a fat book of curses in alphabetical order.

CHAPTER 4

A Good Fellow—Nissel Schwalb

Food and people—forgive the comparison—have this in common: what one likes, another can't abide. As much as Holtzman disliked Nissel Schwalb, to that extent and more did Rafalesco adore him. A friendly, lively soul, he was always talking and laughing loudly, with a slap on the back, addressing everyone with the familiar *du*. In a word, he was a good fellow, and that was enough for Rafalesco.

Our young hero had always been attracted to lively people. Back in Holeneshti, when Holtzman was Hotzmach and working for Shchupak, he too had been a happy, lively sort. But now that he was the director of his own troupe, he had become a worrier and fretter and continually suspected people of plotting to take away his Rafalesco and thereby ruin him.

Noisy London made his worries and suspicions even greater. In Rafalesco's eyes, Holtzman's actions diminished him. The more Holtzman ridiculed and cursed Nissel Schwalb, the more Rafalesco was drawn to him, and just to spite Holtzman, he made Nissel his close friend.

Rafalesco took to the man from the start, drawn by his expressive gesticulations and mannerisms and even his way of speaking. When Nissel spoke, one word tumbled out after another so that it was hard to understand him. And he was no mean liar—even as he kept insisting on his trustworthiness, swearing oath upon oath upon his total honesty, rattling them off so quickly in one breath that your mind didn't have time to grasp the meaning of what your ears had heard.

At first Nissel Schwalb undertook to show our young hero what London was like. He promised to show him all of London in one day.

True, that was a bit much, but no matter. Wasn't tomorrow another day, and the day after tomorrow? The point was, Nissel Schwalb knew London by heart, and if you went with him, it wouldn't be dull. His mouth never shut. Everywhere, on every street, and at almost about every house, he could tell a story, some historical fact or scandal, and not just any scandal but a true story that had either happened before his very eyes or else involved him. When Nissel Schwalb told you something, he hypnotized you. He held on to your hand, or he grabbed you by your buttonhole, and looked deeply into your eyes, and his fully detailed story penetrated your heart.

Here's a fine example: he once met a very upper-class man, he said, almost a lord, in Hyde Park, and fell into conversation with him. You knew for sure that Nissel had invented the story, but he was so animated while telling it and laughed so hard that unwillingly you began to think, *Who knows, maybe he's telling the truth?*

Our young hero befriended this character, became one soul with him, and visited all of London's little out-of-the-way places and especially all the theaters, opera houses, and concert halls. They had plenty of time because the visiting acting troupe Holtzman, Schwalb & Co. were engaged at the Pavilion Theater for only two performances a week.

Rafalesco felt like a fish in water with his new friend. He would have felt even better had not Nissel Schwalb gotten it into his head to include his sister, Henrietta Schwalb, on their rambles. Nissel wanted his sister to see something of the world and to hear some music. "Who knows, it might come in handy for her?" he said, but he really had something else in mind. On the first day Itzik had told him that they had to marry off the kid to their sister, or else Holtzman would betroth him to his own little sister.

"To whom? To that green gooseberry?" Nissel cried, and began to pace the room.

"A green gooseberry, you say? A little apple!" said Itzik Schwalb, red-faced.

"You could chew her up and spit her out in one breath!" his brother answered, pacing back and forth with long strides.

In Nissel's mind a plan was being hatched.

CHAPTER 5

A Person with Plans

Nissel Schwalb was always planning and scheming. By profession he was a promoter, but in London you can't make a living as a promoter. You have to be a clever schemer as well. And Nissel could think up a scheme to serve any purpose. To tell the truth, his schemes at first appeared crazy and wild, byzantine and complicated, truly mad. But afterward somehow they would come out straight and smooth. Should a scheme somehow not go smoothly, well then, he was no more than a person, and people make mistakes.

Many a firm had gone broke following one of his plans, Nissel explained, but that was not his fault; had they followed his plan to the end, everything would have turned out fine. The problem, according to him, was that people didn't follow his plans closely because they didn't understand him. Let's face it, people were fools, oxen, and asses. No one understood business the way he did, and no one realized what a good plan could accomplish.

That the Yiddish Pavilion Theater had fallen into the hands of a Gentile was according to Nissel Schwalb's plan. That the only Jewish newspaper in London, the *Jewish Courier*, was published by a Gentile, not a Jew, was also Nissel's plan. What was the sense in that? That's what Nissel Schwalb wanted, and that's how it happened.

True, the *Jewish Courier* looked like a rag you used for cleaning dishes in the kitchen, and the Gentile publisher went broke. He had lost as many pounds sterling on the newspaper as he'd made from it. If he'd had more money, he would have lost more. But who was to blame for its failure? His goyish head—he wouldn't follow Nissel Schwalb's plan to publish the *Jewish Courier* twice a day, morning and evening, as the English did. But if the London Jews didn't want to buy the Jewish paper once a day, you will ask, why would they buy it twice a day? Nissel replied that they'd buy it twice a day because they'd want to see what a Jewish paper could find to print twice a day.

The story of how the Pavilion Theater fell into Gentile hands is so interesting that we here give our readers at least the shortened version.

Nissel Schwalb, like his brother, was a lover of theater. It apparently ran in the family. But Nissel had his own reasons. And he was a frequent patron of the Jewish Pavilion Theater, a steady visitor, practically living there. In the old days the Jewish London public sat in the theater like sheep, listening to nonsense that turned your stomach and singing that outraged your ears. Back then Nissel's mind had been busy with all kinds of plans. *Why,* he thought, *shouldn't the London Jewish public have a proper theater? And not just one, but three theaters: one for drama, one for operetta, and one for serious opera?* With three theaters, he thought one could make a huge killing. It would befit aristocrats, even Rothschild himself, to attend three theaters. The most important thing was to have a beautiful building and real artists. And there was no more beautiful building than the Pavilion Theater. If he could fix it up a bit, it would be a paradise. And artists? Not a problem! Besides, America had plenty of stars. For money you could bring over not only Adler from New York but Sarah Bernhardt from Paris. In the meantime, if he had to, he could get along with the hacks in London and toss in his sister, the leading lady from his brother's troupe, plus the young artist Leo Rafalesco from Bucharest, who would be the biggest attraction.

This was during the time when Nissel was trying to persuade his brother to bring his troupe to London as a visiting company. At that time Nissel had given up on almost all his other clients and was devoting himself to his three-theater scheme. Letters were flying to his brother in Galitzia, to America, to Russia, and even to Johannesburg and Buenos Aires. Nissel did not overlook a single Yiddish theater or famous personage. Messages arrived from everywhere with good news. People were willing to come to London. Just one thing remained for him to work out, just one detail: *Where to get the money?*

But Nissel Schwalb was not one to stop halfway. Our promoter forged straight ahead and hated to bother about details. He was also a very lucky man. Just listen to this, you'll enjoy it.

CHAPTER 6

You Need to Have Luck

On one cloudy, foggy, sunless day London was transformed into Egypt during the three dark days of the last plagues; even lighted lamps at midday were inadequate to prevent pedestrians from bumping foreheads. That was the day our genial promoter made his way to Hetchkins Bros. Ltd. in the City of London, an agency for selling sewing machines, bicycles, automobiles, et cetera.

The house of Hetchkins Bros. Ltd. belonged to two wealthy English brothers, the elder of whom spent most of his time in Switzerland risking his life climbing the Alps. The younger Hetchkins, the one we met at the railroad station, ran the business.

Nissel found Hetchkins the younger standing behind a tall desk looking over his correspondence. Schwalb said "Good morning" and asked him to set aside his business and hear him out. He had a proposition for him, a deal the likes of which he would find only once in seven hundred years.

The young Hetchkins laid aside his mail, sat down opposite Nissel, and pulled up his wide, checked trousers over his thin ankles. Distantly, wordlessly, he indicated that he was ready to hear about a deal the likes of which you found only once in seven hundred years.

Delivering his lengthy presentation with great panache, Nissel painted a colorful picture of the current state of Yiddish theater in general and of the London Pavilion Theater in particular. He laid out his plan for the three theaters devoted to opera, operetta, and drama, exhibiting a rare proficiency in matters pertaining to theater, acting, and music. Then he spread out a collection of clippings from journals, letters, and telegrams from artists all over the world. All this he translated from Yiddish into English. He ended by presenting a feasible calculation: how many pounds sterling would be needed to invest, and how many pounds sterling the investors could expect to earn.

According to his calculations, in several years they could sell not only the Pavilion Theater but the building itself plus three more buildings in the City of London.

While Nissel was talking, Mr. Hetchkins was wondering what this all had to do with Hetchkins Bros. Ltd. You didn't need sewing machines or bicycles for a theater. Maybe you needed an automobile, but why so much talk over one automobile?

Mr. Hetchkins gazed out the window at the street and tapped his three gold teeth with a finger, waiting for the promoter to finish. When Nissel finally finished, Mr. Hetchkins turned his face to him and looked him in the eyes, as if to say: *So what do you want of me?*

Nissel grasped the meaning of that look and, concisely and sharply, clarified what he wanted. He wanted Hetchkins to go in on the deal. Saying so, he examined Hetchkins's expression to see what effect this offer was having on him.

But that distant expression contained nothing to read, not so much as a letter. It was as distant and cold as the peak of Mont Blanc and as calm as a frozen lake. Mr. Hetchkins sighed, stood up, scratched his Adam's apple with one finger, and sleepily said: "All right." He offered the promoter two fingers of his right hand and told him to come back for an answer to his offer the following day at a quarter to twelve.

The answer Mr. Hetchkins gave, we don't need to tell you. Only a lucky person like Nissel Schwalb could have successfully pulled off such a wild scheme.

You don't need brains, dear reader, you don't need learning— you only need luck.

CHAPTER 7

The Musical Family

"Tonight we are going to visit the cantor," Nissel Schwalb said to his new young friend Rafalesco.

Hearing the word *cantor*, Rafalesco felt his heart skip a beat as he rose from his seat. His former *rebbe*, Yisroyeli the cantor from Holeneshti, suddenly came to mind. With a beating heart, he asked: "What cantor?"

"I mean the Lomzher cantor, the one who was with his gang at the theater. Have you forgotten?"

"Ah?" Rafalesco remembered that once in the Pavilion Theater between acts, Nissel had introduced him to a jaundiced-faced Jew with cotton in his ears. Trailing this Jew was a large retinue of boys and girls of all ages. He did not remember how many, but he did remember that there were more redheads than brunettes and that all had smiling faces and shy eyes.

When Nissel introduced the family, he had praised them to the skies, relating exaggerated stories and telling bits of gossip rapidly. His words tumbled over one another with the usual passionate intensity. Nissel's introductions were lost on Rafalesco in the usual racket of a theater backstage. Rafalesco knew that Nissel had a story to tell about everyone, and every story ended with a scandal of some sort.

On their way to visit the cantor, Nissel repeated what a rare musical family they were: a family of true singers and musicians. From the father the cantor on down to the smallest child, who was not even four years old, they sang and they all played instruments.

"Do you think anyone taught them? Ha ha! They were born ready-made musicians from their mother's womb." Nissel Schwalb stepped into a Jewish shop with Rafalesco and asked to be served bread and Warsaw sausages and anything salty.

"What's this all about?" asked Rafalesco with surprise.

"Refreshments," Nissel said quite earnestly. "They have to have something to welcome us with, and in the meantime they'll also have a little something to eat. They're poor people, really paupers. If someone didn't help them out, they would die of hunger right here in London. That's no small matter."

Nissel bought some packages of food, and a little farther on they came to a doorway. "It's quite a family, *kayn eyn horeh*! Lots of good eaters, but as for money-earners, God bless them, not a one. But that's just for now, while the children are children. Once they learn to stand on their own feet, they'll fill the house with money. Watch where you're going—it's dark here and slippery."

Nissel lit one match after another as both carefully descended into a cellar, really a hole in the ground, then stepped into what appeared to be an apartment. It was hard to tell exactly what it was. The kitchen wasn't really a kitchen, and the room was hardly a room, but the place was wide and long, with beds lined up like in a hospital. The walls were festooned with musical instruments. In the center of the room was a large wreck of a piano. A redheaded girl of seven or maybe eight (Nissel said she was not yet four, ha ha—let us go along with him) was sitting next to the piano and managed to produce terrible, screechy sounds on it. Clearly they weren't the sounds the child wanted to produce, but you must forgive the old piano. It had once had its day. Another one that old would long ago have been put away in an attic.

When the seven- or-eight-year-old girl, who was not yet four, saw the guests arriving, she stopped playing and threw herself into Nissel's arms, crying, "Uncle Nissel is here! Uncle Nissel!!"

As if making an entrance onto a stage, boys and girls suddenly appeared from behind a door, in single file, the same children Rafalesco had seen backstage. They all possessed laughing faces and bashful eyes. Their father, the Lomzher cantor, followed. His red hair was turning gray—in a year or two no red hair would remain. He held himself resolutely erect and immaculately neat. His eyes glinted, and his hands trembled like those of all hungry people, but he refused to allow his face to show what was going on in his stomach.

"First let's have a bite to eat." Nissel rubbed his hands together and licked his lips. "I am starved to death."

He untied the packages of food he had bought and began eating with such an appetite, one would truly believe he was just ending a long fast.

"Why are you all sitting around like in-laws at a wedding?" he scolded the musical family. The Lomzher cantor nonchalantly went over to the food. After all, if someone invites you, you can't be rude . . . and right behind him came all the children, whose appetites were quite evident. As the food began disappearing quickly, the atmosphere became more and more lively. Our Rafalesco thought that the food must be very good and decided to partake of it.

Nissel encouraged him: "Sit, take, slice, cut, chew. Don't hold back! You're among your own." The children gazed at the young artist with their friendly, curious eyes, and Rafalesco felt at home, as if among family. Where had he suddenly developed such an appetite? Why did he feel so comfortable, so free, so energetic? It was a strange, strange family!

Nissel kept up his endless flood of talk during the meal. He had something to say and a nickname for each one. As he talked, the family, continuing to eat, bent over with laughter. Only the father ate with dignity, wiping his lips after each bite. During all his days of wandering, our young hero had never felt as content as he did with this family, as happy, comfortable, at home, free, and lively.

Finishing off the food, Nissel winked to the cantor, who, after thoroughly wiping his lips and replacing the cotton in his ears, ordered the family to pick up their instruments and give a little concert in honor of their guests.

CHAPTER 8
Nissel's Story

The "little concert" that the musical family gave was not little at all but a complete never-to-be-forgotten concert. They played a full complement of instruments—violins, flutes, piano, basses, cymbals, harp, and kettledrums—with masterful artistry, marked by the best ensemble playing. This family orchestra, consisting of half-naked, barefoot children, moved our young hero to tears. Looking at that God-blessed but poverty-stricken ensemble, many thoughts came to his mind. During his wanderings through the world he had seen plenty of talent land on the garbage heap. No one was interested, no one paid any attention. *There are no patrons, none at all,* he thought. The Lemberg patron, Dr. Levyus-Levyusn, had been worth maybe half a million, Rafalesco remembered, and at first had made himself out to be a lover of art, a patron. But all Holtzman had to do was ask him for support, and his face changed. He promised to come to the theater and that was it—you never saw him again. *If,* thought Rafalesco, *I became self-supporting and had a lot of money, I would take this family out of the mud and show the world what they could do.*

Rafalesco as always gave himself over to his fantasies, his golden dreams, as the barefoot orchestra continued to display its wonders. Nissel sat in a corner with the mother of these gifted children, a woman with a red wig that would never turn gray, animatedly recounting his endless stories.

It was late at night by the time Nissel and Rafalesco made their way home. The Whitechapel lamps were brightly lit, but except for a tall policeman with big feet, no one was to be seen. Our young hero, who was usually quiet and weighed his words carefully, had not for a long time been as stirred up as he was that evening.

He was talkative and complained to his friend, gesticulating broadly: "Why? Why? Such gifted children, such golden hands, wallowing in the mud, living in such a hole! How is it possible that in a city like London there isn't one Jewish patron to support this musical family?"

"What are you saying, my child—a patron?" Nissel's loud voice echoed through all of Whitechapel. "Let me tell you a better story, it will drive you crazy! We do have among us someone you might call a patron, a Russian Jew. He was once, *kayn eyn horeh*, a pauper. Today he's a millionaire, may it happen to both of us. That patron's name is Stelmach."

"Stelmach?"

Rafalesco stopped walking. He seemed to remember hearing that name somewhere before, having to do with Reizel, but he couldn't remember where.

Observing that Rafalesco had stopped walking, Nissel said: "Look at this, I haven't even yet started my story, and already you're out of your mind. Better keep on listening. I met this Stelmach not too long ago at the Pavilion Theater. He's a frequent theatergoer, a great fan of Yiddish theater and a connoisseur of music because his young son, Grisha Stelmach, is a famous violinist, a prodigy. He's played who-knows-how-many times at the king's court. It's the son who's made him rich."

"So where is he, this famous violinist?"

"Not so fast!" said Nissel. "I haven't gotten to the son yet. I'm just at the father, the patron, and how we met. I met this blockhead at the buffet between acts. I spotted him walking nearby, chewing and staring at me as I stared back. We had a friendly exchange: 'Where are you from? You look familiar to me.' 'I am Stelmach,' he said. 'So are you really Stelmach himself? Tell me, Mr. Stelmach, which Stelmachs do you come from?' He looked at me as if I were an idiot and responded with an angry little laugh: 'What do you mean, from which Stelmachs? Haven't you ever heard the name Grisha Stelmach? Ha ha, a Jew lives in London and doesn't know there exists a Grisha Stelmach, who has played who-knows-how-many times at the king's court.' I shot back, 'That there is here in London a Grisha Stelmach who has played at the king's court, I know, though I am not too frequent a visitor there myself. But what does he have to do with you?' He laughed even harder and cried out with great pride: 'What does he have to do with me? Ha ha! I am his father.'

" '*Mazel tov*,' I said, 'Lucky is the son who has such a father.' And that was how we started talking—that is to say, this buffoon did the talking. He hates when someone else speaks, especially when he gets going about his Grisha. Ten horses couldn't stop him . . . Grisha-king-concert-music . . . a tale without an end! I finally interrupted him: 'I see you are a connoisseur and a lover of music. If you want to hear some really good music, I will take you to a place free of charge, and you will hear what good music really is!' He answered: 'Ach, with the greatest pleasure. To me, Yiddish theater, music, and the like are so precious that I will go with you three miles on foot.' *Excellent!* I thought. *God Himself has sent you, you fat belly! Maybe it's fated that through your interest this poor family can be helped?* In short, we set a date, and I brought the fellow to the Lomzher cantor once, twice, three times.

"My Stelmach was dazzled! Every time he went there, he didn't want to leave. He sat with them and ate with them and told them wonders about his son, miracles you would not believe! He was so taken by them, I decided to ask him, 'Perhaps it would be possible, Mr. Stelmach, for you to give some thought to this family. We must,' I said, hinting, 'send these gifted children to a conservatory, make something of them.' He looked at me confused and blinked his eyes as if he did not understand what I was saying. I said it to him in plain language: 'Mr. Stelmach, we need MONEY!' Hearing the word *money*, my Stelmach became, what can I say, ha ha ha, pale as a ghost. What good did it do? He quickly said goodbye, and from that time on, no more Stelmach! I waited for him the next night at the theater, the second night, the third night—my man was not there. I thought, *No! No one can escape from Nissel Schwalb's clutches!* I asked around and found out where he lived and marched over to his house. I knocked on the door and heard a voice from inside, his voice that I recognized. 'See who's there,' he said. 'If it's a tall, fat man, tell him I'm not at home.' Those were his very words, ha ha!" Hearing him say this, I thought to myself, *Ay! Before you squirm your way out of my hands, it'll cost you plenty!*"

Nissel's story went on as he made up yet another intrigue and scandal, two scandals, three, clutching his young friend's hand, heating up, spitting fire. Out of politeness Rafalesco acted impressed, but in truth he was thinking of something completely different. The name Grisha Stelmach was sticking in his mind. Was it possible that this Grisha Stelmach was Reizel's fiancé? If so, he was on the right track. But one thing remained: to find this Grisha Stelmach.

CHAPTER 9

They Are Off to America

The brilliant plan for three Yiddish theaters in London that our genial schemer, Nissel Schwalb, had proposed did not work out.

One of the three already-functioning theaters, the Pavilion Theater, was not doing as well as expected. The London public flocked to see the famous Leo Rafalesco from Bucharest and the famous leading lady Henrietta Schwalb from Buenos Aires. But the audience was the same one as always, the Whitechapel inhabitants, the same pregnant women with the same nursing babies disturbing the theater with their crying, the same boys and girls throwing orange peels at each other, talking and laughing so loudly, and making themselves so at home that the Pavilion Theater looked more like a small-town synagogue courtyard on a warm holiday morning when the Torah service was going on inside. The West End Jews, the London Jewish aristocracy of Lord Rothschild, on which Nissel Schwalb had staked this venture, did not so much as stick their noses into the Whitechapel theater, any more than they had before, and they would not do so until the Messiah arrived. An Orthodox English rabbi would sooner convert to Christianity, and a modern Reform reverend would learn how to pray in Hebrew, before a London Jew from the West End would so demean himself as to mingle with the Whitechapel *shnorrers* in a Jewish theater where Jews spoke Yiddish, acted in Yiddish, sang in Yiddish, and danced in Yiddish.

In a word, the business was not going well. The little bit of money had been eaten up by the traveling troupe Holtzman, Schwalb & Co., and the theater had nothing left to support its own actors. The Gentile Mr. Hetchkins was down to the very last of his pounds sterling and was preparing to shut down midseason.

Understandably, this prospect greatly disheartened our promoter, Nissel Schwalb. A goy is still a goy—Hetchkins did not want to accept Schwalb's theory that "the bigger the head, the bigger the

hat, and the bigger the pot, the bigger the fire"—that starting big
was the only way to ensure a big success.

Schwalb argued with Hetchkins that they mustn't lower their
expectations, and they mustn't quit. On the contrary, they had to
enlarge the theater and make it still more beautiful. They had to
write to Adler in America, have him tour England, not spare any
money. He proved with figures, as obvious as two times two, that
every pound sterling that Mr. Hetchkins put into the theater now
would in time bring in three pounds, ten pounds, twenty pounds,
endless amounts of pounds!

But Mr. Hetchkins was deaf to these happy predictions. Going
off on his own goyish path, he wasted no words, not even considering it necessary to convince his hotheaded salesman. Mr. Hetchkins
heard him out to the end, tapped his fingernail on his three gold
teeth, and looked out the window onto the street. When Nissel finished, he rose with a sigh, offered two limp fingers, and responded
coldly and sleepily: "All right, not a shilling more."

What could Nissel do? He couldn't replace this dried-up Englishman's goyish head with his own Jewish head. Nor was he going
to take his own life over such a thing. *The sky hasn't fallen yet. God
is God and London is London. If not this, something else will work
out*, thought Nissel, and his optimistic mind did not rest until he
came up with yet another scheme.

That scheme consisted of one word, only one word, but that
word had in it such power, such magnetism, such magic, that no
sooner did it escape from one's lips than the sleeper awakened, the
laziest became industrious, and the nonbelieving skeptic was filled
with faith and hope.

AMERICA was that word.

America was a great ocean into which flowed all rivers. It was a
wonderful dream that, to be sure, did not always come true; it was
the farthest point, beyond which one could go no farther; the ulti-
mate remedy that, if it could not help you, no doctor on earth could.

Our impetuous schemer had always been drawn to the "golden
land." From childhood he had dreamed that he must become rich,
and one could become rich only in the land of the dollar. At times
he had saved enough money for a ship's ticket, but some new scheme
always held him back. Whenever such a scheme fell through, he
would head for the ticket counter to reserve a ticket on the first ship
to New York. But even on the way to buy the ticket, a new scheme

would fly into his head, and he would turn around and get to work. Then that too would fall through, and he was off again to buy a ticket, and again turn back with another scheme in his head.

But this time he was firmly resolved, even if stones were to fall from the sky. God Himself had told him to go to America. The conditions were now propitious, preparing for him a way to New York. He had conceived that heaven-sent scheme to get to the golden land in the musical family's cellar flat. The Lomzher cantor had recently received a letter from America urging him to bring all his children there, the sooner the better. They would make him rich. "Song and music," the letter read, "is what America lacks and must import from Europe. An old musician who spent all his life back home with torn pants and worn-out boots in America can become a professor of music in two weeks."

The Lomzher cantor read the letter to Nissel, who sprang up as if singed and slapped his forehead as well as the Lomzher cantor's back.

"We're going to America! We're going to America! I have, do you hear, a scheme, a delicious, rare scheme! Tomorrow or the day after, we will meet. It will work out. Goodbye!"

A minute later Nissel Schwalb was on the street. Lively, happy, and cheerful, he strode through Whitechapel, his hat cocked to the side. Whistling a tune, he pushed his broad shoulders through the dense London crowd jamming the sidewalks like a thick fog without beginning or end.

What a city this is! he thought, whistling. *What a pleasure, so full of life! What a blessing to be alive here!*

CHAPTER 10

Breyndele Causes Mischief

The reader must remember how shamefully our director Bernard Holtzman had treated poor Breyndele Kozak. She had vowed that she would avenge herself on that director who had so humiliated her. He seemed to have completely forgotten that he had once been called Hotzmach and had polished Shchupak's boots. But what could she do to him? She was a poor, lonely wanderer created to serve others, to be exploited and then insulted. She had wandered over Europe for years, encountering false, deceiving men who mis-treated her. Finally she betook herself to America, a move she never regretted. She was no longer called Breyndele Kozak but went back to her old name, Madame Cherniak. In a letter to Henrietta Schwalb, written in large, round characters like bagels, she wrote that she had a very good job. True, she was no longer an actress, because in that blessed land of Columbus every trade had its union. The Yiddish actors' union didn't allow foreign actors on the stage. So she now had a different job, one that was respectable and also in the Yiddish theater.

What kind of job, she did not mention. She wrote only that, thank God, she was making a living, was happy, and had given up all hope of marriage. She ended with a curse: "Let all men go to hell, and above all that Yadashviler director. Is he still alive?"

"You cannot imagine my joy, my friend," Madame Cherniak continued in her letter to Henrietta,

> when I found out you were in London, the last stop in Europe before America. Ah, how good it would be, I thought, if you would come to America! Here you would be in your element. I have taken the liberty of talking about you with a few man-agers from the local Yiddish theaters. They listened intently and asked for your picture, which they went wild over. They begged me for your address and received it eagerly. They will surely write you, if they haven't already done so, and proba-bly engage you as a leading lady. My advice: do not state any conditions, and do not even answer them, but pick up and come here without delay. How long can you wander around? I won't tell you how other actors have managed. The union makes it difficult, but with stars like you, or Rafalesco, it is more than certain they will carry you on their shoulders. But it must be a secret. Aside from your brother and Rafalesco, no one must know, and especially that Yadashviler director who will so manipulate you, you will never be able to untan-gle yourself from him. So remember, for God's sake, don't write to anyone, don't speak to anyone, and come here. I've told a few people that you're coming, and they lost no time in printing up the news in the papers along with your picture. I'm sending them to you. Know that you have on this side of the ocean a faithful, a most loyal friend whose name is
>
> *Breyne Cherniak*

In this way Breyndele Kozak quietly undermined her mortal enemy, Holtzman. But she wasn't satisfied with delivering only one blow. Taking away his leading lady, she thought, was still not enough. She had to rip out of his hands his most valuable asset, the only one that would open the door to the world for him, the goose that laid the golden egg. In a word—she had to take Rafalesco from right under his nose, just as he had once stolen Henrietta from Getzel ben Getzel in Lemberg, and just as they had stolen from her other enemy, Shchupak, the other golden goose, Rosa Spivak.

This is what Breyndele Kozak decided, and God Himself came to her assistance.

CHAPTER 11

Two with One Blow

Back home in Europe Breyndele Kozak had never in her life read a tenth as much as she had read in the short time since she'd settled in the "blessed land of Columbus." In the Old Country she had enjoyed the printed word, but when had she had time to read? Once in a blue moon she had found a highly interesting novel to read through the night, weeping silently so no one would hear. But in Columbus's blessed land, you didn't need books. You went out onto the street, and they accosted you with one newspaper after another. Each newspaper was as almost as large as a bedsheet, cost a cent, and was full of fascinating articles. Oh my, what couldn't you find there? The very latest news from back home and from the whole world appeared under large, catchy headlines that you could read a mile away. And what romance novels! Two serialized romances at a time were printed in every paper throughout the year, one better than the other, a true paradise!

One fine evening, in one of these papers, our Breyndele Kozak read under the heading "Drama, Art and Music" the news that soon to arrive in the wealthy uptown West Side of New York were two visitors from Paris, two renowned stars: the great violinist from the English king's court, Grisha Stelmach, and the international singer who had surpassed Patti, the world-famous Rosalia Spayvak.

"Rosalia Spayvak?" Breyndele cried, slapping her cheeks in astonishment. "God in heaven, that has to be Rosa—Rosa Spivak!"

Madame Cherniak was in seventh heaven. *Can you believe it? Rosa, Rosa Spivak is coming!* And her mind filled with exciting thoughts and happy fantasies. Ah, what a joy it would be when Rosa saw her! First they would fall into each other's arms and kiss, and then Rosa would want to know all about her. Had she been in America long? In which theater was she working? Which roles was she playing? Ah, what roles! She was working in the theater, but she wasn't acting any longer. Here in Columbus's blessed country, there was a union for every profession, and the actors' union didn't allow foreign actors. She was working in the theater, but not on the stage. She had a job combing young actresses' hair and helping them change their costumes. Well, what difference did it make? So long as you earned a living. Wasn't that so? "Certainly, certainly!" Rosa would answer, and look at her with her radiant gypsy-eyes. Madame Cherniak knew that look. She knew that girl through and through. She would surely be thinking: *Wouldn't Madame Cherniak be better off with me? Certainly. Why should she work for strangers when she could have a job with one of her own, with whom she had once lived like a sister?*

Poor Breyndele was almost feverish from the happy dreams that she spent the entire night enjoying. She could barely wait till daylight, when she threw on a robe, sat down, and wrote a letter to Leo Rafalesco, Pavilion Theater, Whitechapel, London, in large, round characters that resembled bagels:

> *My dear Leo Rafalesco!*
> You certainly haven't forgotten your old acquaintance and devoted friend Breyndele Kozak, who once wandered through Europe with you, worked with you in the same troupe, sharing the same joys and sorrows. Ah, what a happy time that was! We weren't lacking in troubles. We all had our own worries. But let us not speak of what once was. Let us better speak of now. In the local newspapers I read that your troupe is now in London and that you are enjoying the greatest success. You can imagine, this made me so happy that I sat down to write you a letter and to send you the warmest regards from this distant land, where I am now living and earning money. I don't regret leaving Holtzman and the company, and I hope to God that will continue. America

is truly the Land of Yiddish Theater. If you were to come here, they wouldn't know what to do with you. True, not every actor is gladly welcomed. Here in the blessed land of Columbus, every profession has its own union, as do actors, and they don't let in foreign actors—unless they are famous stars. If you were to come, you would have no problem with the union. I can prove it. I asked the local theater managers what would happen if a star like Rafalesco were to come here as a guest artist. They laughed at me. "We wish it could be," they said. "If he would come, we would make it worth his while!" I am repeating their very words. I am of the opinion that London is not the best place for you. Your place is here in the golden land, where you would not be a guest for long but one of the greatest stars ever, with thousands of people honoring you, among the first of whom would be myself.

Your most devoted friend
Breyne Cherniak

Oh, by the way, I just remembered something. It is likely that any day now my old girlfriend Rosa Spivak will be arriving from Paris. You haven't forgotten her, I hope? In the local newspapers she is called Rosalia Spayvak, no longer Rosa Spivak. I am enclosing a clipping from the paper with her picture, where you can see that she is more beautiful than ever. Obviously my letter to you must be a holy secret, only for me and you and God to know. If you wish to answer my letter, here is my address . . .

Breyne Cherniak

CHAPTER 12

What Is Wrong with the Kid?

Breyndele Kozak's letters exactly hit their marks. Her success was helped along by the fact that both letters arrived exactly at the time when the London Pavilion Theater was about to be shut down, and Holtzman, Schwalb & Co. was on the verge of falling apart. Her letter to Rafalesco literally opened his eyes.

A few days before he received the letter, Rafalesco had been strolling with the prompter Benny Gorgel on one of those fashionable avenues in the upper-class quarter. There he had spotted the name Rosalia Spayvak, together with the name Grisha Stelmach, on a large poster printed in oversize letters. He stopped dead in his tracks and clutched his heart.

"God be with you, what's the matter?" the prompter cried. "What did you see on that out-of-date poster?"

"Just stand here, let's read what it says," said Rafalesco. They read that two or three months earlier a concert by two sensations, Rosalia Spayvak and Master Grisha Stelmach, had taken place in one of London's great halls.

A storm rose up in our young hero's soul. He was in London at the same time as she? How could he be in the same city as Reizel and have missed the opportunity to see her? Who knew, she might still be in London.

He began asking after her, hoping he would find out something.

The first person he asked was his new friend and guide around London, Nissel Schwalb. He didn't come right out and ask him— rather, he approached him from another angle. He asked him which famous performers and singers he had heard in his life.

Like a true theater enthusiast, Nissel did not need too much prodding. He began to enumerate the names on his fingers. It was astonishing how many there were.

True, among them were many that Nissel only knew by name, he said. But some he did know well, if not intimately. Take Patti—

"Leave Patti out of this!" Rafalesco interrupted. "Just tell me if you've ever heard the name Spivak?"

"Which Spivak? There are two Spivaks."

Two Spivaks? Rafalesco had not counted on this. "Her name is Rosa Spivak, or Rosalia Spayvak," he said.

"Ha ha ha!" Nissel broke out in his hearty laughter, which could mean that he knew only one of them, or that neither was worth knowing.

After this laughter he told a long tale about Patti, how he had met her, how a scandal had almost erupted over a grandchild of Patti's—

"Over Patti's grandchild?"

"Oho! That one has great-grandchildren already and great-great-grandchildren!"

That day Rafalesco did not rest. He could not sit still for a moment. All he wanted was to go out. He could barely hear what was being said to him.

"What is wrong with the kid?" Holtzman inquired of his partner, Itzik Schwalb.

"He's your kid, why are you asking me?"

Holtzman left him and went to see his mother. "What is wrong with the kid?" he asked Sora-Brucha as she went to prepare dinner in the kitchen.

But she interrupted him: "Leave me be about the *kid*. I have to go into the *kitchen*, pluck two *chickens* and make *dinner*, so don't *bother* me about the *kid*!" (Let us note that as much as the old woman hated London, she still enjoyed throwing in an occasional English word.)

Holtzman spat, "You're speaking English?"

He turned to his sister: "What's wrong with the kid?" he asked her.

Suddenly Zlatke turned so pale that Holtzman almost forgot about the kid, he was so alarmed. Why had she turned so pale? He locked the door, took her by the hand, and looked searchingly into her eyes:

"Zlatke, what's the trouble?"

"Nothing," poor Zlatke answered. Then she laid her head on the table and began crying like a small child, with silent, warm tears.

CHAPTER 13

The New Company

Like a true Englishman, Mr. Hetchkins of Hetchkins Bros. Ltd. kept his promise. He figured out exactly how many pounds sterling he had lost in the business, and he honored the agent with a distant, drowsy-eyed, "All right." He didn't even honor him, as usual, with two cold extended fingers but turned his back to him, ducked into a waiting automobile, and was gone.

Another time Nissel might have been deeply offended and taken it to heart, but now he did not give it a second thought. He was too busy with a new scheme to care whether a cold Englishman had turned stubborn after investing a few hundred pounds sterling in a Yiddish theater and then would not go one pence further. No, a Gentile is not a Jew. Once a Jew becomes involved in a business, he's in it till the bitter end, win or lose. Whoever said that Englishmen understood business? Hetchkins didn't begin to understand. Don't think Nissel didn't tell him this to his face—he certainly did! "Mr. Hetchkins!" he said. "I have more brains in my left foot than you have under your hat."

That at least was how Nissel boasted to his friends. Soon he began hatching his new scheme, deciding how he would get to America with a company consisting of the very best artist (by this he meant Rafalesco), the best singer (his sister), and the best musicians (the Lomzher cantor and his children). And where did he, Nissel Schwalb, fit? Do you think he no longer had any connection with the Yiddish theater? Oho! What a connection! In all likelihood, Nissel had once been an usher in the London Pavilion Theater. He expanded on what it meant to be an usher:

"To you he is just a ticket-taker. To us he is an usher. An usher's work, you understand, is more outside than inside. The fact is, you can't manage without him. The usher's post is at the very entrance to the theater, where he not only takes your ticket, but tells you where you are seated. Most of all, he keeps order. In a word, on the usher the entire theater depends, as all of London depends on the policeman. Try removing the policeman from London, and it's all over."

He steamed ahead: "And I was, you must know, *the* usher among all the ushers, the head man at the Pavilion Theater. Oho! On *my* watch there was no throwing orange peels from the loges and no nursing babies crying in the orchestra. If anything at all went wrong, I took them by the collar, and one, two, three, they were marched outside! Once this scandal happened . . ."

And Nissel rolled up his sleeves and began to relate an awful scandal in which he had been involved. The story would have been very interesting, except that there was very little truth to it. Nissel made it up from start to finish, inventing it while swearing it was true.

After telling the "scandal" story, Nissel moved on to expound his great plans for that land of gold. He painted the great wonders of America in the brightest colors. He portrayed his troupe's future life there as a paradise. After all, their company possessed the greatest artists!

"Tell me, what could be greater than a theater that has its own orchestra, its own artists, its own musicians, its own ushers—everything its own! Whatever money comes in is divided equally, not one more and another less, as in a commune. Well? Isn't that right?"

Nissel was holding forth in the cellar of the musical family. The first to be moved by Nissel's eloquence was the Lomzher cantor, who announced that he was ready to sign a contract that very moment with both hands if necessary, for as many years as they wanted, even forever. "In the contract," he said, "you can state specifically that my children agree to perform whenever and wherever they wish and for as much as they are willing to pay, and we share all earnings."

But then Itzik Schwalb stepped forward. His red face sweating heavily, he protested that the plan wasn't altogether fair. How could you compare Rafalesco or his sister, the leading lady, to just anyone? There had to be some standards, some limits.

Brother Nissel sprang up and gave his brother a piece of his mind: "You are nothing but a miserable slave! You've become completely enslaved by those fine entrepreneurs. You've become accustomed to those exploiters like Getzel ben Getzel, Bernard Holtzman, and their ilk. But I am not Getzel ben Getzel nor Bernard Holtzman, who ride on other people's backs. I am a fair and humane person. It is more than right for some to work for a year or two or three or more in America for the benefit of others!

Understandably, Nissel had his way. A large majority adopted the idea of a commune, and that was the way a new company of art, music, and theater was founded.

CHAPTER 14

The Capitalist

Now but one issue remained: where to get the money to relocate the new company to America? That problem was solved much more easily and quickly than anyone could have imagined.

The reader, who by now is well acquainted with our genial schemer, knows that Nissel had no difficulty when it came to money. So long as he had a good scheme, "Money," he said, "is my least worry." He had never had to go looking for money, he said—money came looking for him. This time money came to him in the most wondrous way.

It happened at the Café National, involving our good friend, Mr. Klammer.

As we know, Mr. Klammer considered himself to be a good friend to everyone and a humanitarian. But with Nissel Schwalb he had established a solid, long-lasting friendship. Nissel kept no secrets from Mr. Klammer. He entrusted his plans first to Klammer and then to the rest of the world.

Over a glass of beer Nissel described his bold plan for the new company, identifying all its members. They would be ready to leave for America the very next morning, except for the one thing—they had no money for the ship tickets, travel expenses, and other costs. Not a small matter, *kayn eyn horeh,* it was a sizable company!

As Schwalb spoke, Mr. Klammer kept his eyes shut as he stroked his Theodor Herzl beard. When he ended, Mr. Klammer addressed him in a leisurely fashion:

"All right. Mr. Schwalb, do you have anything else to say, or is that all? If you are finished, let me pose just one question. If I were to offer you, let us say, a capitalist, would you agree to share all your profits with him, fifty-fifty?"

By temperament, Nissel was the kind of man who hated to dwell on details. He believed that if you spotted a rabbit in the woods, you shouldn't waste time deciding from which angle to shoot it. You should shoot—*pif-pof*—and that'd be the end of it. But out of politeness he diplomatically rubbed his forehead like a person in the midst of financing a business. After two or three seconds' thought, he stated firmly: "I would agree with the greatest pleasure, with the greatest respect, and with the deepest thanks."

"All right. Give me your hand, and may it be with good fortune and a blessing. I'm your capitalist."

Mr. Klammer pointed to himself, and with unassuming dignity he bestowed upon his friend a tender, affectionate, magnanimous smile. Had Lord Rothschild himself been in his place, he could not have been more tender, more affectionate, or more magnanimous.

Nissel was so taken aback he forgot to extend his hand to close the deal with a handshake. He had known Mr. Klammer for many years and knew him to be a Zionist, a Territorialist, a pillar of the community, and something of a busybody, a good brother and a successful innkeeper, always ready with advice. But that Mr. Klammer was a capitalist—that was unexpected, almost unbelievable news.

Mr. Klammer was quick to read Schwalb's thoughts, and with the same magnanimous little smile he said, "Don't be surprised that I am ready to invest capital in this business. I am a beginner, but I am not as green as you might think. I am not going in with my entire capital. I am leaving my business to my wife. I've long been fed up with selling noodle soup. Everyone must decide where he best belongs and know where his abilities lie. As the Englishman says, 'Everyone in his place.' Mr. Schwalb, please give me your hand before I change my mind. I have a principle: If I decide something, let it be done, or as the Englishman says: 'If you want to do a thing . . .' "

There was much celebrating that evening in the Lomzher cantor's cellar. His neighbors, accustomed to the continuous music and noise coming from the sizable musical family, gathered outside and peered into the cellar through the curtainless windows. They witnessed that a tall, heavyset fellow stood with a glass in his hand giving a speech to a crowd of guests sitting and drinking. Following the speech the family took to their instruments. The tall, heavyset fellow removed his jacket and began dancing with the passion and fire that only a happy father could show at his youngest daughter's wedding.

CHAPTER 15

This Dog Deserves to Be Beaten

The news that the Pavilion Theater would be closing was for our Holtzman like a pistol shot to the heart. He fell upon his partner, accusing him of dragging him into a quagmire. He assaulted him with more dreadful curses than his partner could absorb.

Schwalb had an easy disposition—if he was being cursed out, he usually took it silently. You could abuse him however you wished, and he would not contradict you. As if he were deserving of the curses, he would look at you and perspire. But this time he could not hold his tongue. His brother's honor had been impugned! Holtzman had called him an ugly name, and to defend his brother, he would strike back.

Our poor director continued to curse away at his partner, furious about the unsuccessful dealings in London, upset with the clamorous, cloudy city with its mists and fogs, its gray, cold walls and its gray, cold people, and aggravated by his persistent cough which had grown worse in London. At least the curses relieved some of the pain in his heart.

"This London, together with you, should have been swallowed

up in the earth before I came here! I would have been better off breaking a leg, and you both your legs and your neck into the bargain. Bad enough that I have one partner—now I have two!"

"Why do you always throw up to me that there are two partners now?" Schwalb demanded.

"Once this theater is no longer a theater, there's no longer a partnership. Why do I need two such leeches like you and your brother?"

"Is that so? Then we're through!" Schwalb stood up. "We're going off to America anyway."

"You're going to America?" Holtzman looked fiercely into his eyes. "That's fine with me. You can go to hell for all I care!"

Schwalb started to leave, then stopped and turned his red face toward Holtzman: "Our sister is coming with us."

Holtzman slapped his cheeks in mock horror: "Oo-vah! I'm going to rend my garments, sit down, and cry my eyes out right in the middle of Whitechapel."

Already at the door, Schwalb retorted: "You will cry plenty when you hear who else is coming with us—"

Here Holtzman turned all colors, and his eyes blazed with fury: "Your brother will not live to see the day, that bison!"

Why would "bison" be more insulting than the names Holtzman called him every day like "buffalo" and "water ox"? Go ask Itzik Schwalb. He heard the word *bison* and flared up. His always-red face turned green. Full of rage, he came close up to Holtzman and said quietly but menacingly: "Listen, louse that you are! Say that word once more about my brother, and I promise you'll leave this place a corpse!"

"A corpse?"

"A dead man!!"

Holtzman was apparently not at all frightened by his former partner. He broke into laughter, wracked by a coughing fit. "You? You will turn me into a corpse? Ha ha! *Pche-che-che!* Fool! Before you make a move with your bearish hulk, I assure you I will smack your red snout and make an omelet of it!"

A good part of what these two were threatening to do to each other was surely believable. But suddenly on the scene appeared old Sora-Brucha. She placed her thin but broad-boned shoulders between the two of them and settled the matter. She pushed her son aside, she shoved Schwalb out the door and locked it.

Then the real hell began for our Holtzman. Schwalb's words now sank deep into his heart: "*You will cry plenty when you hear who else is coming with us.*" Exact words, clear words—did he need an explanation?

Now the director understood why the kid was going around as if he were on another planet. The brothers Schwalb had led him astray. Their sister had turned his head. It was clear as day. Perhaps the kid himself wasn't even willing to go. No, he could not accept this. Didn't they realize that? Oh! They knew it very well.

Hotzmach, where were your eyes? Holtzman said to himself, sparing no curses. But curses alone were insufficient. If only he could slap himself, or if someone else would break his bones.

Hotzmach, you deserve this! Holtzman berated himself, pacing like a wild animal, his eyes ablaze. *It serves you right, Hotzmach! This dog deserves to be beaten!*

Out of heartache and anger at himself, he kicked a chair that stood innocently along the wall.

Hearing the clatter, his mother came running from the kitchen, pale as a ghost. "What now? What made that bang I heard in the kitchen?" she asked.

Sora-Brucha did not come in alone empty-handed. In her hands she held a chicken, almost plucked. The chicken's head was thrown back, revealing its slaughtered neck. The dead chicken seemed to look with its pale, glazed eyes right at him. Thought Holtzman, *Everyone is looking at me, everyone!*

Overcome with rage, he felt that at any moment his heart would tear in two. He attacked the old woman with his fists and cried out in a voice not his own: "Go back to the kitchen! To the kitchen! To the kitchen!"

Sora-Brucha remained standing, spat, and turned back to the kitchen with the almost-plucked chicken.

It serves you right! Holtzman said again to himself. *This dog deserves to be beaten!*

CHAPTER 16

An Imminent Catastrophe

Ever since he arrived in that accursed city of eternal fog and mist, a grim foreboding had taken hold of Holtzman. Something catastrophic was bound to happen, only he did not know from which direction it would strike. Almost at once the close relationship between that bison, Nissel Schwalb, and the kid displeased him, but there was nothing he could do about it. He had to accept that the kid had grown up and was a serious person in his own right. Who would have thought that this naïve lamb, who not so long ago couldn't count to two and didn't know the value of a coin, would suddenly develop ambition, insights, a serious attitude, and his own way of doing things, with aspirations for education, for knowledge, for learning languages, and who knew what else?

And who was to blame, if not he himself, Holtzman? What evil spirit had possessed him, back in Lemberg with Getzel ben Getzel, to snatch away the leading lady and those two *shlimazels* Breyndele Kozak and the prompter, Benny Gorgel, whom the actors called the "person of education"? As soon as Holtzman had sensed that Breyndele was cozying up to the kid, whispering secrets to him, he sent her on her way, and good riddance.

But that was not the way it had gone with the second *shlimazel,* the prompter. Gorgel was Holtzman's only confidant, and it was he who caused him more grief than he could have imagined. He had taught the kid everything he knew, and that had been the ruination of Holtzman. How could the director look into Rafalesco's eyes now that he could speak several languages, read books, and declaim entire passages from Shakespeare by memory? He was already dreaming of a new world, he had said, with new horizons. What new world, what horizons was he talking about? It was as if he were speaking Turkish, all about "independence" and a new reformed theater with a new repertoire, new plays, everything new, new, new! And what should be done with the old? Should it all be thrown to the dogs? And who would create all that new stuff? These were all strange words he had picked up from the "person of education," may cholera strike him this very day, him and the bison at the same time!

And so Holtzman ended with a curse. His deep, gloomy ruminations then carried him from the kid to his sister, Zlatke.

His sister! His sister! For her sake Holtzman had woes to spare. Poor Zlatke was quietly wasting away like a guttering candle before his very eyes, and again, who was to blame if not he himself? Who had arranged to bring her and their old mother to Lemberg if not him? Who had torn her away from her home, her honest work, made an actress of her, a wanderer, and awakened in her false, false hopes? He had tried to bring her and the kid closer together, but in vain. He'd thought it would be a match, but it turned out—what would happen to his little sister now if the kid was to get up one fine morning and leave, as Schwalb had said, for America?

Holtzman tortured himself, considering the worst that could happen. But he soon took hold of himself: *Ach! Nonsense!* Rafalesco would not possibly desert them and go without him all the way to America. It was nonsense! Nonsense! He had too good a heart, too gentle a character, and too honest a soul to do that. If they were going, let them all go together. What better way was there?

Holtzman consoled himself with these thoughts, but they soon clouded over again: *This cough, may it go to hell along with the bison.*

Yes, Holtzman's illness had recently worsened in bleak London. Only God knew when he would be up to a long journey. The doctors recommended that he go to Switzerland, if possible, or to Italy, where there was clean air and warm sun. Ha ha ha, those fools! Idiots! Real idiots! What did Holtzman need clean air and warm sun for, without a theater and without a stage, ha ha ha?

In the depths of his misery, paradoxically, Holtzman laughed very hard. It set off a coughing fit so powerful that old Sora-Brucha came running from the kitchen once again, her sleeves rolled up, with a large bowl in her hands instead of the chicken: "That old cough again?"

She reeked of onions and pepper, which made Holtzman's cough all the worse, but he suppressed it. Shouting at his mother, he ordered her back into the kitchen, back to the onions. In the midst of his laughing and coughing, he grimaced, spat into a cloth, and shoved it deep into a pocket so the old woman would not see that he was spitting blood. But no one could fool Sora-Brucha. A mother has a sharp eye and sees her tragedy very clearly. She wrung her hands: "Woe is me! What suffering I have! How miserable I am!" She forced her sick son into bed and sent Zlatke for the doctor.

Terrified, more worried and pale than usual, with tear-filled, swollen eyes, Zlatke threw on her cape and ran to get the doctor.

Hurrying through the noisy, busy streets of London, Zlatke thought in her heart: *What a hell this is—so many horses, trams, and automobiles everywhere. Why doesn't someone take pity on me and run me over and kill me?*

A black, thick fog was settling over the Holtzmans' heads—an imminent, unavoidable catastrophe.

CHAPTER 17
Happy Passengers

Like a gigantic beast, the huge, white ship *Atlantic* moved through the sea. This strange creature made its stubborn way through the water, fought with all its might, wrestled with the wind, cut through the angry waves of the Atlantic Ocean, and forged ever farther ahead on its course from Southampton to New York.

At first the passengers were fascinated by the prospect of this grand journey. They could not tear themselves away from the deck, contemplating the divine beauty of nature and extolling God's wonders surrounding them. But gradually they became seasick. Feeling as if their heads were spinning, they quit gazing at the infinite expanse of sky and water, water and sky, without beginning or end.

One by one they retreated to their cabins to lie down with heavy hearts, alone with sad thoughts and feelings.

A very few forced themselves to stroll up and down the decks, or gathered in groups drinking beer and smoking cigars. They talked, laughed loudly, and told stories, anecdotes, and tall tales, as if nothing were affecting them.

Among those few happy passengers were a pair of our good friends: Mr. Klammer from London, with his Theodor Herzl beard, and his partner, Nissel Schwalb, the former producer, now owner, manager, entrepreneur, director, and treasurer of the new theater troupe Klammer, Schwalb & Co.

Yes, dear reader, gone was Holtzman, Schwalb & Co. The name Holtzman was thrown out, and in its place was the name Klammer, a fact that affected no one but Holtzman. The world seems to consist of a huge army marching off to war. The army will not halt because one soldier falls along the way. The fallen one has a choice. If God grants him strength, he will stand up; if not, no one will bother with him. They will step over him or trample him underfoot with their boots. True, it was a tragedy. But who was to blame for Holtzman's illness if not Holtzman? He had neglected his cough for so long that his doctors weren't allowing him to leave his bed. They were taking his temperature and pulse and ordering him not to speak. Not to speak?! Of all things! What was the difference between a person and a beast if he could not speak? No, there is nothing we can do about it—we must part from our Holtzman for a time and wish him a speedy recovery. We will instead accompany our new troupe, traveling on the ship from London to that land that has drawn to itself people from all over the world ever since Columbus discovered it more than four hundred years ago.

Mr. Klammer and Nissel Schwalb sat together at a table, drinking beer and talking, talking, and talking. Their mouths never shut. What could they have been talking about? Nothing much— apparently they were trying to outdo each other.

Mr. Klammer told old stories about his Café National and about the Russian *shnorrers* and the London charities of which he was a regular member. He peppered his stories and anecdotes with choice witticisms and always with a concluding "As the Englishman says . . ." to drive home the final point.

To Nissel these stories and anecdotes were far from new. On the contrary, he had already heard every one. Not only had he heard the story, he had in fact been there himself when it all happened, and if not for him, a terrible scandal would have occurred. Just listen . . .

And Nissel recounted with his usual passion the scandal he had nipped in the bud. Meanwhile the waves chased the ship like uncaged wild animals, keeping up a steady rhythm. They rose steadily higher and higher until they threatened to leap over the deck, inundate the ship, and capsize it, swallowing it up with everyone on it. But our pair hardly noticed. And on they went. They continued drinking their beer, smoking cigars, and talking, talking, endlessly talking.

Happy passengers!

CHAPTER 18

Between Sky and Water

Another person remained sitting on the upper deck of the ship *Atlantic,* but he wasn't drinking beer or smoking a cigar. He was just reclining on a deck chair, wrapped in a warm plaid lap robe and covered with a red blanket. He was a rather young passenger with a pale, very likable face. His pallor told one that he had long been seasick. With half-open eyes he lay stretched out, holding his aching head and peering at the sky. It was so low, it seemed to merge with the sea. He had thought the sky was lighter-colored, illuminated by the sun. There was not a trace of cloud or hint of wind. Why then were fearsome waves chasing the ship on both sides and becoming ever more ferocious, angry, and wild? Why was the ocean so stormy? Why was God so angry? Why was the ship tossing back and forth, up and down? Or was he imagining it? Why couldn't he lift his head or move so much as a finger? Why did he feel worse and worse, to the point of fainting? Fainting? No. Of dying, dying, dying!

He tried to remember how many days they had been traveling in between sky and water but could not. He could not even remember from where and to where he was going. Worst of all, he could not remember his name. That he was called Rafalesco he knew, but was what his *real* name? He could not have remembered even if you threatened to cut off his head. Oy, his head! His head!

"You don't feel well? Why don't you lie down in your room? Come." Nissel Schwalb bent over him and gazed tenderly into his eyes. But Rafalesco looked back as if he did not know who was speaking to him. Who was standing over him? He wanted to sit up but could not. He strained desperately to remember who this man was. *Reboynu shel oylem!* What was happening to him? Where in the world was he? Why couldn't he remember his own name? His friends in *cheder,* his brothers and sisters, his parents used to call him by a name. His parents? Where were they now?

"Listen, I have a little flask of cognac. Just touch your lips to it, and you'll feel much better."

Rafalesco did not begin to understand who was leaning over him. Who was the man looking into his eyes? He seemed familiar, had familiar eyes, but who was he? Why was his head so heavy? Who was groaning so? That was the ship groaning. Who was whistling so? That was the wind whistling. And the waves chased one another, rising higher than the tallest building. Suddenly there was a clap of thunder, and a bolt of lightning flew by his eyes. Imaginings! The thunder was no thunder. That was the sea talking, those were the waves rising up and falling back. That was not lightning but a sunbeam glancing off the swirling water of the unbridled, angry sea.

"Listen to me—suck a piece of lemon. It will calm your heart."

Ah! Now he knew who that was. Holtzman. Bernard Holtzman? But why was his face so ruddy and fat and fresh-looking? In one hand he held a flask of cognac, in the other a lemon, and he was begging Rafalesco to have some: "Listen to me. Put a little lemon in your mouth. Give me your hand, lean on me. I'll take you down to your cabin."

Nissel called out for his friend Mr. Klammer to help. But Mr. Klammer was already where Nissel's brother was, where his sister and the Lomzher cantor and his musical family were. All of them were lying on their beds, groaning, gasping, seeing the Angel of Death before them. Only he, Nissel, was standing on his feet. He was the only one of the new troupe who remained hale and hearty. The driving rain and snow had beaten on faces and chased even the few remaining passengers belowdecks, except for those much accustomed to these conditions—the stewards, the sailors, and the captain, who stuck a pipe in his mouth and gazed with a dry smile at the angry sea as if it were a naughty child. And the huge, white creature they called *Atlantic* shouldered its way stubbornly, farther and farther, into the deep, wide, infinitely limitless void made up of sky and water, water and sky, without beginning or end.

CHAPTER 19

A Woman's Hand

Once Rafalesco began to recover from his stupor and the fog slowly lifted, he sensed more than saw that he was in a bed, undressed, in his stateroom. He felt someone's hand on his forehead, a gentle, warm woman's hand. But whose hand it was, he couldn't tell.

That he was on the ocean, he knew from the acrid smell of the angry sea and from the roaring of the waves, which were playing like animals in the light of the bright sun. The still-rampant waves, tossing the ship higher than tall buildings, slapped at Rafalesco's porthole, telling him to get up, go out onto the upper deck, and observe God's wonders. "*Enough, enough of this lying in bed,*" he imagined the ocean waves saying to him. He marshaled his memory as best as he could and thought: *How did I come here? Not long ago I was on the upper deck, sitting in a deck chair so comfortably, in awe of divine Nature, warming myself in the setting sun reflected in the foam of the playful waves and musing about the endless merging of water and sky.* He tried to sit up but was afraid he would fall back again. He was also afraid to open his eyes all the way lest he become dizzy from the ship's rocking motion. He let out a heavy sigh: "Oy, my head! My head!"

"Still complaining about your head?" It was a woman's voice, a familiar voice, but he didn't know whose. He felt a hand on him, a gentle hand, a warm, woman's hand stroking his forehead, brushing back his mussed-up hair. Who could this be? Whose hand? Sometime earlier, he did not remember when, he had felt exactly the same hand stroking his forehead and brushing his hair back.

That had been Holtzman's little sister, Zlatke. One evening in London Rafalesco had been lying on a sofa in his room, daydreaming those sweet dreams that were always devoted to the cantor's daughter, Reizel.

No one was in the house, he remembered, but himself and Zlatke. He had never felt as miserable as on that night. A strange longing, he remembered, had crept into his soul and pressed and pulled at him like tongs. He had felt like crying.

Whether he had cried, he did not remember. But Zlatke had appeared near him—perhaps he had called her over—and sat near him and stroked his forehead, just like now, and smoothed his disheveled hair just like now. A warmth had suffused all his limbs. He had felt the warm hand of a devoted sister, and he was endlessly grateful. He put his arm around her, he remembered, drew her close, buried his face in her lap, cried his bitter heart out to her, and confessed that there was one whom he loved with all his life, for whom he was prepared to go through fire and water, whom he could not forget whether dreaming or awake. "What is her name? Where is she?" Zlatke had quietly asked, and her voice, he remembered, trembled, as did she herself. He did not want to reveal her name. But where was she? If he knew where she was, he would not be there now with the traveling troupe. He would no longer be wandering, he would throw everything away and fly to her, because they had given each other their word, long ago, as children, that wherever they might be and whatever might happen to them, they would always be together, always and forever!

No, he did not know where she was. He only knew that she was famous, that she was great and rich, and that she was known worldwide for her singing. "Have you ever heard the name Patti?" "Is she greater than Patti?" "Much greater than Patti, there's no comparison!"

He praised his Reizel to the skies, holding nothing back. She was

an angel sent by God! And now he was so happy to have found someone to whom he could sing her praises and boast of his beloved. Who
else but Zlatke would be willing to hear him out? But he couldn't see
that his every word was to her holy, or feel that her heart was beating.
He couldn't feel her fluttering in his hands like a little bird.

Rafalesco had no inkling of what Zlatke was going through.
His only thought was to pour out his heart to her, to confide in her
his secret, and to ease his soul.

He went on to tell her what his future plans were. He would one
day meet his beloved, he said, and never again would he part from her,
never. He had taken Zlatke in his arms, drawn her tightly to him, and
promised her that when he was together with his Reizel (the name had
already slipped out—too late!), he would bring Zlatke with him, because
he felt that she was loyal and devoted to him, like his own sister.

"Are you as devoted to me as a sister?" he said as he embraced
her warmly, much more warmly than a brotherly embrace requires,
but Zlatke remained silent. Rafalesco did not understand why
Zlatke was silent. He embraced her more tightly and asked her why
she didn't answer him. Was he mistaken? Did she not love him?

"Not love you?!" And Zlatke threw herself on him, put her arms
around him, and kissed him as tears streamed from her eyes.

"Why are you crying, little silly? Why are you crying? Why are
you crying?"

From that time on, Rafalesco remembered, he had often wished
to be alone with Zlatke, to talk to her about Reizel. This was not
too difficult because Holtzman, it seemed, had made every effort to
arrange for them to be alone more often. Could he have been mistaken? No, he was not mistaken—otherwise why would Holtzman
leave him alone with his sister, then quickly return to see if they
were sitting close together, then quickly depart? Ach, Holtzman!
Holtzman! How hard it had been to part with Holtzman, how hard!

"It's time to get up, dearest! You can already see land. We're
almost in America, dearest, dearest!"

It was a familiar voice, a woman's voice. Who was that speaking to him? Who was calling him "dearest"? But he was still afraid
of sitting up, lest he fall back. He was still afraid of opening his
eyes, fearing the rocking of the ship, the merging of water and sky
that would again make him dizzy. He sank into his own heavy,
leaden thoughts and relived the trying moments of his parting with
Holtzman. And he wanted to beat his breast in penitence.

CHAPTER 20

Farewell, Bernard

It had been a cold, cloudy morning of rain, chill, and fog, a typically dismal, smoky London morning.

Rafalesco's things had been packed, and he was ready for the journey. He had eaten, dressed, smoked a Havana cigar, ordered a cab, and ran back in for a quick goodbye to Holtzman.

"Be well, Bernard!"

Be well, Holtzman had answered—with his eyes, as he was strictly forbidden to speak. Oh, if only he could speak to Rafalesco, he would at least have snapped at him, reproached him angrily as he deserved, cursed him out as only he could do, and Rafalesco's leaving would have been easier to take. But no, Holtzman simply fixed on him his keen, searching eyes and—ach, how much sorrow, how much endless sorrow was contained in that look! Holtzman extended a frail, thin hand that seemed to Rafalesco rather too warm.

Never had Rafalesco been so eager to leave Holtzman as at that moment. He could simply have gotten into his cab and been done with it. But instead of moving toward the door, he had sat back down on a chair next to the bed where Holtzman, covered with a blanket, lay in a fever amid the medicinal stench of sickness and death.

As long as Rafalesco had known Holtzman, he had never seen him in such bad condition. Death hung on his lips, flickered in his glazed-over eyes, and hovered over the room. Rafalesco imagined his friend lying dead, his blanket drawn over his dead face, his feet toward the door, his face not visible, only his toes showing. And a candle would be burning at his head, his mother and sister on either side of him rocking back and forth and mourning over him, keening and weeping, wringing their hands, chanting plaintively: "Beloved son! Dear brother, devoted brother! Who will take ca-a-are of us now?!"

He remembered that sad chanting from Holeneshti. Leah the cantor's wife had chanted like that when her own mother had died in her seventies. He sensed the presence of death in the reek of medicines and in Holtzman himself. All he wanted to do was to flee as far as he could go.

But instead of fleeing, he remained sitting. He bent over Holtzman and spoke to him warmly, comforting him, promising that as soon as he arrived in America, he would write to him every day. And when Holtzman got out of bed, which he would surely do soon, he and his sister and mother must come immediately to him in New York, right to him.

Rafalesco kept looking down at his boots. He felt his face burning, because he knew he was lying. Holtzman would never recover. He would never go to America, and even if he were to regain his health and go, the new company would not hire him or his sister. It was a complete lie from beginning to end! But once Rafalesco began lying, he kept on. "Of course," he said, "it would be better if your sister could travel right now with the troupe, but it isn't possible. How could she leave you alone in London?"

Here Holtzman grabbed him by the hand, and his keen eyes lit up and he barely managed to say hoarsely, "An orphan, a poor orphan." More he was not able to utter. He choked on his tears.

"Goodbye, Bernard!" Rafalesco again said, now for the last time. Finally he was relieved to be on the other side of the door, no longer seeing before him the dying Holtzman and no longer smelling the nauseating stench of illness. He looked around and thanked God that he had not at that moment run into Zlatke or the old Sora-Brucha. Where were they? Should he wait for them? No. He had better go on. He wanted to run but held himself back, walked slowly to the cab, and carefully negotiated the high step into the cab, which whisked him away to the station. The whole company—both brothers Schwalb, their sister, the Lomzher cantor, and his musical family—were awaiting him impatiently: "What took you so long? We might miss the ship."

Only when he stood on the upper deck of the *Atlantic* did he breathe more freely. The ship departed from Southampton calmly, proudly, confidently, beautifully. The weather too was beautiful. Gone were the cold clouds and the thick fog of icy London. From a clear sky the warm, friendly sun looked down on them. The sea was calm and as smooth as a mirror. The ship glided over the water, barely touching the waves that were just forming, bowing and bending, making themselves felt, bringing regards from the vast ocean beyond, which moved yet remained in place from time immemorial. A sweet warmth spread through Rafalesco's limbs. He felt free. He was on his way to his beloved, to his only beloved. But suddenly, standing close to him, appeared Henrietta Schwalb, dressed up and bejeweled as usual in real and custom gems. She gave him her hand, and they strolled together on the upper deck. Henrietta held his hand fast; she gazed into his eyes and laughed her high-pitched, coquettish laugh, showing for all the world to see her fine pearly teeth. And the world looked at this couple and wondered who they were—brother and sister, bride and groom, or perhaps man and wife?

Thus our hero bade farewell to Holtzman, his closest friend who had been as loyal to him as a brother, and to Zlatke, who had been as devoted to him as a sister, much more than a sister. "Be well, Bernard" was all Rafalesco had had to say to his friend, Bernard Holtzman.

CHAPTER 21

An Unfortunate Kiss

If Rafalesco behaved toward Zlatke as a brother, he did not know how to behave toward Henrietta. In London the leading lady had seemed always to be at his side, casting flirtatious, coquettish glances his way. In her heart she knew he was as cold as ice to her, but to the world she pretended she thought that he was madly in love with her and that she was his soon-to-be fiancée.

Everybody knew this. There had even been talk of breaking the engagement platters and putting up a wedding canopy. But how could that be worked out? The problem had been named Holtzman. The brothers Schwalb realized that as long as Rafalesco was close to his friend and impresario, Holtzman would not permit the kid to fall into Henrietta's clutches. They had sought ways to be rid of that *shlimazel* Holtzman. Then God had come to their assistance, and they had succeeded beyond their wildest dreams. They hardly needed to convince Rafalesco to go with them to the golden land. When he heard they were preparing to go to America, he immediately offered to join them. The brothers Schwalb were in seventh heaven. They even decided the kid must be crazy about their sister. Fools! They didn't realize whom they had to thank. They didn't know that the same Breyndele Kozak, who had written to their sister from New York, had also drawn Rafalesco there with the promise that he would find his beloved, the cantor's daughter from Holeneshti. And so the brothers Schwalb decided that as soon as they arrived in America, they would put up the wedding canopy, and it would be a done deal. But for now it had to be a secret, not a soul must know of it.

Understandably, the secret was not kept from everyone. From Mr. Klammer, as we know, Nissel Schwalb had no secrets. He was the first to be entrusted with this great plan. Mr. Klammer heard him out, as was his way, with closed eyes, as he stroked his Herzl beard. When Nissel finished, Mr. Klammer said that to him it was not news, he had known it long ago. He had nothing against the match, except for one thing—there must be no delays—one two three. As the Englishman says, "Slow at the start, fast at the finish." They had to see to it that the betrothal took place immediately because actors are quite unreliable in such matters. Mr. Klammer waved his fingers back and forth to show how unreliable actors were.

The same opinion was expressed by their third companion, the Lomzher cantor. Nissel had locked himself and the cantor in their basement room and secretly told him of the great plan. And since that room was also the kitchen where the cantor's wife was cooking dinner, she was in on the secret too, and the cantor's entire family was soon anticipating a wedding.

Only one person had no idea about this plan: Leo Rafalesco. He was oblivious to what was going on. His head and his heart were elsewhere, with the cantor's daughter, Rosa Spivak, whom he saw both in his dreams and in his waking thoughts. It was for her sake that he had deserted on his deathbed his dear friend who had sacrificed so much in his behalf. It was for her sake that he had left behind his little sister who was so overcome with feeling, she could not bring herself to say goodbye to him. Ach! What ugly sins he had recently committed! He could not forgive himself.

And now, lying alone on his bed in his cabin, where he was slowly coming back to himself, he thought: *How did I fall so low? How could I have acted so badly with two such close good friends?*

Like a panorama of woeful images, each one darker than the next, his entire life passed before his eyes, and he saw not a single ray of light, only vileness. He had robbed his father, run away from home, and killed his mother; he had lied to Holtzman; he had betrayed Zlatke in the ugliest way, pretending to be a brother, promising her his love, broken her young, innocent heart. And now he was going to a distant, unknown land forever, forever! No, he was the lowest of the low. He deserved to be reviled, and he felt the deepest revulsion toward himself. As he beat his breast in contrition, suddenly the seasickness came over him, "Oy, my head! My head!"

"Your head still hurts?" asked that familiar voice, the voice of a woman sitting next to his bed. She laid her hand on his forehead, brushed back his hair, and gazed into his eyes warmly, lovingly, full of concern. Who could she be? He smelled face powder and perfume, familiar perfume. He could swear it was Henrietta Schwalb. He opened his eyes slowly and saw sitting close to him a familiar white-powdered face with red-painted lips. Yes, it was Henrietta Schwalb. Her face was close, very close to his. Her eyes looked deeply into his eyes, and the red, brightly painted lips were quietly whispering near him: "Dearest! My handsome boy! Darling!"

At that moment all was forgotten. He forgot that he had just beat his breast in repentance, forgot where and for what reason he was going and who he was. He felt her hand caressing him, saw her eyes gazing at him, heard her lips whispering: "Beloved! Dearest!" He took her in his arms. Her red lips bent down closer to him and came together with his lips, pressed in a long, long kiss.

You can be sure that that kiss would come back to haunt him. It wasn't a calculated kiss, but it was a kiss before witnesses. Because at that very moment three people were at the door: Nissel Schwalb, Mr. Klammer, and the Lomzher cantor.

CHAPTER 22

America! America!

Of all the passengers who arrived that day in New York on the ship *Atlantic,* none pushed as urgently toward the exit, none were more frantic and distraught, than our Children of Israel. It was easy to understand why. The majority of the Jewish passengers were emigrants. They were coming to America to find a new home, after leaving their old home where they had been treated cruelly and from which they had been mercilessly evicted. They were looking toward this new country as they would toward the coming of the Messiah. They huddled together like sheep, their hearts pounding, pulses racing. Dear God! What awaited them in that blessed land?

Almost all the new arrivals had a son or daughter, a husband or wife, a relative, redeemer, or friend who was waiting for them on the shore and who was prepared to "claim" them from the ship, to ease the pain they had to endure at their first entry station, aptly called the Island of Tears.

For Jewish emigrants the entry was torture, an ordeal, a foretaste of *gehennam*, a purgatory where sinners had to purify their souls in order to enter paradise. Once this purgatory had been called Castle Garden, but today it was known as Ellis Island. The name had changed, but the woes and sufferings, the sighs and the tears, the humiliations and the torments remained the same, and with God's help they would remain so as long as some people lorded over others, as long as some people needed to demonstrate that they could still be bestial.

Among the passengers who went out onto the upper deck to view the golden land from afar were the itinerant artists of our wandering troupe. In contrast to the many anxious passengers, this troupe of happy emigrants had gotten all dressed up, each according to his means, ready to greet "the golden land of Columbus" properly, in a celebratory, holiday mood.

The brothers Schwalb were dressed in their finest clothes, after seeing to it that not a trace of facial hair remained. Who needed a beard? Who needed a mustache? Their faces were as smooth and clean as platters. The brothers had very different faces. Nissel looked like a German sausage eater going to church on Sunday, and Isaac looked like a Russian corporal who had just completed his term of duty and had promised himself never again to drink whiskey, only beer.

Mr. Klammer outdid them both—he parted his Herzl beard and combed it horizontally, one half to the right, the other to the left. He wore a snow-white shirt and white tie under his sharply tailored smoking jacket, all of which was supposed to lend him the charm of a true gentleman—but he most resembled a headwaiter in a fancy hotel. As he walked through the ship's dining room, he caught a glimpse of himself in a mirror and remained awhile, apparently quite satisfied with his appearance. Of all the passengers on the ship, he felt himself by far the handsomest. What would New York say? Perhaps in America there were handsomer men than he, but perhaps not. Mr. Klammer could not keep from saying to himself with a very modest little smile:

"Mr. Klammer! You are all right."

It was quite otherwise with the fourth partner of the company. We are speaking of the Lomzher cantor, who had long been away from his shtetl in Poland and whose Orthodox sidelocks had long ago disappeared. But if you force me, just between us, I will let you in on a secret—his beard was again beginning to show. But why should we speak ill of anyone? In short, he brought out his old cantor's *Shabbes* gabardine and satin sash, buttoned the vest all the way to his chin, and put on a pious face, so that neither the Schwalbs nor Mr. Klammer could keep from exclaiming: "What is this?"

"America!" he answered them in one word, then explained his reasoning. "America, you understand, is not Europe, and New York is not London. America is a country where you must make up your mind. If you are an artist, you're an artist. If you are a cantor, you're a cantor. Do you understand?"

Whether they understood or not, we do not know, but the Lomzher cantor was above all a practical man. Until his children one day began to earn money in America, until the group of artists started to bring in gold in the golden land, he would do some cantorial chanting on the pulpit for his countrymen, the Lomzher Jews who had sponsored him and his musical family, especially as the High Holidays were approaching. Thank God he was still feeling strong and the voyage had not diminished his vocal powers. On the contrary, the journey, he felt, had improved his voice. His throat was itching to warble and chant. He had been practicing all morning, ever since they had first spotted land. In a word, the Lomzher cantor was once again a cantor, dressed like a cantor, wearing a cantor's expression on his face suitable for the High Holidays.

The cantor's wife also dressed for the holidays. Over her blond wig she tied a silk head scarf, exposing her ears so people would see the gold-plated earrings dangling from her earlobes (which she had worn since the day of her wedding) and a few wisps of her own blond hair from under the wig. Who knew which counted more in America: piety or vanity? Maybe one needed to have both. Anything could happen in America.

Their children were all clad in European style. From the eldest to the youngest they were dressed in children's clothes: short pants, bare thighs, small caps over long hair. They were the outfits worn by all the famous prodigies like Huberman, Fidelman, and Grisha Stelmach, who hid their young beards and whiskers as long as they could, but despite all efforts, no matter whether you shaved it, cut it, or did what you will, facial hair began to sprout and grow at a fast rate.

The musical family was more delighted with the voyage than any of the others. More was awaiting them in the golden land than anyone. When they were told the good news that land had been sighted, they all ran to the upper deck, embraced one another, joined hands, and in unison loudly sang an American song to the rhythm of the waves, which now beat less strongly but more regularly:

"Ame-ri-ca! Ame-ri-ca!"

CHAPTER 23

The Calm Sea

The once angry sea calmed as the ship approached New York.

It breathed quietly, like an exhausted beast. The vastness of the sea is awesome when it lets itself loose and tosses its great waves about. But when it is becalmed, it is majestically, quietly beautiful.

A riot of color, revealed only when nature is tranquil, was now mirrored in the sea. Delighting the eye of the happy passengers, it repaid them for the anxieties it had caused them during those few hard days of the stormy crossing. With grateful hearts and with enthusiasm for that eternal power that had created so vast, beautiful, and pleasant a world, they forgave the sea and again poured out on the upper deck to contemplate and admire God's work. They could once again be content, satisfied, and happy, as if nothing frightening had happened.

As thrilled as all the passengers were by the approaching shores of New York, two particular young people standing close together, arm in arm on the upper deck, were the happiest of all. At least, that was the way it appeared. They were young, attractive, in the flush of health, and for all the world to see, happy. Many looked at them with envy—a happy, happy pair!

Who was that young pair? Obviously it was none other than the leading lady, Henrietta Schwalb, and her lover, Leo Rafalesco. Whether Rafalesco was happy, we do not know, but Henrietta was certainly in seventh heaven.

Happy, happy Henrietta—she had finally succeeded. She had pursued this handsome young man from their first meeting long ago in Lemberg. And at last now, on the ship, she had caught him. He was hers, he was hers!

Only she knew the sweet taste of that triumph. Her eyes shone, and her face radiated the most intense happiness. Her entire manner proclaimed: *Do you see this handsome young man with the gentle, mild eyes, with his beautiful blond locks? Don't be envious, but he is mine! Mine! Mine!*

She nestled herself closer to him, looking up deeply into his eyes, wishing to assure herself that the little fire burning in them and the thoughts reflected in them were about her. Ha ha, of course they were about her, who else?

If you were to stroll from one end of the ship to the other, through all the classes, you would not find another beauty the equal of Henrietta Schwalb. You would not find another to match her fair complexion, her cherry-red lips, or her luminous eyes, squinting to make her look nearsighted, and her pearly-white teeth that made men crazy for her when she laughed! Try to find another on the ship whose clothes lay on her so elegantly, whose hair was so stylishly combed, whose hat so suited her hairdo, whose collar so perfectly hugged her neck, whose gloves so lovingly embraced her little hands. And who could afford her jewels, her gems?

Possibly there were on the ship fashionable ladies who owned more expensive, finer jewelry. Take that tall, thin, dried-up Englishwoman with gold teeth who was wearing jewelry Henrietta would have been happy to possess. This Englishwoman wore pearls around her neck and emeralds on her ears; a medallion of emeralds was pinned on her bosom; on her fingers were diamonds, sapphires, rubies, and more emeralds! But what a face! Poor thing! How could those jewels look on her? What charm could they have? If Henrietta were to put on those emeralds, oh! But soon she herself would have emeralds, as many as she wanted. Let them get settled in America. Let Rafalesco play a few of his great roles. Let the public see what a treasure he was, and the diamonds, sapphires, rubies, and emeralds . . . her fantasy flowed over into a question to Rafalesco:

"Do you like emeralds?"

Henrietta cuddled up to Rafalesco, not taking her nearsighted eyes from his face.

"What emeralds?" asked Rafalesco.

"Blind bat! Don't you see?"

No, he didn't see, not an Englishwoman, not any emeralds. He wasn't even looking where she was pointing. He was altogether distracted.

Henrietta laughed, not because there was anything to laugh about, but in order to again show off her pearly teeth. She gazed at Rafalesco with her new way of looking, which she had recently perfected in front of her mirror. She had picked this up in London from observing a nearsighted woman with a lorgnette. The woman looked very seductive as she peered intently through the lorgnette with her nearsighted, half-shut eyes while squeezing her eyebrows together. Henrietta soon adopted that pose. She had set herself before the mirror, half-shut her eyes, and squeezed her eyebrows together, and from that time on that was her look.

"Yentl, what is it with you?" her brother Isaac had once confronted her.

"What do you mean, Itzik?"

"Why are you doing that with your eyes?"

Henrietta turned red and disregarded what her brother said, but she kept on trying to look like that nearsighted woman with the lorgnette.

Not too long ago, when Rafalesco was still far from being hers, it was Zlatke who had stood in her way—that little nothing, that wisp of a scullery maid with the upturned little nose. Henrietta had not noticed anything, but her brothers had opened her eyes. They had told her that Zlatke's eyes shined too brightly when she caught sight of Rafalesco, that she blushed when she saw Rafalesco looking at her, and that they were too often alone together. On these matters Isaac made her more observant. One time he told her, "Come with me, you ninny, and I'll show you something." He took her by the hand, led her to a door, and told her to look through the keyhole. But what Henrietta saw was exactly the opposite of what her brother had in mind. She saw Rafalesco pacing, his head bowed, his hands deep in his pockets, and the scullery maid with the upturned little nose sitting on a stool crying. Isaac later explained to her that maybe she was crying because her brother was seriously ill, in critical condition, the doctors said. But he had been spying on them and knew that was just an excuse.

"If the brother is critically ill," he asked Henrietta, "why is the sister sitting on a strange man's lap and crying her eyes out?"

"You're a lying dog!" Henrietta threw in his face, and left in a huff. But the worm of jealousy had entered deeply into her heart and was quietly gnawing away at her. Thank God she was now out of that London hell. Now she would have him all to herself. Now no one else was in the way, no one, no one!

The first thing they would do when they arrived in New York, Henrietta decided, was to be photographed together in various poses. Pose number one: They are going for a stroll, arm in arm. He is wearing his elegant gray overcoat, she a boa around her throat, her hat cocked to the side. Pose number two: They are sitting across from each other at a round little table. He is holding her hand in his and looking at her *en face*, and her eyes are half-shut, her eyebrows pressed together, just like that nearsighted lady with the lorgnette. Pose number three: Against a lit background, two heads—his head and her head—are close together. Here her eyes have to be wide open, looking up like a holy madonna. Pose number four—how can she wait for them to arrive in America?

"Are we still far from America?"

He didn't hear her. She returned to her thoughts about being photographed upon their arrival. Even her brother Nissel had said that the first thing they would do in New York was get married. If he weren't afraid of the embarrassment, he would have put up a wedding canopy right there on the ship. But that was not what Henrietta wanted. She wanted to be a fiancée for at least a few weeks. What was her rush? She had looked forward to this so long. Why shouldn't she enjoy it?

"Are we still far from America?" she asked again, but he did not hear. Was he in another world? Yes, he was in another world. Soon he would be where he had striven to be for so long. Soon he would be with the one he had not forgotten for even a moment. How would their first meeting be in that country, after so many years? Would she recognize him? He would certainly recognize her. He had her picture that Madame Cherniak had recently sent. It was in his breast pocket that he was pressing with his hand. Henrietta was certain it was about her he was thinking. Who else could it be? And she moved closer and closer to him, looked into his eyes, and cuddled up to him like a kitten.

"Soon we'll be in America, isn't that so?" she asked a third time, and flicked his nose, laughing: "Ha ha ha!"

Rafalesco looked directly at her. He could not understand why she was laughing. He had been interrupted right in the middle of his best thoughts. He had already forgotten who was leaning against him. She had reminded him. He looked her over, thinking: *Why am I with this flirt? What makes her think I could be in love with her? That would be like out of the frying pan into the fire!*

Unwillingly, Zlatke came into his thoughts with her eternal melancholy appearance, her eyes swollen from weeping. Unwillingly, he remembered Holtzman's last, barely audible, choked words at their parting: "An orphan, a poor orphan." He wished he could forget, but could not. He wished his entire past, his life since he had become a wanderer, could remain on the other side of the ocean, in the Old World, so that he could arrive in this new land newborn, pure, clean, guiltless, as he once was long ago, in his bygone innocent childhood years. But he could not forget, and his worst thoughts kept coming back into his mind, along with the very saddest feelings.

He tried to drive away those thoughts and feelings by looking out at the sea. He could not tear his gaze away from it. All the passengers were again on the upper deck, also gazing at the sea, unable to get their fill of its beauty and luster. There was no limit to its might when it was angry. There was no comparison to its beauty when it was calm.

The sea was calm as they approached the shores of New York, not quiet, but calm.

CHAPTER 24

The Lomzher Cantor in Trouble

As is well known, entering paradise is not easy. First you must be purified, go through all seven levels of *gehennam*. As in the paradise in the next world, so here in the nether paradise called America. Not for everyone are the doors open, and not for everyone is entry smooth.

Before leaving home, those who know what to expect use all means at their disposal to prepare and protect themselves. Even so their hearts start pounding miles from New York, and they are beset with anxiety. Their teeth chatter, they yawn, they stretch, they make sure to look their best, they check each other out, they pray to God they won't be rejected at the hearing. May they quickly go through the seven levels of *gehennam* on the Island of Tears and peacefully enter through the doors of paradise into the golden land.

Our wandering artists of the itinerant troupe Klammer, Schwalb & Co. laughed at the entry ritual. Some bargain, America! They could, they said, if they wanted, get in and out of America three times over.

"Fools have thought up all these difficulties. There are no difficulties. So long as you are healthy, young, happy, decently dressed,

and can show a few dollars, and name a few American friends—
what else do you need?"

Did America worry about a gentleman like Mr. Klammer, who
wore an elegant smoking jacket and whose mother tongue was
English? And how about that giant Nissel Schwalb—what did he
have to fear? Or Isaac Schwalb? May all emigrants have it so easy.

We certainly need not worry about the artistic couple, Rafalesco and Henrietta. For such young, handsome, elegantly clad
people all doors are open. But all that did not apply to the Lomzher
cantor and his musical family.

Some people are fated to have problems. The entry should have
gone smoothly for the family. They were, thank God, all healthy
and strong and had good appetites—if only there was food to be
had. But a misfortune occurred to the cantor, and he himself was
responsible for it. With a large group of children like his, *kayn eyn
horeh,* he should have talked to his companions earlier, and they
might have advised him to have in hand a few dollars to show on the
Island of Tears.

He protested that he had had no idea he had to show money.
He had thought that America was America and not Lomzhe. In the
end it was, forgive me, worse than Lomzhe. Many poor people come
to Lomzhe, but would anyone ask them whether they had money?
Who would even think of it?

The poor Lomzher cantor sweated even more than when he was
chanting on the pulpit. Imagine, you take a Jew aside and demand
that he show you money. What did they mean by money? They meant
American dollars. English pounds were acceptable, and even Russian
rubles, so long as it was money. That was how it was explained to
him later. He had to produce real money to prove he had something
to live on at the beginning and not become dependent on strangers.
"On strangers? God forbid!" the poor cantor defended himself as
best he could, half in English, half in German. He explained, gesturing with his hands, that he was not alone, that he was accompanied,
kayn eyn horeh, by a large family. Then, they informed him, would
he please show how he would support that family?

In short, our cantor dug himself in deeper and deeper. They
were just about to escort him back to the ship. His halting efforts
at English and German were futile, as were his gesticulations and
appeals to his partner, Mr. Klammer, who could speak English.

Mr. Klammer pretended not to notice. He was an expert at giv-

ing advice in Whitechapel at his Café Nationale. But at the debarka-
tion, with all the tumult and chaos mainly on account of the "cursed
Russian *shnorrers*," enough to drive you mad! our Mr. Klammer
slowly turned away, smoothed his smoking jacket, parted his Herzl
beard in two, and went off, as the Englishman says: "I disown it bag
and baggage."

Luckily there was a second partner on the ship, Nissel Schwalb,
a master of schemes. Sniffing out from afar that the cantor was in
trouble, our genial schemer gathered what was going on. He called
the cantor's wife to the side, whispered to her, and winked at her as
he seemed to be pointing to her bosom. He winked again at her and
her children, saying: "Come!"

Under other circumstances, you can imagine that the cantor's
wife would have rebuked our schemer. The modest but occasionally
impudent Lomzher cantor's wife was entering America with a company of artists—true enough. However, she was not, God forbid, a
chorus girl or a dancer or even a leading lady like Henrietta, who
kissed men like Rafalesco whether they were engaged or not. She
was still the legal wife of the Lomzher cantor. A fellow like Nissel
Schwalb must show respect. But now, with all the upheaval, and
upon hearing that her husband was in trouble, she had no time to
consider those things. And here that fellow Schwalb grabbed her by
the hand, led her straight to the table, and like a person who spoke
proper English, put himself forward as the protector of the cantor
and his wife and their musical family, announcing:

"Gentlemen! I am honored to present to you the wife of this man,
neither of whom speaks a word of English. Do you see this large
family? This is, with God's help, a family of exceptional musicians,
amazing talents. All, as you see them, from the father to the youngest
child, earn their bread and are worth their weight in gold. Only one,
this one, she is the only one who earns nothing. She is a devoted wife
to her husband, a mother to her children, a good homemaker, and
she looks after the money. All the money is safely kept by her. To get
a cent from this woman is like crossing the Red Sea!"

Those were the words that he spoke to the officials in English.
To the cantor's wife he spoke in plain Yiddish: "Dear lady! Would
you please unbutton your blouse and take out the money!" It was
not necessary.

Not until they set foot on dry land, on the American shore, did
the Lomzher cantor realize in what danger he had been and from

what peril he had been delivered. He embraced his savior and protector, insofar as it was possible to embrace a man of Nissel Schwalb's dimensions. He hugged and kissed him and thanked him with tears in his eyes: "You are a genius, a King Solomon, an angel of God!" And again he lunged to kiss him.

"Enough! Enough!" Nissel tore himself away. *What does this man want from me? He's going to choke me, this Jew, right here on the American shore!*

CHAPTER 25

God Bless This Country

At that affecting moment when the Lomzher cantor embraced his protector and savior, his savior pushed him away abruptly with both hands. He had just spotted a round, moon-faced woman. Wrapped in a red cape, a broad smile displaying her large white teeth, she was throwing herself upon his sister and then planting a hearty kiss on his brother Isaac. She then threw herself on Rafalesco, clasped him with her short, chubby hands, and lavished on him the hugs and kisses that only a devoted mother might give.

"Who is this creature?" Nissel inquired of the cantor and his wife. But they were already in the clutches of their transplanted Lomzher countrymen. Among the Lomzher Jews living in America, some had long become adjusted to life here, and some were still newcomers and had not lost so much as a drop of their newness, even down to the laborers' red knotted kerchiefs they wore around their necks.

The women were also of various kinds: Some were all or part Yankee and called themselves "missus" and "lady," wore large hats, and had gold teeth; and some could not part with the wigs they wore back in Lomzhe—real *Yente-Mirels*, as they were called.

All those types, the greenhorns and former greenhorns, the missuses and *Yente-Mirels*—all were delighted to see their countrymen, the Lomzher cantor and his family. They shouted, cried out, whistled, waved their arms, and lunged forward, as if this were not New York at all but the center of Lomzhe on the Jewish Street.

The Lomzhe men and women besieged their countrymen with

invitations for breakfast, dinner, and supper. "Please, come to me! No, to me! Without fail, come to me!"

The Lomzher cantor and his family were overwhelmed. Ever since they had left Lomzhe to wander the world and live in abysmal poverty in London's Whitechapel, they had never received as enthusiastic and heartfelt a welcome as on the American shore. Moreover, in Lomzhe they had never been treated as such welcome guests as in that happy, free land of Columbus. On the contrary, back home among their own, they were considered a bit too many to handle. Even on the way over, they had heard insinuations they were too large a family. Mr. Klammer, one of their own, had asked several times, albeit with a sweet smile, why they had brought their whole family with them. They should have left several of the children, he said, behind with relatives in Lomzhe. And now they had suddenly become esteemed guests, so beloved that people were fighting over them! God bless this country! God bless this country!

The cantor and his wife looked at each other and shed a tear as the children swelled with pride. They were elated, not knowing whose invitation to accept first. They wished to visit everyone, why not? They wished to have breakfast with this one, lunch with that one, dinner and supper with all of them. True, a person cannot divide himself up, but with this large a group, it would work out! It would work out!

Nissel stood and observed the scene, his heart brimming with joy. Who else but he knew how poor and lonely this clan had been in London? Now so many friends had materialized, and good friends too! He had known ahead of time that it would be this way. That was America for you. God bless this land! Too bad he didn't have time to thank them, to get to know them better and discuss America, "Yankee Doodle," Columbus's country—too bad! Nissel Schwalb's mind was at the moment preoccupied with another, less pleasant matter. The apparition in the red cape had first greeted his sister, then his brother, and was now showering Rafalesco with kisses.

No, Nissel could take it no more. He went up to the red cape and tore her away from Rafalesco. "Who is this creature?" he whispered to Rafalesco.

Rafalesco seemed relieved to be rescued from this annoyance. He smoothed his hair, straightened his creased cap, and made introductions: "My friend Schwalb . . . my old acquaintance Breyn—Madame Cherniak."

Rafalesco had come very close to disclosing her real name: Breyndele Kozak.

That was she.

CHAPTER 26

A Time of Trumpets and the Sound of the Shofar

Our new itinerant troupe, Klammer, Schwalb & Co., had chosen to come to America at the height of the year's activity in bustling, noisy, busy, commercial New York.

During that month Jewish life in the United States of America roused itself from the long, sleepy weeks of summer vacation, its pulse beating stronger, the Jewish streets more crowded than ever. The Jewish newspapers burst with screaming headlines, and countless announcements urged Jews to attend *shul* and stated which cantors would be leading services at which *shuls*. There were ads for *shofars, lulavs, esrogs,* and New Year's cards. It was the time of the High Holidays, *erev* Rosh Hashanah, a time of trumpets and the sound of the *shofar*.

It was a time of transition from the old to the new Jewish year, from summer to winter. It was a time to be rid of all that was old and used, to shine and polish what was worn and faded, to refurbish clothing and shoes. It was a time to change jobs, to hire and fire workers, to change teachers and schools, to change where you lived—to "move," as they called it in America. It was time to start afresh with the upcoming New Year. In a word—the Jewish world was the same all over.

They had a good word for those exciting days: the Season. It was an apt word, suiting the spirit of that land of work for everyone alike: for those who offered jobs and for those seeking jobs, for those who sweated and for those who made them sweat, for those who were paid in a handful of coins and for those who were paid in bundles of dollars, for those seeking a crust of bread and for those seeking pleasure, for those who languished through the hot summer with wife and children on the top floor of a walk-up tenement or downstairs in an airless, dank basement, as well as for those who spent the summer lounging in a lakeside cottage in the Catskills, as they called it, playing poker and pinochle day and night, or a game called Flirtation that consisted of seducing another man's wife secretly or swapping wives openly—what is mine is yours, and what is yours is mine.

The Season was also the time of renewal and revival of the theater, and especially of the Yiddish theater, which was heralded in the New York Jewish press. There were regularly appearing columns called "News from the Yiddish Theater World," filled mostly with short notices, bits of news items, innocent lies circulating backstage, and outrageous gossip. They announced, for instance, that this or that theater manager would be returning next week from Europe with the greatest singers from the Paris Opera in tow; or that this or that manager had rented this or that theater; or that this or that manager had stolen away this one's or that one's star; or that this or that prima donna was leaving the Yiddish stage for the American stage; or that this or that noted playwright, who had become immortal for his musical-realistic-dramatic works, had written for the new season three patriotic-musical-realistic-dramatic pieces that would outdo anything ever seen before in the country. This all served to tickle the ribs of some star, pinch the cheek of some leading lady, quickly brush the lips of some theater manager, and bring a smile to some playwright. It was all nothing more than chattering the press permitted itself before the Season really began.

Once the theatrical Season was in full swing, the press took on a different aspect. Then if you opened a Yiddish newspaper, your eye was assaulted by a series of frenetic articles with bold headlines. Full pages shimmered before you in large letters, finely written words and high-sounding phrases, all slick and smooth as honey, speaking to you of the heavenly pleasure that this or that manager had prepared for your benefit and of the veritable paradise that you would enjoy in this or that theater. Those articles were so expertly, so cleverly put together, that the ordinary naïve reader's eyes popped, and his jaw dropped. You couldn't tell whether these were news items or editorials, raves from critics or paeans from satisfied, impressed reviewers. Never would it occur to you that you were reading an expensive advertisement, a paid-for page in which a theater manager could write whatever his heart desired, in which he could boast about his theater with trumpets and the sound of the *shofar*.

"Do you wish to see something spectacular, something you have never seen before?" a journalist trilled like a nightingale. "Do you wish to enjoy an hour in paradise? Do you want to know the meaning of celestial pleasure? Do you wish to hear the sound of authentic Jewish singing? If you wish to weep with authentic Jewish tears, then see *The Broken Hearts*. If you want to laugh heartily at original humor and pure Jewish wit, then see *The Alrightniks*. If you wish to feast your Jewish eye on modern, elegant scenery and patriotic settings, then see *The Jewish Essence*. If you wish to see exotic dancers as you have never seen them before, then see *Four Sticks Make a Canopy*, the most beautiful and moving Jewish tragic-comic-melodramatic-patriotic operetta that has ever been seen on a Jewish stage, performances evenings and matinees all through the holidays."

"Among all the pieces in all the Jewish theaters, this holiday *Menorah* shines so brightly that it has cast into the shadows every other piece," modestly wrote another manager of his own production. *The Menorah,* he added with rare reserve, "stands out among the others like a giant among dwarfs. At no other production will you witness so many tears shed on the stage over the plight of desolate widows and miserable orphans, over lost children and butchered babies, over Jewish daughters murdered and Jewish wives dishonored in bestial pogroms. And the rib-tickling humor, laughter, and Jewish wit heard on our stage cannot be beat. At no other production will you hear such sweet melodies sung by famous leading ladies and see such exciting dances by the loveliest dancers in the world. Such amazingly outstanding and heavenly grace has never been seen or heard before in New York!"

A third manager, delivering a no-nonsense appraisal like a city boss, informed his readers that he had spent a profitable summer in Europe, during which time he had visited all the great cities, all the theaters, kept his eyes and ears open, and busy as a bee had sampled bits of honey from everywhere. That gave him the idea that he should put together for the New York Jewish public a holiday piece that would astound the playgoer with never-before-seen national costumes and fill their hearts with real Jewish pride. It would be a piece bringing together the finest, most authentic Jewish types from the Old Country with the most modern swashbucklers of the twentieth century, a piece that would contain authentic biblical themes, the most uplifting Jewish national melodies and patriotic songs, and the very latest dances from the Paris ballet. Putting this all together, the manager-dramaturge wrote, had cost him a great deal of effort and considerable money, and he was prepared to invest even more effort at great cost to produce it. Only then would he undertake to find the most suitable name for his masterpiece. Imagine, the most difficult thing in a musical dramatic work is not the music, not the dramatization, the characters, the sets, or the staging, but the title. A musical drama must have a title that rings like a bell, plays like a fiddle, and sings like a prima donna. And thank God, he decided that the most fitting title for this huge musical-dramatic-national-patriotic tragic-comedy had to be nothing other than *Moishe*.

CHAPTER 27

Moishe

The name Moishe was popular in the Yiddish theater world in America.

Moishe was the name given to Jewish theater patrons.

Moishe was the symbol of naïveté, coarseness, and vulgarity.

Moishe was the ordinary man-on-the-street with whom you did not have to stand on ceremony. Give him hay and straw to chew—you could rely on Moishe's strong stomach to digest it.

They say—and that makes it as good as true—that the name was thought up by none other than the so-called father of the Yiddish theater, the sainted Goldfaden, may he forgive me for passing this on.

But whoever thought up the name Moishe has much to answer for, because it quickly became associated with another word that cannot be printed but that most Jewish Americans don't hesitate to rhyme with *kadoches* (*toches* to my many, I hope, refined readers).

True, some objected to that word. One fine day in the Yiddish press one of them stepped forward with a fiery protest against this crude, blasphemous desecration of the holiest historical name we possess. But that did no good. People read the protest and had a good laugh. The name Moishe remains to this day, not only in Columbus's land but back in the Old Country, associated with its companion word, so that whenever one of our Yiddish actors said "Moishe," everyone knew what would follow.

In a word, the author of the national-holiday-musical-dramatic-patriotic spectacle with the title *Moishe* was right on the mark. In the show the prima donna led the cast and chorus in performing a patriotic song so charmingly and with such a sweet melodious voice that the audience received it with the loudest applause. The entire audience joined the leading lady, cast, and chorus in singing along. Of course, "Moishe" was the name of the song.

The prima donna, a picture-perfect woman wearing an officer's uniform, sang in a beautiful mezzo-soprano voice:

> *Have you seen my Moishe?*
> *Moishe? Moishe? Moishe?*
> *He's the greatest ever.*
> *Great! Great! Great!*
> *Oh, my, Jewish children, Moishe!*
> *Have you seen my Moishe?*

At this point the leading lady cast her eyes searchingly through the orchestra, the boxes, and the gallery. A voice from the boxes would cry out:

"I am Moishe!"

The prima donna would reply in her charming manner:

"No! You are not my Moishe!"

A voice from the audience would cry out:

"I am Moishe."

Then the prima donna, joined by the choir and the audience, sang out:

> *Moishe here and Moishe there—*
> *There's a Moishe everywhere.*

After the first two or three performances of the song, "Moishe" could be heard all over the ninth district of New York. It was sung in homes and on the streets, in kitchens and in shops, in all Jewish restaurants, in stores and in factories—"Moishe," "Moishe," "Moishe" was heard everywhere. A greater success could not have been hoped for. Once the public picks up a song from a national-musical-dramatic-patriotic spectacle, it will be a long-running hit. The manager of that theater could be certain that "Moishe" would not be removed from the repertoire so long as Moishe did not tire of singing "Moishe." Let the critics inveigh as much as their hearts desired. Let journalists joke about the holiday fare, mocking it as "a parade of silly spectacles." The managers of the Jewish theaters insisted that they knew what Moishe liked and how to satisfy him. And if it came down to it, they said, who was really corrupting the public's taste, the theater or the press? Let the critics leaf through the Jewish newspapers and see what kind of trashy novels were printed in honor of Moishe. A fiery polemic ensued between representatives of the two great powers of the world's largest Jewish community—the Jewish press and the Jewish theater—and all on account of *Moishe*. Moishe read what was being written about him and could not have cared less. Where did he have time, in the land of "hurry up" and "help yourself," to busy himself with such foolishness? Worn out, preoccupied, and confused, the overworked public, exhausted from a day's labor, looked forward to the evening and went out onto the Jewish street. There they bought tickets, filled the gallery, the orchestra, and the boxes, and drank in that sweet, charming, patriotic song "Moishe," sung by that charming prima donna as she searched through the audience with her eyes:

> *Help me, Jewish children!*
> *Tell me, where is Moishe?*

And the audience helped her out:

> *Moishe's here and Moishe's there –*
> *Moishe, Moishe is everywhere.*

CHAPTER 28

The Cooperative Crumbles

The holiday season, with its unrefined, artless holiday pieces, was about to come to an end. The New York Jewish theaters were moving on to more serious fare. Large billboards and the second pages of Jewish newspapers featured well-known names from the Jewish American theater world. New dramas would be produced, as well as works from the Old World that were renamed and ingeniously rewritten. Old pieces brought across the ocean were expertly adapted to the American style, designed to suit current Jewish tastes, so their true origins were indiscernible. In a word, they were now "all right."

The critics wrote quite earnestly about these plays, dedicated entire pages to them, and compared their authors to the greatest playwrights. One they likened to Sudermann, another to Hauptmann, a third they blessed with the name Ibsen, and a fourth was anointed the Jewish Shakespeare—even greater than Shakespeare!

Not all the reviewers were in agreement—their reviews reflected sharply different opinions. One critic lauded a play to the skies and deified its author; another critic pitilessly ripped it apart, stomped it underfoot, and made hash of its author, asserting with absolute conviction that since Columbus had discovered America such trash had never been written. In a word, the Season was at its climax—and *Moishe* still reigned on the Jewish street. The manager of the theater where it was playing kept his hands nonchalantly in his pockets and lamented things were not going well at all: "My theater is too small to accommodate the crowds coming every night to see my *Moishe*." He said this with the sad grimace of a Rockefeller who didn't know what to do with all the many millions descending like manna from heaven.

One can imagine how the other managers envied him, but nothing they produced could equal *Moishe*. They dug out of their chests the best plays by the best dramatists in the world. They advertised that their theaters were "the true home of the Jewish drama." But to no avail—*Moishe* confounded and defeated them all. The poor managers were in despair—when suddenly there appeared a source of hope for revival.

That source of hope was our cooperative, Klammer, Schwalb & Co.

After arriving in New York, the itinerant company had waited and watched from the sidelines, observing the goings-on in the Jewish theater of Columbus's land. When a stranger sets foot in a strange country, he is like a swimmer in unfamiliar waters. First he has to look around to see where he is, get his bearings, learn the language, and become acclimatized.

But to continue on the sidelines was not the best plan. Our artists easily ate up the little money Mr. Klammer had brought from London. With every pound sterling he had to exchange for American dollars, he groaned and chided his partners for not getting to work. In his usual gentle way he let them know that his pockets were emptying and that very soon, before they turned around, it would be, as the Englishman said, "No pay—no show."

The partners resented these hints, especially the head of the company, Nissel Schwalb. All eyes were fixed on the genial schemer, wondering what he would come up with this time. Nissel, for his part, was not about to shame himself or diminish his reputation. He merely asked for patience, and just as two times two equals four, they would soon be raking it in, making a fortune, outdoing Jacob Schiff, putting away three Rockefellers. Nissel Schwalb, with his keen mind, had figured out that in America the rules of the Old World did not apply, that what worked in Europe was a disaster in America. To perform with the whole troupe, as once planned, he concluded, could lead to ruination. Far better for the company to come out gradually, one performer at a time, so that each would have a chance to be seen and cause a "sensation." Nissel Schwalb, a practical businessman, knew that you didn't display your best merchandise first—you led with your staples. First, he put forward his sister, Henrietta, the leading lady, and her brother, Isaac, the tragedian.

For Isaac it did not go too well. Besides the fact that he was an unknown and the critics decided that he was better suited to be a butcher or a milkman or a vendor carrying a barrel of ice cream on his head than an actor playing tragic roles—besides all those compliments, there was the problem with unions in the Yankee country. No foreign actor was allowed in, no matter what they did. Isaac Schwalb had no choice but to take another job, which we will find out about later. Meanwhile we will turn our attention to Henrietta, the famous prima donna from Buenos Aires.

CHAPTER 29

The Star from Buenos Aires

In her letters to Henrietta, Breyndele Kozak had not exaggerated when she wrote that in America Henrietta would be warmly welcomed and that the Jewish theater managers would all be fighting over her. In one theater after another Nissel Schwalb's sister was a rave hit; audiences everywhere were at her feet. Henrietta was at the peak of her enchanting beauty. She was elegantly appareled, her hat was at the height of fashion, and her jewels, more fake than real, sparkled invitingly. When her brother brought her backstage after one of her successful appearances to introduce her to the actors and actresses with whom she would next perform, her fame preceded her; they already knew that she was the famous prima donna, the rising star in the firmament of the Jewish stage. Who she was and where she came from, no one knew as yet. Only later did they learn from newspaper articles announcing in large headlines that appearing soon in such-and-such a theater was a new star from Buenos Aires named Henrietta Schwalb, who with her attractive appearance and slender figure would put to shame all the beauties who trod before her not only on the Jewish stage but on all the stages in the world. And while the author of the article—actually the theater manager—was speaking of beauty, he permitted himself to add that in a Parisian beauty contest, Henrietta Schwalb had won first prize.

Enough said. The articles hinted at other remarkable qualities as well. The article ensured that the public would come in droves to welcome the Star from Buenos Aires who had won first prize in a Parisian beauty contest. The public, which by now was accustomed to being deceived, was in fact completely satisfied and welcomed the Star from Buenos Aires with the kind of thunderous applause that could hitherto only be imagined in a New York Jewish theater.

When Nissel arrived at the second performance to negotiate a contract, he saw the SOLD OUT sign hanging over the box office. It is easy to imagine the tone in which he spoke to the theater manager. Forgetting that the manager himself had invented the beauty contest story, he related, with his usual passion and heat, how wonderful and miraculous it was that his sister had won the prize. All the other picture-perfect beauties in Paris had envied her, he said, and could not forgive her for winning. The directors had been upset when they found out she was Jewish, he said, and had almost taken the first prize away from her. Luckily he, Nissel Schwalb, had stepped forward and threatened to make a scandal. He had not only threatened but had actually done so. He told them so-and-so . . .

Nissel stopped abruptly in midstory because just then someone stomped on his foot so heavily, it could have been the foot of a giant. But it was Breyndele's foot. She had stomped on it to quiet him. What was Breyndele Kozak doing there? Remember that she was the one who had arranged for "the Star from Buenos Aires" to come from London. No one could hire Henrietta without Breyndele being a party to it. Nissel, who had been carried away by his own tales, simply wondered how a woman could have such a strong foot.

Happy Henrietta! Never since she had been on the stage, never since she had been a leading lady, had she received such a welcome as she did in New York. Such applause she had not heard in her life.

No, human hands were incapable of creating that incredible amount of noise. We must confess that hired claques sat in the balcony, with noisemakers in their hands initiating the clamor every time the Star from Buenos Aires appeared or left the stage. The theater was in danger of collapsing from the thunderous ovation. At first the people in the orchestra looked up in fright, but then they joined the made-to-order ovation. Audiences everywhere, once given a push in the right direction, are ready to break loose. Who has to know where that push is coming from? Who would have thought that the people in the balcony with noisemakers were engineering the success of the leading lady, and that the leader of that claque was her own brother?

Yes, the leader of the claque was none other than the tragedian Isaac Schwalb. That was the job his brother Nissel had found for him in America.

Sic transit gloria mundi is a Latin saying that in Yiddish, translated loosely, is: This is how a tragedian becomes a leader of a claque.

CHAPTER 30

The Lomzher Nightingale

Once it made its breakthrough, our cooperative Klammer, Schwalb & Co. was able to climb the ladder of success. Even as the "Star from Buenos Aires" was rising in the firmament of the Jewish stage, the Jewish press was also singing the praises of the "Lomzher Nightingale." Soon the news was trumpeted all over America.

It was all a matter of luck. In London the cantor and his family had been starving in a cellar, begging favors from the London charities and depending on the advice of good people like Mr. Klammer. But in New York the cantor suddenly became a celebrity. He stood three feet taller, and his reputation resounded from one end of the city to the other.

All the newspapers and posters on every day that season carried the following urgent announcement:

Don't Wait! Hurry to Our Theater!
Hear the Lomzher Nightingale Chant
"Kol Nidrei" with his Own Choir
Acclaimed by King George!

How did poor, innocent King George get into the picture? Dear reader, you must not ask such questions. You must remind yourself that we are no longer in Yehupetz but in the golden land of Columbus—a country blessed with freedom and happiness for all.

Say what you will about our brethren in this golden land—that they are a bit too greedy for business, they throw themselves too eagerly into the American way of life, they become too quickly Americanized, they wish to appear more American than the Americans themselves. Some see these qualities as faults, others as virtues, but you must grant that even after they have become totally Americanized, they will never forget the old verse from our own Bible: "Love thy neighbor because you were once strangers yourselves." I will venture to say that in the commandment to welcome guests, every Jew sees himself as Father Abraham. They will extend the same welcome to strangers as to relatives or friends. Every American Jew knows what it is to be downtrodden and a stranger in a foreign land. No sooner is he able to improve his lot in life than he must bring his family to America one at a time. If he were able, he would pack up his whole shtetl, along with the rabbi, the ritual slaughterer, and the cantor, and bring them over to his new blessed home. Let them all see what a good living he is making in the golden land of Columbus, and let them also make a good living.

Still we need not sing a paean of praise about our American brethren or make them out to be pious saints. People are always and everywhere no more than human. When a newcomer arrived, his countrymen already here welcomed him with the greatest hospitality and made a great deal of him. They were delighted to see him and proud to show him off. They gave him the best advice, showed him the right way to do things, and helped him out with a few dollars if they could. But that was still in the first blush of arrival. Time does not stand still. They had a motto, a tough motto: "Time is money." Once the first blush of arrival was gone, he was told: "Now, mister, get to work! The land of opportunity is open for you. Go, little brother, make a living."

And the newly arrived guest, having rested and had a chance to look around, went out on the crowded streets and found he was thoroughly flustered and confused.

What was the problem?

In that turbulent, noisy land of "hurry up," no one had any time and everyone was busy from early morning to late at night. If a newly arrived guest had waited till someone stopped him on the street, greeted him, honored him with a pinch of tobacco, and asked him, "What can I do for you?" he would have waited a long time. No, this was a land of self-reliance, where everyone was his own boss, a land that worked on the ironclad principle "Help yourself." In the old country that might mean, "Uncle, don't stand in my way!" or "Uncle, you can die of hunger if you have nothing to eat." But in this land you must not stand on ceremony or expect miracles. You yourself must stop passersby and announce, "Sir! I am so-and-so and know this-and-that. Maybe you can use a pair of hands?" Hands— that was the main thing. There were no people, only hands, hands talking, hands begging, hands shouting "Hands! Hands!" And the louder you shouted "Hands," the better were your chances.

But you mustn't be so naïve as to think that you are to go alone into the streets and literally cry "Hands! Hands!" No, for that pur- pose newspapers were created, with pages filled from top to bottom with ads and announcements. Whoever wanted to make a living in this land and avoid dying quietly of hunger had to avail himself of the newspapers. Whether he wanted to or not, he had to advertise himself, praise his wares to the skies, ring all the bells, and blow his own horn.

This situation was well understood by our cooperative leader. Nissel's keen sense for what was important and his sharp eye for an opportunity told him that one didn't dare dilly-dally, one had to take the reins in one hand, the whip in the other—and take off! This atti- tude on Nissel's part, plus good luck, played into the Lomzher can- tor's hands. They had arrived in New York at the time of the High Holidays, when cantors were in demand. A certain benevolent soci- ety had found itself without a cantor. It posted an advertisement for the opening, and a flood of cantors applied. Our Lomzher cantor faced stiff competition. Once his Lomzher countrymen interceded on his behalf, however, the Lomzher cantor turned out to be "all right."

But this step was no more than a prelude to the Lomzher Night- ingale's career. An American benevolent society needs a cantor only for the High Holidays, and from that alone you cannot make a liv- ing. Here our schemer Nissel Schwalb displayed his enterprising tal- ent. He rented a hall and had distributed fliers and placed ads in the newspapers with this message:

**COME HEAR THE LOMZHER NIGHTINGALE
A THROAT LIKE A CLARINET
A VOICE LIKE A VIOLIN**
*The world-renowned Lomzher Cantor with his
own choir will sing "Kol Nidrei" in such-and-such a
music hall accompanied by his own ensemble of
musicians who played before King George.*

This first concert was also the last at that music hall, because the following morning our Nissel Schwalb and his financial partner, Mr. Klammer, sat with a glass of beer and a Havana cigar and signed an agreement with a Jewish theater manager. By this agreement the Lomzher Nightingale and his ensemble were to sing "Kol Nidrei" for thirty performances in the famous operetta actually called *Kol Nidrei*.

The agreement was signed, and the manager put it in his breast pocket. But then Mr. Klammer had regrets about the arrangement and reproached his companion for rushing in to make a deal dirt cheap. He proved to be right—after the first few performances the same theater manager signed a new agreement with them for thirty additional performances for three times as much. That led to a quarrel between the two partners, who called each other unprintable names unsuited to gentlemen. It could have deteriorated into an ugly fight, but luckily the cantor and his wife interceded, reminding them that they faced a more important task—providing for Rafalesco. In the meantime the cantor's wife prepared a very fine supper for the entire group. She invited Madame Cherniak (Breyndele) and a few Lomzher friends, who brought along their "missuses" to spend an evening with the Lomzher Nightingale, so that everyone could get acquainted and enjoy themselves, as God had commanded.

CHAPTER 31

A Strange Biography

Providing for Rafalesco was not as easy as our partners had imagined. First of all, ever since arriving in America, they had hardly laid eyes on him. He had spent entire days with Madame Cherniak. "Can you tell me what he has in common with that creature?" Nissel

Schwalb wondered. At night he went to concerts in theaters located in the wealthy, Gentile New York that was called uptown. It was as if he had come to America to hobnob with the Gentiles, not with the Jews, as if the Jewish theater had no interest for him, as if he were not a Jewish actor, a wandering star from the Jewish traveling theater, a child of the Jewish ghetto.

At first the partners didn't attach much importance to his behavior. A young fellow, they figured, in a strange country for the first time—let him enjoy himself. But as time went by, they looked askance at it, asking Rafalesco where he was going and what he was doing, and criticizing him for not tending to what needed to be done. Why wasn't he studying the stage in Jewish New York, which was located "downtown," and why wasn't he picking up acting tips from the famous American Jewish stars?

Rafalesco responded that he already knew the Jewish stage through and through, and speaking of picking up acting tips, it was only possible to do so in the Gentile world, in the great American theaters.

But that was no more than an excuse. Rafalesco was busy with his own concerns, about which we will soon find out. But the cooperative was not pleased. They wanted their prize actor to step out before the New York Jewish public as soon as possible, to show *who* he was and *what* he could do.

In the meantime, naturally, Nissel Schwalb prepared the way. First he acquainted all the reporters for Jewish newspapers with the biography of Leo Rafalesco. He told each one, secretly, that Rafalesco had come from the most renowned Jewish family in Bucharest and that his father, Samuel Rafalesco, was one of the richest bankers in Romania and was accorded citizenship by the king himself. It had cost him a small fortune. Ever since childhood the young Leo had exhibited remarkable artistic talent and dreamed of studying art, but the fanatically religious parents wouldn't hear of it. Leo had decided to present himself to the Romanian queen, who was also a famous dramatist writing under the name of Carmen Silva.

"Carmen Silva is a writer of novels," a reporter interrupted him, but Nissel, undeterred, went on:

"Will you agree that the queen is a connoisseur of drama? Our Leo Rafalesco introduced himself to her and recited several monologues. The queen was so taken by him that she paid to have him study in the greatest Romanian theater. But the young Rafalesco had always had his heart set on acting in the Jewish theater. 'I am,' he said, 'a child of the Jewish people, and I must serve my people and my language, not a foreign one.' One fine morning he left with a Jewish traveling acting company that wandered over all of Romania from city to city. The director of that troupe was a well-known artist and a highly educated dramaturg, Holtzman, Bernard Holtzman, the noted author of the famous work *Uriel Acosta*.

Here the reporter had to cut him off: "Excuse me, Mr. Schwalb. The author of *Uriel Acosta* was not Holtzman but Karl Gutzkow."

Nissel Schwalb was not one of those who lost his bearings easily. He explained: "I know the author is Karl Gutzkow. I mean the Yiddish translator."

"I beg your pardon!" the persistent reporter cut him off again. "The translator of *Uriel Acosta* is not Holtzman but Yosef Lerner."

Nissel charged ahead. "I know that Lerner was the first translator, but Holtzman was dissatisfied with that translation, and he sat down for a whole night and translated the entire work all over again, especially for Rafalesco's sake, and it worked out very well for him. No one had ever translated *Uriel Acosta* like Holtzman, and no one had ever played the role like Rafalesco. You can understand from the fact that in Vienna, Sonnenthal, the great Sonnenthal, once saw Rafalesco in the role of Uriel Acosta—and broke into tears like a small child, vowing that he would never play that role again! And do you know he kept his word. He never again, to the day he died, played that role."

The American reporters were not children—they knew bluff when they heard it. They fixed up what Nissel Schwalb had told them, and a wonderful biography emerged.

One day when Rafalesco opened the paper, he read his own biography with the heading in large letters as follows:

THE JEWISH STAGE DISCOVERS A NEW STAR!
CARMEN SILVA CRAZY ABOUT HIM!
QUEEN CROWNS YOUNG STAR.
SONNENTHAL SHEDS TEARS.

Our young hero laughed so hard, he almost had to be revived.

CHAPTER 32

In the Kibitzarni

Kibitz is a Yiddish American word, born on American soil, in the Jewish press and the Jewish theater. Its meanings are multiple, hard to translate, but let us try to get close to its true sense. A *kibitz* properly used can do many things for you even while seeming to remain simply a *kibitz*. It can deliver a barb hard to remove, or stick a needle deep in the flesh, or tell a person off to his face, or one-up someone, or turn a person's guts inside out, or rub salt into an open wound, or drive someone completely mad, or simply offer unasked-for advice, or transmit a bit of gossip. Our language is, thank God, rich enough in shades of meaning and subtle innuendos to accomplish all this and a great deal more just with the word *kibitz*. But no matter how many more ways I could list in which *kibitz* is used, they would not come close to its actual meaning, which could only blossom and thrive on American soil. It remains difficult for me to convey what a *kibitzarni* really is. It's a kind of club, or café on the Lower East Side of New York, where a certain class of intelligentsia gathered, involved in literature, theater, and politics. These people belonged to opposing camps, factions, and political parties, were often rivals, and almost without exception detested one another, could not bear the sight or sound of one another's names. Such bitter, sworn enemies were they that if one of them were to die, the other would dance a merry jig on his grave. These characters would gather at the *kibitzarni* and seat themselves at their customary tables, surrounded by their devoted followers and others belonging to their faction. They would order something to eat and smoke a cigar, and the kibitzing would begin. First they would exchange pleasantries and compliments and chitchat a bit across the tables; then they'd progress to barbs, mockery, malicious jokes, and wicked gossip. They would then move on to washing someone's dirty linen in public, with devastating critiques and humorous exaggerations; stepping on toes; and enjoying the sight of another's squirming to the point of apoplexy—all in good fellowship, all while joking, grinning, and laughing. The *kibitzarni* was a sort of a free-for-all *gehennam* where people roasted and broiled one another, a kind of steam bath where they beat one another black and blue. In the *kibitzarni* opinions were formed, reputations made and broken, and careers of writers, artists, and actors were advanced or crushed. Opinions came thick and fast, and verdicts were pronounced—dead or alive, no good or all right. Now that you know what the *kibitzarni* is, we invite you to step in for a while at your own risk.

It was a cloudy fall day, one of those days when the unpredictable New York skies—obstructed by the tall, faceless buildings called skyscrapers and the iron sky trains they call elevated lines— were smoky and damp, almost resembling a London sky.

At noon the second-largest city in the world was at its noisiest and busiest—all rush, all work, all running, all buying, all business—a bubbling cauldron.

It was the busiest time of day, but the *kibitzarni* was packed to the rafters, all the tables occupied. A blue haze, thick enough to cut with a knife, hung in the air. Everyone was talking, and the kibitzing was reaching its peak.

At one of the tables sat three people drinking beer, so absorbed in conversation that they were oblivious to the fact that their names were at that very moment on everyone's tongue, that they were being kibitzed in the sharpest language. The three were talking all at once, boasting and telling outrageous lies about themselves. Of the three, two we know very well from the Old World and London.

They were our best friends, Mr. Klammer and Nissel Schwalb. Now we must introduce you to the third person, who was not a Londoner but a real American. You can spot an American a mile away. He has a different appearance, different ways of expressing and handling himself. Whereas the Englishman is a worried, long-faced melancholic, the American is a lively, happy Yankee with clever, shrewd eyes, engaging manners, and gold teeth.

The man we are describing was a Jewish American theater manager named Mr. Nickel.

Nickel was one of the most popular personalities in Jewish New York, a likable person of the kind known in America as "a really good guy" and who in the Old Country would be called a "nice fellow." Nickel would give you the shirt off his back. You would always find him with a friendly smile on his always young-looking, open, happy face. He always had a good word for you and was ready to offer you a small loan if he had the means—something that rarely happened. More often it was Nickel who was seeking a loan. His "missus," he complained, was too demanding. It was well known that she wore the pants in the family. His enemies and rivals took full advantage of it in the *kibitzarni*, multiplying his marital woes by three. But he laughed it off. If Nickel were to take everything to heart, where would he be now!

Nickel knew he was considered the biggest bluffer in Greater New York.

He knew that if someone told an extravagant lie in the *kibitzarni*, another would ask: "Who told you that—Nickel?"

He knew that the *kibitzarni* made things up about him that didn't begin to be true.

For example, they said that Nickel had once boasted of driving an automobile over Niagara Falls when it was frozen during spring.

What the *kibitzarni* could think up! Chatterers! Idlers! Enemies! Rivals! Why was that story so remarkable? Try to find another theater manager who would boast of a feat like Nickel's. Let someone else try, as Nickel had, to travel with an acting troupe across the country in one week, giving twelve performances in eight cities from Philadelphia to Chicago and then twelve performances in the same eight cities on the return trip!

That was how our new acquaintance, Nickel, bragged to our two old friends, who both responded with tall tales of their own. Not in the least did they feel outdone by Nickel's motor trip across the country in one week over eight cities from Philadelphia to Chicago and back.

One might say that as the three of them listened to one another's bluff and humbug, they tried to see who would outbluff the others.

CHAPTER 33

Bluff and Humbug

Bluff and humbug—these authentic American notions are not easily translated into another language. Bluffing is not just telling a fat lie, or lying just to tell a lie, or making up a tall tale, or telling something that could never be. No, America hates that. The American is too smart, too much of a businessman, to offer something so crude. No, when the American cocks his hat to the side, hooks both thumbs in his vest, and offers you a lie, it is smooth and cleverly plausible—and, most important, it pertains to the business at hand.

The aforementioned people sitting in the *kibitzarni* and kibitzing were not idlers, like those sages back home who sat around the hearth at the synagogue with nothing to do but talk. No, kibitzing itself was a vocation or, as it could be called, a business.

Nissel Schwalb, Mr. Klammer, and Nickel, as they sat that morning in the *kibitzarni*, were talking of important business, and it was about the business they were bluffing. Our two old bluffers from the Old World had to admit in their hearts that when it came to bluffing, their new friend could teach them a few things. With his stories and braggadocio, Nickel so drew them in, so addled their brains and confused their minds, that they became helpless and finally had to remain silent. They were negotiating a very important matter. For his theater Nickel had just engaged the famous young star from Bucharest, the one the Queen of Romania had called the greatest tragedian in the world.

Nissel and Mr. Klammer, speaking at the same time, described the marvels performed by this great young artist. Mr. Klammer related how Rafalesco had astounded the London public. He had amazed even a man like himself, who never went to see the traveling companies, whom he considered gypsies, at the London Pavilion Theater. Nissel interrupted him: "What more do you need to hear? Real Englishmen, Christians all of them, couldn't get enough of him. Irving, they said, was a dog compared to him, I swear!"

But Nickel wasn't hearing them. While those two were bluffing, he smiled, showed his gold teeth, and thought up boastful new tales about himself and his own troupe, which had won first place in the United States of America. "So," he said, "show me a Jewish theater that can boast that it had the president of the United States sitting in a box seat applauding enthusiastically and shouting, 'Bravo!'" That could only have happened to him. Nickel had made sure to introduce himself to Teddy Roosevelt, who shook his hand before the whole theater and slapped him on the back: "Nickel, you are all right!" And in front of everyone, Teddy had removed his gold watch and chain and offered them to him as a gift. Nickel drew out an old steel watch to show that he never wore the gold watch and chain that the president had given him during the week. Never!

Behind Nickel the group was in full *kibitz* about him and his company. They ridiculed the Bucharest fly-by-night and criticized him even before they had seen him act. There in the *kibitzarni* they dubbed our Leo Rafalesco a greenhorn, a blackbird, a nothing, a Chaim-Yenkl, Romanian farm boy, a curiosity, and other nicknames meant to prove that only they had the right to an opinion about him.

These envious kibitzers were either theater managers themselves, who had been unsuccessful in signing up the young "Star from Bucharest," or else reporters who had been left out of the first reporting, which had lauded the rising star to the skies, and could not abide it.

And some may have been young actors, Leo's rivals, who had been living in New York for years, waiting for the union to one day have mercy on them and accept them—when along came this young pipsqueak, just a kid, who was grabbed up like a precious jewel. He got the best engagements and was elevated by the press to the highest rank. Wouldn't that have eaten your heart out? Shouldn't he be kibitzed for all he was worth?

No, kibitzing in itself was not enough; the kibitzers had to mount a conspiracy against this injustice. They had to make sure the greenhorn had a fitting downfall, that he was hounded off the stage at his first performance, in proper style. In a word, he had to suffer Haman's fate and desire only to flee from Columbus's land back to Bucharest, and the sooner the better.

America is a blessed land where anything can happen. A person can be raised on high and ensconced in heaven, or he can be sent right down into the underworld. A midpoint, a golden mean, did not exist.

Poor Rafalesco! He had no idea what surprise awaited him in this golden land. But he heard nothing of their plots. His head was uptown on Fifth Avenue, in the wealthiest section of New York.

That was where the renowned singer from the Paris Opera, Miss Rosalia Spayvak, dwelled, whose name resounded across the length and breadth of America.

CHAPTER 34

A Little about Our Heroine

In her youth, you might say almost from childhood, our heroine had knocked about with Albert Shchupak's troupe, entertaining the

Jewish public with popular songs like "Celebrating *Shabbes*" and "Oy-oy-oy, Chava!" and "Every Friday Night," without any inkling that her name would one day take its place among the most famous in the world. Never did she dream that she would one day live on one of the wealthiest streets, Fifth Avenue, in the great, prosperous city of New York, or that she would ride in her own automobile with a black chauffeur at the wheel, or that dozens of reporters from the greatest international newspapers would clamor to follow her and would lie in wait for her for hours with cameras, in order to be honored with a two- or three-minute interview and a photograph.

How did this exaltation happen? A transformation of this magnitude does not happen just between yes and no. Fame isn't achieved overnight. An actor, a singer, a musician, a painter, a writer, or a multimillionaire—anyone who has achieved fame has had to make a continuous march uphill; the path is long and difficult and is strewn less often with flowers than with thorns. If one knew the problems and frustrations that our young heroine had had to live through, and the quiet tears she had shed secretly in her bed, then one might not begrudge her the blazing success she had achieved—the loud applause that the culturally aware public was showering on her so generously, the bouquets of flowers they were tossing at her feet, and the many expensive gifts they bestowed on her.

What we will now relate was taken from several American newspapers, English and Yiddish. You yourself will realize what is true and what is a bit of bluffing for the sake of publicity:

> Born in a small shtetl in Bessarabia of poor Orthodox parents, Miss Rosalia Spayvak was kidnapped as a child by a troupe of itinerant actors, Jewish gypsies, who wandered from city to city and made their living from stealing young girls and making them into actresses. Had they not been caught, they would have taken her across the border and forced her to sing popular songs, first on the street, then in the cabarets, coffeehouses, and music halls. Possibly her career would have ended with a tragic epilogue, as happens to all street singers. But a lucky circumstance brought her to the attention of the world-renowned singer Marcella Embrich, who was charmed by her seductive gypsy-songs as well as her fiery gypsy-eyes. This singer's rare voice evoked such great enthusiasm in the Austrian court that Franz Josef himself honored her with a stipend to study music.

In a remarkably short time, she completed her studies brilliantly in the Vienna Conservatory. At the recommendation of a Hungarian magnate, she was sent off to Berlin, and from there to Paris for two years. In Paris she so impressed Jacques Reszko, a French patron of the arts, that he championed her acceptance into the Paris Opera, where she debuted in the new opera *Elektra* under the direction of Richard Strauss. Her debut was a huge success, and the Opera soon engaged her for three months with a salary of a half-million francs. A short time later she was engaged in Vienna and in Budapest, where she received ten thousand crowns a night. Not long afterward she was engaged in London for two hundred pounds a night, and now in New York she receives two thousand dollars for each performance— a price that only the great Melba had commanded.

Finally we bring you a few letters written at different times by different people. We hope these letters, which bear on our heroine's intimate life, will reveal more than all the publicity biographies and newspaper articles.

Chapter 35

From Rosa Spivak to Marcella Embrich

Dear Mütterchen *Marcella!*
I have been in my birthplace for three weeks and haven't written you a single letter. It is my fault, and I deserve to be punished for it. A long letter will be my punishment. I want to write you, beloved *Mütterchen,* everything, the pure, unvarnished truth. My *Mütterchen* knows I have no secrets from her any more than I have secrets from myself. I will start at the very beginning—about my hometown.
I found Holeneshti as I left it, the same tiny, poor shtetl it had always been, the same poor, simple people. And yet my heart pounded when I first saw the old, familiar, dear shtetl, and when I heard the beloved, sweet name Holeneshti.
Ho-le-nesh-ti! Do you believe me, *Mütterchen*? I was ready to kiss the earth itself, the gray dust of the unpaved,

unswept streets, and I would surely have done so had I been alone, without the crowd following me, without my maestro Solfanini, and without my girlfriends. Ach, why did I bring them along? Why did I need the bother? Why didn't I come by myself? I must admit, *Mütterchen,* as hateful as this might be, but when my mother and father embraced me, hugged me, and kissed me, my face burned with shame. My mother wept and laughed and couldn't stop talking— she loves to talk—and my father was as pale as death and his hands trembled. I don't know why, but I could not feel comfortable. Was it because they were dressed in old-fashioned clothing, as in all our small towns, or was it because they understood no language other than Yiddish? I know it was vile, but it is a fact, dear *Mütterchen,* that I was ashamed, ashamed of my dear, devoted parents who suffered so much humiliation, anguish, heartache, and woe on account of me. True, I am now penitent, and with all my might I wish to repay them. But what worth does that have? The bit of pleasure that I can now offer them doesn't begin to compensate for even a tenth of the grief I caused them by going off with the traveling troupe. That crime I will never be able to atone for, even if I were to be ten times as loving and kind as I am to them. For every hundred, every thousand that I spend on them, I hear myself crying out: *Too late! Too late!* And I look at my poor sick father whom I once loved devotedly, and I imagine his large, dark eyes reproaching me: *Where were you, daughter, during the long, bleak nights when I could not shut an eye and prayed for death? One letter from you, one line, one good word, would have made me the happiest man!* And I remind myself, dear *Mütterchen,* that I wanted to deny that I had parents, and that afterward you scolded me for it. My face still burns with shame, as no one else on earth is as bad a sinner as I am. I am prepared to make any sacrifice on earth now for my poor, humiliated parents. I wanted to bring them back with me, but it isn't possible. My father is sick, and my mother wouldn't leave him even if she were paid a houseful of gold and the English queen's crown jewels. I promised myself that I would provide for them in their old age. I would buy them a house, give them an income. As poor as he is, every man here strives to have his own income. But in this resolve as well, I did not behave in a seemly fashion. I did it more for myself than for them, knowing that I had come home more for my sake than for theirs, because I was drawn there by only one person.

My *Mütterchen* Marcella knows whom I mean. Not only didn't I find him there, I couldn't even find out where he was. There was not a trace of him, not a sign. His whole family was a shambles. His mother was dead, his father out of his mind. His brothers and sisters were dispersed. All that remained was the courtyard, which once looked to me so large and so beautiful, and the house, which once looked to me so rich and bright and festive. When I visited it for the first time, it seemed to me like an unattainable paradise. It was once full of life, laughter, and happiness. Now it struck me as low, small, poor, ordinary, and sad. All that remained were the old grandmother, who was now senile; an idiot of a son-in-law; and an old dog blind in one eye named Terkush.

This courtyard and house—I resolved I must buy it all for my parents. But I meant it for myself, not because I was so pleased with it—what on earth did I need it for? When would I be here? No, it was just a whim, a whim of a gypsy like myself.

Back then, when I stepped over the threshold with torn shoes for the first time, I envied the family terribly and begrudged them their brightness, happiness, and wealth. Why did those rich people have so much while we had so little? I promised myself that, with God's help, this house and courtyard would one day be mine, mine! And perhaps it is precious to me now because in it was born and raised the one who first ignited passion in my heart, the one who I cannot, am not capable of forgetting.

And so, without much haggling, I bought the house, even though my mother protested. Why did she need such a fancy place? she complained. Obviously I got my way. The house is now mine! Mine! That was what I told myself, almost forgetting that I had bought it for my parents as an estate, a provision for their old age. I hired people to refurbish the house, clean up the courtyard, landscape the grounds, and turn it into a palace. Now I almost regret the whole business. My mother was right when she asked why she needed such a big place. I don't know either. No wonder *Mütterchen* Marcella calls me a gypsy! I have earned that name. I live like a gypsy, I burn money like a gypsy, I love *shmattes* like a gypsy, and like a gypsy I can't stay in one place and am full of gypsy longings. I am even spending my time here like a gypsy. The whole shtetl (and my mother and father among them) looks at me as if I were crazy. Day after day we drive around in an automobile, I and my girlfriends and my maestro. We have picnics in nearby woods. We sing gypsy songs, dance gypsy dances, and cavort in ways that have led the local police to keep an eye on us. But who takes notice of police? By day by automobile, at night by boat—ach, what can compare with our Bessarabian summer nights? One at a time the stars light up like candles in the sky. From among the trees in the woods the moon peeks through and silvers the little pond and the orchard. The entire shtetl sleeps as peacefully, as innocently, as only such poor souls can who don't need anything more to make them happy. Only we interlopers from the outside world, gypsies from across the border, our stomachs full, drunk, sated with all kinds of pleasure and luxury, disturb the holy silence of the magical night. The splashing of our oars echoes through the nearby woods. But it is a time for silence, a time to gaze at the sky, to seek familiar and unfamiliar little stars, and to wander about aimlessly. It is a time for longing for the one who appears but once in a lifetime. It is a time for Maestro Solfanini to declare his love for me. I am all that his heart yearns for. Ach! I fear he is my twenty-first love sacrifice! But I hope that along with the other twenty sacrifices, he will not be found drowned in some lake. My twenty-second will have no more luck with me than did the others.

That is how life goes on in this quiet, pious, poor shtetl, far from the great, wealthy, wanton world.

I kiss my dear *Mütterchen* Marcella again and again!

Your most devoted friend,
Gypsy Rosa

CHAPTER 36

From Meyer Stelmach to His Good Friend

My dear friend!

Can you imagine my delight when I received your dear letter? First of all, it meant you are alive, thank God. I hadn't heard from you in so long. Since I've been in London, I haven't received anything from you. And second of all, reading a letter from you is pure pleasure. I imagine no one writes as tenderly, as articulately, as intelligently, and as heartfelt as you. One wants to kiss each word. You know, I've always been fond of *jhargon,* especially coming from a good friend like yourself with whom I grew up, suffered with, ate a herring and bread with, drank from the same glass, and shared a bed.

Oh, the years, the years, do you remember them? I remember them very well and think of them frequently. I dislike it when others deny who and what they are. I am the way I am, an ordinary, simple man. I don't exaggerate, and I hate lies. I tell everyone about my good fortune. When correspondents from the newspapers come to question me, feel me out about Grisha—who and what and how he is—I tell them: "Fellows, Grisha is not Grisha. Grisha—that's me. If not for me, there would be no Grisha. Oh, there would be a Hershel, or a Yenkel, or a Yossel, or a Motl, but there would be no Grisha Stelmach who would cause such a sensation, impress the queen herself, who would invite him to perform for her, to shake his hand, and ask him all about himself. Did he have parents, brothers, sisters? Yes, I may boast that only with my humble understanding, and with the strength God has given me, could I have come so far that cities and countries would battle over my son, all in one voice: Grisha Stelmach! And once again, Grisha Stelmach!

Whoever heard that in one week he would receive invitations from eight cities from all corners of the world: from Paris and Manchester, from Vienna and St. Petersburg, from Antwerp and New York, from Leipzig and Chicago. We don't know who to answer first, even if we had ten hands!

And wouldn't you know, just now I am alone. My partner, the former manager I wrote you about—I fired him, thank God. His contract ran out, and he wanted to renew it for another five years, but I told him: "What nerve! You've sucked enough of my blood." He'll never have another such sweet deal in his life because there is only *one* Grisha Stelmach on earth. Now I am my own boss, it's *my* wedding, it's *my* musicians. Whatever I do is done, and whatever I say goes. That is what I established from the beginning—a father is a father and a child is a child.

The burden I carried on my back, and what I went through until Grisha became the Grisha Stelmach he is today, I don't know if anyone else in the world could have done that. Another in my place would long ago have grown impatient and quit. But nobody needs to know this, and nobody should know it. The world thinks a star like Grisha Stelmach is made overnight. They envy me, begrudge me, and point their fingers at me: "See how that Stelmach is raking in the money with his fat paws!" My so-called friends come forth with advice, worrying that I am not sending my son to school. My fine-feathered friends, where were you when my stomach swelled three times a day from hunger? Where were you when I was worried sick that my Grisha didn't have a pair of decent boots? Why didn't you worry then about my child when I was going around hungry and ignored, a prodigy on my hands, crying out, "Jews, look, I possess a million here!" Who heard me then?

Oh, I know the Jews! I can boast that I've traveled the world, and there is no one, do you hear, not another people on earth like our Jews, may they thrive! May God not punish me for these words—we have so many rich people among us who throw money away, spend thousands, hundreds of thousands, on only the devil-knows-what—to have another carriage, to win favors from the goyim—and not a single one of our own would even notice that here was a precious talent among us. He could be Moses himself, but with torn boots, he's in trouble. Now all doors are open to us, and it's an honor, a joy, that my son bestows a glance on them. The biggest magnate would now consider himself to be lucky if my son would say he wanted to marry his daughter. They would cover him with gold, and if I were to give as much as an approving wink, I would also be given a hatful of gold. But there is a God on earth. Listen to what happened. I will pour my heart out a bit to you, my dear friend. It's a long story.

If you remember, I once told you about a beautiful girl, a Yiddish actress named Rosa Spivak. I met her through Shchupak. He boasted that she was a niece of his from Warsaw. What did I care? He says a niece from Warsaw, let it be a niece from Warsaw. But I liked this girl from the first minute. I mean, I really liked her! First of all, she was pretty, a beauty, with flashing eyes, dark-skinned like a gypsy, and full of charm! She wasn't a foolish girl, she had some education and was lively and hot-tempered. But there was her voice, her singing! You know how enamored I am of song and of Yiddish theater, and since I have enough money, I've probably heard enough singers in my lifetime to be sick of it. But singing like Rosa Spivak's I have never heard before and will not hear again. Her singing touches your soul! I mean the girl really captivated me. From her way of speaking I quickly realized that this was no born actress, as Shchupak had claimed, not his niece, but someone's beloved child. And that's how it turned out to be. His story had all been made up.

She was not a niece but a complete stranger, not from Warsaw but from a small shtetl somewhere in Bessarabia, a cantor's daughter. I found out later that Shchupak had been there with his troupe. He had heard her sing, liked her voice, spirited her away from home, promising her heaps of money and music lessons abroad. As you might have expected, after he crossed the border with her, it was he himself who began teaching her music, to sing in public songs like "Chava," "Making *Shabbes*," "Every Friday Night," and other pretty ditties, and teaching her a few dance steps. God knows what would have happened to her if I hadn't talked with her and introduced her to the famous singer Marcella Embrich, who was giving concerts together with my Grisha. It was a stroke of luck for this girl to talk to me and entreat me to introduce her to Embrich. And when Embrich heard this girl sing, she became deeply attached to her and wouldn't let go of her. The first thing Embrich did was to tear her out of Shchupak's hands and take charge of her. Then she enrolled her in the Vienna Conservatory, hired the best professors for her, and made her into one of the finest singers in the world. It is no secret that today she is three times as good as Embrich. Why should I go on like this? Understand that she now appears with my Grisha in concerts and makes almost as much as he does. People now fight over her as much as over my Grisha, and she has me to thank for all of that. How do you think she thanks me? You will hear what kind of thanks I get. It's a good story, but before I tell you the story, I must first say a few words about my son.

I don't think I have written to you yet about my Grisha, what a genius he is! As great as he is to others, to himself he is modest, simple, and quiet. He knows only the violin and concertizing and nothing else. Ask him how much the concert earned? Did they lose money? How much were the expenses? Was there a profit? It's not his business. All he knows is the violin, and beyond that—nothing. Maybe you think he's a shallow boy? May I be as shallow as he is. But he doesn't bother with those kinds of things. He doesn't bother his head with worldly affairs. Why should he? As far as the "business," as they call it here, there are others to bother their heads over it. That's what he has a father for. For the rest there is a mother by his side. But most important of all is the violin. And there is nothing else left to say. But be a prophet and predict that some cantor's daughter, a Rosa Spivak, a nuisance, would show up and that he would fall in love with her.

When I found out about this affair—and I found out about it from a letter of hers that miraculously fell into my hands, that is, I took it from the mailman—it made me furious at her. After all, I led her to Embrich, I introduced her and opened the way for her to the wide world, and through my connections she became elevated and crowned—and then she repays me by leading my son astray? I did not hesitate. I sat right down and sent off a letter to her in plain language, spelling it out word for word, how come and how dare you and where is justice and where is God! I really gave it to her, gave her what was on my heart! I am not a writer, just a father who when he is hurt is worth eighteen writers.

Guess what this young snip answered? If you had eighteen heads, you could not guess! First, she really gave it to me for miraculously intercepting her letter. The letter, she said, was addressed to someone else. If she had wanted to write to me, she said, she knew my address. Second, what made me think, she said—do you hear her language?—she had designs on my son? "All your thoughts are always focused on only one point named Grisha Stelmach. You are making a big mistake if you think that point is the center of the universe around which everything else revolves. There are," she said, "people, and their number is great, who think of him only while he is on the stage and his violin speaks for him in a language that not many can speak as well as he. From the moment he puts down the violin and steps down from the stage, he is to the world no more and perhaps less than a pleasant dream." How do you like that last sentence? And she went on: How did I know that her letter to my son was not an answer to one of his to her? And maybe it wasn't the first or the only letter? The only difference was, she said, that all the letters from my son to her went straight to her hands, whereas her letters to him apparently had to go through a censor. If that is so, she said she would do everything possible to ensure that her letters reached the party to whom they were addressed and no miracles. She would do it, she said, not because she was so eager to correspond with my son but because even if she was, as I say, a small-town Bessarabian girl, she would show me that my paternal despotism, which comes from my exaggerated devotion, is not as powerful as I think, and that everything on earth has a limit. What do you think of that nerve?

No, listen to what else she writes! She assures me, she says, that when she feels the same toward my son as he feels toward her, they will inform me when they are good and ready and will have no concerns about me. They will be "all right." What do you think of that? Now she's speaking to me in English!

I won't go on at length, dear friend. I answered her

letter, and she answered mine, and so developed between us a correspondence. The upshot was that we became friends. But what friends! When she came to London for a concert with my son, my wife and I had to go down on our knees before she would agree to honor us with a visit. What won't a mother and father do for a child? Would it have been any better to try to break them up even if we could? If you are talking about love, there's nothing more to say. From that time on, the girl became so endearing to us, so beloved, that we would have been happy if they had decided to get married. But no—not he and not she. Modern children! You cannot talk straight to them. They aren't your ordinary boyfriend and girlfriend. They are two international stars. There are very few like them. To speak to them of a wedding—heaven forbid! What more do you need to know—the words *bride* and *groom* cannot be uttered, and that's that. So we must wait, what else can we do? But my wife complains that she wants to live to have a little pleasure from her son. I tell her to be patient, she won't miss out.

As for me, I too am eager. It isn't the pleasure I want. I am not a woman. It's something else. I don't know if I can say it right: my son, you understand, is a great artist, and yet he is still a child, an innocent lamb, and his lover is a terror, too pretty, too clever, too spirited, and we know anything "too" is, as they say, excessive. Now they are both running around London, not on foot, God forbid, but in a motorcar, shopping everywhere. What worth has money to them? I ask you. Luckily I am around to keep on eye on them, or they would burn up thousands! We are preparing to leave for America. They are both engaged for a season and, thank God, under conditions you could wish on all your loved ones. May they both be granted health and success, as they have had till now, and many years to both of them, and may we live to see it and enjoy it, because today they are both equally beloved by us, there is no difference. She is, you must believe me, as dear to me as my own child, perhaps dearer, although truth to tell, she still isn't altogether on good terms with me. Apparently, because of my first letter, I am not on her good side, and she can be a bit contrary with me. She tolerates my talking about money. She takes me for a miser. Children are fools. They don't understand that everything is for their sake. For instance, there is nothing dearer to me than money. She herself tells me that, usually in a snide remark. She thinks she knows me through and through. We are often at odds with each other, so we often have words. I laugh, and my son gets upset about it, so it isn't pleasant, but maybe in time it will straighten out. All children are like that. They think that there is nothing in the world worse than parents. But I am going on too long. I am almost running out of paper, but I feel better for having talked it out. I wouldn't have trusted anyone else but you. You are different. You can keep a secret. It will remain between us.

Be very well, and may your business thrive, and write me often. I look forward to your great letters, as only you can write,

From me, your old friend,
Meyer Stelmach

Just remembered: My wife asks me to send regards. And my son wants to know if you are still playing the violin.

Meyer Stelmach

CHAPTER 37

From Sholom-Meyer Murovchik to Rosa Spivak

To my dear, respected friend, Rosa Spivak, may she be well,
What is going on? You've become so distant from me that you don't even want to answer all my letters that I sent and on the contrary it seems after all I've had to put up with I don't deserve for you to thank me in this way because if not for me you would still be with Shchupak devil take him he wouldn't pay me what he owes me on account of you because he says it is my fault because if not for me you wouldn't have known about Embrich and he wouldn't have remained without a penny he swears that because of you he's become utterly destitute he writes me

and cries his eyes out you know I believe him no more than a dog but when someone is down you have to think maybe he's right I only know all he has now is nothing at all not any medallions and the few diamond rings are also gone and the gold watch I think he pawned somewhere and all because of you because the Jew sewed himself too big a purse for you to fill in addition to which he got it into his head the idiot that God would make it all right he would be rid of all his wives and would turn your head with his jewels and it would go smoothly from then on if you can imagine it and only I he says am guilty no one else in the meantime I'm stuck the little bit you first gave me was enough to fill a tooth and I also had a problem with my poor sister she had to be sent off to America and I was sick myself a long time almost was visited by the Angel of Death so if not for you and your little support I would now be in the next world so I thank you but why won't you do me the favor of answering me at least with a few words it seems I haven't earned it of you to chase you like a dog from Paris to London and from London to Paris and from there to Antwerp and you won't even see me God knows the truth that I always listened to you when you said go I went when you said Murovchik run I ran and not only when you first left Shchupak and went to Italy do you remember I didn't spare any effort and when we had to throw out that *shlimazel* who wanted to shoot himself who sacrificed himself if not Muravchik and now you've altogether forgotten who he is how many times did I try to see you and they wouldn't let me near you I once waited for you at your salon for three clock hours heard you talking to some Frenchman and finally they came out and told me you weren't at home and I almost fainted and I could barely find the doorknob woe is me what has happened to you and I told myself that when a person is successful is this the way to behave when you promised you would never leave me and in the end when I ran after you in London at the dacha I saw you fly by in a car with Stelmach's boy and I removed my hat but you pretended not to see me so I wrote to you once and twice and you don't answer me why I don't know but now I hope you will answer me

because I have a certain matter to ask you about this person found a packet of your letters that he brought me and
asked me to pay a lot of money for them but really a lot he
says he knows you are now in the money and since he has
all kinds of letters you probably won't let him carry them
around too long so I told him do you know what uncle I
will write a letter to her right away and so I am asking you
my dear worthy friend Rosa to send me a letter right away
if you want your letters back and if you need them write
me and I will see this person and I hope with God's help
I will be able to get them so write me to my name in care
of the director Waxman of the Paris Jewish Theater how
much to offer him because the person doesn't know how
much to ask from me your devoted servant who wishes
you much happiness and success eighteen-fold

Sholom-Meyer Murovchik

CHAPTER 38

From Rosa Spivak to Marcella Embrich

My dearest Mütterchen *Marcella!*

This time I will take up a bit more of your time than
usual because I haven't written for a long time and I have so
much to tell you. I don't know where to begin. First of all,
I am, as you can see, not in Paris. No more Paris. No more
Opera. I am again a free little bird, again a gypsy, again a
wanderer over the wide world. And, as you can see from
the enclosed newspaper cuttings, I am singing in guest roles
to the greatest acclaim, and not alone but together with our
former famous wonder-child, now the even more famous
virtuoso, Grisha Stelmach, whom I first met at your concert, that unforgettable concert that made a life-changing
impression on me. Ach! It is a whole romance. I will try to
describe in short form as well as I can because, first of all,
I don't want to take much of your time and, second of all, I
am writing this letter on the ship carrying me to America.
The day after tomorrow we will be in New York.

"We"—that means I am not traveling alone but with someone, as I have always wanted, as I have always striven to achieve. In that I have my triumph. Ach! How I long to embrace you now, to draw you close to my heart and kiss you, dear, dear *Mütterchen*! Do you think I am drunk? Yes, I am drunk, *Mütterchen*, drunk, but not drunk with love, no. Call me a gypsy, call me a dreamer, call me an adventuress, call me what you will, but hear me out and perhaps you will understand me. You, only you, can understand me. What I will tell you now is an episode in my life that I could never tell you about till now because in the episode you play the main role. It happened early morning on the day of your remarkable matinee concert that I will never ever forget. That was the happiest morning of my life, the start of my career.

Dazed, excited, lost, and enchanted by your singing and acting, I was swept out of the hall by the stream of people, and along with most of them I remained standing at the door waiting for the two heroes of the hour, the famous Marcella Embrich and Grisha Stelmach.

Whether the waiting lasted a minute, an hour, or a day, I do not recall, because my soul was in another world, a world of heavenly song and otherworldly sounds. Suddenly loud applause broke out, and the crowd lurched forward. I raised my eyes and saw approaching a shiny, elegant automobile. Like a flash of lightning, both of you streaked before my eyes, first you, then he, then joined by a third party, and as in a lovely dream, you vanished in triumph amid loud applause.

But in my memory that moment remains fixed. All I need to do is shut my eyes to have that precious dream materialize, in which you are the queen and he is the prince and I and all the other people who wander the earth are your subjects, your slaves, and both of you rule over us.

After the automobile sped off, the crowd vanished like smoke. Remaining were only a few local people, and I too still stood in a daze, stunned, full of fantasies that caught me up on their wings and carried me to where you were, my magnificent queen, together with that young handsome prince. And I, the small, lonesome, poor Rosa, suddenly saw my own triumph and heard my own name together with Grisha Stelmach's, and I began to shiver. A storm stirred in my brain and a fire in my heart, and I told myself: *This dream must be realized!*

The dream, as you see, has been realized. It has been realized in the best possible way. Not only have I been honored with a triumph I have not deserved, but I have attained much more: the young prince himself, who grew up, changing from a wonder-child to become a great artist. And that great artist is now mine, all mine!

Now do you want to know if I am happy? Ach, dear, dear, don't ask me! I am not worthy of the love that people grant me. I am unworthy even of the hundredth part of what you, *Mütterchen,* have given me. I carry within me a wicked heart. I am possessed by an evil spirit. I love no one, no one! I am only doing what I feel like doing at the moment, only what caprice dictates. Other people's worries are a joke to me. Another's tragedy is a game to me. An evil spirit has lodged itself in my heart, in my soul. Nothing pleases me. The more life gives me, the more I demand. The luckier I am, the more capricious I become. Moments, no more than moments, exalted, uplifting moments, make up my life, and those are the moments when my prince, my magician, is onstage. Ach, how imposing, how tall, how handsome he is then, heavenly, godly handsome. There is no comparing him to anyone, except . . . Ach! Why is he not the other, the other whom you know?!

Tell me, *Mütterchen,* what must I do to become happy? Teach me where I should seek my happiness. Will I find my happiness in the New World, where I am going now? Is there happiness to be found in this world at all? Am I not right when I tell you I am a wicked being, a lost soul? That is what I have always been, and that is what I will remain.

Your lost, wanton, capricious

Gypsy Rosa

CHAPTER 39

From Meyer Stelmach to His Good Friend

Dearest friend!

I could not wait for your answer and so I am writing to you again. You can believe me or not, but I feel some need, a great urge, to pour my heart out to you, because first of all, you are almost the only one in the world who understands me properly. You once told me that since I was capable of having a son like Grisha, it is evidence that I myself am no ordinary person as the world might think. Hearing those words from a knowledgeable person like yourself means a great deal to me, as you can well understand. And second of all, I simply enjoy talking with you as I would to my own brother because with you I can speak frankly and write everything that is in my heart. I hold you, as I have said, to be the best person in the world to trust with a secret. I know your lips are sealed, and I am certain that the letters I write you will never be seen by anyone else and not a soul will know.

Well, guess where I am writing this letter from? From a ship, my dear friend, I am writing from a ship. We are on our way to America. When I say *we,* I mean *I,* Grisha, Rosa, and the manager, an American character who has arranged for us to tour America at his expense, naturally first class, and for a certain minimum fee. The minimum is guaranteed, meaning that we cannot make less than a certain amount, and if there is more, that too is ours. Does that make sense to you? In plain Yiddish we can say he has hired us—or to speak the pure truth, he has bought us for a certain time—and that's the whole of it. To belong to someone, dear friend, to be sold to someone, is not what I call a good thing, something I learned very well from my German, may his name be obliterated! But what can one do? The minimum is substantial, and God knows money is always a great temptation. At first I didn't want to hear of any minimum-shminimum. Do you think someone is going to tell me what to do? Where am *I* in all this? Don't I know the business? But that American character latched on to me like a leech, demanding to know how much pure profit I wanted to make, and how much was the very least I was figuring on. What could I say to that character? Noticing I was hesitating, he told me it wasn't necessary to answer right away. He told me I had twenty-four hours to make a decision. How do you like that! He gave me a gift of twenty-four hours! Naturally, I didn't sleep that night, thinking this way, thinking that way, conferring with my wife, talking it over with the children. But what do children know? As I have already written you, my son is not interested in these things. He knows very well that more is better, but he doesn't interfere. He relies on his father. He knows, you understand, that his father will not allow anyone to spit in his kasha. Rosa is much more practical than my son. Money is as nothing to her, and when it comes to spending, squandering, and throwing away money, she is easily the equal of my son and can certainly outdo him. But she does understand business, has an appetite for money, *kayn eyn horeh,* and can demand a fee to make someone see stars! I agree with her that every person must know his worth. I just wonder where she got that from. If you talk to her, she says I'm the one who loves money!

To make a long story short, the twenty-four hours passed, and my American character was right on time, clean-shaven, a perfectionist, every button buttoned up, waiting for me to close the deal. I gave him my minimum price, which if I told you, you would surely think I was telling a lie. Do you think he was shocked? After not so much as a minute this fellow extended his hand and said, "All right." You can imagine I became quite despondent. That fellow had taken me in. If he had at least shown that he wanted to bargain a bit, ask more for himself—but no, he never bargained. I told him I wanted the minimum to be guaranteed, meaning he had to put a certain amount in the bank in my name. Do you think he was surprised? Not a bit. "All right!" he said again, stood up, and went to cable New York to send him the money—and that's the way the deal was struck.

You can be sure that Rosa later teased me for asking for so little. Do you hear that? She said I had small expectations.

I lacked, she said, that knack for business. What do you say to that impudence? I was feeling enough aggravation from that American character, and she rubs salt in my wounds! I wanted to ask her how I was supposed to have that knack. Did I go through Albert Shchupak's school? But I decided to let it go. I didn't want my son to know about Shchupak and other such matters from the past. And to tell the truth, why is she responsible for Shchupak's misusing her the way a gypsy is made to dance with a bear so he could make money off her? Then again, what is the shame? As you say, it's no shame to be poor. I once was wandering from town to town with my Grisha without a pair of shoes to my name, playing six tunes for three *groshens* just for Jews. They had a musician named Moshe-Noach who could play rings around anyone. No, my dear friend, I am not ashamed of what once was. Rather, I can happily tell you that God's help is for me a blessing. I am happy when we all get together and I can tell them stories from long ago when we smiled at little things, when a glass of tea with sugar was something to celebrate, a quarter of a chicken was seen only in a dream, and for an apple and two plums Grisha would play the most beautiful tune for you!

More than anyone else Rosa loved those stories. Her eyes would light up, and she would become even more beautiful as she told stories from her own past. She loved to include all the details. You would hold your sides laughing at her stories from her shtetl, Holeneshti. She imitated the Jewish women in the market or pretended to be a hoarse cantor trying to chant. I tell you, dear friend, you didn't need a theater. You could hear the laughter three streets away. The problem was that she wasn't always so inclined. I believe I've already written you that she is a capricious girl. She does as she pleases. Sometimes she is lively and happy, singing and dancing so that the whole house dances along with her. Other times a cloud moves across her face and she goes off to her room alone for the whole day, or she can sit down and write letters all day. It's fruitless to ask her to whom she is writing so often and so much. Sometimes she will suddenly demand that Grisha play for her even if he doesn't feel like it. But if Rosa wants something, can you deny her? And if she should get up in the middle of the night, for instance, and ask him to play? If you are in love, what difference does it make? He takes the violin, and she sits down opposite him, leaning her head on both hands, never taking her eyes off him, and at that time, I tell you, she looks like an angel! A beauty! If you ask her to sing she will never comply. On the contrary, the more you ask her, the more she will refuse. But if she feels like it, she will sing for you like a nightingale. Do you think she sings arias, concert pieces? Not at all! She sings gypsy songs, or a Hungarian tune, or maybe a Yiddish song. You should hear her singing Chasidic songs. You would walk ten miles to hear it. I know you are a lover of Yiddish songs, so I will write you the words of a Chasidic song she sings to a lively tune. Too bad I don't know how to read music, but here are the words:

> *From Chaslavitch to Libavitch*
> *Ay, who listens to you?*
> *From Libavitch to Chaslavitch—*
> *Ay, I laugh at you!*
> *I lift my pack and don't look back.*
> *Ay, who listens to you?*
> *I stuff my* tallis *in my sack.*
> *Ay, who needs you!*
> *From Chaslavitch to Libavitch, etc.*

> *I'm off to the* rebbe *in Libavitch.*
> *Ay, who listens to you!*
> *I'm off to the* rebbe *in Chaslavitch.*
> *Ay, I laugh at you.*
> *From Chaslavitch to Libavitch, etc.*

> *I have a wife and seven children.*
> *Ay, who listens to you!*
> *I bought a goat for seven gulden.*
> *Ay, who needs you!*
> *From Chaslavitch to Libavitch, etc.*

> *I have a house without a roof.*
> *Ay, who listens to you!*
> *I have a succah that's not rainproof.*

Ay, who needs you!
From Chaslavitch to Libavitch, etc.

On my window pelts the rain.
Ay, who listens to you!
In the chimney whistles my pain.
Ay, I laugh at you!
From Chaslavitch to Libavitch, etc.

On my heart a sadness falls.
Ay, who listens to you!
I'm off to the rebbe, *ay, to the* rebbe,
Ay, who needs you!
From Chaslavitch to Libavitch—
Ay, who listens to you!
From Libavitch to Chaslavitch
Ay, I laugh at you!

Dear friend, I would give seventeen concerts and eighteen symphonies for her one Yiddish song, or to hear her sing bits from all the famous cantors in the world, from Nissi Beltzer, Yorachum Hakaton, Pinni Minkovski, Razumne, Kvartin, Sirota, and anyone else you can name. She can stand up and chant the beloved prayers with all the trills and tremolos so sweetly that you can, I tell you, melt in her hands. A regular devil! In addition to all that, you should hear how she speaks German, how she speaks French! And if you want English, she also speaks English. How can you dislike someone so capable and talented! But her one fault is that she is a bit short-tempered, and how short-tempered! You have to watch every word, every look, because if it isn't just so, your life is in danger. She is a rare, shining jewel! So we are careful, we give in to her, and all because of my son. Thank God we were blessed with his temperament. If he were different, he could ask for anything and magnates would consider themselves lucky. They would cover me with money! But it's too late. Maybe it was fated to be a match. May God grant that I will hear something fairly soon. Meantime there is nothing, absolutely nothing, no more than a romance. Too bad, dear friend, you are not here by my side. We would have so much to talk about. We would sit for days and nights, and I would tell you and tell you about this pearl. She is a world in herself. But I must end my letter because the bell is ringing for the passengers to eat, and eating on a ship, you must know, is quite a treat. The appetite of passengers is, *kayn eyn horeh,* great. Until they live to hear the mealtime bell, they must put something in their mouths at least two times. What a pity you are not here with us on the ship! I promise to write you an even longer letter from New York. May God grant we arrive safely. Meanwhile be well, and write your welcome letters to my New York address, which I enclose.

From me, your best friend,
Meyer Stelmach

Almost Forgot: That American character included a point in the contract that almost killed the whole deal. Listen to what an American can think up! The contract stipulated that neither my son nor Rosa is allowed to talk to anyone else without his knowledge. That means if someone wants to entertain them, he has to know who it is. If they want to go somewhere, he has to know where. And even letters to them he has to know from whom they come. How do you like that? Naturally, I had second thoughts but finally signed the contract with all its conditions. This last condition I kept from the children because if Rosa knew of it, she would hit the ceiling! I beg you to keep it our secret. I would not trust anyone else with it but you.

Meyer

CHAPTER 40

From Sholom-Meyer Murovchik to His Friend Albert Shchupak

Dear friend I am writing this letter to tell you that I am in London blessed be His name for the second time and you are in Odessa so I am writing you this letter to Odessa so you

will know Albert that things are not good with the bread falling butter side down nothing is working out even if you tear
yourself to pieces I am sick to death that I didn't go that time
back home with you now it's too late it's the devil's work so I
remained stuck first in Vienna afterward in Paris now in London all because of our great beauty thinking I would make
out like a bandit with her money and instead I was fobbed
off and humiliated when she came back from Italy she put on
airs I almost had a fit when I heard her singing and she sings
Albert so that neither you nor your grandmother and not
your grandmother's grandmother ever heard before in their
dreams and now you should see the fame and the jewels she
wears you would die on the spot and whose fault is it that you
behaved with her like an idiot and on account of you I am left
high and dry almost dying of hunger just lucky that in Paris
there's a Jewish theater Waxman is the director a bitter young
man who barely eked out a few cents for me and off again to
London it turns out the next morning she is actually in Antwerp and in Brussels so we must get to Antwerp and Brussels and we don't have a cent what to do so I went and left
my satchel in London with some idiot named Klammer and
when I went to pick up my satchel it turned out Klammer was
gone the devil had carried him off to America and Rosa went
there first do you know with whom with our Stelmach's boy
Grisha she sings and he plays and they say they make in one
night what we would wish to earn in three months and for
me it's a big problem because in my satchel there were papers
actually her papers very important I haven't read them but I
understand they must be very important because she writes
to me in a letter Rosa to send her the papers and money is
not a problem so it is just my luck it happened that her letters
were for three months in Waxman's hands, may the cholera
afflict him they all vanished like salt in water now the question is what shall I do and where should I turn but to you my
dear Albert you should trust me and send me right away for
God's sake a hundred to London here is my address so I can
get to America there I don't have a problem just let me get to
that Klammer and get my satchel back with the papers you
know I have earned more than a hundred from you remember and I look forward to your sending me a few *groshens* till

now I didn't nag you because I didn't need it but now I am in
need and am about to go to America my sister has long been
there I have a letter from her and she writes that everyone
is already in America even Breyndele Kozak is there too and
you can surely believe me that I will pay back your money
and more with many thanks may God grant me luck I don't
need yours and when you write me a letter I want you to write
me everything in detail how you are with your business and
do you have a proper troupe and what pieces are you putting
on in Odessa and how are things with you and how are our
other buddies it's no secret Hotzmach is here in London with
his own troupe and what do you say to his father who is sick
I hate that Jew like pork but to hell with him, you have to just
forget him and be well with eighteen times best wishes

Sholom-Meyer Murovchik

CHAPTER 41

From Albert Shchupak to Sholom-Meyer Murovchik

Most valued friend Sholom-Meyer whom I had nightmares
about last night and the night before are you mad or crazy
to ask me to add the living to the dead and send you hundreds I barely lived to see you on the other side of the door
do you think money is growing in my garden I have hundreds like you have a brain in your head because whoever
has God in his heart is pulling tearing biting sucking money
from me from all sides they are ruining me I barely got rid
of the old pain-in-the-necks and there's always a new one
but no one burns me up as much as your cantor's daughter who you dragged me into a quagmire for besides having
reduced me to absolute poverty and cost me a fortune she
also insulted me in front of my friend Stelmach and called
me a whore if she had called me a bandit and evil or what
have you it would not have hurt as much as whore I will
never forgive her for it even when I am lying with my feet
pointed to the door and as for your wanting to go to her in

America that plan appeals to me and I can lend you money for expenses but not a whole hundred and on the condition I send you the bills she ran up maybe you can shake out of her what I am owed because if she is making as much money as you say why shouldn't she give me back what I spent on her I will forgive her the interest and for calling me a whore I am not that kind of person God forbid who carries a grudge in my heart and you God help you must help me you know I don't hold a grudge against you and may you succeed they say America is a land of gold see to it you write a letter once in a while not like until now you were silent as a dummy and suddenly there you are so why didn't you write sooner you bastard but waited till now maybe a little earlier I could have sent you a whole hundred now I can't as God is my witness send more than fifty because the competition is great and the expenses are even greater and new problems keep popping up and if God will help then you will probably pay me back money doesn't come too easy God knows how hard you have to work till you earn fifty and if you see that beauty, remind her of the candies and chocolates and the second-class trains and the new clothes she always had to have she took the shirt off my back it's lucky I was able to come here to Odessa my old home I used to do good business here I can't complain today too if not for the competition three theaters in one city but my theater is the best because I have my acting school and my claques on the cheap but the problem is that we are three troupes here and times are hard, the cholera is raging and the wind is biting and we have here in Odessa a rich man a Haman and even worse but still I'm putting on a successful production of *The Jew* thank God which is still playing and *Khinke Pinke* is good stuff and *Velvele Eats Compote* is tasty as ever and I have a fine name in Odessa am considered a success and bought back a few of my diamonds and have my own *Sefer Torah* to hell with all of them but the problem is you are never sure with your life and enemies there are many and they come to my present wife and they tell her a bald-faced lie that I have a cantor's girl somewhere else a girlfriend who is costing me a fortune and how can you defend yourself to hell with them all together with that girlfriend that's all I need no more news to write be well and write immediately about the fifty I am sending you and write me how those papers got to you she really lost them Rosa did you find them in her locked table drawer because you were sort of a secretary to her do you think I don't remember how you two used to whisper together behind my back but still and all give my regards to her and to Breyndele may she keel over dead and also give my regards if you should see Hotzmach tell him I wish him a miserable death with best wishes *director*

Albert Shchupak

CHAPTER 42

From Leah the Cantor's Wife to Her Daughter, Rosa Spivak

To my Daughter the Worthy, Intelligent Reizel, Long Life to You

First of all I must tell you that I am in good health, blessed be His name. God grant the same to you and may we hear news of much joy and happiness from you, amen.

Second of all, my dear, beloved daughter, I did not want to upset you with the tragedy that has struck me like a bullet from a gun or a thunderbolt from heaven. As God is my witness, I would not write you about it because as long as you are doing well, you mustn't be disturbed. I know very well that as bitter and hopeless as my life is since I have become a lonely widow in my old age, it will be a thousand times worse when you learn you are now an orphan, having lost a father whom you so loved, as he did you, who till his final minutes did not fail to speak your name, Reizele and again Reizele. What could we do when God ordained that from the very day you left us, he would so take it to heart that he felt the whole world had collapsed around him. Everything was all the same to him, eating or not, sleeping or not, however hard we tried to talk him out of it. If a child dies, may it never happen, it's a thousand times worse than when a child leaves. God can help, and the child might someday return, but when a child dies, God forbid, it will never return because what the earth covers is no more. Our wealthy Rafalovitch will not even allow anyone to speak of his bright son. The worthy name Leibel is not allowed to be spoken in the house, a blessing on his head, because what good did it do his poor mother when she wept and lamented over him until, may she forgive me for saying this, she went out like a candle and so it was all for nothing. That is what I tried to tell your father, but it was useless. Your father would not hear any of my comforting words and would only bring up the example of the poor man and the little lamb set down in the holy books. He compared himself to the wealthy Rafalovitch, who had many sheep and cattle and so could spare one cow, but he was like the poor man who only had one little lamb, his most precious possession, the apple of his eye which was taken (away) from him, and how could he bear it? That was how he argued and maybe he was right. I will never forget as long as I live the nights he would wake up and go behind the curtain and kiss your pillow so I wouldn't see him and weep silently, swallowing his tears. And I said, "Yisroyeli, you are sinning before God, a person must not grieve so much." I said, "You'll see, God willing we will soon receive a letter from her with good news." He would put on a smile and try to convince me he was beginning to forget his pain but I could see the man was going downhill, was shriveling up from day to day. I am not trying to make you feel guilty, my dear daughter. I know your heart was drawn to him as was his to you, as I know from your first letters that were for him better than all the remedies and herbs that the doctor prescribed for him to drink. And when he lived long enough to see you visit us, he was not to be recognized, literally rising from the dead to life again. I thought the sun had risen and angels were dancing with me, an end to my woes. But it turned out I was misled, woe is me; it wasn't enough that he had enjoyed the small bit of pleasure you gave him before his death, your showing your devotion to him by your visit and generosity that nobody had counted on. "Now you must live, Reb Yisroyeli," the elders of the town all told him, and envied him the house you bought us and the honor that came with it even though it was too large a property for us and about which I wonder even now, what will I do with it, one person alone in so many rooms. I will go out of my mind like old Rafalovitch's mother who still lives in the house to this day. Rather than live to be as old as she, it is better to die as your father did, may he rest in peace. Exactly twenty-two days in the month of Av he died, and today it is twenty-one days in Elul already, the thirty days of mourning have passed so you don't need to sit shiva any more than one hour a day because if you have a job you cannot do otherwise. You've already earned enough grace by coming home and lengthening his days even if only a little. You must know, my dear daughter, that two hours before he died, your father spoke well of you, may he be your protector and mine and all of Israel in the next world. God did not give him the privilege of leaving a son to say kaddish for him, so I appointed Chaim Shayeh the beadle, the one you gave money to buy a cow, to say it every morning and evening. Nachum, his son, is writing this very letter for me, so it's fated that his father should say kaddish for your father every morning and evening. I don't know if any rich man could have had a bigger funeral than his and he was given a highly honored grave site at the cemetery thirteen places from the old rabbi. On one side lies Boruch Ber the *shochet* and on the other lies Reb Shlyome from Telenesht, and from there on they're all wealthy townsfolk. After all, he earned it and if I live to see the anniversary of his death, God willing, I will enclose the grave as he deserves. I beg you, my dear child, to give me permission to rent out at least half the house, because what will I do, one person alone in so many rooms? Write me good letters often, as you have till now, because the dear letter you wrote bidding us farewell when you left for America and the one you wrote when you got there telling your father to take care of his health till your return he was not fated to read because by then they already placed the shards on his eyes in his coffin. They read me your letter after the shiva and they brought the money to the house so you no longer need to send money, dear daughter. There will be enough for the whole winter till Passover because when I think of it, what do I need, a widow all alone. I ask no more from God than that I live to see you at least one more time when you come back, God willing, in good health, and I need no more than that other than asking that I live to see you under the wedding canopy, and be well and strong and don't cry too long, my child, for your father, and take care of your health and I hope the One Above will send you your intended one soon and I will live to see you make your mother's heart happy as I pray God for you day and night.

From me, your devoted mother who kisses you a thousand times,

Leah Spivak

CHAPTER 43

From Meyer Stelmach to His Good Friend

My dear friend!

I received your warm, caring letter. You ask what America is like, and I had wanted to sit down to describe Columbus's land to you in all its details. But first you wish to know how I am and how my Grisha is. What can I write you, dear friend, except that we wish our problems on all Jewish children. The prestige that those two, Grisha and Rosa, have here, can it be described? The whole country, from one end to the other, all the newspapers—the greatest, the Gentile ones—are full of them. You open a paper and all you see is Grisha Stelmach and Rosalia Spayvak, Rosalia Spayvak and Grisha Stelmach! To get to hear them is a rare privilege. Whoever does not have a reservation eight days in advance might as well try buying it from a bear. I will tell you the truth—I don't know which of them is more popular. We have reviews from Washington, Philadelphia, Chicago, Canada, and the ends of the earth. We are no longer talking of money, that's settled. The managers implore us, "Take as much as you want, strip us down to our shirts, just come!" The problem is that our manager, that American character, skims off the cream, damn him.

But I don't begrudge him at all because he spent plenty
just to bring us all over to New York. But don't worry. He
won't lose in the end. We've already made him rich. We did
have one interruption during the holidays. Do you think
it was on account of religious observance? You needn't
worry about America. America is, God bless it, a free
land, even freer than London. Here everyone does what he
wants. Come the High Holidays, this one runs to the synagogue, another goes to work in a shop. Come Yom Kippur
to Kol Nidrei, this one weeps at the Ya'ales, another goes
to a ball, a Yom Kippur Ball, it's called. A group of young
people gather together and over a glass of beer and a pork
sausage they make their peace with the old Jewish God for
His evil deeds, for His edicts, and for His pogroms, and
take him to task so he will have what to remember till next
year's Kol Nidrei! If you're talking about a free country,
here you can do anything!

Anyhow, the interruption we had this holiday was over
another matter. Our poor Rosa, long life to her, became
an orphan. Her father, who was a cantor in a small town,
died. Yes, he died—rest in peace. It happens that a father
dies. But you should see how that girl carried on! First she
canceled her performances several nights in a row. Do you
have any idea what a loss we had to take? You might wish
to earn as much. According to the contract, we have to pay
double for every missed performance. What didn't we say
to her, my son and I and the American agent? She refused
to hear. And she was quite angry at us too, saying if we told
her what to do one more time, she would break the contract, and do her something! Finally a few days later she
came around and agreed to go on. If she hadn't, we might
as well leave America. Still and all, at her last performance
she sang so beautifully, the walls wept and the earth shook.
Old fool that I am, I wiped the tears from my eyes and
my Grisha—you can only imagine! So that was the first
thing. Then she decided she had to sit shiva, but what kind
of shiva? She simply removed her shoes and sat down on
the floor. "In God's name," I said, "dear Rosa, what are
you doing? You're among Christians, Gentiles, aristocrats,
millionaires!" Does the wall listen? And you can't say a

word to her. She is a temperamental thing, God help me! I wouldn't write this to anyone else, but I know you are discreet and would never show my letters to anyone. I tell you, she blows hot and cold! Imagine this outrage, what this girl can do. It was the High Holidays; she gets dressed and wants to go to *shul.* "What is this?" "I want to go to memorial services!" she said. "Are you out of your mind?" I said, "Do you want to slaughter us? Here's a knife!" And she said, "Don't you go to *shul* on the High Holidays?" "She-devil! How can you compare yourself to me? I can go anywhere. I can go to *shul,* I can go to the theater, but not you. Tomorrow it will be in all the papers!" "What of it? Why isn't Melba or Embrich or Caruso or eighteen others like them ashamed to go to church when there is a holiday?" How do you like those words? In a way, she is right, but what can we do? We are, after all, Jews in a Christian world. She would not be convinced. A Gentile is a Gentile and a Jew is a Jew. I love being a Jew, believe me, with all my heart. I love Jewish theater, Jewish food, as you know, and love *jhargon,* and I have a Jewish home, and my wife, long life to her, is a kosher woman, my children are, thank God, Jews, and, beyond that, I must insist that, let my Grisha just once go downtown to the Jewish neighborhoods and step out onto a Jewish stage or go into a synagogue, that would be the end of it, everything lost, no more leader of the band! No more Grisha Stelmach! And the same would be true for Rosa Spivak. So long as she is among Gentiles, though they all know she is Jewish, the wealthiest Jews will run to hear her sing. But if she were to behave foolishly and appear just for Jews, they would say, "Eh! So you're just one of us, what's so special?!"

In short, we finally convinced her to at least put on a thick veil over her face so no one would know her. My dear friend, we had our hands full with her. She did calm down a bit, but at first I thought I would have a heart attack! And I had to give in to her because what doesn't one do for a child?

And now do you want me to describe this country? After writing the above, you can understand what a coun-

try this is. I am afraid to say this, but I believe America is
not America but Eretz Yisroel. The Jews, I think, cannot
complain about Columbus. Whoever wants to and is able
to work can make a living. And music is highly esteemed.
I am certain that if you were to come here, you would not
regret it. You would make a good living and feel at home
among Jews. There are so many Jewish newspapers here.
For a reader like me, it is a true paradise. I can safely say
I swim in *jhargon* like a fish in water, and at night I cannot decide which theater to go to first. Coming to town
this week is a guest star in the Yiddish theater, a Rafalesco
from Bucharest, they say, a sensation! Everyone is going
wild!

For the most part, my friend, I am very knowledgeable
about America. I just wish I could report some progress about
the children because for those two it seems to be a story without an end. I will tell you the simple truth—you are the only
one I would write this to since you are so discreet. I do not
like this love affair. Make up your mind, I say, one way or the
other. How long does a love affair go on? Now there's a good
reason. She is in mourning for her father. She says she wants
to send a telegram to her mother asking her to come to America, and once she decides something, she won't budge! What
will happen if she does come here? What will we do with the
cantor's wife from Holeneshti? I haven't the faintest idea! One
consolation is if she does come, she might be able to exert a
mother's influence, and out of respect for her mother, we may
soon be able to announce an engagement and together put up
a wedding canopy.

Don't be offended, dear friend, if I am writing only
about myself. It helps to pour out your heart a little to a
good friend. I am growing old and gray from this romance
which I cannot fully describe. People urge me to leave it go
its own way. They tell me I am too involved, too emotional
a father; it may very well be. But what can I do? That's
the way I am. No one will change me now. So be well and
happy, and write me if you are really thinking of coming
to America. For me it would be, I really mean it, a celebration! I would at least have someone to bare my heart to,

because not everyone is a true friend and not everyone can
be trusted with what I have entrusted in you . . .

From me, your best friend,

Meyer Stelmach

Almost Forgot: You can run into many old acquaintances
here, but I avoid them. When I go to a Jewish theater, I must
hide myself, pull my hat down over my face, and find myself a
corner. What can one do? That's our crazy livelihood!

Meyer Stelmach

CHAPTER 44

Introspection

Our hero Rafalesco had been carried along by the current of life further and further into an unclear future without any reckoning on his
part. He never asked himself where he had come from or where he
was going—until he reached the shores of America. There for the
first time he looked back and saw the frightening ordeal he had survived after his early boyhood years, and the point he had now
reached—and he was amazed.

When we review our past, we realize we have lived through
and endured a great deal and have more or less achieved something.
Although Rafalesco was amazed that he had lived through and
accomplished so much, his deeper amazement came from another
source. He could not fathom how he had found the strength, courage, and energy to endure his life voyage. Who had shown him the
way? Who had been his guide? What was the name of his teacher?
What school did he attend, and what books did he study?

He asked himself, who had ignited the first spark of his art?
Who was the first to push him onto the stage? And whose light had
illuminated the way during the long dark night of wandering on his
artistic voyage?

A procession of figures passed before his eyes. First there were
childhood friends and classmates with whom he had put on little
plays between the afternoon and evening prayers so the rabbi would
not catch them. Then there was Albert Shchupak in Holeneshti with
his renowned troupe, and afterward Hotzmach, his first intimate

friend. After him came the director of the Lemberg theater, Getzel ben Getzel, the brothers Schwalb, and on and on, people from whom it had been impossible to learn anything. The only bright stars that did appear in his dark sky were the prompter Benny, the "person of education," who had opened his eyes; and Dr. Levyus-Levyusn, the Lemberg magnate, who had uncovered new worlds for him but, when he heard the word *money* from Hotzmach, fled the scene as fast as he could; and the great Sonnenthal, who like a meteor had flashed by and vanished. Beyond these few he could not remember anyone else.

Alone, alone, all by himself, without a rabbi, without a prayer book, without an alphabet, he had become what he was.

Alone, alone, he had grown into Leo Rafalesco, and if what was written about him was true, he was a rising, shining, glowing star on the Jewish stage.

Our hero paused in his thoughts and considered the other great stars of the New York Jewish stage. Who were they? Where had they come from? What had they been before? And again he was amazed. He had heard of their remarkable life stories. If they were written down, each could be a book of the highest interest.

As he reflected on his own life story, many things became clear. Schools did exist where you could learn how to become an actor, but there were none for Jews. Philanthropists did exist in the world who gave away fortunes to the arts, but none had yet been born for Jews. We had no schools for Jewish artists, no teachers, no texts, no alphabets, no philanthropists, no art. We had theaters, actors, talent, great bright stars whose light reached far, far beyond the Jewish stage, even to the Gentile nation. And sometimes it happened that they learned of such a star. They traveled down to the Jewish theater, smiled knowingly at one another, and latched onto this star until they seduced him to come over to them, and he was lost to the Jewish stage forever. The Gentile temptation is too great for a Jewish actor or actress to resist once they hear compliments from a non-Jew such as "Your place is not among Jews" and "Awaiting you are great opportunities, a large stage, a Christian public."

Great and mighty is the Gentile temptation everywhere and especially for those on the Jewish stage. Rare is the Jewish star who does not dream of one day finding a place in the non-Jewish firmament. Rare is the Jewish actor who with luck and considerable effort has the chance to tear himself away from his small Jewish circle and step into the larger, broader, foreign world.

Our hero Rafalesco was one of those fortunate ones who could easily and without effort have stepped into one of the largest non-Jewish theaters in New York and made a brilliant career. And if he resisted the Gentile temptation, if he vanquished that urge, it was only because certain life events occurred that will be described in the following chapters of our novel.

CHAPTER 45

Our Hero Is Lost in a Void

The large traveling company Klammer, Schwalb & Co., whose Star from Buenos Aires and whose Lomzher Nightingale had made it famous in America, was in a holiday mood, preparing itself for its last and greatest triumph—the debut of the world-renowned Star from Bucharest, the young artist Leo Rafalesco.

Our good friends Nissel Schwalb and Nickel did everything in their power to see to it that this debut would sound the death knell for all the other Yiddish theaters in New York. Two weeks in a row the announcements in the Jewish newspapers loudly proclaimed the arrival of the young star whom "Queen Carmen Silva had crowned with her own hands" and who had brought the great Sonnenthal to tears upon seeing him in the role of Uriel Acosta. All this was the work of our schemer, Nissel Schwalb.

Nickel was not sitting idly by. Walking nonchalantly around the *kibitzarni* with his hands in his pockets, he told everyone that he had invited prominent Jews like Jacob Schiff, Louis Marshall, Nathan Bijur, and many others for the debut. He confided to a few people that the governor of New York State and a few highly placed Christians might also be coming to the theater that night, but he would prefer it not be noised about, because they were already running out of tickets at the box office. His face shone, his cheeks glowed, and his gold teeth sparkled. Rockefeller, Carnegie, and Vanderbilt in their Wall Street offices could not have felt happier than Nickel.

But Nissel Schwalb was not feeling overly thrilled. His plan for the match between his sister and Rafalesco was not progressing. America was a land of "hurry up," business, rush, and noise. The cooperative was taking up all his time. Talking about it to his sister was a waste of

time. She said he shouldn't worry, it was their business. She was preoccupied with toilettes and photographs. As for the kid, as Holtzman
used to call him, something about him simply did not feel right. Since
they had come to New York, there was something wrong with him.
He seemed to be distracted, asking ten times a day if any letters had
arrived for him. From whom was he expecting letters so anxiously?
And what business did he have with that comical woman in the red
cape who would rush in "just for a little while" and sit either with him
or with Nissel's sister for hours at a time? To ask Henrietta was the
same as asking the doorknob. What did she know, the silly ninny? Her
success on the stage and the bluff about her beauty pageant prize in
Paris had so turned her head that you couldn't say a word to her. She
would simply dismiss you. Her brother Isaac said to Nissel: "Don't
tangle with that dumb cow. She'll cause you nothing but trouble!"

Isaac was right. She really was a dumb cow. If she'd had an
ounce of sense in her head, she would think of other things besides
foolishly having herself photographed with Rafalesco in a dozen different poses. She should better get him quick under the wedding canopy. How long could she wait? Mr. Klammer said the same: "Bake
bagels while the oven is hot or as the Englishman says: 'If you want
to do a thing, do it.' But who is to blame if not you, idiots?"

That was Mr. Klammer's opinion on the matter. Everyone had
something to say about this match and put in his two cents' worth,
including the Lomzher cantor's wife. She came to visit always wearing the new overcoat her husband had bought her in New York and
would raise the same question: "When will the Messiah be born?"

*What does that imbecile of a cantor's wife with the red wig mean
by that?* Nissel wondered. *And why should she worry her head over our
sister?* That woman's nose had been up in the air ever since her husband
struck it rich! And the cantor himself was not the same man. When he
had still been just the Lomzher cantor, who lived in Whitechapel and
longed for challah, he kissed your boots and held himself as the least
of the least. In America he was now the Lomzher Nightingale, and you
couldn't recognize him. He never had any time for you. He stood there
with his skullcap, a baton in his hand during rehearsals, shouting at the
choir, "C-flat, fa minor, E-flat major," acting like a regular conductor!
Soon he'd be refusing to speak a word to Nissel.

Such were the troubled thoughts that our genial schemer entertained during those early days in New York, as he argued continually
with his brother and sister and his partners. But none of it seemed to

touch our young hero. Rafalesco continued to walk the streets of New York sunk deep in his thoughts and dreams, as if the vast city around him were a dense, dark forest, a limitless void. What did he care about the company and its accounts, its rivalries, wrangling, and infighting? What did he care about his first American appearance on the stage, which would without a doubt prove to be a triumph, as it had always and everywhere? For whom did he need to show off, when at his debut the one he wanted most to see would not be there? And that she would not be there, he knew for certain. It was a foregone conclusion. Of all his dreams, not one had been realized. All his hopes for America had been shattered. Madame Cherniak had led him astray. Ever since Rosa Spivak had been in America, Madame Cherniak hadn't bothered to see her. She blamed it on her new job, which kept her busy. If she were able to get away for a day or two to see Rosa, she said, everything would be "all right." After *Shabbes,* when she had a day off, she would go uptown, and then everything would really be "all right."

Every day it was a new lie. She'd promise that tomorrow she would get him a ticket to the opera where Rosa Spivak was singing or to a concert where she was performing with the famous Grisha Stelmach, but nothing ever came of it. You couldn't buy a ticket for a million dollars!

Madame Cherniak was getting on his nerves to so much that he could barely stand to look at her. He went uptown himself to buy a ticket in the hall where Rosa was singing. It turned out she had been there the day before, but today she was no longer in New York. She was touring the country doing guest appearances. No one knew when she would be back. *You were always a loser, and you'll always be a loser!* Rafalesco berated himself, eating himself up alive. The company members kept bothering him about his first appearance. Reporters asked for interviews, while streetwalkers smiled at him and made tempting propositions. And Henrietta pestered him with her toilettes and photographs. He did not know what was happening to him. He was lost in a void.

CHAPTER 46

Mephistopheles in a Dress

"I wish to inform you, Reizel, that I, Leibel, Benny Rafalovitch's son from Holeneshti—do you remember him?—am here downtown in

New York, an artist with the Yiddish Nickel Theater, and my name is now Rafalesco."

That was the content of the letter that our young hero intended to send Miss Rosalia Spayvak, brief and to the point. What more was there to write?

But writing this first serious letter took on a life of its own and tapped into a hidden source. From it poured his life story, all of what had happened to him, from the time they parted on that magical night of the fire on God's Street in Holeneshti until the present moment. From his pen flowed an account of what he had lived through on his artistic journey, all his dreams and hopes, thoughts and feelings, joys and suffering.

No, it was not a love letter. The word *love* did not flow from his pen once. It was too banal, too commonplace. The threads that bound her name to his, their past with the present, were too sacred. And if some affectionate words loosen to escape from his pen, they were cloaked, wrapped, disguised.

He asked her to remember that starry night in Holeneshti when she had asked him about the falling stars raining from the sky and to remember what he had answered: *"Stars do not fall, stars wander."* And he asked her to remember her visit later to a gypsy fortune-teller who had foreseen wandering stars traveling in opposite directions that could never meet.

His letter was full of hints wrapped in allegories, and dots trailing after unfinished sentences.

At the end of the letter he asked her not to question why he was speaking to her through a letter and not in person. For one, he had heard that it was impossible to approach her. First you had to apply to a Mr. Bohrman, and you had to tell him who you were and what your business was. The word *business* was in quotes, underlined three times, and followed by an exclamation mark. Also, he let her know, delicately and again with interspersed dots, that he was afraid he might upset "certain people" who were with her and who were appearing on the stage with her to such acclaim.

Here our young diplomat intentionally used the word *people* in the plural, though the merest child in New York knew that Miss Rosalia Spayvak performed only with one Grisha Stelmach.

Ach, Grisha Stelmach! That name had long preyed on our young hero's mind and would not allow him to sleep. *Who is he? What does he look like?* As much as he longed to see Reizel, he would rather have first met this Grisha Stelmach, at least to see him from afar. Whenever he heard the name, he felt a stab in his heart. Madame Cherniak thrust the dagger deeper by saying she knew for certain that those two were betrothed and that they would marry any day now.

What had led Breyndele Kozak to take on the role of Mephistopheles? It was simply a matter of revenge on her sworn enemy, Hotzmach. Her goal had been to take away his leading lady and to trick the kid to come as well, and this had been achieved. Now what more did she need to do? I ask you, was it her duty to solve the problems of the world? Where was it written that she had to intercede on Rafalesco's and Rosa's behalf? Let them work it out themselves. How many people were worrying their heads over her? If she were to lose her job, who would look after her in that cauldron of New York? Forget about men, may the devil take them one at a time and leave not a trace! But maybe not even Rosa Spivak, to whom she had been as close as a sister, wandering together with Shchupak, eating together, almost sharing a bed. Breyndele went to visit her in New York, and they wouldn't even let her near! She wrote a few words to her: "My Rosa dear, my soul, Madame Cherniak wants to see you." And she didn't answer! She wrote her again—still no reply! Rafalesco came to New York, and Madame Cherniak went to greet him, embraced and kissed him, took him in like a member of her family, pampered him, opened up her soul, and he still wasn't satisfied. What did he want? He wanted her to deliver Rosa Spivak and Grisha Stelmach on a silver platter! Men! When they wanted something, the ground could split and the sky crack open! May they all be consumed in one fire!

"Be patient, my dear Rafalesco. Let's talk a little first. How is Hotzmach, may he drop dead? And how about that homely little sister of his? And that old mare, his mother—is that witch still living?"

When Breyndele Kozak put off Rafalesco in this manner, she could not understand why he looked offended. Why was he making such a tragedy over that Spivak?

Whenever Breyndele thought of "that Spivak," her blood boiled. She could not forget her shame and embarrassment that they did not welcome *her*, Madame Cherniak, and did not allow her to see them, nor even answer her letters. Who was this shtetl cantor's daughter! So her luck had turned, and she became famous—what of it? You can be rich and famous, but the other person is not a dog. If you fly too high, you have farther to fall. It could happen. Henrietta Schwalb was also a leading lady, also famous. They also trumpeted her in the newspapers, and a riot broke out whenever she stepped off the stage, but still and all, bless her, she was simple, decent, and devoted to her, like her own sister. That's why she, Madame Cherniak, was also loyal like a sister, ready to listen to all her secrets, visited Henrietta every day if she had time, and sat and chatted with her. There was always enough to talk about, plenty! They talked until it started to turn dark. Then Madame Cherniak slapped her fat thighs and grabbed her red cape: "Oh my God! It's almost pitch-dark!" And Breyndele Kozak skipped out the door and over the streets of New York, caught a cab, and flew off to her job in the theater, while in her mind she was hatching a Mephistophelean plot for a hasty wedding between Henrietta and Rafalesco.

No, may her name not be Breyne Cherniak if there would not be a wedding! It would be a joyous, stylish wedding. The newspapers would drum it up, they would talk about it in the *kibitzarni,* and she, Madame Cherniak, would be the most important relative—but from which side, the bride's or the groom's? No, it would be from both sides. And she would dance with that trickster, Nissel Schwalb. The whole troupe would get drunk, carouse, and dance until the wee hours. Then she would come home, sit down, and write a fine Mephistophelean note to Rosa Spivak and give her a *mazel tov,* or wait, maybe not. In the most lurid romantic serials she was reading, it went differently: Rosa would get an invitation timed so that she arrived at the exact moment when the bride and groom were standing under the wedding canopy. He would be putting the ring on her finger. Rosa faints away . . . Uproar . . . Her fiancé Grisha Stelmach runs to her and shoots himself in the heart. Do not ask why the young Stelmach should get a bullet in his heart. When a person seeks revenge he does not care who is guilty or not guilty, only that blood flows like water.

CHAPTER 47

Breyndele Kozak—A Matchmaker

In a few days the new star from Bucharest was to step out before the New York public for the first time. All the preparations, rehearsals, and sets were complete. In the theater Nickel informed the company every two minutes by phone that it was "all right," that there were hardly any tickets left for Rafalesco's performance, people were tearing them out of one another's hands, fighting for them at the box office. He was afraid they might demolish the house, storm the doors. The company wasn't frightened by this information. They very well knew that the greater half of what Nickel said you could dismiss outright, a third you could throw into the river, and the rest you could give away to the poor.

The brothers Schwalb, Mr. Klammer, and the Lomzher cantor were talking. Rafalesco and Henrietta had gone to have themselves photographed in a new pose. The company's mood was not good. Not because the business was going badly—on the contrary, brilliant prospects were predicted, and shares of the company were going up from day to day. What was lacking, what was everywhere and always lacking in any human community, was unanimity, peace, and tranquillity. What one said, the other contradicted. Each considered himself to be infallible and the other wrong.

On this day Nissel boasted that coming to America had been entirely his idea. If not for him and his plan, where would they be now? Mr. Klammer claimed that if not for him and his deep pockets, they would be begging from house to house. The Lomzher cantor interrupted him and asserted that no one was getting anything from Klammer's pockets. Thank God, he could now manage without anyone's help, and he could certainly support his family.

The cantor's boasting hurt everyone's feelings, especially Isaac Schwalb's. He bristled and asked the cantor if he remembered when he was living in London Whitechapel in a damp cellar, where the large stove always desperately needed some wood, and he never saw a full pot except *Shabbes* and holidays, or when his brother collected a few shillings from a few good people with soft hearts?

Naturally, the cantor wasn't too pleased to hear that, so he reminded Schwalb quite pointedly that his place in the theater was in the aisles and that his work consisted of clapping his hands, not his tongue.

To this Isaac retorted that if the time came when the Lomzher cantor needed his hands to clap for him, and one of those times might happen soon, the Lomzher cantor would be in deep trouble.

This exchange might have resulted in a bit of a ruckus if someone had not come in with the information that a lady was asking for someone.

"A lady? For me?"

All four men sprang up.

"The lady is asking for the elder Mr. Schwalb."

Nissel Schwalb straightened his tie, opened the door, and when he saw his visitor, he cursed his fate. Seeing that Nissel was upset, Breyndele Kozak, the lady in question, made a little curtsy and told him she had something important to tell him.

"About business?"

"About business."

"In private?"

"In private."

As it was about business and in private, he had to invite the lady into a separate room, where they sat down to talk.

Breyndele started with a long introduction, going back to the days when she had been a young woman and had not yet met Shchu-pak, may he perish. At the time she had never dreamed she would one day be in Columbus's land holding down a menial job. She wasn't complaining, God forbid, about her luck. She knew there were many who would wish to have that job. She had a few dollars saved up, not a lot, so long as she didn't have to ask for help and could make a living.

Nissel saw that the lady was going on a bit and apologized for cutting her off. He said he was wondering what she wanted of him. He was happy she was making a living, he said, and didn't have to depend on others, but he was very busy now. They were going out of their minds today preparing for the debut of their star, Leo Rafalesco.

"It was him I came to you about," Breyndele said.

Nissel looked at her small Oriental eyes and her perspiring red moon-shaped face. "What can you tell me about Leo Rafalesco?"

"What can I tell you about Leo Rafalesco? First give me your hand."

"Here are both my hands."

Breyndele grasped both his hands and moved her chair so close to Nissel's that he felt her warmth and smelled an aroma of mint drops and patchouli soap mixed with perspiration and young onions. As succinctly as possible, she told him she was a match-maker, but without any personal interest. Her only interest was for Henrietta, her very good friend. May she herself have half of what she wished for her, and if he, Nissel, wanted his sister to carry the name of Rafalesco, he had better see to it that it happened soon, or else it would be too late . . .

With those words Breyndele moved her chair a few feet back, wiped her perspiring moon-shaped face, fixed her small Oriental eyes on Schwalb, and smiled with severely pursed lips, like a person who knows a very important thing but cannot put it into words . . .

Nissel insisted she tell him what she meant, but she refused. No matter how many vows he swore that he would keep it a secret, Breyndele kept silent. She wrapped herself in her red cape and hastened to leave.

"Not a word, do you hear?" she said at the door. She put her finger to her lips and smiled broadly, showing her excellent, healthy white teeth. "Remember now, the sooner the better, and not a word to anyone. Goodbye!"

CHAPTER 48

Leah the Cantor's Wife in New York

It is more than natural that a lover of Yiddish theater like Stelmach would be among the first to rush to see the new Star from Bucharest. The surprise was that he would risk bringing along the "children," whom he normally kept closeted and feared showing in public, especially in downtown Jewish New York, where they could, according to his theory, arouse the evil eye. To solve the riddle, we must return to our heroine and see what has happened to her recently.

As we know from Stelmach's letter to his good friend, Rosa wished to bring her widowed mother to America. Not one to spend too much time thinking, she sent several telegrams to Holeneshti, but there was no reply from the cantor's wife. You can imagine that simply the arrival of telegrams threw Leah into a panic. She reckoned that something awful must have happened to her daughter, or that she had, God forbid, died. Why else would she be bombarding her with telegrams that cost a fortune for each word? Leah admitted afterward that if not for her fears she would surely not have left for America. She wanted to know what she was missing—but what would happen to the bomb while she was gone?

"What bomb?"

"The rich man's house you saddled me with in Holeneshti, what else? I would have liked to rent it, but in Holeneshti very few are interested in renting palaces, except perhaps Christians. But in Bessarabia they've become such scoundrels, I wouldn't trust them," she said.

On the same day that her mother was supposed to arrive, a conflict sprang up between Rosa and the elder Stelmach. Always practical, he had asked her what she planned to do with her mother. In answer Rosa shot him a scathing look with her black gypsy-eyes. He would rather have been insulted in words than receive that look—Meyer hated Rosa's silences. They were the calm before the storm. He hurried to explain that he had meant no harm—he merely wanted to know where the poor woman would stay and especially what she would eat.

"Oh, is that what you meant?" Rosa, without thinking, stood up and called for a car to take her downtown, where she would rent a Jewish lodging with a kosher kitchen for her mother.

Meyer Stelmach, upset that Rosa was going downtown, sprang up like one who has been scalded with boiling water. *That's the last thing I need!* he thought. He summoned Grisha to help him, and finally Rosa agreed to stay at home while he went downtown. He would arrange lodgings for her mother and see to it that everything would be, as they say in America, "all right."

And it was "all right," but of course until he worked all the details out, he had his hands full. For once the Holeneshti cantor's wife arrived, she had many requirements. Luckily he could pour out his heart to his good friend, at least on paper. He sent off a three-page letter, as was his style, written on all sides in tiny letters, pouring out all the troubles, woes, and heartaches he was suffering at the hands of Rosa's mother.

Imagine, he had to secure lodgings—but only from a Bessarabian Jew, a ritual slaughterer. He had to introduce her to all the neighbors. Then he had to buy her two secondhand candlesticks for *Shabbes* candle blessing. They had to be brass, as for as long as she had run a household, Leah claimed, she had had only had brass candlesticks for the blessing. He had to drop everything and go to East Broadway searching for a pair! Poor Meyer Stelmach, after much effort, succeeded in finding brass candlesticks. What was next? You'll never guess, he wrote his friend. He had to search out a synagogue for her. Then, it turned out that in her great hurry to leave, she had left her prayer book at the bookbinder's in Holeneshti. He had to find a Jewish bookseller who had the one particular prayer book like hers. And the fuss she made about the food! When they sat down together at the first restaurant he found for her, they had suggested a dish called brekfish. She would eat fish, she said, but not brekfish. Who knew? It might be lobster. They insisted it wasn't lobster, and it wasn't even fish, it was just meat, and it wasn't brekfish, but breakfast, the morning meal. She said they could call it what they wished, she had never eaten anything so disgusting and was not about to eat it now.

In short, Meyer Stelmach was at the end of his rope. He didn't want Rosa to be seen taking her mother around the Jewish Hester Street—that was all he needed! But most of all he was hoping the cantor's wife would exert some influence in favor of a speedy marriage, please God.

At first he had to struggle just to get her to agree to the match. A fine kettle of fish—Stelmach had to get down on bended knee to a Holeneshti cantor's wife to beg her to let her daughter marry his son! But that's what a father does for a child. The cantor's wife said that Grisha was a fine young man, one couldn't deny it, and would be a good provider as well. "Who could say no? But what good is it if he's a mere *klezmer*?" Poor Stelmach, taken aback, exclaimed, "May it happen to all Jews—my son is a *klezmer* as much as I am a rabbi." "What else does he do?" she asked. "Does he write books?" His son was an artist, he explained. "He can be an artist thirty times over," she said, "if he plays the fiddle, he's a *klezmer*. He's a fine young man and a good provider, who would say no? Let God send him the bride he deserves, and let him send my daughter someone else. Because my husband, of blessed memory, never played the fiddle, and his father never played the fiddle, and his father's father never played the fiddle."

One cannot describe the invectives Stelmach hurled at her in his mind!

But Stelmach finally persuaded Leah to agree to the match. After a brief period of consideration, she convinced herself that the young man was made to order for her daughter. Then she became what Stelmach regarded as a real treasure. She began pestering Rosa: Once and for all, how long can a person carouse? In her family it had never happened that a girl should, God forbid, be single till she went gray. If her father, of blessed memory, were alive, he would have been so proud of her. He would surely have said the match was made in heaven. But since God had punished him and he was not given the honor to see it, then she, his widow, would be there, as long as her legs could carry her sinful body.

"In short, why should I bore you?" Meyer Stelmach wrote to his dear friend. "We have a great God, a powerful God, and I thank and praise Him every day for sending me this Jewess to nag her daughter. She will nag her until she gives in. I will soon be sending you a good reason for a *mazel tov* and an invitation to a wedding, either in London or New York. As a close dear friend, I am sure you will accept. But oh, how does one live to see the day, God in heaven!"

With those words Meyer Stelmach ended one of his longest, most loquacious, and heartfelt letters to his truest friend.

CHAPTER 49

Mazel Tov!

Good news never comes when you are waiting for it—but always when you least expect it. Meyer Stelmach was sitting at his desk in his hotel writing a letter to his wife in London, lamenting that America was a world apart, noisy, tumultuous, a perpetual carnival. And especially he bemoaned the children, who were taking so long to make up their minds.

"What can I write you, my dear? They seem to be back where they started," he confided. "It's a story with no end in sight, a drawn-out agony, a protracted love aff—"

He was about to write *love affair,* when a knock on the door interrupted him.

"Come in!" Stelmach cried out in Yiddish-accented English— that singsong trope that often happens when our brethren "Yiddishize" the local language. In came the children, Grisha and Rosa, both dressed in sports clothes, their faces glowing, their eyes shining.

"Papa, give us a *mazel tov* . . ."

For a moment Stelmach stood as if paralyzed, and the blood drained from his face. He had never seen his Grisha so happy, and Rosa too had never had so glowing a face as that morning. Both children were blossoming like flowers in springtime. Stelmach, rooted to the spot, looked from Grisha to Rosa and back: "Has it really happened at last?" He broke into a sweat. He sighed, leaned back in his chair, and could barely speak:

"Really, is it true you deserve a *mazel tov*?" he said. "Listen, why don't you say something? Why am I sitting here like a fool? Come here, and I will give you a real *mazel tov*."

With those words, he jumped up, embraced the children one at a time, and kissed them, as tears filled in his eyes.

More than a little moved himself, his son noticed his father's tears. "Why are you crying, Papa?"

"Am I crying?" the father said, wiping his moist eyes. "Who told you I was crying, silly?"

"God forbid, who said you were crying?" said Rosa, laughing. "You aren't crying, but the tears are flowing just like my mother's when she has her crying days. What will happen when she hears the good news! Grisha! Let's go tell my mother." Meyer Stelmach's heart almost melted for joy.

"Go to your mother. At once go to your mother!" Stelmach echoed Rosa's words. He rushed around the room, patting his pockets, looking for something. In his hurry he forgot to cable his wife about the good news. He joined the children in their automobile, and all three drove downtown to Jewish New York to give Leah the cantor's wife a *mazel tov*.

As she did every morning, Leah was sitting over her prayer book moving her lips in silent prayer, when a fancy motorcar driven by a black driver wearing cuffed white boots pulled up in front of her lodgings.

Anywhere else in New York a chauffeur-driven automobile would arouse no surprise, but for the Jewish ragamuffins here it was a rare spectacle, something to look over carefully and comment on admiringly. They ran their hands over it while sticking their tongues out at the black chauffeur with the cuffed boots. The chauffeur, sporting a huge visor, chased them off—otherwise they would have jumped into the enormous vehicle and taken it for a spin so that the Jews of Hester Street could see them driving this live beast on wheels, the devil take them.

First to step out of the automobile was Stelmach, who wanted to tell Leah the good news and give her the first *mazel tov*. He flew into her house like a whirlwind. "Good morning to you, *mazel tov*! We are now in-laws!" he cried.

Stelmach had assumed that when Leah heard this news, she

would join the celebration. But he was mistaken. She indicated a chair where he could wait while she stood with her face to the wall praying. Stelmach sat down to one side. The children entered with a loud "good morning," but when they saw the cantor's wife praying, they also had to sit down and wait till she finished.

Only then, after hearing the *mazel tov*, did Leah dog-ear a page in her prayer book and say to her children: "*Mazel tov* to you, and may good luck attend your life. May God grant you good fortune and a happy life—what else does a person live for? If the One Above grants us children, one must receive fulfillment from them. The only one for whom it is bad lies in the earth. If he were only here, may he rest in peace." she hid her face in her apron.

"Leave the dead be!" Stelmach interrupted, hoping to cheer her up. "Let us better speak of happier things."

The cantor's wife leveled her reddened face and tear-filled eyes at him. "Happier? Some are happier, but some are sad, don't you know! Some laugh, and some cry. Some have broken hearts, but some feel like dancing. So it is written in the Rosh Hashanah litany."

The cantor's wife was preparing to give a sermon to impress her new in-law, but her daughter, tense yet happy, stepped in. "Mama! Leave that prayer for Rosh Hashanah. Now that you have the privilege of seeing your daughter about to be married, and you helped convince me to do it, we must decide how to best spend this day and evening."

"My child, what is there to decide?" Leah said. "We have to call people together, write the engagement contract, and break the engagement platters. We are, after all, Jews, don't you know?"

But her daughter said that no people were to be called, no platters broken, no engagement contract written. It had all been decided by the two of them, they had declared their intentions, and it was final.

Astonished, the pious mother considered the handsome, elegant, happy pair. Yes, she saw, everything was good, everything fine, *kayn eyn horeh*. They were young, handsome, rich, and famous, praised be God. She had no complaints to Him. But would it be too much trouble for them to observe some *Yiddishkeit* in the old-fashioned way? Wouldn't it be nicer to have a *minyan* of ten Jews, real Jews, from the Old Country, with beards and black hats, to gather in their home with a rabbi, a cantor, and a *shamesh*? The rabbi should bless the young couple. The cantor should read the contract, and the *shamesh* should smash the first platter on the ground, and then the whole crowd should cry out: *"Mazel tov!"* What was so attractive about a bride and groom holding hands? The groom wasn't even wearing a hat—and apparently a hat was too heavy even for his father. What a wasteland this America was!

So thought the poor pious Leah, who poured out her bitter heart by scolding Meyer for going without a hat. "I can see the young ones living loosely in today's world," she said to him, "artists, as you call them. But you, a man with a beard—what can I say?"

Rosa, Grisha, and Stelmach exchanged glances. Stelmach's beard had recently received a very bad trim, so only stubble remained. The cantor's wife raised her pious eyes and saw the remains of her in-law's beard and said no more. She sighed, turned the page of her prayer book, and softly and quickly intoned a prayer: "Thou Guardian of Israel, watch over the remnant of Israel and do not overlook those who proclaim, 'Hear O Israel . . .'"

CHAPTER 50

A Happy Day

Success and bad luck—once these guests make themselves at home, they settle in and forget to leave. When things start going someone's way, they keep on going. It's no laughing matter!

Meyer Stelmach was one of the luckier ones—success sought him out and took up residence in his home. Money and recognition poured down on him from heaven. He had lacked but one thing: to see his son married—and now he would see it!

If there ever existed on earth a happy father, it was on that day none other than Meyer Stelmach. Floating on air, he barely felt the ground under him. Joyfully, he brought the children to the finest jeweler and asked to see only diamonds. He told Rosa to select the best and costliest jewel, not to spare his expense. And Rosa complied, paying no heed to cost.

That day Meyer admitted that he had never squandered so much money so lightheartedly. That day there was nothing in the world too good for Rosa. "Darling! I will give you half my kingdom!"

They ate a good meal, and feeling all was well with the world, Meyer sat in a soft chair at his son's place, his jacket unbuttoned, a Havana cigar in his mouth. Grisha paced about the room playing on his Stradivarius violin. Meyer leaned over to Rosa and whispered: "Do you know how much of a fortune Grisha has?"

Rosa was sitting with her chin in her hand, never letting her eyes leave Grisha and his violin. She did not hear the secret nor wish to hear it. Her soul was now entirely in that other world, where it had been transported by the divine sounds that the great magician Grisha Stelmach so smoothly and effortlessly elicited from the priceless Stradivarius.

No elegant, illuminated hall anywhere in the world; no flashy, select audience of pure-blooded aristocrats, magnates, millionaires, and fine ladies; and no royal palaces could have so swept the maestro and his Stradivarius into a heaven of celestial, divine melodies as that one word, that sweet *yes*, that Rosa had uttered earlier that day. Now that one word was moving the great young magician to perform wonders on his violin.

His violin did not play—it spoke a divine language, one that only a great artist can speak and that only another great artist can understand. Angels might have hovered above that vast sea of heavenly song, sung rapturously by unearthly voices. Gliding upward and downward, offering their welcome, the voices of thousands upon thousands lifted in song. They praised and gave thanks to the One who had created this great wonder of song, music, beauty, magic, and love. No, that morning Grisha Stelmach played as he had never played before. On that morning he celebrated a festival in his heart, a joy in his soul, where hundreds of gardens blossomed. And the divine language he spoke was always sweeter, always stronger. He told Rosa lovely stories on his violin. He dreamed sweet dreams, wove tapestries of gold for Rosa. She understood his divine language better than anyone, listening to the stories, to the sweet dreams woven with gold. She imagined she was about to faint, her soul about to fly from her body and be united with that world of song, or else drown in that sea of celestial music and unearthly melodies.

Grisha ended, and Rosa, forgetting that the elder Stelmach was present, fell on his neck. She would have fallen at his feet, so moved was she by his playing. But she quickly pulled herself together, ran over to the piano, raised the lid, and played a few mighty chords. Without any particular plan, without a score, simply improvising, she began singing. Not one but many voices poured from her throat, spilling a stream of trills and roulades. Emerging were songs no ear had ever heard before, that no concert hall had had the privilege of hearing.

Only a lone nightingale in the woods might sing like this,

warbling its hidden feelings, the deep longing of its lonely soul. It was a strange, rare impromptu concert.

How many thousands of dollars would those American Yankees pay for such a concert? the happy father, the only listener present, thought, almost dissolving with joy.

"I have something to tell you, children," he said after the concert. "I have a great idea." "What is it?" they asked, turning their young, shining faces to him with eyes radiant with love. The happy father clasped the place where his beard had been and said in a singsong, "The burden we carry is heavy, and our God is good—and He has granted us a beautiful day and a free evening. Perhaps we can all go to the Yiddish theater tonight. I can ask my American agent to free up our time to be entirely alone. What do you say to that, my dear little lovebirds?"

The lovebirds exchanged glances and agreed wholeheartedly: "All right! To a Yiddish theater. All right!"

"And from the theater, my little canaries, shall we go to a Yiddish restaurant for Jewish fish and Jewish roast and Jewish stuffed derma?"

"Bravo, bravo!" the dear canaries applauded, laughing. A plan had to be decided upon. To which theater would they go? New York had a few Yiddish theaters. What was on tonight?

"What's on tonight? I'll tell you." Stelmach, as a Yiddish theater expert and a lover of *jhargon,* bought all the Yiddish newspapers every day. His room overflowed with Yiddish newspapers, magazines, and pamphlets. What would he do with them all? It would be a sin to throw them away—Yiddish words were sacred to him. But to take them with him wherever he went, to buy chests to hold all that baggage, would require Vanderbilt's fortune!

Meyer went to the mountain of Yiddish papers strewn on the table and chairs, scanned through them, and slapped his forehead:

"Children, we have a great God! This is a day to celebrate in the Yiddish theater. Today is the first appearance at the Nickel Theater of a famous artist from Bucharest, someone called Rafalesco. I think I already told you about him. The papers have been full of this star for a long time. He must be quite something, this Rafalesco, because they describe wonders about him. See for yourselves: 'The Queen of Romania, Carmen Silva' . . . 'The great Sonnenthal from Vienna,' Possart, Barnay, Irving, Rossi, all hailing him. See, children, we do have a great God!" said the happy father.

He proposed a plan for the evening: first they would go to the

Nickel Theater, then afterward to Sholem's restaurant for Romanian paprika fish and Bessarabian *pomyak*. Sholem was famous; his picture was in all the Jewish papers. You opened a Jewish newspaper, and Sholem and his restaurant jumped out at you.

"So what do you have to say about that?"

The children were enthusiastic and had never been as happy as that morning. Nor had they ever seen Stelmach as happy, as lively, as relaxed as he was now. All that remained was for him to arrange a theater box for three.

"I won't have it!" cried Stelmach. "I agree to everything but that. I will arrange for the best box in the house, but only for the two of you. You will sit in the box, and I will sit in the orchestra. Why? Simple: I cannot be seen with you in the Yiddish theater. I am forbidden to be seen with you. Someone might recognize me and immediately know who is with me. No one has to know who is sitting in that box. Grisha, I want you to pull your big, soft hat down over your eyes, and you, Rosa, please be so kind to wear the largest hat you own, so a person would need to bend down to see your face. You have to beware of a Jew, ha ha. It's no joke, really! Let one Jew sniff out who is in the box, and tomorrow all the Jewish papers will be full of big headlines: THE GREATEST STARS IN THE WORLD, GRISHA STELMACH AND ROSALIA SPAYVAK, AT THE YIDDISH THEATER—ha ha! Those who don't know will surely think you are performing in the Yiddish theater. That's all I need—ha ha!"

So began that happy day for our happy Stelmach.

CHAPTER 51

A Return Visit

Dear reader, you must remember the visit of Madame Cherniak to Nissel Schwalb, and her warning to him that if his sister were to bear the name Rafalesco, it had to happen soon, else it would be too late.

That warning had left our schemer quite shaken. He could not calm down and wanted a much more detailed and thorough understanding of what was going on. He decided one morning to visit that creature with the red cape and monkey face.

His sister provided him with Madame Cherniak's address,

somewhere in Brooklyn, and an idea about when he might find her home. Then our Schwalb made his way through avenues and streets, located the building, climbed up to the twelfth floor, and found the tiny tenement apartment. He had to bend over his large bulk before he could enter it.

"Hello! Does Mrs. Cherniak live here?"

Madame Cherniak was wearing a dressing gown with wide sleeves and a very low-cut neckline and house slippers on her feet. Her hair was not yet combed, and the room was not quite cleaned up. The bed was unmade, the trash not removed, and the remains of last night's supper were on the table. The arrival of this unexpected guest (Nissel Schwalb was the first man to have crossed her threshold in America) sent her into a dither. What should she do first? Should she throw on a dress, cover the bed, empty the trash, or remove the supper remains? Frozen in place, she forgot to ask the guest to sit down. She stood holding her hands awkwardly at her sides, waiting to see what he would say.

Nissel realized she was confused, and so he seated himself and also offered Madame Cherniak a chair. He tried to put her at ease with small talk, telling her sincerely that he had long wanted to get to know her better. Especially after her visit to him, he felt she deserved a return visit. He also would enjoy chatting about things that only people with their background in the Old Country could share. He would speak openly and frankly because he was a gentleman and an outgoing person. Here he unbuttoned his jacket and stuck out his round belly, which boasted a white vest and a large, thick, gold chain.

"You can rest assured," he said, "that everything we talk about will remain here, in these four walls."

Nissel indicated the walls of Madame Cherniak's small room with both hands, while complimenting her on its taste and cleanliness. He had not seen such a clean place in a long time. Did she live there alone?

"All alone, alone as a stone," she answered with a deep sigh, turning red as a beet.

"I am also a person all alone, alone as a stone," Schwalb echoed her. Madame Cherniak understood him differently. She moved her chair closer and faced her dear guest and arranged her hair with both hands. Forming the prettiest, most coquettish-naïve little smile she could manage on her round moon-face with Oriental eyes, she asked him as if in passing, "Are you single?" She used the English word.

He answered with an English word, "Sure!" and then added in Yiddish, "And what a single man!"

Madame Cherniak became even friendlier and more cordial. Both sleeves of her dressing gown somehow rolled up above her elbows, and drops of perspiration appeared on her upper lip, above the slight growth of black hair that was beginning to show.

"How come?" she asked affably, with curiosity and sympathy.

"That's just the way it is. I'm busy day and night, always on the go. Come morning, I'm again on the run, with no time even for a shave, a drink, or a sandwich. Don't even ask about sleep. I sometimes nod off while I'm walking. Believe me, weeks go by, months, when I don't eat, drink, or sleep."

Madame Cherniak, listening most attentively, nodded and moved even closer to him. She crossed her bare arms over the high, full breasts that were peeking out above her corset—they resembled not so much the two gazelles of Shulamit in the "Song of Songs" as two pillows.

"That's not good," she chided him like a devoted mother, "not good. A person shouldn't neglect himself. One must think of oneself too."

"How can I think of myself when I have such a burden on my back? I am talking of my sister, the prima donna. She has her good looks going for her, but she is too pretty. Anything 'too' is excessive. May God help me and get my sister married and get my brother a good job, and then maybe I would be able to think of myself. It's time, although I'm still . . . how old do you think I am? Go on, guess."

Is it any surprise that Madame Cherniak's heart melted like butter? Ah, what a man this was! What a gentleman, a real gentleman! You could not judge a person by his appearance. Never would she have guessed that this tall, burly gentleman would possess such a tender soul. And his face, his language, his little smile, his gestures! Many a man would envy even his smallest fingernail!

Breyndele hadn't felt so happy or at ease in a long time. She had not spoken with anyone as openly as she had with that gentleman. She had opened her heart to him, one could say. She had not kept anything from him.

Nor did Nissel Schwalb regret his visit to the creature with the monkey face. It had opened his eyes, and many things had become clear. The quiet Rafalesco with his secret romance, his constant going around in a fog, and the amazing cantor's daughter who now played such a large role in the theater world—everything was now as clear to him as if laid out on a platter.

As he was returning from his visit and whistling a happy tune, his ingenious brain was already working on a new scheme.

CHAPTER 52

At the Lomzher Cantor's for a Glass of Tea

Nissel Schwalb did not go directly home. He made his way to his partner and adviser Mr. Klammer, and the two of them then went off to the Lomzher cantor about a very urgent business matter—a spanking-new scheme.

What kind of business? Mr. Klammer asked his partner. What kind of scheme? But he was unable to extract this scheme from him, neither gently nor with anger. Nissel asked simply for his patience and almost had to force him to come along to the Lomzher Nightingale. Still, he talked with emphatic gesticulations, as was his manner.

As they approached the house where the cantor lived, Mr. Klammer refused to go farther. He had a principle: as the Englishman says, "I do not buy a pig in a poke."

"Speak English, speak Turkish, speak Persian," Schwalb said, grabbing him by the shoulders, "but you will come."

They found the cantor hatless and not wearing his gabardine. The fringes of his small prayer shawl were visible. Surrounded by his family of choristers, he was preparing a new concert.

The gang rushed over to Nissel. The older ones shook his hand, and the younger ones climbed onto his back like playful kittens. At first he tolerated it in good spirits and even smiled, but he soon shook them off and shouted, "Get away, you imps! All of you go outside, every one of you, but fast! We have business to discuss here. Where is your wife, cantor? Call her in. We have to have a conference."

Rest assured that no one but Nissel could have gotten away with this bluntness. Uncle Nissel, as they called him, was special. They all loved him because he was a "great guy." He had a good word for each of them every time. He slapped one on the back, pinched another's cheek, and gave another a shove. Or he would would throw off his jacket and assume a boxing stance, ready to trade punches with them. He never arrived empty-handed but always brought something to chew on. This time he brought candy. In the blink of an eye the cantor's gang grabbed it and fled the room. The cantor put on his gabardine, stepped next door to his neighbor's, and summoned his wife. Then behind locked doors, they held a conference.

That evening a large group of invited guests turned up at the Lomzher cantor's for a tea party. As we all know, a tea party involves not only a glass of tea but a meal. The main part, however, comes between the tea and the meal, and that is what we call a game of cards.

Many people think that if ever cards were somehow to disappear from the world, no human society could exist. What would one do between tea and supper? The host and the hostess would yawn. The guests would fall asleep. People would stop congregating, renewing friendships, and conducting business. Little by little the world would come to a halt. Let the moralists say what they want—card playing is not an idle activity. During a card game the world becomes, you could say, one city. Everywhere in the world, even in far-off places, wherever you find at least two people, you will find a game of cards. Every place has its own game, and every game has its own name. Back home, actually, they don't play cards anymore—it went out of style, it's finished. So now when they get together for a glass of tea, they play Preference or Okeh, or they make fools of themselves playing Tertle-Mertle. In the New World it is the same—they don't play cards anymore. Feh! That's for professional gamblers. When proper folks come together for a tea party, they take out the same cards, but now they play poker or pinochle. They do it to pass the time or to do some business. Everyone sits down at the table convinced that this evening he will surely be a winner. And afterward, as luck has it, he either loses or he wins. It's a matter of chance.

Now that we know what a tea party is, let us see who this group was that had gathered at the Lomzher cantor's for a glass of tea.

CHAPTER 53

A Mixed Group

It is difficult to describe the people who gathered that night at the Lomzher Nightingale's tea party, just as it is difficult to describe the American people who live in this large, worldly city of New York.

It was a mishmash of types, most of them Lomzher countrymen of the cantor's, Jews of all types and occupations.

At first glance they appeared to have nothing in common. What, for instance, would a "reverend," meaning a rabbi and a *mohel* combined, wearing a yarmulke and with earlocks tucked behind his ears, have to say to an asthmatic Yadeshviler Jewish salesman? Or what would a typewriter salesman, a fine youth with teary eyes, say to a Hebrew teacher, a small man with a pimply face?

What could be the connection between a druggist with angry eyes and a butcher from Essex Street who reeked of meat, or the landlord of a house in the Bronx, a dark-skinned man with a bulbous nose who spoke with a deep, hoarse voice, and a tailor from the Bowery with false teeth? And what did all these people have in common with a cantor and his wife, with actors, actresses, musicians, and ushers of the Yiddish theater?

As different as they were, all of them felt at home, all equal, all proud to be in America, to have a business, and to be making a living. No one turned up his nose, as some of us used to do in the Old Country, when we got together for a meeting or a celebration. The democratic spirit of the American republic is felt at every step in this land, and our brethren, who arrive here daily from all over the world, become acclimated as easily as anyone in this melting pot and readily absorb that spirit of equality.

All three furnished rooms in the cantor's apartment—the parlor, the dining room, and the bedroom—were packed with guests. People were drinking tea, smoking, or playing chess or pinochle, or they were listening, chatting, laughing, or rattling on. One complained about a janitor who made new rules and regulations every week for his tenants. Another recounted that his union wanted to suspend him and give him the sack, but he had brought them to court. A third told of a near-fire in their factory. A fourth talked about real estate, stocks, lots, and other Wall Street business. Actors and actresses chatted about roles, stars, plays, unions, full houses, and benefits. All spoke at once in a lively manner, as Jews do, and all felt free and at home. And because the noise was so loud, the smoke as thick as in a bar, and the air as hot as in a bathhouse, people's faces were hard to make out.

But we can say that besides the cantor, his wife, and his children, Mr. Klammer was there, dressed in his holiday dinner jacket, his Herzl beard combed to the right and left. He sat in a chair opposite his new partner, Mr. Nickel, who was today wearing his real gold watch and chain, the gift from the president of the United States of America. Both spoke English, and bragged about their great achievements and successes, which any eavesdropper would recognize as pure bluff.

Also present were Isaac Schwalb and Breyndele Kozak, who stood at a table watching a card game. Among the cardplayers was the leading lady, Henrietta Schwalb, wearing all her jewelry. She sparkled, spoke, laughed, and glittered more than anyone. She was having a run of good luck. A pile of money lay on the table beside her, and all the ladies envied her. The men winked at one another, exchanged comments at her expense, and openly pressed themselves against her. A gentleman with a red clean-shaven face, a pointy nose, and a diamond ring on his finger was sitting opposite her—several times he pressed her foot under the table, even though we know for sure he was a married man.

To the side, sitting in a rocking chair, was Leo Rafalesco, smoking. Around him several actors recounted theater anecdotes, one after another, erupting into such loud laughter that the walls trembled. One particular comedian, bald, with an expressive face and laughing eyes, had everyone in stitches even before he spoke. He joined in, laughing so hard that he grabbed his sides with both hands and bent over double.

"Ladies and gentlemen!" the Lomzher cantor announced in his sweet voice. He had already become so Americanized that he spoke half-English, half-Yiddish. "Ladies and gentlemen! Come to the table, please. Supper is served!"

The crowd did not need a second invitation. Those lounging about were eager to take their places at the table, and those who had amused themselves playing pinochle took time to count their money and exchange reports on what they'd won or lost.

CHAPTER 54

Nissel Schwalb, Toastmaster

Our leading lady, Henrietta Schwalb, had not only won—she had made a killing. Intoxicated, she counted her winnings, her face aflame, seeing no one around her, just dollars and more dollars. Her

brother Isaac and Breyndele Kozak looked on enviously as she swept
the money into her purse and asked her what she was planning to do
with it all. Would she buy a motorcar, or diamonds, or a house on
Fifth Avenue? But Henrietta ignored their questions as well as the
flat-footed compliments of her partners, who joked that she played
cards as well as she sang in the theater.

"Beautiful!" the gentleman with the red shaven face and the
pointy nose enthused. He had been moving ever closer to her, raking her with his flirtatious, moist eyes, smiling and licking his chops
like a tomcat. He tried to sit close to her at the table, as he was
very much attracted to her, but it was not to be. Our well-known
schemer, as toastmaster of the evening, took charge of seating the
guests around the table, and he fulfilled this role with the earnestness of a businessman, exhibiting no less expertise here than he did
in his schemes. He seated them so artfully that each lady had a gentleman to either side of her. The Lomzher cantor's wife had as dinner partners the typewriter salesman with the teary eyes and the
butcher who smelled of meat. An actress with a large chignon had to
her right the rabbi-*mohel* with earlocks curled behind his ears and
to her left the tailor from the Bowery, whose false teeth knocked
together when he ate.

The ladies and the gentlemen were not entirely happy with
their neighbors. What would a cantor's wife say to a salesman or a
butcher? Or what would an actress say to a *mohel* or a tailor? But
then again, Nissel had seen to it that the leading lady Schwalb was
sitting between Rafalesco and her brother Isaac. He wanted that
couple to sit together, for reasons we will soon learn about.

Feeling altogether frustrated was our gentleman with the red
face and pointy nose who had fallen in love with the leading lady.
He was seated next to Madame Cherniak, who perspired like a
steam engine and was overly perfumed with patchouli soap and
other strong scents. Nonetheless he conducted himself as a true gentleman, very politely. He pushed her plate closer, offered her bread,
poured water into her glass, and asked which wine she preferred—
but in truth he wished she were elsewhere. Breyndele, for her part,
was satisfied in every way, but let us not speak of her now. Let us
return to her clean-shaven gentleman.

Providence came to his aid. The table turned out to be a bit too
crowded, and so Nissel Schwalb directed the guests to move. This
they did, with the result that our gentleman found himself seated

opposite the leading lady. His eyes lit up. Now he could work his feet under the table as much as his heart desired. True, it took a little time for him to find what he sought. A few times he tapped Rafalesco's feet or Isaac Schwalb's. Finally, when he discerned a smile on the leading lady's face, he saw that he was now "all right."

But the young newcomer, Rafalesco, enraged him. He was still seated next to this beauty. As if to taunt him, the leading lady kept bending over to whisper things into his ear, then laughed and threw her head back, displaying two rows of perfect pearly teeth. The gentleman, who had drunk a glass of wine both before and after the fish, was overcome by jealousy and envy. (He had apparently forgotten he was a married man.) Such angry, murderous looks did he cast at Rafalesco that Henrietta laughed even harder.

Why is she laughing? And who's that strange young man she's whispering to? I'll bet he's a greenhorn, thought the jealous gentleman. But the riddle was solved for him soon after the first speech.

"Ladies and gentlemen!" Nissel announced to the crowd. "I wish to inform *meine Damen und Herren* that the first speech will be made by our friend Mr. Klammer. I beg our worthy host and his wife, the worthy hostess, to fill the wineglasses of our worthy guests. Mr. Klammer, you have the floor!"

CHAPTER 55

Mr. Klammer's Speech

Now that he had the floor, Mr. Klammer rose and coughed; adjusted his dinner jacket, shirt, and tie; parted his Herzl beard; wiped his dry forehead with a silk handkerchief; leaned forward on the table with his thumbs; took in the room with one look; bit his lip; and after a long pause, began his speech.

Our friend Mr. Klammer had always considered himself a good speaker. Since coming to America he had heard many excellent lectures, sermons, and speeches, and he could hardly wait for the opportunity to show the Americans what an orator really was. To tell the truth, Mr. Klammer was indeed a fine speaker. His speech may not have been as rich in content as it was in words, not as rich in words as in delivery. As for his voice, Mr. Klammer knew when to make it thunder, and when to make it so soft that it was barely audible. And the way he held himself! And used his hands! His hands played a very important role, perhaps as much as his mouth. A speaker has to know what to do with his hands, when to raise them and when to lower them, when to clasp them to his breast, when to hook them into his vest, and when to shove them into his trouser pockets. And occasionally, after making a thunderous pronouncement, he has to take two steps back, holding his hands behind himself, tilting his head a bit to the side, and after a pregnant pause, striking a pose to "make the point." Those points, as the Americans call them—the holding of hands in pockets and all the other fine oratorical flourishes—our Mr. Klammer had picked up from American orators and had adopted in every detail.

Regretfully we cannot relate Mr. Klammer's entire speech, for it is too long and too interspersed with elevated poetry and flowery language; it is too permeated with high-sounding prose and verses, aphorisms that he attributed to learned people (who actually never spoke or wrote them), and English proverbs that were very clever and highly seasoned (but unfortunately had little to do with the subject).

We can only transmit the contents in brief:

"A person's life span," he began, "can be divided, like our year, into four epochs: spring, summer, autumn, and winter. Spring, my dear ladies and gentlemen, is the very best, the most beloved or, as Moses called it, the most poetic time of the year. Spring is the time when everything starts to blossom, to grow, to awaken, when the nightingale, as Heine said, is 'all right,' when the hearts of young people begin to beat with a feeling of love. Ah! Love! said Voltaire. Who among us has not drunk from that goblet the sweet potion whose name is love? Who among us, said Tolstoy, was not once young and fresh and, after a great search and effort, found the one who would be his sole guide on his life's way? What could be finer, more sublime, and more sacred than that feeling that our immortal Shakespeare crowned with the name of sympathy? According to the great scholars of yore, like Kant, Socrates, Diogenes, Mephistopheles, and also our own Talmudists, there are three things upon which the world stands: on love, on love, and on love! Without money, said Ibsen, a man can still be 'all right,' but without love, our lives are empty, stale, and wretched, like a ship without a rudder, or as the Englishman says, 'Like a body without a soul.'

"Ladies and gentlemen! Do you not feel here, this very evening, at this table, the presence of that sacred feeling of love and sympathy that drew together two young hearts when they were still on the other side of the Atlantic? Yes, *meine Damen und Herren*, on the other side of the Atlantic, in secret their love was kindled, to burn like a bright flame. Their romance, *meine Damen und Herren*, like all great romances, was carried on in secret. But heaven and earth decreed, as Émile Zola said, that nothing can be concealed in this world, or as the Englishman says, 'You cannot hide an eel in a sack.'

"Ladies and gentlemen! You know my principles. I am independent, not a man to poke into another's pot, and it is not in my character to expose another's secrets. Their business is not my business. As the Englishman says, 'When friends quarrel, all else keep aside.'

"Ladies and gentlemen! The great writer Milton once said: 'Don't think we are so dumb as to consider it wrong for a boy to love a girl and for a girl to love a boy.' I repeat his words, and with particular pride I can share with you, *meine Damen und Herren*, that I and some of my friends who are present tonight had the good fortune to be on the same ship at that most exalted moment when their sacred love was sealed, as Byron says, with the oath of freedom, eternal devotion, and eternity, when their souls were fused together, as Zangwill says, in the melting pot.

"Ladies and gentlemen! That was the first act of a glorious romance, of a heartfelt drama, a drama, *meine Damen und Herren*, that began in the Old World, a drama whose last act is destined to take place here, as Theodor Herzl says, right here in the happy land of the dollar. Here in this land the final word will be spoken. Here in this land the final curtain will fall. Here in this land they will be 'all right' or, as Schiller said, '*Finita la commedia.*'

"Ladies and gentlemen! It gives me great pleasure to inform you that—besides the fact that the heroes of this romance are both 'all right,' that is, young and handsome and fresh—they are equally famous and well known to the whole world from one end to the other in the spheres of art and Jewish theater, he with his acting, she with her singing.

"Ladies and gentlemen! May I call them by name? It is unnecessary, as they are known to us all. Here they sit, hand in hand, like two little doves. You have all surely heard her sing. You have admired her and recognized the Star from Buenos Aires. And he— her chosen one—is the young but already famous Star from Bucharest, whom we will have the pleasure to hear and to admire no later than tomorrow at this time, in his first appearance at the renowned Nickel Theater. If you already have tickets, you are 'all right,' and if not, know that by early tomorrow morning they may be gone and you may need to buy them from scalpers.

"Ladies and gentlemen! I look at this couple and see their faces glowing with a bright flame, and I can understand their emotions at this moment, when our eyes are turned to this happy betrothed pair. Let us hope they will be 'all right' in their life together no less than they are 'all right' on the stage. Long live Yiddish art! Long live its priests! Long live our stars! Long live the loving couple! I raise my glass and end with the words of King Solomon: 'The voice of the bride and groom'—hooray for Mr. Rafalesco! Hooray for Miss Henrietta Schwalb! Hooray!!!"

"Hooray!" all the guests cried, raising their glasses and toasting the happy couple.

CHAPTER 56
The Broken Platter

The shouts of "hooray" and the clinking of the glasses after Mr. Klammer's brilliant speech were no more than the response prescribed by custom and etiquette. The real celebration began when the Lomzher cantor's wife, pleased that this event was taking place in her home, became so excited that she grabbed a platter in both hands, raised it over her head, and flung it down, shattering it to pieces. And as if she were the true mother-in-law who had seen her dream come true, she cried out:

"*Mazel tov!*"

"*Mazel tov! Mazel tov!*" echoed the crowd, rushing to kiss the couple. The future brother-in-law, Nissel Schwalb, got there first, then his brother, Isaac, Mr. Klammer, Mr. Nickel, the cantor, his wife, and Breyndele Kozak. The kissing procedure became a bit disorderly, everyone kissing everyone else, as is customary at these occasions. The gentleman with the red face and the pointy nose kissed and embraced the engaged couple enthusiastically, not so much the groom as the bride.

After the breaking of the platter, the celebration became so great that people soon started dancing.

"The devil take it!" Nissel exclaimed, opening another few bottles of wine. He poured everyone's glass full, not forgetting his own. "The devil take it, I haven't had a drop to drink tonight! Mr. Klammer and Mr. Nickel, let us drink to Columbus, who discovered such a wonderful land as America, a sweet, a golden land! Say, cantor, why are you sitting there like a Lomzher shop owner? Where are the noisemakers? Why isn't anyone singing a happy song? Brother Isaac, get Madame Cherniak up from the table, and do a little dance—show us what you can do! Ladies and gentlemen! Despite his big heavy feet, my brother dances like a ballerina!"

At those words Madame Cherniak's face turned fiery red, and Isaac, already a bit tipsy, stood up, ready to show what he could do. It was a fine celebration, a joyous party at the Lomzher cantor's house. And the happy couple? The happy couple sat at the head of the table, hand in hand, their faces shining, as befit a newly engaged couple.

Nissel had every right to feel exultant. Of all the schemes his genial head had ever concocted, this ingenious one—the tea party at the cantor's and Mr. Klammer's speech—was the best and most successful. Luck had played a part as well—Nissel had chosen the very moment when our young man, as we have seen, was at his lowest point, wandering about New York as if in the wilderness. New people were making a fuss over him, he had an altogether new lifestyle to which a newcomer cannot always quickly adapt, and at the same time the newspapers were trumpeting his greatness and miraculous acting, publishing things about him that were entirely untrue. On top of it all, Gentile managers were following him, making him tempting offers, usually in secret. As soon as he left the Yiddish stage, they said, and came with them, a new world would open up for him. Famous stars from English theaters and opera houses, they said, compared to him were as nothing. Yet today one cannot afford to see them act, and they have their own houses, villas, automobiles and the most beautiful women. And it happened to them quickly, because this isn't Europe, this is America, the land of "hurry up."

Certainly these tales spun our hero's head around and strengthened his resolve. He was eager to step out onto the stage to prove who he was, what he was worth, and what he was capable of doing.

Contributing to this eagerness was the fact that he had not received a reply to his letter to Rosa. He had bared his soul to her—it was the first important letter of his life, written to the one who was dearer to him than anyone else in the world, whom he had enshrined in his imagination.

Reading the New York newspapers, he always saw the name Rosa Spivak paired with the name Grisha Stelmach. It was as if this Stelmach were her shadow—the thought was like a stab in the heart. *Let her be happy with her Grisha,* he thought. *Let them grow old together in honor and riches. But she could still answer my letter.* Or had she become so arrogant and involved in herself that she had forgotten her old home? Or perhaps she did not want to remember. Maybe she wanted to forget him like a bad dream! *Why then am I suffering so much for her? Wouldn't it make more sense for me to also forget her like a bad dream?*

Rafalesco was finally ready to forget the one who had drawn him to this land. He now wanted to persuade himself that he had come for the sake of his career. And as usual, now as in happier times, our young man went around in a world of dreams and fantasies. He imagined that his brilliant first night in America went so well that, before the second performance, he was picked up—or as they called it here, "kidnapped"—and taken from the Yiddish stage. Paid whatever he asked, he was now on the English-speaking stage, performing in one of the largest theaters in New York. The name Rafalesco was on everyone's lips, even reaching the ears of the famous but arrogant Spivak. Then he would repay her. He would tell her plainly what was in his heart, that she was not worthy of him, not worthy of the long sleepless nights he had spent over her. He had been drunk and now he was sober, he'd been a fool and now he was wiser, he was sick and now he was healed, entirely healed.

Caught up in this fantasy, our bridegroom drank glass after glass, laughed and celebrated with everyone else at his own party. Still, he did not fully grasp in the significance of what had taken place that evening, nor the meaning of the broken platter.

CHAPTER 57

In the Nickel Theater

The following morning Rafalesco awoke with a rare headache, and before he could clear his head of the fog from the previous evening and pull himself together, he was taken to the Nickel Theater for a rehearsal. Several stars from other Yiddish theaters would be attending the rehearsal, he was informed, as well as several reporters from English newspapers.

Never, since Rafalesco had been an artist, had he been so eager to impress with his acting. At his first appearance in New York that evening he would go before a full house in the Nickel Theater. He was burning for success, for recognition, for fame. His heart beat like a student about to take a test. He must pass with flying colors, he told himself.

For the moment, all his other interests had to be put aside, leaving but one remaining interest: to please the New York Jews, to capture the New York audience. That evening the real artist in him would awaken. The fever of an artist that made the eyes burn and his blood boil would give him the strength and power to create greatness.

* * *

If you live long enough, you achieve your goal. The day of the big test arrived for the "Yiddish Star from Bucharest," whom the press had elevated to a place among the greatest actors like Sonnenthal, Schildkraut, Irving, Possart, and Rossi.

The magnificent, vast Nickel Theater was packed to the rafters and beautifully decorated. From the directors to the ushers, everyone was elegantly decked out for the occasion. The audience radiated confidence. It felt more like a benefit, an award-giving evening, than an actor's debut. And it was indeed a large audience. In addition to the usual crowd that filled the galleries every night, a large number of new faces appeared in the boxes as well as the orchestra, among them many of the New York Jewish intelligentsia and a number of Gentiles. Nickel attended to them personally with great respect and humility, showing them to their seats and providing them with programs, a task usually left to ushers. But after all Mr. Nickel was a Jew, and a free citizen in America, yet he felt more respect for a Gentile than for a Jew, especially when the Gentile treated him as someone special by lowering himself to attend his Yiddish theater.

Naturally, Mr. Klammer used the Gentiles' attendance as good publicity for the Nickel Theater. He whispered made-up names into people's ears—except for the names of two brothers who were managers of a large American dramatic theater.

The New York newspapers trumpeted the advent of the "Star from Bucharest" so loudly and insistently that those two well-known managers became interested in the young Jewish star, thinking that if even half of what was said about him was true, they would "kidnap" him. Why did Jews need a Sonnenthal, a Schildkraut, an Irving, a Possart, or a Rossi? Jews themselves wouldn't deny that they were a people of contractors, not connoisseurs, who somehow knew how to put under contract and present to the world the best and finest they could afford.

Obviously, reporters abounded at the Nickel Theater that night, American as well as Yiddish. They were fine young men, every one of them, clean-shaven, with lively eyes, ambitious, smoking pipes. They wrote and ate on the run, and they slept sitting up with a fountain pen in hand.

Amid the army of reporters were our acquaintances from the *kibitzarni*, noted headliners, politicians, poets, publicists, and newspaper editors, armed with weapons to wage war against the new star. Some might think him a genius, but others knew he was an amateur. Some might consider him a Sonnenthal, an Irving, a Possart, and a Rossi, but others were certain that he was a greenhorn, a "Chaim-Yenkl," a Romanian shepherd, a funny little nobody.

Indeed, Rafalesco's debut really got things hopping in New York's Yiddish theater world. On one side were the supporters of the Nickel Theater, and on the other were the supporters of competing theaters. All had arrived with already-written reviews, ready for the morning papers they represented.

For these special occasions, editors generally take on the role of reviewers. Here is one newspaper review that was to come out the following morning:

> It has been a long time since the walls of the Nickel Theater thundered with such extraordinary applause. The enthusiasm of the enraptured audience was something to behold and proved to our bought-and-sold adversaries that . . .

Another editor began his review with these words:

> Last night's terrible failure at the Nickel Theater will be a good lesson for the two-legged jackasses who made so much out of so little, taking a penny for a dollar.

In a word, people at the Nickel Theater were in a state of heightened expectations and high spirits. All eyes were focused on the curtain, waiting for it to rise. Then all the lights went down, and the curtain rose.

At that moment three elegantly dressed people, who had been driven to the theater entrance in an elegant chauffeured automobile, silently entered and asked to be taken to Loge Three—the most expensive in the Nickel Theater.

The three were an older man with a substantial paunch, a rather young man wearing a wide-brimmed hat pulled down over his eyes, and on his arm, a young woman heavily veiled. The young couple led the older man to the door of Loge Three. While a black driver stood to the side of the door, holding a woman's coat and a lap blanket, the couple entered the loge. The older man turned and made his way down the vestibule to the orchestra.

At that moment Nissel Schwalb ran down that small corridor and bumped into the older man. Both jerked backward, stood stock-still for a moment, eyed each other, parted, and again stood still, and again eyed each other. After a few seconds of this stopping and looking and not remembering who the other was, they separated. The older man headed to the orchestra, and Nissel, pausing, said to himself: *Isn't that the same boring boaster who was trying to pull a fast one on me?*

He went to the box office and found his partner, the owner of the theater, Mr. Nickel himself. A short, intense conversation followed, which we will set down word for word:

"Who is that couple sitting in Loge Three with a black man at the door?" Nissel asked.

Mr. Nickel hated to waste time thinking too long: "In Loge Three? If it isn't Jacob Schiff, then it's Louis Marshall."

"If you're not a bluffer, then you're an idiot."

Mr. Nickel placed both hands in his pockets and gave his companion the friendliest look—you would think he had just received the highest compliment. "Who else can it be?"

"Now you're talking! I could swear that fellow who brought that couple to Loge Three is Stelmach."

Mr. Nickel, confused, failed to understand what Nissel was saying. "Who is Stelmach?"

"Why are you acting as if you don't know? Don't you live here? Haven't you heard the name Grisha Stelmach?

"Grisha Stelmach!?" Mr. Nickel jumped up, slapped his cheeks, and called himself an unprintable name. Then he shouted out three times, quite loudly: "I am an idiot and an idiot and an idiot!"

"That's what I've been telling you."

Mr. Nickel let this pass and was suddenly filled with joy. "If that is Grisha Stelmach," he said, "now I know who that beauty was, may I live so long."

"Amen. Who then is she?"

"Miss Rosalia Spayvak."

"Rosalia Spayvak?" Now it was Nissel's turn to slap himself on the forehead.

He left Nickel at the box office and went into the orchestra to have another look at his old acquaintance, to prove to himself that this was indeed the cheat.

CHAPTER 58

Rafalesco Creates a Role

When the heavy curtain of the Nickel Theater rose with a loud *swoosh,* the sea of heads in the dimly lit great hall seemed to sway, and a cool breeze wafted over it. For the span of a minute, with a quiet rustle, the audience prepared itself to watch and to hear. But soon that longed-for hush descended, that pleasant, gentle, blessed stillness that embraces the actor from all sides, elevates him as if he were on wings, and lifts him from the stage, sailing him over the sea of heads in the auditorium. That blessed stillness touches the noblest strings of the soul and draws out the finest overtones of talent.

That evening Leo Rafalesco dominated the New York public at the Nickel Theater.

As always for his opening nights, they performed *Uriel Acosta.* From the first moment that Uriel appeared on the scene, he was the focal point. That silky young man with the fine, noble, pallid face, the long hair, the large, tired-looking eyes, the newly sprouted blond beard, and the open-necked shirt begged comparison to Jesus Christ.

With an uncanny power, he drew the sympathy of the entire audience. Something about his demeanor and the vigor of his voice endeared him to the listener. A particular charm emanated from his every step and move, and his characterizations were the most natural and rich in color. One moment a young thoughtful man was standing before you, chatting with Dr. Da Silva as in a synagogue, the next moment he was a philosopher discussing the deepest mysteries of the universe.

"I will not say that I know the absolute truth that all must accept—oh no! I only know that my not-knowing forces me to inquire. My blindness forces me to look more deeply. My deafness forces me to listen harder." Saying the words *my blindness*, this silken young man pointed to his eyes; *my deafness*, he indicated his ears with the gesture of a Jewish scholar, a learned skeptical *maskil;* he spoke with rare charm and authentic feeling.

When the betrothed bridegroom of his beloved Yehudit arrived on the scene, his physiognomy altered completely. No longer did you see the philosopher before you, but a young man in love, speaking rapturously of his beloved who was falling into the hands of another:

"She is a heaven-sent treasure," he said to his rival, Ben Yochanan. Suddenly he drew near his rival and lovingly, prayerfully, as a humble supplicant, took his hand. *"Oh, do not touch her with the same hand that trades in gold!"* he said. *"With humility beseech her, beg her. Repent before her!"*

When Rabbi Da Silva and the beadles came to the Jewish Tribunal to present Uriel Acosta's book as evidence of his apostasy, Acosta's face and appearance again changed. Now he was a martyr. Pious people, blind fanatics, oblivious to the rest of the world, were set on his excommunication and desired either to force him to think as they did or to sacrifice his life.

Here Rafalesco's face changed from moment to moment, expressing the tragedy of his life, the suffering in his heart, the pain of his soul—all without needless, trite gestures, without wild gesticulations, without grabbing his heart or tearing the hair from his wig, wringing his hands, striding across the stage, or contorting his face.

Everyone had to admit that he was a born master, a great performer, a poet, an artist favored by God, who did not so much act a role as live and create a human being before your eyes. There was no doubt Rafalesco was bringing something new to the stage.

The Acosta that Rafalesco had given the audience was his own, not one learned from a book, not a type, but a man who with much effort and study he himself had created.

Near the end of the first act, when Acosta remains alone onstage, Rafalesco was again transformed. Now the oppressed martyr was replaced by a hero who was ready to wage war, not against the heart, but against understanding.

"Oh, Ben Yochanan, you are in great error! He who is accustomed to battle for the truth will not permit his golden crown to be trampled upon."

Here Rafalesco raised his arm, seeming to wear not a golden crown but a crown of sorrows, of misery and pain. Everyone's sympathies were with him, everyone's heart beat for him, and they were sorry to see the curtain drop so soon for the first intermission. All craved to continue looking at that handsome, noble, beloved Uriel Acosta. There was no stopping their exultant cries of "Rafalesco! Rafalesco!" And Rafalesco appeared in front of the curtain again and again.

No, the Nickel Theater had never before heard such cheers and shouting and applause. The theater managers and the members of Klammer, Schwalb & Co. were in seventh heaven. Meanwhile their enemies, the supporters of the other theaters, who had gathered to humiliate the "greenhorn," and the skeptical *kibitzarni* critics who had been sharpening their teeth to put this Possart-Barnay-Irving-Rossi in his place, were gnashing their teeth.

But they weren't altogether losing hope. "Wait, the night isn't over," they comforted themselves. "Karl Gutzkow's tragedy has five acts."

CHAPTER 59

Between Acts

During intermission, as in all debut performances, the Nickel Theater was buzzing with people talking excitedly, some voices rising almost to a shout, as each tried to impress on the others the powerful impression that this new "star" had made. The name Rafalesco was heard everywhere, downstairs in the orchestra and in the boxes, as well as upstairs in the gallery. His new fans mentioned bits of the young artist's biography that had appeared in the papers—testimony to how closely the theater and the press are tied in New York. Not all the papers were of the same mind about the biography, and not all the opinions of the artist were the same. And not everyone knew what *Uriel Acosta* was about or who had written that tragedy. Some were expecting in the later acts a musical similar to the popular *Moishe,* so low had fallen the general public's taste in art. Nevertheless all found themselves under the influence of this new power, a power that not everyone understood intellectually but that all felt with their inmost beings.

But one person sitting by himself had no one with whom to share the sheer joy that the evening was providing him. Sadly, our lover of Yiddish theater, Meyer Stelmach, had not a soul to speak to. He decided to quietly slip into Loge Three to visit the children and to hear what they had to say about this rarity, this Rafalesco.

No sooner had he taken three steps then he was stopped in his tracks. Standing in front of him was the same giant who had earlier run into him in the corridor—a very familiar person. His happy, smiling face looked Stelmach right in the eyes.

This was Nissel Schwalb.

"*Sholom aleichem* to you!" Nissel said. "You didn't recognize me? How come? In London we were close pals. I even visited you, do you remember? That is, I stood outside your door and heard you send word that you weren't at home. I even heard your voice. I wanted to make a fuss about it, you can be sure, but I decided, *Never mind, let someone else take him on.* I visited you, if you recall, not for my sake but for the sake of the Lomzher cantor and his family. Do you remember that bunch? You should see them now—heh heh! They don't need your favors anymore. They're 'all right.' And how about you, how are you, Mr. Dragon? If not for your Grisha sitting with Rosa Spivak in Loge Three, I would never in my life have recognized you."

It was a miracle that this character and his abusive language did not provoke Stelmach into having a stroke right on the spot. How had he found out about Grisha and Spivak? And what connection did this oaf really have to him?

We can only imagine what Stelmach silently wished on this oaf's head. But what good did that do? A person stops you and says he knows you. You can't just spit in his face. But Stelmach's evening was ruined. It was too late to visit the children. He would have to put that off till the second intermission, which he would anticipate as if sitting on pins and needles. Had he been sitting in the box with the children during the first act, most likely he would not have encountered the oaf, and everything would have turned out differently.

CHAPTER 60

What Took Place in Loge Three?

In Loge Three, to all appearances, nothing was happening except that the famous couple Grisha Stelmach and Rosa Spivak were enjoying the first act, never taking their eyes from the honored guest artist, Leo Rafalesco. He impressed them even more than he had the rest of the audience. It was a gratifying surprise to see this truly talented artist, clearly a rising star on the Yiddish stage.

For Rosa in particular, pleasure was mixed with feelings of revenge and triumph. She herself had had her experience on the Yiddish stage. It had been a long time since she had so fully enjoyed herself as on that evening. She was truly grateful to the elder Stelmach for suggesting that they attend.

As the first act wore on, her astonishment grew. She could hardly believe her eyes. She had never imagined that the Yiddish theater would attain this high level of true art. Least of all had she expected that a Rafalesco would emerge from the likes of the Jewish actors she had known. He was a towering figure, a giant, a hero of an artist. With the greatest interest and suspense, she followed every step, every movement of this great artist, who with his supreme naturalism transported her to long-ago Amsterdam. The illusion was so powerful that Rosa joined in spirit with this Old World hero, sharing his joys and sufferings in that time when free thought and fanaticism were pitted against each other, the time of Baruch Spinoza. It was a pity that people talking in the adjoining box were making it difficult for her to hear properly. Some women seated in the loge were chatting quietly as if they were at services in *shul* when people talk in low voices so as not to disturb the rabbi.

The women apparently had some connection to the Nickel Theater and to Klammer, Schwalb & Co. Among them were (unknown to Rosa) the Lomzher cantor's wife and a few no-longer-young but elegantly dressed women with wrinkled, heavily made-up faces. If they were not actresses, they were probably actors' wives. But what was so important about their conversation that they could not put it off till later? It's always like that—when you should be silent, that's when you feel you must speak. That's human nature.

Still, these women alone would have been bearable. But right in the middle of the first act the door of the box opened, and a young beauty swooped in wearing a large hat so wide, it could easily have covered all the women there. That was when the real fuss began.

Rosa would gladly have torn that beauty with the fearsome hat limb from limb. She could evidently not sit still for a moment! Surely some spiteful devil had deposited her in the adjoining box. Her mouth never stopped moving. She whispered first to this one, then to that one. She giggled and moved constantly, drawing her sleeves up above her elbows to show off her bracelets and jewels—and at the same time display her pretty white hands. Rosa looked over at her sternly several times, condemning her with her eyes, while thinking, *What kind of creature is this?*

At the end of the first act the curtain fell, and the whole theater was shaking with applause and shouts of "Ra-fa-les-co!" But even then this creature did not stop chatting with her women friends, laughing, jerking her body about, so that one wanted to have her removed from the theater.

When Rafalesco was called out for the third time, and was bowing politely to the enraptured audience, Rosa noticed that the creature stuck out her tongue at him, and the other women burst out laughing. Rosa could no longer restrain herself. She leaned over to the woman with the hat and said to her in Yiddish: "Didn't you like that artist's performance?"

"Which artist? Rafalesco? Ha ha! He is my fiancé, ha ha ha!"

She said it so plainly and with such guileless laughter that Rosa suddenly felt a liking for this creature. She moved closer to her: "Your fiancé? Are you an actress too?"

"Am I an actress?" She stopped laughing. "I am a leading lady. My name is Henrietta Schwalb."

"I am happy to meet you."

Rosa did not mention her own name but moved closer to the prima donna so that they were face to face. Only the low partition between the boxes separated them, and no third party could overhear them.

"Let me ask you something," Rosa said to the prima donna in a friendly way. "Is it true what they write about this Rafalesco from Bucharest, that Queen Carmen Silva—"

"All lies!" Henrietta interrupted her, laughing." "First of all, he isn't from Bucharest. He's from Holeneshti."

"Holeneshti?"

Rosa did not so much utter the word *Holeneshti* as it was torn from her heart. She clasped Henrietta's large, bare, cold hand. But she quickly caught herself and pretended to be studying Henrietta's bracelet. "You wear quite a bit of jewelry. I like your bracelet."

"It's a present from my fiancé."

"What did you say was the name of that city, again?" Rosa kept staring at Henrietta's bracelet and jewels.

"Did you say city? It's a shtetl. It's called Holeneshti, in Bessarabia. There they eat *mameligeh,* ha ha ha!"

The conversation between the two prima donnas had to be broken off, because the lights dimmed, the curtain rose, and the second act began.

CHAPTER 61

The Theater Goes Wild

Where had her eyes been? How had she not recognized him from the first moment she saw him, from the first word he spoke?

Rosa looked at the program. She read: "Uriel Acosta—Leo Rafalesco."

"Ah, yes—Leo . . ."

"What Leo?" asked Grisha, who saw that Rosa was no longer herself. During the first act she had sat close to him, her hand in his. But during the second act she was a different person. She was leaning forward, peering through her binoculars, and saw onstage a garden, several trees, and among the trees, she saw figures—but the one she was seeking was not to be seen. The figures seemed to be made of the same material as the trees, moving mannequins, talking robots. One old man, elegantly clad, was reading a paper. He spoke with a strange, whiny voice. Near him stood a servant in old-fashioned livery with a braid down his neck. Those wooden figures were chatting, she did not know about what. Then a girl entered, overly made up, with too-black eyebrows. Her hands were too large and red. Who was that girl? What was she doing there? She spoke to the old man in German: *"Vater."* They seemed to be speaking about nonsensical, incongruous things—about the Amsterdam stock exchange, about Rubens and Van Dyck, about Moses and Socrates and Christ, about art and religion, and all in German—nonsensical, incongruous things. The servant left, thank God, another one rid of.

The old man was also no longer there. The girl remained alone. She wandered about the stage as if lost, gazed upward with her badly made-up eyes, clasped her red hands to her false bosom, and continued to speak in German (naturally in German): "*The chains of my despair encircle my heart.*" Stupid nonsense. But—there he was, Uriel Acosta! Rosa could hardly breathe. Her blood was pulsing, her heart almost bursting from her body. For a split second she imagined that Acosta was looking directly at her. Her face burned with a hellish fire. No, she had only imagined it.

Calmly, quietly, and sedately, Uriel spoke to his beloved Yehudit, his voice soft, his gestures fine, elegant, and graceful, every movement weighed and measured. He made not a needless step, not a wasted nuance. The audience hung on every word, as if he were the only one onstage. Suddenly his voice rose and expressed great power—and yet remained tender and full of love, as he held his beloved Yehudit's hand, saying: "*My dearest Yehudit, for the last time—farewell!*"

Ah, how beautiful, how utterly beautiful were his eyes! How much feeling, how much painful love they conveyed! Was he leaving the stage? No, the old man returned with a few others, but Uriel remained, thank God. Rosa set her binoculars on him and saw Yehudit take his hand as they slowly exited. Distant music was heard.

With a sigh, Rosa laid down her binoculars. The young maestro sitting by her side looked into her eyes, trying to understand what was happening to her. He wished to ask her why she was sighing, but Rosa was in another world. She was now alone, facing a crisis in herself. Was this the one for whom she had so long been searching, the one constantly in her thoughts, the one she had seen so often in her dreams? Or was this a dream now? No, it was not a dream. In the next box she heard people whispering. She could make out the voice of the one who had boasted that Rafalesco was her intended bridegroom. Was that possible? She would ask him, that very day! Where could she see him? Right there, in the theater, backstage! As soon as the second act ended, she would ask to see the guest star. Who would they say wanted to see him? A lady wished to see him, tell him a lady. They would all look at her. *Who is that lady asking to see Rafalesco?*

One thing Rosa had lost sight of—she was not alone in the theater. Grisha Stelmach was in the box with her. Ach, Grisha Stelmach! She had forgotten about him, entirely forgotten what he was

to her, what had taken place between them that day, even that someone called Grisha Stelmach was in her life. Poor, poor Grisha!

The sound of a trumpet was heard, startling Rosa as if from sleep.
The stage filled with people, all speaking—as she imagined—strange,
nonsensical, incongruous words. Where was Uriel? There he was,
now altogether a different person. His voice rang with a new power.

Rosa kept the binoculars on her eyes as she listened to Uriel
Acosta's long monologue. She did not comprehend its exact meaning, but every single word had a special meaning for her, not so much
the words, as the voice, *his* voice. How could she forget *his* voice?
How often had she, with her eyes shut, heard him speaking?

*"I want to bear the anguish of all of you! I accept my excom-
munication, but I remain a Jew!"* As Uriel Acosta brought his
monologue to an end, the whole theater broke out in wild applause.
Young people were fired up with the feelings of intense nationalism
that had recently reached our brethren on this side of the Atlantic. They were especially moved by the words *"I want to bear the
anguish of all of you."* Stirred by the young people, the remainder
of the audience also applauded hard. The man on the stage, they
knew, was an extraordinary talent, a true artist, who was carrying
the entire troupe on his back, holding the public in his hand; he had
enchanted the entire theater as if by magic. Yes, this was a star, they
all agreed, a real star rising in the firmament of the Yiddish theater.

The ecstatic cries of "Rafalesco! Bravo, Rafalesco!" continued.

"Shut up! Quiet!" Others tried to still the audience, but to no
avail. Instead of "Bravo, Rafalesco!" they began shouting "Hooray
for Rafalesco!"

"The theater is going crazy!" a voice was heard from the orchestra. Indeed it was.

CHAPTER 62

Mr. Nickel Also Gives a Speech

In America everyone, young and old, fat and thin, likes to speechify.
Unless he is a born mute, everyone, it seems, knows how to give a
speech.

In America there is a speech for every occasion: an engagement party, a wedding, a bar mitzvah, the conclusion of reading the Torah, a divorce, the departure of a guest. That's not to mention meetings, lectures, evening events, visitors, banquets, concerts, and theatrical performances—on these occasions God Himself commanded there be a speech.

Whenever a guest artist, a true star, performs, either the guest himself or one of the actors who has a good voice and stage presence honors him with a speech delivered from the stage. Occasionally the manager himself takes the opportunity to inform the esteemed audience of what he thinks they should know.

At the conclusion of the second act, as the audience continued its applause and shouted "Hooray for Rafalesco!" Rafalesco was too exhausted to go out yet again and bow before his captivated New York public. Instead, the curtain rose to reveal the well-known, happy figure of Mr. Nickel.

Like a man at home in his own house, he was dressed in a simple, ordinary jacket, his hands in his pockets. On his lips hung a slight smile, the familiar, ever-present little smile that made Mr. Nickel a "great guy."

"Ladies and gentlemen!" Mr. Nickel began extemporaneously, "First of all, I must express my deepest gratitude to the esteemed public for the honor they have given me by coming to my theater. I am not surprised that the Nickel Theater is sold out for all these performances, at a time when other theaters in New York have enough empty spaces to drive a car through. I do not, heaven forfend, mean to embarrass my rivals, but one cannot deny the fact that the esteemed public prefers my theater to the others. Perhaps that's because I do everything in my power to please the public. I do not care for money and I do spare no expense, no matter how large. At great expense I am delighted to bring from Bucharest our honored guest artist of this evening for several more performances. He is the king of actors, the world-renowned dramatic artist Leo Rafalesco from Bucharest, who has no equal here or on the other side of the Atlantic. It thrills me to see that the esteemed public appreciates him, and I am prepared to promise that no matter the cost, I will keep our genial guest on longer, to give those hundreds and thousands of people a chance to see him who had to go home heartbroken today because there was not a seat to be had at any price.

"Ladies and gentlemen! With the greatest respect for this esteemed audience, I cannot resist thanking those prominent guests who have honored my theater with their presence. I take particular pleasure that among the prominent guests who have honored my theater with their presence tonight, some have never before been to a Yiddish theater in New York, that is, except for my own theater. Among them are two who are themselves artists of great fame in both worlds, Europe as well as America. You can see them, ladies and gentlemen, right here, in the box on the left. We all have heard the names Grisha Stelmach and Miss Rosalia Spayvak, just as we have all heard the names Washington, Lincoln, and Edison."

The rest of Nickel's speech no one could hear. The already excited public craned their necks to see the two celebrities who had not left the headlines in the last few days. Carried away, the audience rose as one, giving them a clamorous standing ovation. The famous couple was aghast and had no alternative but to flee the Nickel Theater as if they had suffered the greatest disgrace. The elder Stelmach managed to reach their box and forcefully pushed them out. He whispered something to them and led them and the black driver to the automobile, the raucous applause still ringing in their ears. He sped off with the couple, a curse on his lips for all of Yiddish New York, especially for this downtown performance, which had created an unheard-of spectacle, almost like a royal funeral.

Rafalesco did not hear Nickel's successful speech to the end. When the owner began thanking the guests whose "prominent presence honored his theater," Rafalesco could no longer stand it and went off to his dressing room to put on his makeup for the third act.

"What's all that noise about?" he asked his makeup man, who ran in from the orchestra in a sweat.

"Crazies!" answered the makeup man, a young freethinker and socialist who never missed a socialist lecture in Clinton Hall as long as it didn't take place at night when he was busy with his job. "Absolute crazies! They're wild people without an ounce of civilization! Our manager gave a speech in honor of this evening. He should have given a respectable speech, but he is, between us, a boss, a bourgeois, so he has to flatter the capitalists, the prominent guests and their aristocratic artists who honored us, lowered themselves to come down from Fifth Avenue to us downtown. Big deal! If Karl Marx were here, he would bury himself alive!"

"What artists from Fifth Avenue?" Rafalesco asked, looking into the mirror and striking a pose that would best suit him for the third act and his tragic meeting with his family and his blind mother.

"Who are they? He is a violinist, plays the fiddle, and she is a singer, a prima donna. His name is Grisha Stelmach, and she— Rosalia Spayvak, or Rosa Spivak."

Had the socialist makeup man singed him with a hot iron or accidentally slit his throat with a sharp razor, Rafalesco would not have sprung up more quickly then he did at those last words. For a second he stood frozen, confused, as pale as death. Then he yanked the wig from his head and the beard from his face and ran to the door. The makeup man thought the young maestro had gone mad. At that moment there came a knock at the door, and without waiting for the usual "Come in," the person noisily entering Rafalesco's dressing room with a laugh was Henrietta Schwalb.

"Ha ha ha! Our uptown aristocratic colleagues put on a show! They ran away from us as if from a plague. It was a farce, a vaudeville act, ha ha ha!"

CHAPTER 63

Another Meeting

While the excited public was expressing its approval with thunderous applause and standing ovations, first for Rafalesco, then for Grisha Stelmach and Rosa Spivak, in the vestibule of the theater another scene was playing out.

Our elegant friend Mr. Klammer was standing in the vestibule, listening to Mr. Nickel's speech. Keeping one eye shut, he nibbled on the end of his Herzl beard, his whole demeanor conveying that he was not pleased. How could an uneducated man, without an inkling of history, art, or Shakespeare, stand before such an audience and give a speech! Now, if they had let *him* up on the stage, it would have been "all right." It would have been the best of all possible speeches, or as the Englishman says, "I would fire away for all I am worth."

"Ah? *Sholom aleichem*, my fine big shot! How's life going for a Jew in America? I've been looking for you in every corner. It's on account of you that I came to America, I swear it."

Mr. Klammer saw before him a short man with shrewd eyes, wearing a new suit straight from the tailor and a pair of strange, large lacquered shoes. His shirt had overly long sleeves that kept slipping down over his hands, requiring that he constantly push them back up. This person spoke rapidly, in a slightly hoarse voice, and all in one breath without waiting for an answer.

"Tell me, my dear Englishman with the checkered trousers, how is it going for you in this country? How is your health? How is your business? And why are you looking at me like a starved bridegroom waiting for the wedding feast? You don't recognize me? Come on, try to remember. My name is Murovchik, Sholom-Meyer Murovchik. I stayed with you in London when I was in big trouble, may it never happen again. I had to come to you for a loan, to borrow a few shillings, and I gave you a package to hold for me as collateral. Now there is peace at home, I have money in the pocket, and I have come to repay my debt and take back my package. I hate to carry a burden of debt on my back, besides which I need the papers."

"What papers?"

Mr. Klammer apparently did not recognize him. The man with the shrewd eyes laughed in a hoarse voice, still waging battle with his shirtsleeves.

"How about this Jew who is playing dumb! You forgot? A small satchel, reddish, bulging, packed full of papers, important papers. Maybe they weren't worth much to you, but to me they're worth a fortune. Either give me back my papers or give me a thousand dollars."

"Haven't you made some error and gone through the wrong door?"

The other man laughed. "Nice try, but it won't work! Listen here, I have never made a mistake, and I always find my way to the right person. I have never bothered someone who didn't deserve it. To prove it, I will tell you that they call you Mr. Klammer and that you lived in Whitechapel and ran an inn with the fancy name of Café Nationale. Now is it clear to you that I haven't made a mistake? Here's more proof. You took my satchel with papers from my hand, carried it upstairs, and locked it in a closet. What do you have to say now, Mr. Snake-in-the-Grass—I mean, Mr. Klammer?"

At this point, Mr. Klammer apparently did remember that he had at one time possessed such a satchel with papers, but what had become of it, he had forgotten completely. All he could do now was play dumb.

"I don't know about any satchel or any papers. Stop driving me crazy, because all I have to do is whistle, and they will throw you out of the theater right onto the street."

"Is that so? You'll whistle? Go ahead—whistle! Go on! Why aren't you whistling?"

Sholom-Meyer Murovchik moved right up close so that Mr. Klammer's large Herzl beard was almost in his grasp. Who knew what would have come of it if Mr. Klammer had not cried out for help, bringing on the scene Nissel Schwalb (how could there be a ruckus of any kind without Nissel Schwalb?) and the ushers and other theater workers, who grabbed Murovchik by his new suit and cap and threw him out. Peace was restored.

If you think Sholom-Meyer Murovchik came to New York just to have a run-in with Mr. Klammer's Herzl beard and be thrown out onto the street, you are making a big mistake. He came to America, not just for his papers and not just for his business with Rosa Spivak, but also for an important matter concerning our young hero. When Rafalesco heard about it, he . . . But let's not run ahead of ourselves. Let's instead return to London and recount briefly what happened there to our Murovchik.

CHAPTER 64
Still Another Problem

As we learned in one of Sholom-Meyer's letters to his friend Albert Shchupak in Odessa, he was planning to visit his sick onetime colleague, the director Holtzman.

But London is not a city where one can easily find what one is seeking. It takes a great deal of effort. In addition, our Sholom-Meyer was at the time, as he expressed it, in deep trouble. The bit of money he had brought from Paris had melted away in his hands, and his friend Shchupak was not jumping at the chance to send him the few rubles he had asked for. Time was running out. Then one foggy night, as he doggedly continued his search, he found himself in a slum neighborhood that could easily have been in Vilna or Berdichev.

He entered a large courtyard with doors on either side, doors that seemed like open mouths ready to swallow whoever entered. An overpowering reek of onions fried in goose fat, mixed with the smell of overseasoned fish fried in oil, and the sounds of small children and wives arguing and cursing in different Yiddish dialects all testified to the fact that Jews—"our people," as they were called—were living there.

Murovchik mounted some dark, slippery stairs, trusting in God that he would meet someone he could ask for information. But he climbed almost to the top floor without meeting anyone. Then he bumped into a tall, emaciated old Jewish woman with a broad back and the kind of frightful face you would rather not meet at night. She looked like a witch. She was carrying in her arms a large bundle of wood and was gasping heavily.

"*Muhme'nyu!*" Murovchik called to her. "Can you tell me if a Yiddish theater director named Hotzmach, or Holtzman, lives here?"

She stopped, peered into the dark to see who was asking, and then let out a groan. "Come, I'll show you."

A few steps higher they entered a tiny apartment of two rooms and a kitchen. It seemed not to befit a director of a theater, not even a Yiddish theater. In the kitchen the old woman threw down the wood, straightened up her broad back, and gazed with her old red eyes at the visitor. "Who do you want?"

"I want to see the director, Hotzmach, I mean Holtzman. Tell him, please, that a good friend of his has come to pay a sick call."

"You want to see him?" The old woman raised her arms and then dropped them to her sides. "To see him would be very difficult. He is far away now . . ."

"He went away?"

Again she raised and dropped her arms. Then she bent down, because she was two heads taller than he, and shouted into his ear as if he were deaf: "May he rest in peace!"

Sholom-Meyer sprang back and wrung his hands. "He died? Holtzman died? What are you saying?"

"What am I saying? Woe is me! He was my son, an only son, my one and—"

The old woman could not speak the last words. She dropped onto a kitchen chair by the door and hid her old, wrinkled face in her tattered apron. Her broad back heaved with her mournful weeping.

Died is an ugly word that has enormous power. Murovchik was so stricken, he forgot that the one who had died had actually been his mortal enemy. Remarkably, he felt as if he had lost a good friend, a very close friend, one could even say a relative. After all—he and Holtzman! He paused a moment, then seated himself near her.

"So you are his mother? My friend's mother? My friend always used to tell me about his mother—he hardly let the word *mother* leave his lips. 'May I live to see my mama' was his most often said vow. Do you have any idea what a devoted son you had? What a good brother he was! A good brother? He would give away his last bite of bread! As for me, we were as one body, one soul, God help me."

Murovchik had many more virtues and merits with which to praise his dead friend to his bereft old mother. He imagined everything he was saying was God's truth.

To the old mother, his words were a balm for her fresh sorrow. Thank God her poor son had had at least one good friend. He had been extinguished like a candle, all alone, lonely, and far from home in desolate, dark London, which should sink into the ground like Sodom, because if not for desolate, dark London, her son would still be coughing for who knows how many more years.

Poor Sora-Brucha recounted her tragedy to her son's friend as they sat side by side in the kitchen. Her Hershber had coughed blood, and she had rescued him. It had cost her, but what wouldn't a mother do for a son? Such a son he was! And then he had died, and she had not wanted to believe it, because how could her only son die? Such a son! And afterward they had whisked him away, not observing the Jewish rituals for the dead, not cleansing the body, not putting shards on the eyes, not using spices. What did these foreigners know? They came with tall black hats and a high black wagon, picked him up, and took him away, not even letting her have a good cry. It was awful the way they grabbed him—may something awful grab them all one day, God in heaven!

Wah! Wah! Wah! A strange, screechy little voice came from one of the back rooms—it could have been the whining of a puppy or the meowing of a kitten.

Murovchik turned and gave the old woman a questioning look. She suddenly became silent and got up. Unsure of what to do or say, she bowed her head and stood still and forlorn.

Sholom-Meyer, who was no fool, understood what it was. He asked in his hoarse voice: "A baby?" Not receiving a reply, he asked, "Whose baby?"

The poor old woman did not reply but stood in complete desolation, so he decided not to ask any more. He simply said, as if unbidden: "Still another problem?"

"Still another problem!" she repeated, and sat back down beside her son's friend. "You put it very well. It is indeed still another problem—oy, what another problem!"

What did those three words mean, "still another problem"? But she spoke then so appropriately, and with so right a tone, that they became the key to open the old woman's heart. She revealed to her son's friend everything that had been known only to herself and her daughter, and God.

CHAPTER 65

Sholom-Meyer Murovchik—A Good Friend

It is sometimes not easy to know who is your friend and who is your enemy. It was a pity that the director Holtzman could not rise up from the grave and see his mortal enemy, Sholom-Meyer Murovchik, so ready to devote himself to help his mother and sister. He would never have believed his eyes. He would have been amazed to see Murovchik, whose face he could not bear to look at without his blood boiling, now traveling with his mother and sister to America, regularly seeing to it that they had all they required, visiting their second-class cabin to find out what they might lack or what they might want.

But the old Sora-Brucha and her daughter lacked and wanted nothing. They stayed with the small baby who was wrapped in blankets and swaddling clothes, looking like a little doll, peering at God's world with eyes as blue as the sky and as clear as the day. Its mouth was small like that of a hatchling, its little face serious, as if it already had its own thoughts. How lucky they were that the passage was as calm as "*Shabbes* after dinner," praise God. They thanked God, not so much for themselves as for the poor little soul, God's creation—what did it know of its circumstances?

Strange how those two women had managed, not so much Zlatke as Sora-Brucha. When Zlatke was in labor, she had been sure it was the end of her. Surely she was dying, and the Angel of Death was upon her. But once she heard the first wail of the newborn, and laid eyes on it, from that moment a feeling of immeasurable compassion for this little being awoke in her. All her pains vanished, all her wounds healed. The shame that she had earlier thought she would never overcome simply vanished. And her earlier desire to throw herself under a car in that noisy *gehennam* called London, and once and for all to be rid of the humiliation that had, like a fearful cloud, settled over her—all those thoughts and feelings were swept away. Only one thought, one feeling remained—she was now a mother.

But old Sora-Brucha's response had been the real surprise. For her it had been like a thunderbolt in midday, as if ten walls had fallen on her, as if a hundred hammers had been striking her heart.

It had happened exactly at the time when the two were sitting shiva for her beloved son. The week was nearing its end. Their eyes had dried, and an eerie emptiness entered their hearts, and a frightening despondency clutched their souls.

"Today is the sixth day," the mother said to the daughter. "The day after tomorrow, may we live and be well, we can end the shiva. What will we do? Where will we go? To whom will we turn?"

She was about to break down in tears, when Zlatke suddenly fell into her mother's arms and kissed her. She turned very red, grabbed her belly, and let out a scream: "Mama! Save me—I am dying!"

"God be with you, daughter! What's the matter? What's happening?"

Zlatke wrung her hands, then clasped her belly, then beat her head with her fists. She tore at her face, still screaming: "Mama! I am dying!"

Miraculously, old Sora-Brucha summoned the instincts of a woman and a mother. Pulling on her torn cape, she forgot the shame, forgot everything else in the world, and ran to one neighbor after another until she found a midwife. During that difficult night her beloved daughter also wrestled with the Angel of Death, hovering between life and death. But at daybreak God rewarded her with a grandchild.

Exhausted, pale, and drawn, Zlatke lay in bed, her unruly black hair spread out on the white pillow, her eyes glazed over and fixed on her feet. There, bundled in a sheet, a living thing was stirring. She listened with curiosity as it whimpered like a kitten.

The new mother was young and beautiful, her face childlike and pure white, her hands small, her breasts firm and modest. Her demeanor seemed to implore: *Jews! I am not yet eighteen years old!*

Sora-Brucha rolled up her sleeves to her bony elbows, exposing the bulging, gnarled veins of her large hands. She stuck her head scarf behind her ears, tucked her apron in her skirt, and brought in a heavy wooden washtub. Putting up water, she heated it and washed the baby, all the while reviling the city of London and its inhabitants.

"Some city! May it sink into the earth! Some building! May it burn down! Some neighbors! May they never find a resting place!"

In short, the old woman fell into her mother role, as if she had been preparing for it, as if she had known what would be happening. Still her pain was great and her shame even greater. If a grave had opened, she would surely have thrown herself into it. But what could she do? Now was not the time to sit down and rebuke her daughter, who had just lived through so much danger. May the One Above help her to fully recover—then she would scold her as she deserved: "Tell me, my dear daughter, how and when and where and . . . whose?" They were in deep trouble. What could they do? Where should they go? To whom could they turn?

But that conversation must come later. Now Zlatke needed to be pampered, tended to, and fed hot broth twice a day. She was a new mother. And the baby? It was not to blame. It was God's creation, a living creature, pity on it. If it had any sense, it would end its own life here and now. But to strangle it—never. Pour boiling water on it—never. Are we not Jews? Luckily, it was born a girl, so no *bris* was necessary—one less shame. And wouldn't you know, she was a healthy girl, *kayn eyn horeh*! And she was pretty too. The neighbors said they had not seen such a pretty baby in a long time. Whom did she take after?

"Whom? After her father," Sora-Brucha would say. "He is a handsome young man, a tailor, in America now . . ."

Sora-Brucha felt her old face burning with shame. She had lived so many years, and in her old age she had become a liar. Woe unto her gray hairs, and a curse on her enemies' heads, may they all suffer together with him! Who the old woman meant by "him" was not too hard to figure out.

Happily Zlatke, having recovered from childbirth, was soon able to leave the bed and was now walking about. Sora-Brucha had still not berated her. It seemed unnecessary. There was the baby, a little bird, that needed to be bathed. What did Zlatke know about such things? After all she was herself just a child. And now that hoarse *shlimazel* Murovchik had come into their house. He visited twice a day and proposed a plan to the old Sora-Brucha that would save them from all their troubles and disgrace. He had nothing bad in mind, he assured her; on the contrary, his plan came out of pure friendship for her and her son, of blessed memory, who was his best and only friend.

CHAPTER 66

A Good-Hearted Person

At first our Murovchik had hesitated to involve himself further. To stick one's nose in someone else's pot, to sniff out what was in it, and to offer advice comes easily to Jews. Sholom-Meyer's nose was especially adept. What another might need weeks or months to detect, Murovchik could sniff out in a day. This man had in him a certain power. Once you accepted him as a friend, you found yourself trusting him as one of your own. You were ready to confide in him. Not only old Sora-Brucha but even shy Zlatke felt that his hoarsely uttered words found their way directly into their hearts.

He said to them:

"What can I do with you, *Muhme'nyu,* if you are a woman from the Old World, and your daughter is an innocent lamb? If you ask me, I will tell you exactly what is going on. I will tell it to you as if I were reading it from a book. I am myself an actor. The fellow goes back to the old days in Holeneshti. I recall him as if he came to me in a dream. He is a young man who threw off his shackles and went off to America, forgetting to say goodbye. As we say, out of sight, out of mind. But in America there is law that if a boy gets a girl in trouble, he has to answer for it. It's one two three, no nonsense, and off to the wedding canopy. And if he refuses, there is the clink or, as they call it, Sing Sing."

Zlatke turned red as a beet and lowered her eyes.

"I've never been there, but I'm about to go there, because I have business to attend to with a famous singer. If it works out, I will be saying grace with honey and will fill my hat with gold, or dollars, as they call it. Dollars, you must know, are good to have. A dollar is worth two rubles . . . So, what was I telling you? Yes, I believe we should all go together because if I talk to that young man, he will listen to me. I hate pussyfooting. When an actor talks sense to an actor, you can be sure it will work out. Why do you think I am doing this? Out of sympathy. I am sorry for your daughter, and I want her baby to have a father. That's all I want, as God is my witness."

Murovchik wasn't content with words alone. When he dedicated himself to someone, it was with body and soul. When he saw old Sora-Brucha lugging a load of wood or a bin of trash by herself, he could not bear it. "Let me show you how to carry the wood so it will seem as light as a feather," he'd say. Or: "That's not the way to carry the trash. Do it this way."

He could not bear to see Zlatke attending the baby day and night. True, he had never had a baby, may it always be so, but he did have a sister. She was very poor but fiercely fertile! She believed in the two-child system. Every year she gave birth to twins. That's why he was so experienced. He even knew how to stop a child from crying. Without giving it a moment's thought, he would grab the screaming baby from Zlatke's arms and toss it up and down until the baby quieted, while Zlatke's heart almost stopped beating out of fright.

Zlatke had never in her life trusted anyone as she did Murovchik. She told him what she had not told her own mother.

It was one early morning, when Sora-Brucha was at the market shopping for dinner. Zlatke had remained alone with Murovchik. She was strangely agitated.

"I have a favor to ask of you," she said, her voice breaking, then regretted what she had just said, but having started, it was too late.

"What is the favor, little kitten? I'll go through fire and water for you."

With trembling hands, Zlatke removed from her bosom a small packet wrapped in a yellow kerchief. Her brother had given it to her an hour before his death, telling her, with stumbling words, to guard it with her life and not to show it to anyone, not even her mother. With these words Holtzman had his final coughing fit, spoke no more, and shortly thereafter died.

Handing the packet to her new friend, Zlatke felt as if a stone had been lifted from her heart. "I am giving you all we have in the world," she said to him. "I trust you with my soul. Take it, and do what you think best, only bring me to *him*, as you said . . ."

More than that the poor Zlatke could not speak. A storm raged in her heart, and she was choked with tears. Sholom-Meyer was so moved that he did not look inside the packet, but, as if by sleight of hand, it disappeared into his pocket. Then the old woman arrived, and he could do no more than shake Zlatke's hand. "You can rest assured, my dearest," he said to her, "may my name not be Murovchik."

The following morning he arrived, neatly shaved and dressed from head to toe in brand-new clothes, like a bridegroom on his wedding day, and announced with a sweep of his hand:

"Listen to me, *Muhme'nyu*, this is the way it is. Thank God, my business, as I foresaw, is doing very well, but they are summoning me to New York. If you want to forget all your troubles and enjoy your later years, do not dilly-dally. Take your packs and sacks—I mean your daughter and the baby—and let's be off. I'm running out right now to buy ship tickets. I don't want you to mention money. God will help, and we will one day pay Him back."

Sora-Brucha and her daughter exchanged looks. She did not understand what kind of person he was. He seemed like a *shlimazel,* and yet he took so much on his shoulders! Out of great emotion, two round tears rolled down her wrinkled old parchment-face. She wanted to thank her son's good friend, to bless him and wish him all that was good, which he well deserved, but he covered his ears with his hands and left, not wishing to hear.

"Enough! Enough! Good day. I'm running out to buy tickets, and you must get ready to go. We leave tomorrow. Adieu!"

"Did you ever see anything like it? A good-hearted man!" the mother said to her daughter. She raised and lowered her arms as she stood in the middle of the room.

"A good-hearted man," her daughter repeated, and both began to prepare for the journey.

CHAPTER 67

Rafalesco's Disastrous Failure

We left our young hero Rafalesco between the second and third acts of *Uriel Acosta*. Henrietta Schwalb had just barged into his dressing room laughing loudly, at the very moment when he learned from the makeup man that attending his performance that night was Rosa Spivak.

"It's a farce with our uptown aristocratic colleagues, a vaudeville act, ha ha ha! Do you know what happened? They all ran away, ha ha ha!"

Rafalesco had been at the point of running out the door without knowing where he was going. He backed away in a daze. "Who ran away?" he asked.

Henrietta haughtily flicked his nose. "You greenhorn! Don't you realize what high and mighty guests we had? Grisha Stelmach and Rosa Spivak—they were sitting in Loge Three, right next to the director's box. We became acquainted. She admired my bracelet. I told her it was a gift from you. She asked where you were from."

"What did you tell her?"

"What should I tell her? I told her you were from Bucharest, ha ha! The Romanian Queen, and all that rubbish! But that's nothing compared to how they ran out of the theater. Whoever did not see them running really missed something, ha ha ha!"

Rafalesco wiped the cold sweat from his forehead and spoke in as controlled a voice as he could manage. "Why did they have to run away?"

"I guess they didn't like us, ha ha, those aristocrats! I can tell you, I watched them during your performance, and that couple just sat and laughed, ha ha ha!"

At times during the sorrowful romance between our hero and Henrietta Schwalb, he detested her for her foolishness, could barely look at her. At other times he overlooked her silliness, ignored all her caprices. But at this moment she was so tiresome that he not only detested her, he was ready to attack her, to grab her by the throat and strangle her, or to stuff her mouth with a handkerchief and suffocate her, as Shakespeare's Othello had strangled Desdemona—that was how his blood was boiling. Hammers were pounding in his temples, and strange-colored rings were spinning before his eyes. His nose tickled, and he was grinding his teeth. A wild animal, provoked, arose in him. One had to be a real hero to overcome what our tormented hero lived through in those few very difficult minutes.

Henrietta was in higher spirits than ever. She flung herself before Rafalesco's mirror, threw back her head, and inspected her white teeth in the mirror. Then she broke into gales of laughter. The makeup man thought, *Just what we need—another maniac.*

Henrietta kept repeating her story: "No, you had to see for yourself how those two linked arms and—march, march, from the box down the corridor like lightning, straight out the door to the automobile, with the crowd shouting: 'Bravo, Spivak! Bravo, Stelmach!' Pure farce, a vaudeville act, ha ha ha! Ha ha ha!"

"Hurry up! The third act is starting." A tall gentleman stuck his head into Rafalesco's dressing room, showing his birdlike face without a sign of eyebrows over his red eyes. He was the stage manager of the Nickel Theater, who was in charge of seeing to it that the actors made their entrances on time.

When Henrietta heard "Hurry up," she leaped aside, making room for Rafalesco to sit back down in front of the mirror. The makeup man took to his work with all the seriousness of an artist who knew exactly what he needed to do. He set the wig back in place, reapplied the beard, made a smear here, a rub there—and Uriel Acosta again stood ready to make his entrance on the stage before the public that had calmed down and was looking forward to seeing the young rising star, Leo Rafalesco from Bucharest.

But instead of the rising star from Bucharest, instead of the sympathetic Uriel Acosta sitting at a desk before them on the stage, there sat the unsympathetic Menasha, boring his audience with his monotonous talk of books, accounts, and figures. *How long will that old geezer drone on*? the audience thought, looking toward the door at the rear of the stage. *When will Uriel appear?* Soon the door did open, but instead of Uriel, in came Yehudit who engaged in an endless conversation with her father, Menasha. *Will it ever end? Thank God, here's the servant.*

"*Dr. Da Silva has arrived,*" announced the servant.

"Shut up!" a member of the audience said quietly. "To hell with Dr. Da Silva—give us Uriel Acosta! These pests! Before you get to the sweets, you have to swallow sawdust! Oh, there he is now!"

Uriel Acosta made his entrance and stood at the door with hands folded across his chest. A shiver ran through the audience. It grew quiet. All were ready for great lines to be delivered in elevated language, to bear witness to extraordinary acting. Rafalesco's eyes wandered aimlessly over the audience. One could barely hear a word he said to Da Silva.

"*It is I, Uriel.*"

"A little louder! Louder!" was heard from the upper balcony, and the gallery above added to the chorus: "Speak up! Louder! Louder!"

Rafalesco barely whispered the words: "*May the accursed one approach the holy guardian of pure souls?*"

"Louder! Speak up! Louder! Louder!" the balcony shouted as one.

"Shut up! Quiet! Let it be quiet!" they cried from the orchestra as the uproar grew.

Rafalesco, unaccustomed to this kind of reception, looked up. He did not understand why they were shouting. He thought he was speaking loudly enough. He became confused and lost his place. Before Da Silva could finish his part of the dialogue, in which he explained about the proceedings at Reb Ben-Akiva's, Uriel asked him: *"Renounce? That word sounds so strange to me."* He stopped speaking, because the actor playing the role of Dr. Da Silva, an actor with a heavy step and thick lips, looked at him furiously and whispered to him sotto voce: "In God's name! Why are you jumping ahead?"

He spoke the next line loudly: *"I am coming from the court-house, Acosta. They are a little softer toward you."*

To this Uriel replied: *"I know that very well. I have long been seeking a way. But what does one thing have to do with the other?"*

"Hey, Leo, what's going on?" a voice piped up from the gallery. Laughter began rippling through the audience, growing louder, like thunder gathering strength before the storm breaks. Poor Rafalesco, not accustomed to seeking help from the prompter, now lunged toward him in desperation and saw only wild gesticulations, the waving of arms and winking of eyes, whose meaning he did not understand.

Rafalesco realized he was lost, that the ground beneath him was quaking, and at any moment he might fall. He was now in God's hands. "What the devil! Worse than this it cannot get!" he said under his breath. Out of the blue, he said to Da Silva:

"As I see it, I have nothing to say to you."

"That's right!" the same voice yelled out from the upper balcony, and the whole theater burst into laughter. They no longer heard either Dr. Da Silva or Uriel Acosta's monologue in which he proudly asserted, *"I have no regrets. I will not bow my head to the preachers."* The audience could not stop laughing, even when the blind Esther arrived with her two sons. That didn't help Yehudit, who was new to her role. Finally Rafalesco reclaimed his bearings and brought the third act to a passionate conclusion, but was too late. Even if he had acted like God Himself, it would not have helped. The audience was agitated, angry at the fallen idol to whom they had just knelt. They began hooting, whistling, and hurling ugly catcalls at the dethroned king. Mr. Nickel's rivals, the *kibitzarni* bunch, had been right when they said that the night was still young and that *Uriel Acosta* had five acts. They enjoyed their revenge. But even they could not have foreseen the extent of the rising star's disastrous failure.

CHAPTER 68

Murovchik Backstage

In the last scene of the last act, in which Uriel Acosta leaves, Rafalesco's great artistic form returned. With rare passion and mesmerizing force, he seemed to awaken from sleep as he cried out in a tormented voice: *"Enough! Let me go! Let me go! I am going . . . I am leaving!"*

As he rushed off into the wings, the ground slid beneath his feet, and the scenery spun before his eyes. He fell into the arms of the first person he saw, a man of short stature with shrewd eyes who was unknown to him. He had seen that Uriel Acosta was falling. He ran over, caught him, and called for help in his hoarse voice to the others nearby:

"Why are you standing there like wooden dummies? Bring some water, water!"

Within a few minutes Rafalesco was lying in his dressing room, stretched out on a sofa. Next to him sat Sholom-Meyer Murovchik.

What was Murovchik doing there? The reader will remember the scene that had occurred in the vestibule between Sholom-Meyer and Mr. Klammer, when he had confronted Mr. Klammer's Herzl beard and then was tossed out by Nissel Schwalb's bouncers. Sholom-Meyer was lucky that he didn't fall into the hands of the New York police. America had a very liberal constitution, but it was still better to keep one's distance from the police.

What devil made me get into trouble with that bedbug? As a kosher Jew cannot stand pork, that's how I cannot stand that beard! Murovchik was saying to himself as he was unceremoniously tossed from the theater. Quickly pulling himself together, he made his way through the stage door at the back of the building. There he placed himself among the scenery so cleverly that he was able to see everyone and no one saw him. Eyes focused intently, he studied the stage, seeking among the actors the one he needed.

"Which one of them is Rafalesco?" he quietly asked a stagehand, a worried-looking fellow, a pessimist with expressionless eyes who looked as if the world had fallen on him.

"That's him with the long hair and white collar, playing the role of Uriel Acosta."

"Smart aleck! They all have long hair and white collars."

The worried soul stared at Murovchik expressionlessly: "Am I to blame that you're a moron and all the pigeons look the same to you? To you they're all the same, the old Menasha and Uriel Acosta."

"Very smart, I get the point. Now I know which one is Uriel Acosta." So Murovchik thanked his new friend and winked at him with his shrewd eyes. "Maybe you have a cigarette, my dear fellow?"

The glum stagehand almost annihilated Murovchik with his pessimistic eyes. "Greenhorn! Do you want me to bash your skull in and throw you down the stairs? You want to smoke a cigarette here by the sets?"

"Sha-sha! So I won't have one. What are you getting so worked up about?"

Sholom-Meyer tickled him under the armpits and asked him to move over a bit so he could sit down on the bench with him. "I don't have the strength to stand on my feet for a whole act," he explained. "I've hardly eaten anything at all today. Not because I'm fasting, and not because I don't, God forbid, have money, may all Jews have as much. It's just that I've been on the go all day."

"Here they say 'busy,'" the worried pessimist said, then asked him what business he had in New York, when he had come from Europe, on which ship, and how was the passage?

Sholom-Meyer made up a long list of nonexistent business, which led to a conversation that lasted through the final act and so engaged the stagehand that he almost forgot to lower the curtain—another catastrophe in the making. The audience would have seen Uriel Acosta fall into someone's arms.

When Rafalesco came to himself, he said to his skillful savior, "Your face is somehow very familiar to me."

"That's no surprise! How many times did we see each other in Holeneshti?"

"In Holeneshti?"

That was enough to make our young hero forget the disaster he had just suffered onstage. He asked everyone in his dressing room to leave. When they were alone, he turned to Murovchik, demanding to know who he was and what he was doing here.

"Who I am? I'm also an actor in the Yiddish theater. Where am I coming from? London. What am I doing here? A friend of mine, also a Yiddish actor, took my hand in his an hour before he died. He told me about his little sister, a sweet young girl, and about a young man, also an actor, who had made love to her. What happened because of that lovemaking should not have happened, but it did, and the girl, after nine months, gave birth to a baby. The young man, the father of the baby, in the meantime took himself to America. Therefore I took my dying friend's hand and swore to God, who sits above and knows all our sins, that I would take his sister and her baby to New York, find the fellow, and not leave him for a moment until he stood under the wedding canopy with her in holy matrimony. I had to give him my word and swear on the Bible. Doesn't that sound to you like a novel, a cheap romance?"

Possibly our hero had a premonition, or possibly he was just curious to learn more about this romance. He asked his unknown acquaintance, "Can you tell me the name of your friend who asked you to do this?"

"With the greatest pleasure. They called my friend Hotzmach, but his real name was Holtzman."

Rafalesco sat bolt upright, as pale as death: "Holtzman? Bernard Holtzman, you say, is—"

"Dead. May his memory live on. And his little sister's name is Zlatke. She is here with me in New York. She really wanted to come to the theater tonight to see you act, but she was reluctant to leave the baby—she's a young mother and so devoted, so admirable. Do you want to know who the young man is, the father of the baby?" Murovchik looked him right in the eye. "He comes from Bucharest, that is, he comes from Bucharest like I come from Jerusalem. God be with you! Why do you turn so pale? Why are you shaking? Nothing bad will happen to you, heaven forbid. Believe me, you don't know what kind of person I am. I am Sholom-Meyer Murovchik. I want only to do what is right by my friend who is in the Other World!"

CHAPTER 69

Another Scheme Falls Through

For Nissel Schwalb, Rafalesco's great downfall was a godsend. Now he could get to work on his marital plan with much more promise of success. A beaten dog is far less proud, and if he has fallen in his own eyes, then one can do with him what one wills.

These were Schwalb's thoughts as he went to Rafalesco's home the very next day after our hero returned there from his disaster with a broken heart and a beaten spirit.

When Nissel arrived at his young friend's place, he was amazed to find the short person with the shrewd eyes whom he had pulled away from Mr. Klammer's beard in the theater vestibule.

"You're still alive?" Nissel asked pleasantly, as was his style. "You have a way of showing up where you're least expected."

"What did you think?" Murovchik answered, also agreeably. "Last night it was your dumb luck that you were so many and I was just one, or I would not have let that fine gentleman from London Whitechapel out of my hands in one piece. He'd be lying there without a beard, and I'd have him give me my papers back. You can bet he will give them back to me, as my name is Sholom-Meyer Murovchik."

"Murovchik? A familiar name. Which Murovchiks are you from?" Nissel edged over to his new acquaintance and offered a large, fat, soft hand.

Murovchik retorted hoarsely: "Which Murovchiks am I from? I'm from the real Murovchiks, who never owed anyone any money in their lives, because no one ever lent them any, and if they did, forget about it, it was gone, just like the blows I received last night. You can believe me, it's been a while since I took such blows. Still and all, one thing has nothing to do with the other. I prefer your face to your fists, may they wither. I promise you that when I have time, I'll get to know you a little better. In the meantime, I am busy, I must go. Be well and strong, send regards and write." With these words Sholom-Meyer shook Nissel's large, fat, soft hand.

Nissel said in a very friendly tone, "You cannot imagine how happy I am to make your acquaintance."

"That's what I saw yesterday, and not so much saw as felt in my bones," said Murovchik.

These pleasantries exchanged, Murovchik headed for the door. Rafalesco accompanied his guest as they whispered together.

When he returned, Nissel asked him: "Who is he, that *shlimazel* with the shrewd eyes? He looks like a pickpocket, a horse thief, or a pimp." Not waiting for an answer, he continued in the serious tone of an older brother: "I'd send that *shlimazel* with the hoarse voice on his way if I were you. I wouldn't let a bum like that into my place! He's better off in hell. So, my dear Rafalesco, let us get down to business."

Nissel paced the room, preparing himself to introduce his plan. "I came here, first of all, to tell you how I feel. You don't need to be so despondent. Sometimes mistakes happen, things go wrong, there's a failure."

"Some mistake! Some failure!" Rafalesco answered, and also started pacing the room. "One failure is not the same as another. As long as I've been on the stage, I've never had to resort to the prompter! No, that was a catastrophe!"

"It was far from a catastrophe. With God's help, the day after tomorrow at the next performance, you'll do better. In the meantime, we must in these next few days get down to work, one two three, and get it over with. When do you think the wedding should take place?"

"What wedding?"

"What do you mean, what wedding?"

They stopped pacing, faced each other, and looked at each other as if for the first time.

"Are you joking?" Nissel Schwalb asked his young friend and wanted to smile, but he couldn't manage it.

"I, joking?" Rafalesco answered, "You are the one who is joking. You have all decided to joke with me."

"All of us joking with you?"

"All of you—you and your brother and your sister. What was that speech of Mr. Klammer's at the Lomzher cantor's house, if not a joke, a bad joke, a banal joke? Do you think you've got hold of a provincial yokel you can lead around by the nose? God has blessed you with a sister, a pretty little imbecile, a dumb cow, whom you yourself call blockhead and can't get rid of. So you want to palm her off on me, and I'll be stuck with her forever? I thank you very much, very much! Find yourself another fool!"

Rafalesco delivered this monologue with such artfulness and charm that, had it taken place on the stage, it would have earned him applause. He closed with a polite gracious bow. But as it took place in real life, and touched a matter deeply affecting the honor of a family, one can only imagine how Nissel Schwalb reacted. First he turned pale, then red, then blue. A vein throbbed in his flabby red neck like in an ox a minute after the slaughter. His eyes looked as if they would pop from their sockets, like those of a fish being scaled. Astonished and agitated, Nissel lowered himself onto a chair, breathing heavily.

His mouth became dry and his voice changed. "Let me ask you something, my dear friend," he said to Rafalesco in a lower tone. "Do you know the meaning of the words *breach of promise*?"

Rafalesco stood opposite him, hands behind his back. He was

no less upset than his friend Schwalb, but he kept calm. "What do those words mean?"

"They mean that if a young man makes a promise before witnesses that he will marry a girl and then breaks that promise, he gets a swift kick in the behind and has to marry her."

Rafalesco moved quite close to Schwalb. "When did I make a promise to your sister? Maybe it was that night at the cantor's when you made me drunk with sour champagne and all of you began hugging and kissing me, including Breyndele and the cantor's wife?" And he broke into laughter.

For Nissel, this ironic laughter was even worse than the words he heard. Had his whole scheme fallen through, all that fine work he had put into it, suddenly—*splat!*? He could no longer sit still. He rose, laid his heavy hand on Rafalesco's young shoulder, and said in one breath, as was his way:

"Rafalesco! We will have an ugly lawsuit here in America. America is a country that hates fooling around. We have witnesses, little fool, who will come forward and swear they saw you holding the girl in your arms and kissing her. It was on the ship, do you remember? Or have you already forgotten? And more witnesses will be found to testify that you bought bracelets and other gifts for my sister and put them on her wrist for all to see. Silly fool, listen to me, I am a good friend. Do the right thing, because if you don't, you will make it worse, I promise you. You will thank me, my boy, or else, may you choke." With those words Nissel Schwalb stalked off.

"May you all choke!" Rafalesco called after him with a bitter laugh when Schwalb was on the other side of the door.

After pacing a bit more, our young hero sat down at the window, lit up a cigar, crossed his legs, and sank deep into thought.

CHAPTER 70

Rafalesco Again a Penitent

Rafalesco had much to think about. Thick clouds were gathering in his sky. Everything had happened all at once, above all the previous night's failure at the Nickel Theater. But that was really the least of his misfortunes. Between acts and at closing time, representatives from the English theater had approached and whispered to him that he was "all right," meaning that he should not commit himself to any theater until a certain person came to him the following morning and made him a proposition that no Yiddish theater could afford.

That certain person did not wait long—he came first thing in the morning.

He was a freshly shaved Englishman with a bald head, gold-capped teeth, and long nails. A reporter from a large English newspaper accompanied him, a crafty-looking man with a smiling face, a bit red, who spoke many languages, even Yiddish. The smiling reporter introduced him as Archibald Boyervls, and judging by that name and excellent English he spoke with an American accent, he could have been a born American, a real Yankee. But his nose, the sheen of his hair, and especially his eyes cried out: "What Archibald? What Boyervls? Just call me Archie Berels, and that's it!"

The two gentlemen sat down, arranged their trousers so as to expose the toes of their comfortable American shoes, and got down to business. The bald one talked as if he had just had two wisdom teeth extracted and his mouth was stuffed with cotton. The smiling Archibald translated for him into Yiddish. The gist was that they were proposing that he come right over to the English theater. He could play his roles in Yiddish until he learned English. The terms they offered made Rafalesco's head spin. But he had enough sense and tact to hear them out quite calmly, and he said he needed twenty-four hours to think it over.

"All right!" said the bald gentleman, and got up to leave.

The reporter with the smiling face said to Rafalesco in Yiddish: "Don't let this chance go—it'll never come again. Goodbye!"

That was number one. The second matter that made our hero more thoughtful than ever was Rosa Spivak.

What had brought her to the Nickel Theater the night of his debut? Was it pure coincidence, or had she been following the New York Jewish newspapers and knew it was his first performance? If so, why did she run away between the second and third acts? And was it true that Rosa and her aristocratic escort, Grisha Stelmach, had been sitting in the box exchanging glances and laughing while he was performing his most serious tragic role? True, yesterday he had been weak in the role, but why should one laugh, especially when the first two acts had been such successes? Ah, how much of his life he would willingly give up to find out! At another time he would not have rested till he had finally found his way to her, as he had longed to do for so many years and for which he had come to America in the first place.

And now came the third point, and that was Sholom-Meyer Murovchik with his news and his *mazel tov*.

News of the death of his old friend Holtzman, with whom he had run away from his beloved home and spent his best young years, had made a profound impression on him. He was heartbroken. When the bookkeeper Sison v'Simcha told him the sad news of his mother's death, he had felt tears of pity and some regret, but the death of his unlucky friend made him feel a deep sense of loss. He had betrayed Holtzman without any conscience, without a drop of justice, acted like a murderer. How could he have behaved so indifferently and abandoned a sick friend at whose bedside had stood the Angel of Death?

Unwillingly Rafalesco remembered that morning when he came to say goodbye to his friend, and that sorrowful image that had pursued him on the ship now appeared to him again.

There were other things our young hero remembered as he sat at the window, things that made him shudder, things he wished to forget but could not. The most despicable was how he had acted toward Zlatke, to whom he had not even said goodbye. He had considered himself lucky at the time not to find her at home. He had simply fled from her, like a thief afraid he would be caught with stolen goods. No young man had ever behaved so indifferently toward a girl as he had behaved toward that poor innocent Zlatke. What could she have thought when her sick brother told her that he, Rafalesco, her ideal, her god, had fled to America? What had she lived through and suffered all that time? What could her opinion of him be? Where could one find anywhere in the world a punishment suitable for a thoughtless murderer? His punishment had to be that he ripped from his heart all his youthful dreams and foolish fantasies. He must forget there had ever been a Rosa, and he must give poor Zlatke back her stolen ideal, return to the woebegone woman, fall at her feet, kiss her hands, and say to her: "Zlatke, I am yours, yours forever!"

And he would do so, certainly do so. He would have done it that very morning, but then Murovchik had stopped him. He gave him to understand it must not be done impetuously. Zlatke, he told him, was a plain, honest girl, even though she already had a baby. She had never read any romance novels, and if a young man came to her and sprawled at her feet and began crying, "I have sinned, I repent, absolve me," she would faint of fright and go running to her mother. Rafalesco mustn't forget, Murovchik said: there was an old mother named Sora-Brucha who could make mincemeat of him. No, better that Sholom-Meyer visit the women first and gradually prepare them. Certainly he would not tell them that Rafalesco was ready to beat his chest and declare himself a sinner. Women hated weak men who took things to heart, whined and whimpered, wept crocodile tears, apologized, and groveled—feh! Women liked a man to be a man. Murovchik knew those things very well. He had had more dealings with women than he had hairs on his head, may God help him.

So concluded our solver of all difficult matters, and as we have seen, he left on his mission. And our young hero, now a penitent, had abruptly dismissed his other friend, Nissel Schwalb.

Sitting with a cigar in his mouth, he was alone with his thoughts at the window of his hotel, looking out into the street. There he saw a limousine drive up to the curb. A black man jumped out and walked to the hotel. *Wouldn't it be nice if that were for me,* Rafalesco mused. And so it was—he heard a knock at the door.

"Come in!"

The black man came in with a letter to be personally delivered only to Mr. Rafalesco.

"I am Rafalesco."

With trembling hands Rafalesco took the letter from its scented envelope, carefully opened it, and looked at the signature. His heart began to pound so hard he had to sit down.

CHAPTER 71

The Letter

My dearest wandering star!

The wildest fantasy is incapable of creating such crazily entangled coincidences as life itself. I am still so upset by what I have lived through in the last twelve hours, that I feel I am incapable of conveying a hundredth part of what I have to tell you personally. In short, I must tell you that it was only sheer coincidence that brought me yesterday to your premiere at the Nickel Theater. If my heart had not shattered when I found out that Uriel Acosta was you, it would be a sure sign it was made of steel. I sat petrified till the end of the second act (but no longer than that). Then a disturbance broke out that no one could have predicted. Our disguise was seen through, and we were recognized in a most unnerving way, and I was forced to flee, even though, as God is my witness, I yearned to go back, to look at you once more, to hear again your voice which I never ceased hearing in my mind all those years of our wandering over the world.

But wait—that isn't all. When I arrived home, I found on my table a pack of letters from many people, which according to the postage stamps, had arrived long ago but had not been delivered to me because my manager intercepted them. Though an Englishman and a gentleman, he had concealed them from me and kept them. Today I called him in and gave him to understand that from this day forward I am free of my agreement with him and he can sue me for damages if that is what he wishes. But that is not the point. The point is that in the packet of letters was your letter, which I read and reread I don't know how many times. A terrible pain took hold of my heart. Kissing the very words of your dear letter, I wet them with my tears. *Why tears?* you will ask. I was crying for our lost youth, our happy young years, our precocious love that (possibly) could now be much more passionate than it was then but, one must admit, would never again be so crystal pure, heaven-sent, or childishly naïve as it was then in our small, poor, unforgettable Holeneshti.

Ah, Holeneshti! Do you know I went there and searched for my Leibel, asked about my "rich man's boy"? Alas, no one could tell me anything about you! Like a sweet dream, you had vanished from my heaven, like a dream that happens only once and never again!

My dearest! You ask me in your letter if I remember what the old fortune-teller told me in that shtetl in Galitzia. Oh, I remember quite well. But how did you know about that? Is it possible you asked about me, as I did about you? Why then, you bad person, did you give up on me and fall in love with someone else, also a prima donna, perhaps prettier than I, but much, much more foolish, boast-

ing to everyone that you are her fiancé? But ah, what am
I saying? Who am I to reproach you when I myself have
through many complicated circumstances been driven to
enchain myself? But let us not speak of chains that can
at any moment be broken and cast off, if that is what we
want to do. Let us better speak about where we can meet
today. Below you will find an address. Look for me there
between four and five, and you will find me there. We will
be quite alone and will have time to talk. Be there today
between four and five and look for me. I insist you be there.
No, that's a lie. Why shouldn't I tell you the whole truth?
I don't ask you, I beg you, I long for you, I fall at your feet
and I kiss you, I kiss you! Do you hear? I kiss you!

Reizel

CHAPTER 72

Again Breyndele Kozak

Sholom-Meyer Murovchik arrived at his new friend Rafalesco's
place exactly at the time they had arranged, but he didn't find him at
home. On the table he found a note addressed to him:

My dear Murovchik, I am leaving New York for several
hours and don't know exactly when I will return. We will
have to delay our visit for another time. Please make my
excuses, as you know very well how to do, to the ones we
were going to see, and I will never forget it!

Your L. Rafalesco

*An actor remains an actor, damn him, no matter how refined
he is! A person makes an appointment, is on the verge of a nervous
breakdown, and in the end...*
Sholom-Meyer, trying to calm himself, prepared to spit in
disgust, when he heard a knock on the door. He was elated. *It's
certainly him.* "Come in!" There was another knock, another
"Come in." After the third knock, Murovchik flared up and called
out loud: "Go knock your head on the wall!"

The door opened slowly, and in came Breyndele Kozak.

Had Hotzmach returned from the Other World, our Murov-chik could not have been more stunned. But within half a minute he did find it in himself to come to his senses and become the same lively, happy, chipper Murovchik as always. He greeted the guest with a friendly, outstretched hand and a hoarse little laugh. "Wel-come! Look who's here—a guest! What's the good news, Breyndele, I mean Madame Cherniak?"

Madame Cherniak could not find a single word to say in reply but remained standing at the door in her red cape, paralyzed. She had never dreamed she would meet her old nemesis Murovchik here in New York. And where? At Rafalesco's! And when? When she had come to save the young star from a disaster!

From Nissel Schwalb she had just learned the terrible news that Rafalesco was breaking off with his sister and that Nissel had gone off to a lawyer to bring a breach of promise suit against Rafalesco. The Lomzher cantor and his wife, as well as Mr. Klammer, would swear they saw the prima donna in Rafalesco's arms on the ship to America. Half of New York had been at their official engagement party, broken platters and drunk champagne, and the engaged couple had kissed all the guests. In a word, Nissel had sworn up and down that he would cause a scandal such as had not been seen in New York since Colum-bus discovered America. Well, how could Madame Cherniak allow this to happen? First of all, it was a pity for Rafalesco, a young artist, a star who was just beginning to rise, a flower that was about to blos-som—he could lose his whole career! That was one consideration. And second, Madame Cherniak had her own reasons.

Our readers will remember very well that when Klammer, Schwalb & Co. arrived in New York, a new chapter had begun in the life of Madame Cherniak, called Nissel Schwalb. He was her last hope, the last station of her life's journey, the only star that still shone brightly in her gray sky. She was ready to go through fire and water for him.

Poor Breyndele Kozak! She had fallen in love with Nissel Schwalb with the same passion, if not a greater passion, as when she first fell in love. And that was nothing to be ashamed of. It was high time for her to become the same as everyone else, to have a purpose in life, to stop wan-dering, to stop trying to put a dollar here together with a dollar there.

So she was ready to sacrifice her life for her new idol Nissel Schwalb. He had just conveyed to her the gist of his morning talk with Rafalesco and the story of the previous day's visit in the Nickel Theater with Rosa Spivak and Grisha Stelmach. Breyndele immediately grasped what was happening, and several questions arose for her at once: Who had Rosa gone to see at the Nickel Theater if not Rafalesco? Had they decided in advance that she would come to his premiere? Then what about that charade at the Lomzher cantor's, the breaking of the platters, the *mazel tovs,* and all that kissing? Was that done to throw people off the track? If so, then she must pop in to see that fine fellow, to look him in the eye (that was all she needed to do) and sweet-talk him into arranging a meeting between herself and her old friend Rosa, who had kept at arm's length from her and did not answer her letters. Once Madame Cherniak had had a chance to explain things to her, it would all be straightened out between Henrietta and Rafalesco. The young man would marry Henrietta, and then—oh! then, as they said in this country, it would really be "all right."

For those hopes Madame Cherniak had dressed and powdered herself and then walked into Rafalesco's room—where she found her former bitter enemy, Sholom-Meyer Murovchik.

When Murovchik saw the petrified Breyndele Kozak, now looking more like Lot's wife, he took pity on her and came to her aid. "Well, well, you have certainly blossomed in this country," he said. "You haven't changed so much as a hair! On the contrary, you look younger than ever. If not for your red cape, I would not have recognized you, as God is my witness!"

Madame Cherniak, who was not used to such compliments from "wicked men," melted like butter and her round moon-face quickly changed, becoming red and perspiring. At that moment she was prepared to forget everything, all the insults she had suffered from that hoarse *shlimazel,* the pain he had once caused her, and the old debt he had never repaid—she was prepared to forget and forgive it all. She unbuttoned the red cape and moved a chair close to Murovchik. A conversation ensued that we relate with almost stenographic accuracy.

CHAPTER 73

The Conversation

This was the dialogue that took place between Breyndele Kozak and Sholom-Meyer Murovchik.

BREYNDELE KOZAK: Of all people I never dreamed of meeting you here.

MUROVCHIK: That's a sign I am as good as dead for you, while I think of you day and night, in my dreams and when I'm awake.

BREYNDELE: You should live so long.

MUROVCHIK: Amen.

BREYNDELE: You're the same good-for-nothing you always were. Tell me where that lowlife is now, your boss, may he burn in hell.

MUROVCHIK: Who? Shchupak? He's in Odessa, may the cholera suffocate him this very winter!

BREYNDELE: Don't you mean the plague?

MUROVCHIK: I'll agree to a simple, miserable death in the middle of the day, so long as there isn't a deep frost. What are you doing here, my dear? Do you also need to see our Rafalesco?

BREYNDELE: Who else? I'm surprised he isn't home. He's usually here at this time.

MUROVCHIK: I have a better story. We have an appointment. We set our watches by it. How are things going for you, dearie?

BREYNDELE: It could be worse. I make a living. And you?

MUROVCHIK: No complaints. You work and you slave and barely make enough for water for the kasha. Tell me, my soul . . . what was I going to ask you? Oh, yes, what business do you have with this actor?

BREYNDELE: Ach, our business! Have you been in New York long?

MUROVCHIK: According to the beatings I've received here, you would think I'd come with Columbus. Tell me, dear heart, what sort of business could you possibly have with my boy?

BREYNDELE: Since when has he become your boy?

MUROVCHIK: Since when? Ha ha! It happens. I've known him since he was no more than a head taller than a cat.

BREYNDELE: Everything is possible. If that's so, you might have some influence over him, eh?

MUROVCHIK: Ha ha! If I could!

BREYNDELE: Then why don't you see to it there's a wedding?

MUROVCHIK: It's still quite a long way from a wedding, dearie.

BREYNDELE: Really? Why the delay?

MUROVCHIK: The delay is on account of that tiny little creature!

BREYNDELE: What tiny creature are you talking about?

MUROVCHIK: I am talking about the baby.

BREYNDELE: What baby?

MUROVCHIK: Really? You are asking me what baby? That's a sign you know just a little more than a dead man. So what are you babbling on about?

BREYNDELE: Don't worry. I know very well what I'm talking about. I'm talking about the prima donna, and here you come yammering about a baby.

MUROVCHIK: First of all, the baby isn't mine. And second of all, which prima donna are you talking about?

BREYNDELE: Which one? I know of two prima donnas.

MUROVCHIK: What's all this about two prima donnas?

BREYNDELE: Do you see? You don't know what's what if you don't know about the two prima donnas.

MUROVCHIK: Do you know what? You can choke on your prima donnas!

BREYNDELE: You go first, you're older.

MUROVCHIK: I only see there's no use talking to you. You're even worse than you ever were.

BREYNDELE: You were a good-for-nothing back then, and that's what you'll always be.

MUROVCHIK: With your face you should be a fishwife in a Vilna alley.

BREYNDELE: And you deserve only to shlep around with a snake-in-the-grass like Shchupak and carry on with wives.

MUROVCHIK: You should know as much about your mustache as I know about Shchupak and his wives.

BREYNDELE: And who tricked the cantor's daughter out of Holeneshti if not you and Shchupak?

MUROVCHIK: How do you know about Holeneshti? How do you know the cantor's daughter?

BREYNDELE: Aha! Now do you see I know more than you?

MUROVCHIK: Do you know what? Why should we argue? America is a land of peace. Let's leave it at this: I will tell you the story of the baby, I promise, and you tell me the story about the prima donnas. Is it a deal?

BREYNDELE: Give me your hand on it.

MUROVCHIK: Here's my hand.

BREYNDELE: Swear.

MUROVCHIK: May I . . .

BREYNDELE: May you what?

MUROVCHIK: May I have happiness and good fortune!
BREYNDELE: And if not?
MUROVCHIK: May I rot!
BREYNDELE: Nonsense!
MUROVCHIK: May a barracks collapse on me!
BREYNDELE: Foolish talk!
MUROVCHIK: May Columbus come from the Other World and
     strangle me!
BREYNDELE: That is not a vow!
MUROVCHIK: What are you doing to me? I'm actually sweating!

The upshot was that Breyndele bit by bit told Murovchik everything she knew about Rafalesco and both prima donnas, Henrietta
and Rosa. But when it was Murovchik's turn to tell the story about
the baby, Breyndele realized he was talking around it and making
up tales. She rose, red and sweaty, wrapped herself in her cape, and
laughed harder than a thousand demons.

Murovchik recoiled in fright. "What is it with you? What's come
over you?"

"Ha ha ha!" Breyndele did not stop laughing. "Everything I told
you was lies, falsehoods, never was, never happened. Ha ha ha!"

Sholom-Meyer glared disdainfully at Madame Cherniak, who
had so vilely misled him, but in his heart he was thinking: *Breyndele
Kozak, go tell it to your grandmother!* This interesting couple parted,
each in a different mood. He was very pleased with his meeting with
Breyndele Kozak from which he had obtained what he wanted to
know; and she cursed that hoarse devil of a bastard, may he have a
stroke. She was angry at these "wicked, lying men," for leading her
around by the nose, may a cholera take them all—all but one!

CHAPTER 74

Sholom's Restaurant

The stories Murovchik wheedled out of Breyndele Kozak about
Rafalesco and the prima donna Henrietta Schwalb, and especially
about his romance with Rosa, was a revelation, opening his eyes.
Many questions were now answered. He remembered that Rosa

would jump at the mention of Hotzmach's name and always ask about him—now he knew she was really asking about the kid, Rafalesco, who had always been underfoot back in that hick town Holeneshti. *Ay, Rosa!* he thought, *and a cantor's daughter too.* He deserved to be laid out right here in the middle of America, he thought, and be given at least fifty lashes if he failed to take advantage of the situation and profit from either the bridegroom's or the bride's side. *Even when you laid your hands on the packet of letters from Rosa,* he reproached himself, *you sold them for a few shillings to that London dandy, may he have a heart attack in the middle of New York! He caught me when I was down and out. I could fill my pockets if I still had those papers. But I can't show my face to Rosa because to her I'm a louse and a liar.*

Murovchik sprang up as if from sleep and said aloud to himself:

"May a plague settle on Shchupak in Odessa and on Mr. Klammer in New York if I don't use this story with God's help to my advantage, and if not, Sholom-Meyer, you deserve to eat straw."

Within the hour, he had devised a great scheme, for which he gave himself a pat on the back: "Murovchik, you have a clever mind!"

Meanwhile it was time to eat. He went out to find a Jewish restaurant and came upon the famous Sholom's Restaurant, advertised daily in the New York newspapers and featuring a picture of the owner:

DON'T FORGET YOUR FRIEND SHOLOM, WHO SERVES YOU EVERY DAY
WITH THE BEST ROMANIAN DISHES, KOSHER, FRESH AND DELICIOUS.

Entering, Sholom-Meyer found almost all the tables occupied with businesspeople who had no time and ate in a hurry, as they did everything in America. He looked for a spot where he could sit by himself with his lunch, his plans, and his thoughts.

Before he could look around, an energetic young man approached him, a waiter with a white towel folded over his arm, redheaded and clean-shaven. Like a magician, he produced a fountain pen and a small pad, fixed a pair of coal-black eyes on the customer, and bowed slightly, as if to say: *Mister, order your meal, but don't take up too much of my time. Do you see how many customers we have? Hurry up!*

But Murovchik was not about to be rushed by this redheaded waiter with the folded white towel. He sat down at the table and took off his new cap that the buffoon Nissel Schwalb, may his hands wither, had crushed yesterday. He removed a folding comb from a side pocket, and as he combed his hair back, he began ordering a lunch dictated only by his sharp appetite, without taking a glance at the menu. "I would like a paprika goulash of chicken livers and wings—number one. I want a broth with a hefty quarter of a chicken—number two. And mix it up with *farfel*—number three. A carrot *tsimmes* with a piece of stuffed derma—number four. A small glass of your best cognac with a piece of radish and *shmaltz* next to it, and a fine glass of lager beer—number five. Now get a move on, be quick about it, and look sharp!"

Murovchik spat out those last words in one breath, as was his way. The redheaded waiter with the folded white towel wrote the order down in his little pad as quickly as a stenographer. He looked over the order from top to bottom and asked, "Well! What do you mean, 'mix it up'?"

Murovchik set his shrewd eyes on the waiter. "You don't know what 'mix it up' means?" he said, half-joking. "Don't you know what a stew is either? What kind of servant are you in this restaurant? Maybe you'd better shine shoes on the street for a living, or sweep the—"

Murovchik didn't finish, because the redheaded fellow with the folded towel threw him an angry look with his coal-black eyes, stepped right up to him, and insolently talked back at him in a combination of Yiddish and English slang: "Say, mister, shut your trap! I am not a servant. I am a waiter in a Jewish restaurant! I am a member of a union! I am a—"

Luckily Sholom, the proprietor, came on the scene and made peace, otherwise it would have turned out badly for one of the two.

This set-to did not at all spoil our Murovchik's appetite. He took to his ordered lunch with gusto while his head was buzzing with his scheme:

"That this songbird Rafalesco fell in love with my young lady Rosa is a good thing, a good match. I must see to it that nothing goes wrong with it. I have nothing against them. Let them grow old in honor and in riches. Ay, but what will happen to Zlatke? It will be the same that happens to all girls who get into trouble, put their blind faith in a boy, and give away the dowry before the wedding. Certainly she deserves a lot of pity, but what can one do? She will cry until she stops. And I will step in. I am not Shchupak and don't have a bevy of wives. I don't have even one. Maybe it's time for me to make my own little corner where I can lay my head. How long can I go on wandering, serving other people's false gods? And especially as Zlatke is such a fine girl, quiet, honest, a kosher little lamb, and the poor thing has truly fallen on hard times. To marry a girl like that is a *mitzvah*. It doesn't bother me if she does have a baby, so long as she's honest. Things will go well for her with me, you can be sure of that. I won't berate her for old mistakes, and she won't want for a crust of bread. I am not Shchupak, may his name be erased! Naturally, they will have to help support us, I mean he and she . . . they have enough, it won't be a hardship for them. They both earn good money, especially she. Here in America, they say, she is pulling in money with both hands. He still has to agree to my proposal. After all, I am taking her as she is, with a baby and a mother into the bargain, no small thing. I hope he won't take too much time haggling, but he will probably go along because I have the upper hand. If he tries to get funny with me, I'll bring him a baby as a gift at the wedding canopy.

"Oh, Mr. Noodle Man! The check!"

The redheaded waiter heard those last loud words called out to him by Murovchik, but he pretended not to hear. He gave up his tip and sent for his boss to settle up with the greenhorn.

Murovchik paid for his lunch, threw down a few cents on the chair as a tip for the waiter, smoothed his full belly like a satisfied bourgeois, lit up a cigar, and left with a lift to his step to take a stroll through the streets of New York.

CHAPTER 75

Underground

Our hero hastened well in advance to the rendezvous Rosa had arranged. He forgot to check the time before leaving—not till he was already on his way and read Reizel's letter for the tenth time did it register that the appointed time was four to five. He had enough time to stop in at a barbershop for a shave, and to have a bite to eat at one of the nicer coffee shops. The hour hand moved slowly and lazily. Time had never crept as slowly. He shortened and slowed his steps, pausing at almost every block to read the posters displaying their bold advertisements and screaming headlines. Not quite aware of what he was doing, he descended to that underground world known in America as the subway, which connected all the city streets of New York under the ground. The subway was a city apart, with its own streets that created a new world of iron and electricity. Not a ray of sunshine penetrated its depths, and yet it was brightly lit and lively twenty-four hours a day. Night never fell in this world. For twenty-four hours continuously in this chaotic world people rushed in every direction, each intent on pursuing his own business, and always racing, always "hurry up!"—exactly mirroring New York life aboveground.

Once you went down the stairs into that underground domain you felt you were in another world. Iron and electricity surrounded and possessed you. You imagined you were in touch with the secrets of the abyss. Unwillingly you began to think about things that in another place would be far from your thoughts. Unwillingly you pondered on the eternal, hidden powers above and below you. But not for long—from a distance you suddenly heard the roar of a beast racing toward you in the dark. At any moment it would cut through the deep, dark abyss. And now there before you was that strange giant iron beast with its frightful, huge electric eyes. Now it stretched out in front of you, twisting like a snake over the shiny rails. Like devils, the conductors jumped up and shouted out the name of the station, and the doors opened. Suddenly hundreds and maybe thousands of people spewed out—one stream flowing out, another stream flowing in, all accomplished so quietly, without confusion, and in less than half a minute, because there was no time—hurry up!

Our hero found himself carried along by the ingoing stream, one foot already in the subway car, when suddenly among the outgoing passengers a familiar figure flashed by him, a short man with a small, crushed cap. Could it be Murovchik? Rafalesco stepped to the side.

Catching sight of Rafalesco, Murovchik was surprised to see him. Meeting Rafalesco was just as unexpected as hearing Breyndele Kozak's news had been.

After leaving Sholom's Restaurant, Murovchik came up with a complete plan to take advantage of the remarkable situation in which Rafalesco and his three potential brides found themselves: Henrietta Schwalb, Rosa Spivak, and Zlatke Holtzman. Well, between the first two, Murovchik figured, according to what Breyndele told him, Rafalesco would sacrifice Schwalb; in fact, he would have to be an idiot or a dumb ox to trade a golden little apple like Rosa for a cheap Lemberg Yiddish prima donna. And what about that engagement party?

Call me what you will, but an artist, and a Jewish one at that, doesn't really worry himself over such things. Plenty of Jewish actors have not only three girlfriends but three wives: mine, yours, and ours together. What could happen to him? Absolutely nothing! So who's left is girl-friend number three: Zlatke and the baby, and that's where the dog lay buried. *That's where I get mine . . . Don't be an ox*, Sholom-Meyer admonished himself. *Know what you have to do. God has handed you this great chance on a silver platter right here in New York, and if you don't take advantage of it, you deserve what you get.*

This was what Murovchik was saying to himself when he unex-pectedly ran into Rafalesco underground, but he covered up his joy, pretending indifference.

"If someone like you travels in the underground," he said to Rafalesco, "what should *we* say, we plain meat-and-potatoes paupers?"

CHAPTER 76

Ay, Americhka

If Murovchik found it necessary to hide his joy from Rafalesco, Rafalesco expressed most openly his satisfaction at encountering him once again.

"Hello! How-do-you-do!" he cried out in the American fash-ion, putting out his hand. "It's good to see you. God Himself has brought you here. I really must speak with you."

"With pleasure—here I am, ready for you," Murovchik said coolly. "Where shall we go?"

"Wherever you wish," said Rafalesco, seeking a place to sit down. "Here's a bench. We can talk here awhile."

"Right here underground?"

"Right here under the ground."

"If that's what you want, I'm fine with it."

They sat down on the bench, and Rafalesco began talking while Sholom-Meyer looked into his eyes and listened carefully. Murov-chik had a strange power. He could easily become a close, bosom friend, one you could completely trust. Rafalesco felt closer to him than to a brother. Murovchik had this virtue: you didn't need to spell things out for him. Words were almost superfluous. He looked at you with those shrewd eyes, knew what was in your heart, and took the words from your mouth before you uttered them. A pleasure, a pure pleasure to be with him!

"You don't need to tell me," Murovchik soothed in his hoarse but even voice. "Believe me, I understand the situation completely. I will read it off for you as from a book. May we all be protected from the evil eye, but these things happen to a chap like yourself, a sinner like the rest of us. A girl is a temptation, and sometimes you aren't even to blame. For heaven's sake, how can you be a prophet and know that a baby will come of it? Truth to tell, it's not your fault and not her fault. Do you think she doesn't understand this? She understands better than all of us, I promise you."

For our hero, those words removed a heavy weight from his heart. All his apologies and explanations, he realized, were needless. Murovchik provided a different view: not only did he stand up for the poor fallen Zlatke, but Zlatke herself was ardently not so eager for the match. To further reassure our hero, Murovchik said to him:

"Where do you think I'm coming from right now? From Zlatke's. I told her what you said to me. She cried, 'How can I compare myself to him? He is so famous—who knows where he will be tomorrow? I worry that I might become a hindrance, forced on him.' Do you hear those words?"

Rafalesco was moved. "Is that really true?"

"Did you think I could make up such a thing?"

"No. That's not what I mean. Did she really say that?"

"May I live so. Don't you know what a pure soul she is? She's worth more than eighteen prima donnas!"

Tears came to Rafalesco's eyes, but he hid them for his new friend, who forged ahead:

"So it went, back and forth, and I saw the girl was speaking sense. I thought perhaps she was right. I said to her: 'Listen to me, my dear, this is the story. The young man wants only your happiness, and the happiness of your little baby. But since, I said, you are not so enthusiastic about it, it's another story. You won't be forced or dragged into it. And as for the baby? You never need worry, I said, and remember, Rafalesco is not a nobody, a boy off the street, but a very good earner, *kayn eyn horeh*. So I am sure he will provide for you and the baby, as he should, and even your mother will not need to fall back on strangers. But most important, I said, you won't be alone. I'm not, I said, dead yet. I have been with you, and I will stay with you. Who brought you here, if not Murovchik? Who registered you under his name when we left the ship, if not Murovchik? Make believe you are already mine and I am yours, what's the difference? And if it comes to that, I said, in America you can find four sticks for a canopy, and Sholom-Meyer Murovchik will recite the necessary prayer, and that will be that.' And I myself, as you see me, am not far from taking that step, first of all, because I have pity on her, a poor orphan, and second of all, because she is an honest child, as quiet as a dove. The question is, how will we get along? But God is a benevolent father and, as I said, you probably will not forget us."

"Forget?" Rafalesco grasped Murovchik by the hand. If he hadn't been embarrassed, he would have embraced and kissed him. "I can put it in writing, if you wish."

"Why do you need it in writing? Just make out a few promissory notes in my name, and that will be the end of it. I will be at your place tonight, and I will bring all that's necessary. Now you were probably on your way somewhere."

Rafalesco was so absorbed in the conversation that he did not notice how often the steel snakes with the electric eyes ran past them, ejecting one stream of people and drawing in another. The hands on the clock approached three. In an hour's time he had to be there. The word *there* made his heart jump. He said goodbye in a most amicable way to Murovchik, stepped into one of the long cars, and within half a minute was swallowed up by the underground darkness.

Sholom-Meyer, you are "all right"! Murovchik said to himself as he waited for the next train. *What a great country this is! Ay, Americhka!*

CHAPTER 77

Among the Cages

The place where Rosa Spivak had arranged to meet her beloved Rafalesco was in the Zoological Gardens, which are rarely visited in winter. One could stroll freely among the animals confined to their cages without encountering anyone.

He had arrived a full half-hour early. As he walked among the cages, he surely suffered more than he had in all his wanderings over the world. The significance of this meeting, toward which he had been striving for years, was enough to make him tremble and his heart pound like a hammer. Adding to his discomfort, wild thoughts came into his head—black, mordant thoughts, each one grimmer than the next. Who knew, he thought, whether she would even come? And if she did, who knew what state she might be in? Who knew what she meant by "chains"? Who knew, there might have been a last-minute scene with Grisha Stelmach. The most despondent thoughts, the darkest fantasies shrouded in black, crept into his mind. No matter how hard he tried to drive them away, his efforts failed. He felt he was at a momentous turning point. Unwillingly his thoughts went to what he had almost arranged with Murovchik—he had almost betrayed that pure innocent Zlatke, handing her over as one would an object for sale, a servant, a slave. And to whom? To a person he hardly knew at all. And when? Right after he had that very morning been prepared to run to the same poor Zlatke, to fall at her feet, and swear he was hers, hers forever?! And he imagined someone shouting in his ear, *Cain! Cain! Cain!*

Rafalesco wandered farther into the Zoological Gardens. He wished he could escape from himself, but could not. He wished he could wipe out his whole past life, but could not. On the contrary, all his great and small sins, clear and plain, all his artistic ambitions and ideals, lay before his eyes. As from an open book, he read the balance sheet of his actions. The verdict was plain: As a human being he was little more than a criminal, a Cain, a Cain! As an artist he was small and insignificant, surrounded by petty people who show-ered him with false acclaim. It was all bluff, bluff, and bluff from top to bottom! Much water would flow, many sacrifices would be offered up, many altars would be overthrown, but he would remain forever outside that holy temple, toward which his once-young but now-suffering soul had yearned.

But wait! Who was coming? His heart stopped, and his eyes opened wide, almost bulging. *Can it be? Can it be?* He looked harder. Coming toward him was a beautiful woman who did not so much walk as glide airborne. *Can it be she?*

Yes, it was she.

Never, never, when we meet someone we have long awaited, do we find what we have expected. No, she was not the one Rafalesco had imagined in his dreams. She was neither the Reizel he had known in Holeneshti nor the Rosa he had pictured in his fantasy. She was an entirely different person. She appeared taller, older, and very, very different. In that first moment she struck him as too serious, too severe, too cold. Only the eyes were the same—the black, fiery gypsy-eyes.

To Rosa as well, he was not the same Rafalesco she had imagined in her dreams, and he was not the same Leibel, the rich man's son, whom she remembered from those *cheder* days—he was altogether, altogether changed. But unchanged were his eyes, his kind, blue eyes. For a moment they simply faced each other, not speaking a word, not moving a muscle. Each seemed to read in the other's eyes their entire past, the story of their youth that had so unhappily vanished during their long years of wandering over the world. But it lasted no more than a minute. A little smile, the first smile, suddenly appeared on her face, and he felt his heart skip a beat, and he was once again drawn to her.

* * *

The day ended. The sun set. Stars shimmered in the sky. The moon drifted into view. Our two young heroes, Leibel Rafalovitch and Reizel Spivak, were still sitting and talking, talking. They were remembering Holeneshti, the Yiddish theater, God's Street, the fire, the wandering stars . . .

Epilogue

FROM MEYER STELMACH TO HIS GOOD FRIEND

That's the way it is, my brother, don't ask questions. It is, as they say, a world within worlds. If they had made a clean break of it, it would be over. It happens—a match is no longer a match—what can you do? But no, the match fell through, but they are still good friends. You might ask, in what way they are good friends? They exchange letters every week, Rafalesco is also included. Since my Grisha and Rafalesco met, they have become as close as people can get, and they think the world of each other, call each other by affectionate names. So, what do you say to that? If that were all, I could take it. As they say, if you're happy, I'm happy. But it's the shame of it. And who is to blame if not me? If I had not brought them to the Yiddish theater for Rafalesco's debut, nothing would have happened. For that I have to pay the price and keep my mouth shut! You should hear the gossip around here! They say that it's an old story between Rosa and her old friend Rafalesco, a love affair going back who knows how long, since childhood, and any day now they'll get married. I say this to my Grisha, and he laughs: Nonsense, he says, never, Rosa will never marry Rafalesco, do you hear that? *Never!* Go make heads or tails of it. But then the gossip continues. You feel bitter enough in your heart, and these gossips come along and rub salt into your wounds! Listen to what I tell you, dear friend. Jews are a small folk, but nasty! And if you write me, write to London, as you have till now, and don't feel bad that I've filled your head with all this trouble. If you pour out your heart to a good friend, you imagine it makes it easier.

From me, your good friend, who is confused, torn, and overwhelmed.

Meyer Stelmach

FROM SHOLOM-MEYER
MUROVCHIK TO ALBERT SHCHUPAK

Here is your fifty go to hell with it I can now bless His name lend you fifty if you need money and I am writing to tell you that your cantor's daughter went out of her mind and fixed herself up with two bridegrooms and doesn't know which one to marry if she would listen to me she would marry both of them because that Grisha Stelmach is stuffed with money and the second one I wrote you about is that kid from Holeneshti Rafalovitch who is now called Rafalesco and is very well off because the English have taken him over to them and have showered him with gold coins from head to toe and I am writing you that I have at this time no business I am looking into a little theater not really a theater but a vaudeville house if it makes any money I could turn it into a big business though the Yiddish theater I must tell you very frankly has here in Americhka gone wrong they've begun bringing over from Berlin the best German actors and they pay them good money a curse on Columbus but in the meantime you can make out very well with your troupe in Americhka so I'm writing you Albert if you want to spit on Russia and come here and we'll be partners and if not you can go to hell and bake bagels respectfully

Sholom-Meyer Murovchik

Almost forgot: I just found out some news which if you hear it you will die on the spot just listen to this remember our Holtzman who I wrote you about from London he decided to die bless his *tsimmes* and left a little sister Zlatke is her name a fine girl with one fault I really was considering her almost married her but it happened that she already married you'll never guess even if you had ten heads that fellow Rafalesco may his name be erased and who do you think is crazy about her it's Rosa I mean your cantor's crazy daughter may God give me luck can you figure that something like this could happen so tell me if you don't you have to bury yourself nine feet deep in the ground as I wish you from my deepest heart respectfully

Sholom-Meyer Murovchik

FROM BREYNDELE KOZAK TO HENRIETTA SCHWALB

. . . and write me everything, my dear, how it is going for you in your new place in Johannesburg. I hope you are all right. No evil eye, but everybody says he is a multimillionaire and that he bought you so many diamonds and jewels that only a Rockefeller could afford. You cannot imagine how happy that made me because who, if not I, knows how you suffered all your life at the hands of your brothers. And even recently when you began earning good money and making a living, they wanted to manage your life, one in a good way, the other badly. I don't want to say anything bad about them, they are, after all, your brothers, and I don't mean to flatter you or to put them down but, believe me, they are not worth your little finger. And never mind your Nissel with his sweet talk and his oaths. May God repay him for the honest and decent way he treated me, may it happen to all men, God in heaven,

especially to him. I know very well he has his own bur-
dens. No doubt he is now desperate. Since the company fell
apart, all his schemes have fallen through. But still he has
a new scheme. He's found a man somewhere with a paper
model of the Holy Temple and has put up advertisements
all over New York, but will probably be buried together
with this scheme, just like all the others. May God repay
him for you and for me and for all Israel. Your brother
Isaac is gold compared to him, but he has his own problems. He has a good soul. Just ignore everything he says
about you. He says you sold yourself for money and that
your husband deals in . . . I refuse to repeat his words. And
it's all about filthy money. I advise you to stuff his mouth
with a few dollars. He could lie down in the middle of the
street and not a soul would help him. Who would even
give him the time of day? The Lomzher Nightingale? May
she live so long, his wife with her red hair! She's thrown
off her blond wig and has become a real missus. That's no
small thing! Her children, they say, are raking in money
with both hands. Who could have guessed that a Lomzher
cantor would came here with a gang of brats and strike
it rich? And that cantor has as much of a conscience as
a Russian Cossack. If your brothers were down to their
last penny, he wouldn't give them a cent. What more do
you need to know? Mr. Klammer, who sacrificed everything for him and his family, brought them over here and
set up the company, barely has the fare to go back to London. And do you know who lent him those few dollars?
If you had eighteen heads, you would never guess. It was
that *shlimazel* Murovchik, the one who brought together
that couple, your former fiancé and the singer, who has
her nose up in the air, terrible! She and her first fiancé,
Stelmach, are now, thank God, finished, accompanied by
a big scandal. The elder Stelmach, they say, wanted to sue
her, but his son wouldn't allow it. May my troubles fall on
their heads! How much truth there is in all of this, I do not
know, but that is what I heard. What I hear, I take for what
it is worth. I was not there myself. And with your lover,
she has parted, as they say, forever. They had words and
guess over whom? Over Zlatke, Holtzman's sister. To tell

the truth, I had a part in it. I wrote her a letter, and very frankly laid out the truth for her, wrote everything that was to my advantage to squeeze out from that swindler, Murovchik, about Rafalesco's romance with Holtzman's sister. And though I didn't have the privilege of her inviting me, nevertheless I know everything that is cooking there. For instance, I know that Rosa, to her credit, paid a visit to Zlatke and was quite taken with the baby she had with Rafalesco. I also know that Rafalesco has joined one of the most prestigious English theaters, but that Mr. Nickel, who had a contract with him for the whole season, demanded such a huge sum that even Rafalesco, who understands about money as much as I do about jewels, almost had a stroke. But here again Rosa appeared and said she would pay for it. How do you like that story? How true it is—I do not know. What I hear, I take for what it's worth. I wasn't there myself. But you needn't envy them, my love, you can tell them all to go to hell. God helped you, you are richer than they and have more jewelry than they have, as well as more dresses and you don't have to miss the stage. It is, pardon me, foolish of you to do so. Just see to it that you have a good life with honor and respect and have fun and pleasure and don't forget, my dear, your family, I mean your brothers, though they certainly haven't earned it from you or from me, that I should come to their defense, but to the devil with them. It is better for you to send them something before they need to come to strangers for help. And don't forget your friend, dear heart, who is devoted to you with heart and soul. Write me a letter sometimes and whatever you need, I will try to take care of. And should you come across a good job for me, write me about it and I will come to you in Johannesburg, though it's on the other side of the world. I'm fed up with this land of Columbus and its people and especially our actors, may a pestilence afflict them in one day, leaving no trace of them. Amen. Amen. Amen.

I send you one thousand kisses.

Your most devoted friend,
Breyne Cherniak

FROM LEAH THE CANTOR'S
WIFE TO HER DAUGHTER ROSA

You should know, my child, I look forward, as you wrote me, to your coming to Holeneshti to visit, because if you weren't, I would have sold the house a long time ago. I am one person, so why do I need such a big place with so many rooms? If you think there is a buyer for the house, you're mistaken. Who needs a house with so many rooms in Holeneshti? It's a town of poor people, no one has any money, and whoever did have a little money has left for America. One possible buyer is Henich the winemaker's son-in-law, a new rich man in Holeneshti. He really likes the house, but he's afraid to say he's a buyer in case I ask too high a price. And I don't want it to be known that I am selling the house in case he wants to get a bargain. In the meantime I'm stuck—I'm neither here nor there. I'm looking forward, my daughter, to your coming and making me happy with news of a future husband, one you deserve, not like that *klezmer*, may God not punish me for these words. I have nothing against him, but he is not a match for Yisroyeli the cantor's daughter. May the One Above send him someone else, and he will surely forgive you for breaking your promise, even though for us it is a big sin. And as for what you write about our Leibel, the rich Rafalovitch's son, that he is rich and famous, is certainly welcome news, because his poor sisters and brothers have had no luck at all. The whole family fell apart, children spread out everywhere, who knows where they are? Only Anshel is still around. He comes here often asking me for help, and I give him what I can. Can you stuff a sack with holes in it? In addition, he's a spendthrift, it seems, and has a coarse face, may my worst enemy have it! If Beylke, may she rest in peace, would rise from her grave and see what has become of her house and her children and her husband, God forbid! He has gone completely out of his mind and is living somewhere in a rest home and looks forward to paradise. Sison v'Simcha, who sometimes visits him, brings him a pound of tea and a cone of sugar. Woe unto Benny Rafalovitch, it has come to this, that his bookkeeper is his paradise and provider! He visits me too, that Sison v'Simcha, stays here all day and night and talks and talks and talks, a *nudnik* of a Jew, forgive my words. And their old, blind grandmother, you should see her, she is still alive. It looks like the Master of the Universe has forgotten her. "Who lives and who lies in the ground," as we say in the *U'netaneh tokef* prayer. Wouldn't it have been ten thousand times better for your father, of blessed memory, to be alive and with me so I wouldn't have to roam around through so many rooms? But ask God a question: Why did Yechiel the *klezmer*—do you remember him?—last week decide to drop dead, a young man too? Henich the barkeep also died, but it wasn't as sad—a rich, elderly Jew. He had a fine funeral befitting a good Jew, and do you know for what good deeds? Well, that your blessed father had a fine funeral I can understand, but Henich the winemaker! What was so great about him? Why did he deserve that? Because he was rich, they needed to flatter him after his death? Never mind, I don't begrudge him the honor and won't speak badly of him. He left a widow, poor thing, with four children, a good business, and a lot of money, but still and all, orphans. They will never have a father again. What the earth covers is gone forever. The spade shovels in the dirt and goodnight. More to be pitied is the poor *klezmer*'s wife. She really was left with nothing. She doesn't have enough to get through another day. They took up a collection, and I gave as much as I could, though the trustees of the synagogue complained it was too little. They said I was a rich woman, *kayn eyn horeh*, and I have, they said, such a daughter and live in such a house, with so many rooms. Go tell them that for me, the house and the rooms and all the fuss are more than I can keep up. God above should help me, and I should live to see you come here in good health, and then I would decide with you what to do with the house, why do I need such a house, one person alone with so many rooms? Do you think I am the only one saying this? Everyone here is saying it. Everyone is looking forward to your arrival, all of Holeneshti, even Necha the widow and her younger sisters. They haven't ever married, a plague on them! They keep asking me: "May you be well, Leah'nyu, when is your Reizel coming?" She's forgotten the shame she caused me that time, may it never happen again, when you ran away and they dragged me to the police chief, may his name be erased and forgotten, he's long gone from this world. Be well, my child, and write me if it's true that you are getting ready to go to America again? I don't like that plan. That country is so bad and the people are not so bad, but I don't like their language where a "chicken" is a fowl and a "kitchen" is where you cook. What kind of life is that? But come to Holeneshti beforehand, with God's help, and we'll discuss everything. In the meantime, everyone in Holeneshti sends regards, and Chayim Shayeh's son, Nachum, who is writing this letter, sends you special regards.

> *Your mother, who always prays to God for you, day*
> *and night,*
> *Leah Spivak*

FROM ROSA SPIVAK TO MARCELLA EMBRICH

Mütterchen! As you see, I am back in Europe. The wandering stars that have, as you know, been drifting toward each other without ever meeting have finally met. That was in America. But just met, nothing more! To really meet, to become one— that will never happen, never. Who is responsible for this, I or he? That I do not know. Possibly both of us. We both have made our share of mistakes during our lifetimes, though we hardly lived, hardly lived at all. Late, too late, the wandering stars met. No, dearest, apparently there is no happiness here on earth. There is only the striving toward happiness. But happiness itself is no more than a dream, a fantasy. There is no love, just an image of it, an ideal that we ourselves create in our fantasies. Love is no more than a dream. Oh dearest, too late the wandering stars met. And once again I am alone in my cloud of glory and success, again leading a wandering, homeless gypsy life. I am fated to live this wandering life for a long, long time to come. Write to me, dearest, but do not console me. Do not feel sorry for me, and do not try to convince me to be different. This is the way it has been till now, and that is how it will always be.

> *Your forever, prodigal, wandering gypsy,*
> *Rosa*

Glossary

afikomen—a board of matzo hidden by the head of a household during the Passover seder for the children to "steal" and hold out for "ransom"

bar mitzvah—a boy's coming-of-age and assumption of religious responsibility at the age of thirteen

bris—circumcision rite of eight-day-old males, representing the covenant between God and Abraham

bubbe—grandmother; affectionate term for a little old lady

challah—braided Sabbath and holiday egg bread

Chanukah—the eight-day holiday commemorating the purification of the Temple in Jerusalem by the Maccabees. Candles are lit, latkes eaten, and gifts given to children.

Chasid—adherent of a Jewish religious movement founded in the eighteenth century in Eastern Europe, stressing pious devotion and ecstasy

cheder—a religious elementary school where boys are taught Hebrew prayers and the Bible

chuppa—a wedding canopy

dreydl—a spinning top used in a Chanukah game

esrog—citron, used symbolically at Succos

fraylichs—a celebratory dance

gonef—thief

gehennam—hell

Gemorah—part of the Talmud that contains commentary on the Mishnah

goy, goyim—Gentile(s)

groshen—small Central European coin

Haman—villain in the Purim story

havdalah—ceremony performed at the close of *Shabbes*

jhargon—Yiddish

kaddish—prayer recited by mourners after the death of a close relative

kayn eyn horeh—"knock wood" (literally, "no evil eye")

klezmer—musician

Kol Nidrei—prayer sung to usher in the beginning of Yom Kippur, holiest day of the year

kosher—food or drink that Jews are permitted to consume when proper regulations have been observed

l'chayim—to life!

mameligeh—cornmeal mash

maskil—a student of the Enlightenment

matzo—traditional unleavened flatbread eaten during Passover

mazel tov—congratulations! (literally, good luck)

mensch—a responsible, honorable person

mezuzah—a rolled-up piece of parchment inscribed with biblical passages, placed in a small container and attached to the doorpost of Jewish homes and holy places

minyan—the minimum of ten people required to perform any religious ceremony

mitzvah—commandment, good deed

mohel—performer of ritual circumcision

momzer—bastard

Moshiach—Messiah

Mütterchen—affectionate term for a woman

nebbish—a "nothing" person, dweeb

nudnik—a pain in the neck, a nuisance, a nag

Pesach—Passover, the spring festival commemorating the exodus of the Jews from Egypt

pidyon haben—the ceremony of "buying back" the firstborn male from the priests

Purim—joyous celebration of the Book of Esther

Purim-shpieler—actor of traditional plays relating the story of Purim

reboynu shel oylem—"Oh, God!" our ruler of the universe

rozhinkes mit mandlen—raisins and almonds

Shabbes—sabbath

shamesh—a sexton; caretaker of the synagogue; a rabbi's assistant

shaygetz—Gentile boy

Shevuos—Fall Festival of Weeks, a religious harvest holiday

shiva—weeklong period of mourning following the funeral of a close relative

shlimazel—clumsy person, misfit, bringer of bad luck

shmatte—rag

shnorrer—moocher, beggar

shofar—ram's horn blown in synagogues at the close of High Holiday services

sholom aleichem—traditional greeting, "Peace to you"

shtetl—Jewish town in the Pale of Settlement in Eastern Europe

shul—synagogue

siddur—Hebrew prayer book

Succos (Chol hamoyed)—a fall festival, a religious harvest holiday

Talmud—compilation of religious, ethical, and legal teachings of the rabbis, interpreting the Bible

tsimmes—stew made up of potatoes, yams, and prunes

U'netaneh tokef—a prayer recited during High Holidays asking for another year of life

willkommen—German for "welcome"

yahrtzeit—anniversary of the death of a close relative, commemorated by prayer

yarmulke—a skullcap, a headcovering worn at all times by observant Jews

zloty—small Polish monetary unit